trouble

Trouble Series: Book One

By: Maria Dun

Copyright © 2024 Maria Dun

All rights reserved. No part of this book may be reproduced or transmitted in any form without permission from the author or publisher, except as permitted by the U.S. Copyright law.

To request permission, contact Maria Dun at Mariadunbooks.com for more information.

ISBN: 9798345450543
Imprint: Independently published

ASIN: B0DM6HM8XB

Published by: Kindle Direct Publishing © 1996-2024, Amazon.com, Inc. or its affiliates. All Rights Reserved.

Author's Playlist for Trouble: Book One

Trouble- Cage the Elephant

The Night We Met- Lord Huron

Imagination- Foster the People

It's Ok- Imagine Dragons

Daylight- Taylor Swift

Yellow Love- Citizen

Wild Love- James Bay

Easy Love- Lauv

Those Eyes- New West

Mansion- NF

Invisible String- Taylor Swift

True Love- Coldplay

Nervous- John Legend

Paladin Strait- Twenty One Pilots

Talk Me Down- Troye Sivan

Easy on Me- Adele

I Love You So- The Walters

Exile (ft. Bon Iver)- Taylor Swift

Us Against the World- Coldplay

Maybe IDK- Jon Bellion

3

Warning:

This book contains elements of self harm, domestic violence, as well as depression, anxiety, and other mental illnesses. This book is in no way meant to glamorize mental health or violence, but to bring awareness to it. Other aspects such as sexual content are included, however, the reader is given an option to skip over the sexual content if desired by page labeling within this novel.

Read at your own discretion.

Authors Note:

To my readers, sometimes things don't go as planned in life, and we are not meant to have all the answers. Life is a constant process of learning from the good, but more importantly, the bad. There are plenty of stories that are romantic and have a happily ever after.. This story is not one of them.

Proceed with caution.

-M

<u>To Mady:</u>

Thank you for being such a wonderful friend, my creative confidant, and one of my biggest supporters. So grateful that Ohio University led me to such a wonderful friend. Here's to you being the only person to read this book in the beginning, and here's to your future! Congratulations on your engagement! This book is dedicated to you, friend.

-Grams.

Continued Dedication & Thanks:

To the dreamers and the creators:

Don't let anything stop you from making your dreams happen. Don't sit, don't wait, don't hesitate. Do the damn thing.

To my dad:

Thank you for giving me the tools to fall in love with poetry and creative writing. This all started as something we loved to share, and now you get to watch me publish my first book. (But please don't read this there's some scenes you don't want to read..) love you dad!

To my mom & Emily:

You two always have supported me in everything I have decided to do, and I couldn't go forward in confidence of publishing this without you. You both show me what it is like to be a strong woman and I love you both so much.

Also… Emily can read this, but mom can't. Love you mom!

To my friends:

Thank you for encouraging me to write and share my stories with the world.

Thank you for pushing me to pursue my dreams. Thank you for always being honest with me and helping me through everything. I'd truly be lost without you guys.

To my love:

Thank you for always supporting me, motivating me, and loving me. I wouldn't have been able to finally publish my book if it hadn't been for you. I love you.

Prologue

June 5, 2011

Dear Adam,

I know we haven't spoken in almost a year, but I wanted the news to come from me. Here goes: I'm engaged.

And Pregnant.

I'm so sorry to tell you this through a letter, but it was the only way I knew how.

I'm still taking college classes at GSU, but I am currently living on a military base with my fiance. He was deployed to Africa four months ago, and he will be for two years.

The reason I'm telling you this is because I feel an immense amount of guilt for what happened between us, and what happened with Ricky. I never wanted anything to happen to either of you, and yet everything was taken from me in a blink of an eye.

It's been very hard to believe that I will never be able to see you again, or to hear your voice. And most of the time I just miss your presence. I wish things could have turned out differently for us, but I do know that the time we did have together was beautiful and once in a lifetime.

And I wanted to let you know that I will never forget about how much you loved me. You got me through a lot of things in our short time together, and I could never thank you enough.

I wanted to send this letter to let you know that even though we have moved on, I still want what's best for you and I want you to have so much happiness in your life.. you deserve that.

I wanted to also tell you that I hope I can have your blessing in naming my son after someone we both love dearly.. I could never feel comfortable with naming him without your approval first. His name will be Ricky, and I wanted you to hear that from me first.
I hope that's alright with you.
I wanted to honor him the best way I could. I know he was a brother to you, and he meant so much to the both of us.

I do hope you are well and taking care of yourself. I hope you're finally at peace, and maybe even found someone. Whatever you're doing, I want you to know I will always be in your corner, and you will always be in my mind.
I do love you, I always have.
It's amazing how quickly we came together, and grew apart.
But life has a funny way of teaching us lessons, doesn't it?
It's funny how one moment can change everything..
I can remember the day we met like it was yesterday.. can't you?

       Yours,

         T

September 2010

Chapter One: Tara

Breathe.

That's all I could keep telling myself.

Just breathe.

    I had started incorporating breathwork into my morning routine since the day I began college classes at Georgia State, considering that now being a college student came with a whole different set of responsibilities. Not to mention the neverending fact that my parents continued to remind me that they were *"happily"* paying for my tuition, so I had to major in pre-med, just like my dad.

That wasn't my biggest problem, though.

    I was still living at home with my parents and commuted to my classes. If that wasn't a big slap in the face for a social life, I don't know what is. Most of my days consisted of going to class, then I would go to the sports facilities for swimming practice from four to six. Sometimes I'd even go to practice at five in the morning prior to my eight am lecture. And finally, to top it all off, I would have cheering practice from six to eight in the evening, leaving just enough time for me to go home and shower, do my homework, and then wake up and do it all over again.

    You know that saying, *same shit, different day?* Yeah… That was my life.

    But all in all, college wasn't so bad. I didn't have to spend eight hours, five days a week at school anymore like I had for high school, and I got to drive home from class with a short and easy commute since it was only twenty minutes away. Although, my college experience wasn't all sunshine and rainbows; it did come with a lot of challenges. Challenges like Riley Turner. She was the equivalent to day three period cramps; a bitch to put up with but, nevertheless, something you had to push past. Seeing her at practice and some of my lectures was just about enough for me. Too bad my parents were friends with hers, and I was stuck doing *everything* with her. We were even kind of friends when we were little, but that never diminished the unspoken competition between us set on by our parents.

And if I was being honest, I had a lot of strengths: I was a great student, and I was an even better swimmer.. but the one thing Riley had a one up on against me? Cheerleading. It most definitely was not my strong suit. In fact, I *hated* it.

I did competitive cheerleading from the time I was six years old until now, and when I officially had enough in junior high, I did my best to beg my dad to let me quit. He at first seemed to be on my side, until my mom said no because she thought it was my *dream*. But it was never my dream, *it was hers*.

Rather than fight the situation, I continued to cheer all throughout highschool, and now into college. I was on the varsity squad, shoved in the back of the group for our halftime routines because I was the tallest. That didn't mean I was the most skilled, in fact, Riley made sure to tell me I had no rhythm almost every day at practice. It was kind of hilarious though; the fact that I was twenty years old and still dealing with my middle school bully.

I had thought when I graduated highschool that meant I also graduated from dealing with bullies, but I quickly learned that bullies were *everywhere*, no matter the age.

So, here I was..in the old muggy sports complex at seven pm listening to the same song mix over and over again on a loop. Everyone was doing the choreography for our newest routine which had been a complete disaster.. but truthfully? I no longer cared. My mind had been everywhere else.

"Alright everyone, run through it one more time! Oh, and Tara quit cutting the back tuck off short, it looks sloppy. We're never gonna win the College Conference Competition if you keep flipping like that."

Riley.

Riley was *unfortunately* our cheerleading captain. She was Cruella De Vil and we were the Dalmatians. And that was to put it nicely..

The truth was that Riley Turner was a complete and total bitch.

There was no way to sugarcoat it.

She just *was*.

"Hello? Earth to Tara?"

I watched as her thumb met her middle finger, and her finger swiftly moved down her thumb as the friction ended in a *snap*. Her eyes glared furiously in my direction, showing the type of death glare that only Riley was capable of. "Did you not hear what I said?"

I wasn't in the mood for confrontation, so I simply nodded in reply. "Yes, I heard you Riley. No shorting off my tucks, got it."

She smiled an entirely fake, coy smile, and tapped my shoulder lightly, like I was a damn dog and she was calling me a *"good boy"*.

"Good."

Breathe. Just breathe.

Out of habit, I felt my body turn towards the direction of my friend, Danielle, who I had met freshman year of College. Danielle had always been a good friend; One who I didn't need to worry about feeling judged, she made me feel seen. She just saw me and knew exactly who I was.. and she accepted me. It was also nice knowing that she was on the squad with me and had seemed to be just as annoyed with Riley as I had been. I turned around to look at Danielle, who walked behind me as she patted my shoulder and gave me a knowing glance. "Just let it go, T.." she whispered with wide eyes, and walked towards the benches to grab her water bottle.

Riley watched as Danielle grabbed her water bottle and took a quick drink, before she turned towards the rest of the squad who had taken a break themselves. We had been going at our competition routine for almost three hours. The girls were tired, as was I, but Riley was such a control freak that I knew that the water break wasn't going to last very long.

"Um, girls, did I say you could take a break? Get back into your positions!"

And there it was. Right on the money. It took everything in me not to scream in her smug face right that second, and even though I forced my mouth closed to prevent me from saying something to her, my body didn't completely let it go… I felt my eyes roll at her comment. "Okay, 5..6..7..8".

Even though I went through the motions and continued to act like I was enjoying myself, I could barely keep my head on straight when it came to cheering.

I had been doing this and swimming for the majority of my life, and even though I knew that I hated cheerleading, I still did it. I still did it because I couldn't find the strength within myself to disappoint people. Especially my mom. That was one thing I would never be— a disappointment. I was always the girl who did anything for anyone; the girl who felt like she was stuck in a role that she didn't want to play. And when you act the majority of your life? Well, you get sick of playing the same part.

I had a lot of trauma happen to me in my early years that forced me to pretend that life wasn't horrible. Up until age five, life was challenging for me before I went into the foster system. After that, it seemed as though things finally turned out and I couldn't jeopardize that. There was no way I would risk what I had for something I didn't want to do. It's not like my parents would force me to do anything, I just couldn't let the fear of them being disappointed in me escape my mind. I knew I was being too hard on myself; I always was. Everyone expected perfection out of me, and since the day I came into my mom and dad's world, I made sure that I was nothing but.

The rest of our Sunday evening we continued to practice our cheers and our routine for our county cheering competition for the following weekend.
Riley had worked our asses off, and I knew I would continue to feel completely sore and bruised up for weeks. Not to mention, I also had swim practice every morning before school at five a.m as well as from four to six due to our next meet coming up in a few weeks, so I would be super sore from that, too.

After that dreadful cheer practice I could feel the exhaustion in my entire body. My arms and legs ached, bruises were scattered on my legs and my head felt like a loud bass drum was pounding repeatedly, making me have a dull and painful headache. I wasn't even sure if I could walk to my car in the school parking lot, and I had decided at that moment to do absolutely nothing for the rest of the day.

As I pulled into the familiar subdivision we lived in, past memories began to fill my mind. The now familiar gated community used to be so foreign to me; I didn't even know what a suburb was until I moved in with Jennifer and Garrett. G&J, or so I call them, invited me into their lives when I was just five years old, and for them to do such a thing, well I used to think they came down from heaven. G&J always told me that they wanted kids, but that Garrett had some fertility problems, so Jennifer could never get pregnant. They said that they felt like they had tried everything they could, so that's why they started to look into adoption.

G and J were relatively young when they adopted me; Garrett was only twenty eight and Jennifer was twenty five. I remember how in love they were with one another, I remembered that because I never saw genuine love before. That made me so excited to be a part of their family; knowing that they loved one another, and they were going to love me, too. I still really appreciate everything my adoptive parents have done for me, I felt so blessed to be able to drive a brand new car to my house in the suburbs. But sometimes, it felt like life just wasn't real.
This wasn't the life I thought I was going to have.
This wasn't the life I really thought I wanted, anyway.

Five year old Tara would have never even had this kind of life on her radar. Everything was too perfect and even at five years old, I knew that to expect the picture perfect family would just end in a complete disaster.

Growing up in the foster system changes you. Sometimes you get things and they seem great for a little while, but then the other shoe drops and you're back to a rat infested one bedroom apartment with your heroin addict mother.

The truth is, the system doesn't care about you. They think they're saving you from a bad situation, but the reality is that nine out of ten times, you end up in another bad one. It's a never ending vicious cycle. I should feel lucky though, I was only in the system for two years. Some of the other kids that were in the system with me stayed there until they turned 18, or reconnected with their druggie parents and became a drug addict themselves, or worse. I thanked God every day that my life didn't turn out like that. I was beyond blessed that my life turned out pretty amazing.

As I pulled into the drive, I pressed my security code into the box for the main gate to open. After living with G&J for twelve years, you'd think I'd get used to the beautiful scenic drive through the neighborhood. I never felt like I could get used to any of it, but I could never tell my parents that I felt like I was entering into a place that didn't belong to me.

I pulled up in front of my house and noticed both of my parents' Audi's in the driveway. It was strange, Garrett was usually still out on hospital rounds at this time, so I was surprised he was back already. I parked behind Jennifer's SUV, grabbed my cheering duffle bag, and got out of the driver's side of my car. I continued to walk up the steps to the front door, hearing their voices amplify with every step I took.

"Well what the fuck did you think, Jen?"

I opened the door slowly, hoping that I could slither in and go unnoticed. What I heard up the stairs in their bedroom must have just started, because it was pretty heated.

They had come a long way from the two love birds that I remembered when they adopted me at just five years old. They no longer showed love to one another, their stances were always cold, and they never showed up to an event together. They always fought & screamed at one another; and my mother always would make sure to use hurtful words toward my dad any chance she got. They seemed to be very unhappily married, but so comfortable that they were just used to the patterns they had made.

As I walked through our entryway, I saw Garrett carrying down a purple suitcase and a matching carry on bag with it. Jen followed him down the steps combing through her long blonde hair with her fingers. She had makeup all over her face and tears flooding out of her eyes. I had no idea what was going on. My parents must not have noticed I was home, because as soon as they saw me, Garrett's furious expression immediately changed to a wide smile.

"Hey kiddo, what are you doing home so soon? It's only a quarter to nine."

I wasn't going to pretend like I didn't just hear them screaming at each other. I wasn't sure what kind of game they were playing.

"Yeah, I was gonna stop by the gym and do some laps at the pool, but cheering ran over, so I just decided to come home. I'm pretty beat."

I slid my cheering tennis shoes off of my feet, and placed them in my row of the shoe cubby next to the door.

"Is everything okay?"

I wasn't sure what was going on entirely, all I knew was that Garrett was mad at Jennifer for something, and that her luggage was sitting in the entry way.

"Uh, yeah sweet pea. Everything's fine. We've just had a little spat, and your mom's gonna go down the street to stay with Gran for a few days. You know, until we work some things out." Now things really weren't making sense. *What had happened? Why was J leaving*? I wanted to know, and I didn't want my parents to sugarcoat it, either.

"Yeah....okay. Um, J, why are you going to grandma's?"

She quickly wiped her nose with a tissue, and cleared her throat. She began walking down the grand staircase and walked straight to me.

"Honey, things have just been so complicated lately. And we didn't know what to tell you, but.."

"But, you're an adult, so if you want to know, we can tell you" Garrett butted in as he glared at Jennifer with wide eyes. "Okay, then I want to know. what's going on?" Mom huffed and pulled me in a gentle hug. "I'm so sorry." She pulled away and walked over to her luggage by the end of the stairs as her back faced me, unable to look me in the eye.

"Honey, I had an affair."

My dad's head sunk down, and his eyes remained on the ground. I knew this must of been semi-fresh news for him to hear as well. *When did my mother have an affair? With who? And most importantly, why*? Garrett was the kindest man I've ever known, and despite everything, he loved us both so much. I was so confused.

"Why would you do that to us, J?"

I was surprised I got that question out, because I felt like I had a serious case of cotton mouth and I felt like I couldn't breathe.

Breathe. Just breathe.

I attempted to calm my rising anxiety down, taking in slow deep breaths through my nose and out through my mouth, attempting to regulate my breathing before it got out of control. My family was breaking apart, and there was nothing I could do about it.

"Honey, things haven't been easy with me and your dad, and he's hardly ever home. He's always in surgery or rounds, or constantly on the phone with consults, and I felt lonely. You were always gone, too. Doing your sports and also with school. It was selfish of me, but I didn't want to feel alone."

I had always been the polite, happy, and caring daughter. I always listened to my parents, and was afraid of their disapproval, but *this*? Now this was funny.

"So you felt lonely and that's why you cheated on dad? If you were so lonely you could've gotten a dog." G's head lifted up then, and a small speck of a smirk rose on his face. J noticed, because her face turned red and the arguing began once again.

"See! This is what I told you Garrett. You never take anything seriously, and then when you do try to do something serious, absolutely no one believes you because you constantly have to make everything into a goddamn joke! It was cute when we were younger, but now it's really immature." My moms hands were on her hips now, already shooting her metaphorical bullet, waiting for dad to shoot one right back.

"I'm immature? I'm immature?! You cheated on me with Donny down the street! How many other neighbors do you have 'play dates' with? Are you baking cookies and going to PTA meetings? Oh no. No. You're too busy going over to do Donny Miller at his house!"

"Oh my god you're going to go with that?! Really!? You are so low Garrett!"

I stood there for about five minutes, watching them bicker back and forth over ridiculousness that I couldn't even really begin to sort out in my mind. I'm sure they kept most of their arguments hidden until I wasn't around, but as I got older, I had witnessed quite a lot of them, especially when they'd want me to "chime in" to their argument. Most of their arguments nowadays seemed like a damn telenovela.

I kinda loved it.

Except for the part where my family was ripping apart at the seams.

    I wanted the arguing to stop, I didn't want to hear the constant bullshit and blaming anymore. I decided to just throw a recurring thought out there, because what could be worse than witnessing them arguing ever since I walked through the front door?

"So I'm guessing that this would be a bad time to tell you that I want to quit cheering."

    The immediate silence became deafening. We all stood in the foyer, frozen, staring at one another.

"Excuse me, what?" Jennifer finally said, breaking the silence. I could tell J wasn't all that excited to hear that I wanted to quit cheerleading.

    "I'm just so busy with swimming and the class office meetings, it feels like too much." My dad looked over at my mom with a face full of concern.

J's face had turned so red that I swore she was the same color as a tomato.

"No way. Absolutely not, Tara. If you start something, you finish it. That's what we've always taught you."

    I stood in the doorway of the entryway with my hands crossed over my chest and I was biting my tongue as hard as I could.

This wasn't the first time I've been told what to do by J, and I never talked back to her about it, either.

    I knew that no matter how much I wanted J to finally ease up on me and let me choose my own path, she would always have some kind of control over my life.
She could always grow tired of me and decide to kick me out of their lives forever, and I couldn't jeopardize that.

    "Garrett, say something to your daughter right now. Tell her she's not quitting." Garrett looked between me and my mother a couple times before letting out a large sigh.
Clearly he was being put in the middle here.

    "Kiddo, you've worked so hard, and we want what's best for you. I really think you should stay on the squad, It helps you to stay active and make friends. Plus, you really seem to like those teammates of yours." It would break my parents hearts if they knew the truth. It would break their hearts if they knew that what I presented to people on the outside, wasn't who I was at my core. It was like I was playing a major acting game.
I never wanted to disappoint my parents or anyone, because I had always felt so lucky to receive the kind of life that I have, and I didn't want that to be taken away.

    "It was just an idea. I get overwhelmed with my busy schedule sometimes, but you're right..." I felt myself hesitate with my words, knowing that what I truly wanted and the decisions I wanted to make for myself, despite being an adult, were not entirely mine to make. For the very simple reason that I, Tara, did not want them to regret adopting me. I didn't want them to completely cast me out and never speak to me again just for one stupid choice I had wanted to make. The choice wasn't as important as keeping my family. They were all I had, and without them I would have nothing. I'd have worse than nothing.. I'd probably be dead.

It was at that moment that my wants and needs began to collide in my mind, and I realized quickly that I wouldn't, in fact, be able to stand my ground. It seemed as though my anxiety and my parents had won and there was no reason to fight it.

"..I won't quit if that's what you both want."

My mom came back over towards me and grabbed my hand. She squeezed it as she held it and gave me a wide smile. "No, Tara, we don't want you to quit. We want you to have the best experiences that life can offer, and you've been doing this since you were a little girl. There's no reason to throw it away now." I so badly wanted to roll my eyes. I so badly wanted to tell J that I shouldn't give two shits about what she wanted, because she cheated on G, and she didn't have a right to have an opinion right now. But I told my mind to stop being this way. That the things I didn't like anymore were simply a piece of a puzzle that was young adulthood, and I had begun to outgrow it. I told myself to endure the torture just for a little bit longer, because college and cheerleading didn't last forever.

I simply nodded and gave her a half smile as she kissed the side of my head, and cupped her hands around my cheeks, swiftly combing her fingers through my dark auburn hair. "You're right mom, I don't know what I was thinking." She softly caressed my cheek before kissing my forehead and stepping away.

She grabbed her luggage, and rolled it towards the front door, stopping and turning to face me once more. "That's my girl. Tara, I am so sorry for the pain I've caused you and your dad.."

her voice started to tremble, but she maintained her composure. She cleared her throat and tilted her chin upward, trying to not show weakness.

J was never one to show weakness. She always was the stronger one out of her and my dad. Garrett was always more relaxed and emotional than Jennifer. He was more sensitive in the way he cared about things & the emotions he showed. He took more time talking to me and really understanding me than my mom did. My mom always had a lot of expectations out of me & a lot of expectations of herself. When she wasn't working, she was on phone calls with her management team for her distributing company, which meant very little time for me. So growing up, I very quickly became a "daddy's girl".

J wasn't completely stone cold, but she rarely showed any emotion. She rarely showed love to anyone, so her behavior in this moment was anything but normal.
This wasn't her normal, but it wasn't a normal situation either.

Maybe breaking my dad's heart is what made her realize how important him and I were, and maybe it woke her up to her mistakes. Maybe she was finally realizing that she could've tried more for us, for our family.

She wiped a tear off of her cheek with her knuckle, and then reached out for my hand. I walked to the front door and intertwined my fingers with hers. G was still near the staircase, watching the both of us say our goodbyes. ".. We just need some time to think all of this through. I'll be down at grandma's and you can come down any time, okay?" I nodded and smiled softly, trying to give my mom some inclination that I would be seeing her often, despite her and I both knowing it wouldn't be that easy with my school and sports schedule.

She pulled me into a tight hug as I heard her soft sounds of sniffling on my shoulder, before she pulled away and examined my face, and scanned me with extreme focus while I stood in front of her. "I'll see you soon sweetie, and remember to drink those antioxidant smoothies I put for you in the freezer..you're looking a little bloated in your face and stomach and we don't need that for your cheering competition."

I stood there, stunned. Unsure of what to say, but unfortunately not wanting to say anything at all.

She shouted "love you!" over her shoulder, blew me a kiss, and then she was out the door.

A beat of silence stood between me and my dad, while I was continuing to process my moms final words to me before she left. The sad thing? I was entirely used to it by now. And I was pretty excited to finally have a break from her constant judgment.

"Well...Looks like it's just us two for a while."

Garrett was facing me in the entryway now, hands in his pockets, and bouncing on his feet, like he was in an awkward situation. The thing was, it was an awkward situation. "Yeah dad. I guess so." Was he just going to ignore that entire moment? How awkward and confusing and unsettling it was?

There were a few moments where I could feel the awkward tension start to surface. I never really talked to my dad about things like this— like adult things.. relationships, him and J...and even though I was closer with him, thinking about talking to my dad one on one about what just transpired just seemed uncomfortable, not to mention I don't think either of us had time to fully process it yet.

I guess I needed to make the best out of this new change. It was gonna be just dad and me for awhile.

This new family dynamic was something I would have to get used to, and I knew I would have to take this time to build a new relationship with my dad.
I didn't know how I would get past this awkwardness with him now, but all I knew was that I would never leave him. I knew he was struggling right now, and that this kind of situation couldn't be something that could be dealt with positively.
I couldnt leave my dad, and I didn't want to.

"Well, I'm gonna call and order some pizza for dinner tonight, sound good?"
He pulled his cellphone out, dialing the number to Rob's pizza shack.
I knew he was dialing that number like the back of my hand. There were other pizza places in Covington, of course. But my dad loved Rob's pizza shack more than any other pizza here in Georgia.
I smiled at him as he finished typing the number into his phone.

"Yeah, sounds good. I'm gonna go get a shower before they deliver it, okay?" He smiled at me and simply nodded in my direction. "Hey kiddo, I love you, do you get it?" He placed the phone up to his ear with a smile and walked through the entry way and into his study as he began talking to someone on the other line to place the order.

I let out a large sigh and smiled in the direction he was heading
"I won't forget it."

I whispered, knowing our little saying we had since I was little. He always would use it when I was in need of a smile, and he always used it at the perfect times.. just like now.

I walked up the stairs and tried to take in everything that just occurred when I came home. It was a lot to take in. I couldn't really wrap my brain around it. I had no clue that anything was going on.

Had I been this clueless the whole time?

I felt the shock vibrate in my system, causing my stomach to twist and nausea to take over me. Guilt was also trickling in, making me realize that I had been so wrapped up in my life and my schedule, that I wasn't paying attention to what was around me.

Jennifer cheating on Garrett?

That almost sounded like it was a prank, like someone was playing a sick fucking joke on me.

Along with the nausea and the intensity of feeling guilty, panic came in along with it. I had been used to it; the feeling of panic seemed as though it had become a familiar old friend, peeking its head in unannounced at any given moment. It was like no matter what I did, stressful situations in my life equaled my anxiety spiraling out of control.

I began thinking that maybe once G got tired of me, he would kick me out. My thoughts spiraled into a tornado of anxiety, making me think the most outlandish thoughts, even though in reality, I knew a lot of the things I was fearing, wasn't going to happen.

That's what anxiety does, though. It makes you think of the impossible and it makes whatever you're thinking a million times worse than it really was. It feels like a huge weight on your chest that you can't control, much less get rid of. It stays there, hovering around you, ready to take over whenever you're in a moment of weakness.

I felt my breath quicken and my skin began to feel clammy. I couldn't control my breath and I kept trying and trying to take deep breaths, but I couldn't get the air into my lungs. As much as I tried, it wasn't working. I rushed up the stairs and into my bedroom, locked the door & grabbed my coping mechanism out of my nightstand.

I bit down on the collar of my shirt, preparing to inflict pain to myself in order to calm myself down. It had been the only way that I could stop myself. That I could feel physical pain that outweighed the emotional. It was something that grounded me back to reality, instead of panicking. And no matter how irrational it was, it unfortunately worked.

I began snapping the band on my wrist repeatedly, over and over again. I watched as my skin turned bright red, and then darkened to a deep maroon the more and more I did it. I dug my fingernails into the palm of my hand, not caring about the tears or the muffled shrieks of pain coming from me. The anxiety had to go. The betrayal from my mom had to go. And this was the only way to bring me back to the reality that I wasn't going to let anything break me down or take me away from my family.

Not now, not ever.

As I got out of the shower and walked to the mirror of my bathroom, I could hardly recognize the girl staring back at me.

I had taken a long hot shower to allow myself time to process what had happened today, and the intrusive thoughts that I held inside my mind. I had cleaned off the trace amounts of blood from my palm of my hand, cleaned them with soap and water, and then began the after-self-harming-and-shower routine of medicating my now open scars with antibiotic ointment & bandaids.

I took care of my self-inflicted wounds and covered them up with a long sleeved crop top shirt, and matched it with a pair of dark distressed jeans.

I walked out of the bathroom and into my room, double checking myself in a full length body mirror that had pictures taped to it of my parents and me, as well as my best friend Michelle and I freshman year of college. Seeing the photos of my family made tears rise to the surface, and I felt the self-created habit of snapping my rubber band against my flesh occupy every thought in my mind. Once the thought creeped in, the obsession over it, to fix me, were all I could think about. All I knew was if I did it, it would make me feel better somehow. I needed to take care of my emotions this way before I got too out of control in the wrong place.

I grabbed the rubber band under my long sleeve t-shirt, and snapped it once.

Twice. Three times.

Breathe.

Four. Five. Six. Seven.

Breathe. Just breathe.

   Once my skin was bright red and my wrist began to feel numb, I stopped.

   Tears were streaming down my face as I pulled my long sleeve back down over my wrist, and I glanced in the mirror at myself one more time.

What a mess you've made yourself, Tara.

What a waste.

   And I really believed it, too. Maybe I didn't give any value to anything and maybe that's God's way of telling me that my life was falling apart.

What if you snapped the band so much it made you bleed out?

You'd be better gone.

I squeezed my eyes shut for a few minutes, trying to control my breathing in hopes to control my thoughts. The problem was though, that I couldn't look around this house without memories of my childhood surfacing.

You'd be better gone. No wonder your parents didn't want you. Those words still rang through my ears the same way they did when I was just eleven years old. I remembered a lot of things, hell.. I remembered everything.

I couldn't look at my room without thinking about all the times I had to fall asleep to the sounds of G and J arguing, or the moments when Jennifer thought she was better off without her medication and would spend thousands of dollars on clothes for her and I, just to then blame me for it like I was the one with the impulsiveness. I was just a kid.

Things weren't always bad with Jen though.. Most of the time she was a good mom, and I would often find myself struggling between her being my best friend and being my worst enemy.

Jen's words would come to the surface at any moment of weakness; whenever I was feeling depressed, or anxious, or not believing in myself.. her words were there. All of them; the good ones, and the bad. And right now, it seemed as though the bad ones had taken over in a moment of anger.

I had tried several techniques that i had tried in the past to clear the negative thoughts out of my mind, but the after effects of overthinking had begun to take over. The dull pulses overtook my head and my eyes and filled them both with pressure.. I knew I needed something to make my mind stop spinning in repetitive circles, and I knew that I needed to escape reality just this once. I needed to go to a place where I could just have fun without worrying about anything else in my life.

A place, such as a bar.

 I grabbed my black wristlet off of my dresser and pulled out my fake I.D. out of the third drawer. I had kept it hidden there for the past two years, hoping that my parents would never find it. I remember the moment that I hid it in the pocket of an old pair of gray sweatpants that I hardly ever wore. I didn't want to get caught, so that was the best place I thought to hide it.

I pushed the I.D. into my back jean pocket and headed out of my bedroom and into the entryway hall.

"Hey sweetheart, the pizzas on the counter."

 My dad glanced at me as he sat on the couch in his office, watching a men's soccer game. Once he noticed my outfit, his expression changed into what I could only explain as sadness.

"Oh honey, I didn't know you were going anywhere. You look nice."

I smiled shyly back at my dad and tucked a loose end of hair behind my ear.

"Thanks, dad. I won't be out too late. I'm gonna go to dinner in Atlanta with the squad and then to Rylee's house to study for my physics exam tomorrow."

 I had to come up with some kind of lie, of course my dad wouldn't allow me to go out if I told him I was planning on going out to get drunk. He gave a small smile and ran his hand through his jet black hair as he kept his eyes on the television.

"Okay, sweet pea. Let me know when you're there safe and sound. I love you."

I walked out of the entryway and into his office towards the couch. I leaned over the couch and placed a kiss on my dad's cheek as I patted his shoulder.

"Love you, too. I'll be back soon, dad."

He reached up and held onto my hand on his shoulder. He was gazing at the TV, but didn't say a word. I knew he just needed some comfort for a few minutes, so I let him have it. It took him a moment before he let go, and that was perfectly okay with me. He patted my hand and squeezed it. I smiled down at the vision of my dad, knowing how much he loved me and realizing how much he was hurting. I left the room as soon as I could though, because I wasn't sure if I could take standing in there without breaking down. I was just glad that I was able to make it to the front door without feeling that familiar rise of panic set in.

Today was hard enough as it was, but Garrett had broken my heart in that small moment of needing comfort, and I wasn't sure if I was the one who would be able to comfort my dad. I knew he wasn't okay, but he was holding it together for me.

I knew with everything in me that I couldn't pretend to keep my composure. I could feel my heart break for my dad. He hadn't asked for any of this; and yet, there he was, trying to stay strong for us both. I couldn't take it. Without a second thought, I made sure my rubber band was around my wrist, and ran out the door.

I needed to take a break, and for once, just to try to let everything go.

Chapter Two: Tara

As I drove in my car out of my gated community, I felt a sense of guilt come to the surface. I suddenly felt like I shouldn't have left my dad alone; that I should've been there to comfort him. But I decided to stop second guessing myself, and that dad would be fine. Just this once, I needed to think about myself before other people. I told myself that it was something I needed to do for myself, and that with everything going on, drinking was a fairly acceptable way to cope. I knew I was trying my best to rationalize it and make excuses for it.. but deep down I knew it was something I shouldn't do.

To be honest.. I knew better. But when you get depressed and the panic starts to set in, you'd do anything to mask it or get rid of it, even if it were a few seconds.
And that's exactly why I did it.

I continued driving down our subdivision, repeatedly attempting to convince myself that I deserved it. Only thing was, I wasn't sure I believed it.

I pulled into a mostly deserted parking lot belonging to an old rustic looking bar just fifteen minutes down the road from the center of town in Covington. It was made of wood and the rusted sign was half lit, hanging crooked above the door. The sign read "Skull's Tavern" and even though you could see it right off of the main highway, it still didn't have many cars in the lot. The bar did look a little sketchy, like a bar that motorcycle gangs would go to. Not that I ever really saw a motorcycle gang before, but if I did, I'm sure they'd come here. .

It was a strange feeling, though… I wasn't sure how, but this place felt comforting to me. I wasn't scared, and normally I would have been going to a random bar in the middle of nowhere by myself. But this one? It was like I had been there before and it was the weirdest feeling. I couldn't really understand why I had felt such a sense of peace when I pulled into the lot, but I felt like it was where I needed to go. I thought that maybe I had felt so comfortable because usually the people who would come here for a drink were sad, lonely, or confused. And I could relate to that.. because I was all the above. I felt comfortable going to a small town bar instead of driving into the city and going to a nightclub, but I also felt more comfortable in knowing that everyone in there maybe, just maybe felt the same way as me.

    I parked my car next to a few motorcycles in the parking lot, most of them had an arrow with a lightning bolt through it on the front of their bikes, clearly a symbol for their crew. I got out of the driver's seat, and let in a huge sigh of relief. I needed this. And no matter how I was feeling, I wasn't going to allow my anxiety to talk me out of it.

Not tonight.

    As I entered the tavern, I noticed the burgundy leather booths that had dark brown tables in the center, and there were dark wooden bar stools and a matching countertop just in front of where the bartender stood. This place on the inside was completely different than expected. This was drastically different from the way the outside of the bar looked. It was so beautiful; the deep richness of the burgundy walls, the antique gold accents, and the dark wood floors and bar stools all tied in together perfectly. As I looked around, I noticed several older men in leather jackets sitting on the dark wooden stools and drinking large mugs of beer. I knew that I felt out of place and I knew that I looked the part, too; this wasn't where young adults come to hang out, apparently.

But that also made me happy to know that I wouldn't see any other familiar faces here.

I was glad that no one was here that could possibly tell G or J what I was up to. I was one of the few women inside of the bar, along with a few older women who looked to be in their early sixties. It wasn't difficult to realize that I was the only young person in here. But I didn't mind, in fact it made me feel better that I didn't have to force myself to be outgoing.

I sat myself on a barstool at the far end of the bar, away from the group of motorcyclists and the older women who were with them. I felt okay to be here by myself, I almost felt like I could do anything that I wanted… like I was free to make my own decisions; like an actual adult would. That thought gave me new found confidence, and I felt like I was on top of the world.

I looked at the bartender and politely smiled. "What can I get you?" He said as he furrowed his eyebrows at me, already studying me. I pulled my fake I.D. out of my back pocket knowing he was going to card me irregardless, and put on my fakest smile to play the part. "I'll just have a cranberry and vodka right now, thanks." I slid my ID and my cash towards the bartender as he simply nodded.

I admired the inside of the bar once again, noticing the old wood beams supporting the ceiling, and the way the walls were just as burgundy as the booths. I noticed all of the gold accents; gold colored glasses, gold colored alcohol mixers, and gold colored tables to match. I was admiring the bar so much that the bartender's voice snapped me back to reality. "Do you want anything to eat? We have some great wings here."

I shook my head *no* in response and offered a polite smile, before and grabbing my phone from my back pocket to check the time. 9:45. I knew I was about to have a long night ahead of me, but I was pretty sure I had found my new favorite bar. I felt unbothered, yet comforted here. I felt dangerous, yet safe, and even though it didn't make much sense, it almost felt like I was supposed to be here.

"Here you go hun.." the old bartender stated as he sat down my glass of cranberry vodka on a coaster. "..I don't think I've seen you around these parts before." I smiled as I ducked my head, hoping that no one would look at me and possibly recognize me.

"Yeah, I-uh, just moved back into town to be closer to my family." The bartender nodded his head and rubbed his chin stubble. "Oh would I know any of your family?" He said, keeping his eyes on the bar, watching for empty glasses to refill.

I had to think of a lie, and I had to think of one quickly before the oldie bartender blew my cover. I couldn't risk it. No way was I about to get outed by the bartender within my first ten minutes of being here.

"Um, maybe. Dr. Murphy is my cousin." Dr. Murphy wasn't really my cousin. Dr. Murphy had been my mom's chiropractor for six years, so I was frequently going with her or driving her to the appointments. I couldn't think of anyone else in that split second of time, so Dr. Murphy had to work.

"Oh yeah, I know Ed! He used to be a buddy of mine back when we played ball in high school. Good man... How's Kristy his wife doing?.. I can't believe this! What a small world!" He walked over to the register behind the bar, and quickly pulled out three dollars, then sat it back down on the counter in front of me. "Here, honey. It's on the house. It's the least I can do for the family of an old buddy of mine." I didn't want to lie and this man made me suddenly feel very bad, but I couldn't risk getting caught. I decided to swallow my guilt and just simply smile. "Thank you...Uh.."

The old bartender let out a small, light laugh and turned back behind the bar to grab a glass. "Oh, sorry, Where's my manners?... My name's Joe. I'm the owner-slash-manager of the bar here." I lifted up my drink, nodded and took a small sip.

"Well, thank you, Joe. I'm Tara."

After a few seconds of silence, I thought I would try to keep the conversation going, and ask Joe a question. "So, uh, Joe. Do you get a lot of business from people passing by here?"cJoe finished pouring beer in a mug from the draft, and handed it to one of the older men on the opposite side of the bar, then walked back over to me.

"Yeah. I don't get a whole lot of young people in here, you're one of the few. But I get a lot of people who are just passing through. It's pretty close to the highway, so that's an advantage we've had for years. Place needs major updating though, with all the new contractors coming in to build these hotels in Covington and tv producers wanting to shoot here.. I've kind of hit a wall with the customers lately. All these big city people love to stay in the center of town or go to Atlanta.. they don't really care about the outskirts anymore, so very rarely do I get new customers. I've been serving most of the same guys for over fifteen years. I've just been hoping to gain some more customers sometime soon, cause I don't know when I'm ever gonna get these renovations done."

He pointed up to the ceiling then, gesturing for me to follow his gaze. As I looked at the ceiling, drops of water slowly fell down and hit my cheek. A large yellow stain was permanently stuck on the ceiling tile above me. "Yeah, Joe. I guess I can see what you're saying." I felt bad for him. I truly did.. You could really tell this place wasn't doing too hot from the outside. I'm sure most of the inside had to have been remodeled pretty recently, because it was absolutely beautiful… well apart from the leaky ceiling.

"Well, Joe, do you have any extra help around here? Maybe a few of them could help you renovate this place a little bit."

Joe looked down at the floor, as if he were defeated, and let out a large huff of air before he spoke: "I have three other people working here. Casey, she's a great bartender, but she's so hardheaded, I know she wouldn't help. I have my nephew who helps out a lot but he's always in and out. And then I have Platz, he has always been a little wishy washy. I cut him some slack though, he's raising his two year old by himself, so a buddy of mine let's him stay in the upstairs of his hardware store. He works both here, and over there." I held my index finger up, signaling that I needed a refill and also to be honest, I was curious and wanted to ask Joe another question. "Wait, his name is Platz? What kind of name is that?" I had hoped Platz's name had been a nickname, because damn, that name sounded terrible. It sounded like something getting squished to tiny pieces, and I would never recover from that nickname if I had that last name. Riley would never let me live it down. "His real name is Darien, his last name is Platzmen. Hence, Platz." I shrugged my shoulders and nodded my head simultaneously, realizing that it finally made a little more sense.

I tapped my empty glass to signal that I needed a refill yet again.

I was downing these drinks a little too quickly, and it seemed as though Joe was taking notice too. "You sure you don't want something to eat? You'll get sick without something on your stomach." Joe's eyebrows were furrowed and his arms were crossed, clearly showing me his concern. In truth, I had started to feel the effects of the vodka a few minutes back but I didn't really pay much attention to it. I had felt this way before, I figured I knew how to handle it. What I didn't realize, however, was that this refill was now my fifth. Five cranberry and vodkas? And all within less than an hour?

I was so screwed.

    Deep in my mind, I worried. I started to have a panic attack at the thought of how I was gonna get home without being taken there by an uber, and after all those true crime documentaries I had been watching for the past month? It didn't seem like a great idea to do that, either.

    I decided to quickly throw those fears to the back of my mind and let the warmth of the alcohol take over. My lips felt numb, and my head swirled around in slow circles. I simply shook my head toward Joe, letting him know I didn't want anything to eat, and he shook his head before tapping on the bar table and grabbing the bottle of Grey Goose vodka.

    As Joe finished pouring my drink and sat it in front of me, I slid the money and a couple extra dollars to him and smiled. "This is all you're getting for now, kid. Nothing else until you eat something, so enjoy it. Can't have my customers passing out from alcohol intoxication." I smiled and laughed lightly in reply, knowing that he was just doing his job, and being a really great person while he was at it. He didn't need to show me that kind of kindness tonight, and yet he had. And I was grateful for that. I didn't need someone judging me or asking me my problems.. I just needed to know someone was there. And Joe was.

    "Thank you for taking care of my drinks tonight. I appreciate it. I also think I made a new friend, which is really nice." Joe's smile was so wide it was like his eyes lit up.. I was glad to have met him. It almost felt like I had known him my entire life, like he was the cool uncle I had always wanted. "You sure did, I'm glad I met you as well, kiddo. Are you sure you're okay enough to go home by yourself?"

I downed the last half of my drink, and nodded more times than I could count.

"Absolu-AHH!"

I felt myself slip off of my seat, and my entire body collapse to the floor. I felt a deep laughter escape my throat and continued on for what seemed like hours.

Soon a couple of the older women and Joe were standing in front of me, trying to help me and lift me up off of the ground.

Once they did, they sat me in one of the red booths and sat a metal bucket next to me under the table. *They were so nice*. I allowed myself to slump down into the booth and used my elbow as my pillow. "Someone look in her wallet to see if she has an emergency number somewhere." one lady said. "I'll do it. I could call Dr. Murphy's office but he wouldn't answer there. I could call the cops to give her a ride." Joe replied sternly. I heard a rustle and a sound of a zipper, but my brain felt too fuzzy and too spinny. I couldn't think of anything else except that. I was surprised I even knew my own name at this point,

"Dammit... I can't call the cops." I heard Joe say as he slammed something down on a table nearby. "She's underage. And with the way she was drinking, I bet there was a reason why. I— I don't want the poor kid getting into trouble, and I could get into trouble myself for serving underage." One of the older lady's said something to Joe, but I couldn't really make sense of anything at the moment. I enjoyed my cozy little corner of the booth, it felt pretty warm and inviting over here. "No, no. I know what to do. I'm gonna call one of my workers to give her a ride."

Platz? He's gonna call Platz?

Platz was such a weird name, I didn't want him to drive me home.

Platz.

That was such a funny name.

    I felt a little giggle escape followed by a hiccup that seemed like someone had punched me in the chest. I hated hiccups, I always had. It made me feel like my drinks were making it way back up my throat. I hated puking, and I was determined not to. But as I closed my eyes and my surroundings began to darken, I felt a force rush up from my stomach and to my throat.

Dammit.

    I hated hearing the sound myself, but it made me feel entirely better the second I did it. Only thing was that there was a horrible smell of vomit coming from the bucket below me. I decided to snooze off this feeling of being on a merry go round. That was the only logical thing I could think of this entire evening.

After everything I had experienced today, I didn't think this night could get any worse.

*

    I hadn't known how much time had passed, but I knew I was starting to wake up as my body began to adjust to my surroundings. My vision felt blurred and hazy, my head was pounding and my arms felt weak and heavy. I was trying to adjust to my surroundings and stop myself from feeling like the room was spinning, when I felt two hands reach under me; one under my shoulder blades, and the other at the bed of my knees, and soon I was hoisted up into the air, in some strangers arms, moving away from my safe space of the bar booth. I had no recollection of my surroundings, but it felt like I was being carried only for a short amount of time.

Whoever was carrying me seemed strong; their hold on me never wavered and their body seemed so warm and comfortable that I felt myself sink into them. I opened my eyes and looked around the bar. The only one left was Joe, no one else was here now besides the stranger holding me. I didn't care if I seemed embarrassed, all I wanted was to be close to that safe and warm person who was saving me. I quickly thought that maybe it was a sexy firefighter, causing me to laugh again, which ended in another hiccup, and then nuzzled my head into the stranger's neck and breathed in the scent.

The smell of mahogany and pine filled my senses, and the sudden feeling in my stomach was no longer nausea, but butterflies. I closed my eyes again, too tired to fully focus them on my random savior's face, but I knew I would always have the smell of them, and that was something I would be grateful for forever.

I heard a muffled voice in the background, and soon recognized it to be Joe's. "Make sure you get her home safe, Adam, I mean it. No side-hustle stuff on the way to her house, either. Here's some money. Call yourself an Uber once you drop her off."

I heard a small, yet deep and powerful chuckle escape the stranger's throat and felt the slight movement of his head turning.

"Está bein, tio." Another slight laughter escaped from his lips.

"I'll get her there in one piece, uncle." All that was left to remember was the angelic voice that came out of the random stranger's mouth before I fell into a deep sleep.

And I was completely, and entirely okay with that.

Chapter Three: Adam

What the actual fuck..

I couldn't believe Uncle Joe was making me do this dumb bullshit. This wasn't my problem.

I had been on a supply run with my best friend, Ricky, when Joe called. We had gone just south of the outside of Atlanta to a beat up old trailer back behind one of the railroad tracks and hidden deep in the woods. That's where some of my regulars would meet me for the transfers. It was just easier that way.

I had to relocate too many times; I was always getting chased down by the cops and there was no way I was gonna spend 20+ in a lock up for this shit. This wasn't going to be the rest of my life. I always told myself that.

I always told myself that I would get out of this shit business and get a real job, but that day never came. Hell, that year never fucking came either.

Truth is, I made more money distributing drugs to the same needy users in a week than what I would make at a regular job in a month.

It was basic knowledge, and it was smart business for a guy like me: a guy that wasn't really heading much of anywhere.

So here I was.. with Ricky in this gross ass trailer, and three of my regular customers. They were all women, too.

The first two were druggies. No doubt. They always looked the part, too. My conscience told me I shouldn't judge so much on their appearance, that what they were doing was dangerous, and I happened to be contributing to it, but I threw the thoughts of martyr Adam out quickly.

That's not what I was here for. I was here to do my job and then to get the fuck out of here swiftly before we got caught.

You can't have fuck ups in this business. Mistakes were one and done... and done had you buried six feet deep in a damn ditch.

So whatever these girls did to themselves, well that really wasn't my fucking problem, now was it?

The third girl though, Natasha..she did things to me. I didn't mind coming on runs here because I'd always see her. She was definitely the hottest out of the three girls, and I knew she wasn't into the coke like the other two were. I met her on the first supply run two years ago, and we had been on and off friends with benefits ever since.

I did my usual thing every time we came on a run. I sold the coke to the first two girls, and told Ricky to count the money in the other room and occupy the other two girls while I spoke to Natasha.

There she was, in a navy blue crop top and jean shorts that were really, really short.
The thought of how she looked underneath made a deep groan escape in my throat.
It was one of those bite-your-knuckles-moments: she looked that good.
"Adam.." she said, her voice barely a whisper, "Quit looking at me like that."

Natasha had a sly smile on her lips, and her eyebrow was cocked. She knew what she was doing to me. "No. I don't think so. It's too good of art for me to stop looking." She rolled her eyes and shook her head in response. "Oh, so I'm art now?" A coy smile appeared on her lips as she walked closer to me. "You know you're a certified jackass, right?..I'm not doing this again, I told you that last time."

She had always said that every time we'd meet up to have sex. She always told me that was the last time. It was never the last time.

Something in my stomach bothered me though by the way she was looking at me.
It was different than I had ever seen.
Maybe she *was* serious.

She walked closer towards me and softly stroked her fingers against my chest, then grabbed a fist full of my gray t-shirt and pulled.
"I know you want it. I want it..." she started, but was looking down at the dirty, old tile floor.
"But, Adam.. I can't do it anymore. I mean it. Things are different now."
I was so fucking confused. She was always sending me mixed signals. This girl was always fucking around with my mind like I was nothing.
"I'm engaged."

I felt myself pull away, like a magnet had been behind me pulling me in the opposite direction, and stepped back as far as I could from her. No way in hell was she engaged.

I never knew of another guy this entire two years we had been seeing one another. No, we weren't in a relationship, and that was perfect for me.

But the least she could fucking do was let me know she was fucking another guy while she was fucking me.

This was insane.

"Since when?" That was all I could get out. I wasn't really thinking straight. Even though we weren't committed to one another, I felt betrayed.

Talk about a bruised fucking ego.

I had gotten used to her being there. She was with me for two years, and I couldn't forget shit like that.

I can't forget her like that.

I wouldn't forget her.

"Last month. He's an accountant from Savannah, he said he was gonna help me get out of this lifestyle. And that's what I want. I want a normal life with a normal guy, and I want to have kids."

She look a deep breath then, and met my gaze.

"We were never going to be that, Adam. We were just hooking up. I know you don't want that, and now I know what it's like to be in love with someone. You'll always hold a special place in my heart. You will, I promise." The silence between us was violent.

But I wasn't going to act like it phased me as much as it had.

"You won't see me with the girls again, I'm moving to Savannah with Harry. But I wanted to say bye to you." She stepped closer towards me with a single tear streaming down her cheek.

I took a step back; reluctant at first. I had been hurt and given up on too many times in my life, and this shit was getting pretty fucking pathetic. I didn't know how much more loss I could take, and sometimes it was just easier to turn it off.

Soon her hands were cupping my face and she placed an eager kiss on my lips as she let out a small sigh. I felt myself give in for old times sake, and the heat in me ignited. I took my hands to her ass, and lifted her up around my hips. As I deepened the kiss, I felt a flick of her tongue against mine, and that made me want her.

And *God* did I want her.

    She was letting out the oh so familiar moan from her mouth and I felt her hips starting to thrust in a rhythm against mine. She didn't want to stop this either.

I knew she didn't. "Don't quit this." I said softly, still on her mouth.

That's when my fucking cell phone rang.

Fuck.

Timing was a bitch.. *wasn't it?*

    Like a strike of lightning, she was off of me and fixing her dirty blonde pixie cut hair. The back room door opened then, as Ricky walked out and the two girls followed.

They walked over to Natasha and rubbed her shoulder.

"I'm sorry Adam. I have to go." She turned towards the front door, then quickly turned back around to look at me once more.

This was the end.

"I'll see you." I said that looking straight into her eyes, and I tried my best to convince myself that what I said was true. I wasn't ready to say goodbye to her, but I knew it was fleeting.

    My phone continued to ring, so I pulled it out of my back jean pocket to look at the caller ID.

Joe.

    Damn, he was so fucking needy, but he was the only family I had left and that was important to me. "Tío, que pasa?" I heard a low growl from the other end of the line. I knew something must have been wrong.

 "Uncle, what do you need?"

Joe cleared his throat before he spoke "Adam, you know how I have difficulty with Spanish. I've never learned it. That was on your mother's side, not your dad's and mine. I'm as white as white can be, sorry kid." I heard a small chuckle from his voice, which made me smile.

"I know Tío, that's why I'm glad they decided to give me my mothers last name."

I always spoke in little bits of Spanish as I got older in hopes he'd learn it a little bit, but mostly to mess with him.

Mom and dad were big on teaching me about my mother's heritage in Mexico and what it meant to carry the legacy of the Rodriguez family. I took pride in my heritage as well as speaking the language, even if English was my primary.

"But I do get it can be confusing for you, uncle. Sorry. What's up?"

I heard static and background noise from what I assumed was from the bar. He was always at that damn place, he never did anything else.

"There was a girl who came in here tonight.. A bit too much to drink." I wish he would've been able to see my reaction, because it was a really good *"what the fuck?"* face.

"And that has to do with me, how?"

I knew my uncle was short fused, it sounded like he really did need something, but I couldn't help but throw some sort of sarcasm.

"Adam, just get down here. I need you to take her home. I couldn't call the cops, she had a fake I.D. and is only twenty.. I don't need that reputation for my bar. Not to mention, I doubt she'd want to get caught either since she's underage."

I rolled my eyes in response to what he said. It was around midnight for fucks sake and this random girl didn't know how to hold her alcohol?

"Adam..." Uncle Joe's voice began to sound shaky.

Ricky just standing there in front of me, staring at me like a fucking lost puppy. I nodded at Ricky and threw him the keys to my car. "Go start it" I mouthed. Ricky was a good friend, but he could never take the lead.. he would just stand there and look at me like a lost fucking puppy. "Fine, uncle I'll be there. It'll be a little bit though, I need to take Ricky home. I had to pick him up from his mom's."

There was no sense in lying to my Tío Joe. He had his suspicions and already knew what I was getting myself into. He was a smart guy, I didn't even need to tell him.

"Take him home, then get here." Joe didn't say anything else, he just cleared his throat and hung up the phone.

I just had a big fucking difficult moment in this trailer between trying to do my job, Natasha throwing a big ass bomb on my plans, and my uncle Joe calling for help. And even though I didn't want to be a fucking taxi for a baby twenty year old girl, I knew I would rather do that then to spend time alone with my shitty thoughts, and the constant reminder that I would never see Tasha again.

I walked out of the trailer and headed to the car, ready to get this night over with. Ricky was in the passenger seat lighting a cigarette as I approached the driver's side. "Give me one of those, will you?" I kept my face toward the front windshield, reaching my hand over to get the cigarette from my friend, but my hand remained empty for several seconds. As I turned to meet his gaze since he was taking so fucking long, but I was met with his wide, concerning stare.

"What the fuck happened, man?" All I could do was roll my eyes at him.

Ricky knew me better than anyone, he had known me for almost 14 years. He was my ride or die, quite literally. Ricky knew I had stopped smoking about 7 years ago when I had lost my dad to lung cancer, so for me to bum a cigarette was clearly shocking, since it never fucking happened anymore.

"Nothing, Rick. I don't want to talk about it. Just bum me a fucking cig and don't talk."

Ricky sighed and scratched his head, like he was having an internal war with himself for a minute.. clearly he was unsure of what to do.

Sure, Ricky was my best friend and knew everything about me, but one thing he had to learn was to not fuck with me when I was in a bad mood. I snapped my fingers and shot a heated stare in his direction. I wasn't waiting for him to contemplate, I just wanted a fucking cigarette. I was tired of his concerned puppy dog eyes staring, frozen at me in time. "Fuck, I'm sorry. Did I ask you to make my decisions for me, Rick? Either bum me a cig or you can ask one of those crack whores you like so much for a ride home.."

Ricky shook his head in defeat and pulled an extra cigarette out of his pack, lighting it before handing it to me.

"You didn't need to be such a douchebag Adam. What the fuck man." I put the car in reverse and backed out of the old abandoned driveway and onto the backroad headed towards Covington. "Let's get one thing clear, Rick. You may think you know everything about me, but when I tell you to do something, you shut the fuck up and you do it. Whether it's a cig or a drug deal, you do it. I'm your upline for a reason." For being twenty six, I was one of the best in our business. So much so that our boss made me in charge of most of the distribution in Covington. It was a lot of ground to cover, and a lot of responsibility. Having Rick on my team made it easier to complete. But I'd be damned if I let someone who was under me in this business think they could make decisions for me. Even if it were my best friend.

I was the alpha in this corner of the business, and I was the alpha in my life.

And no one was going to tell me what to fucking do..

Well...except for Tío.

I owed that man *Everything*.

    We drove the rest of the way in silence, me finally reminding Ricky of his place seemed to do its job. He didn't speak a word to me, and despite me feeling as though I had been a little harsh, I knew he needed to know his place. And besides, we'd be cool by morning. That's just how we were. I dropped him off at his house before heading to the Tavern to save my Tío Joe's ass and some teenager who clearly didn't know how to handle her alcohol.

    The night had gone from bad to worse, and I couldn't think of anything else that could fuck up this night more than it already was.

But *fuck* was I wrong.

Chapter Four: Adam

It was a little after 1 a.m. when I got to the skull. I was almost sure that uncle Joe was gonna beat my ass. But that was okay.

I was saving his.

I knew that I was dreading this entire fucking thing, but it was the least I could do for my tío who put a roof over my head. Fifteen years without my mom and seven without my dad carried a shit ton of emotional problems for me, and without Joe, I would've been on the street, or worse.

I owed him my life.

I pressed my car key to lock my corvette before entering the bar. This car was my baby. This wasn't the car I used on supply runs though, I used my first ever car for that: a 2005 Toyota Camry. That beat up piece of shit got me around to where I needed to go, but it wasn't my baby.

After leaving our last buyer on our way back to Covington, I switched my cars at Ricky's apartment. I always left the Camry at his apartment since the lot was usually full, and most people who lived there couldn't avoid luxury cars, no one would be able to point my car from the rest. I was happy to be able to buy a corvette, though. Ever since I was a kid, it had been my dream. Cars were always a hobby dad, Uncle Joe, and I had shared and that car became my prized possession.

I walked into the back room of the skull and sat my gym bag in my uncle's office. I was planning on carrying upstairs to my apartment later on, and I knew I didn't need to worry about it right now. I pushed the rustic barn door that separated the bar from the back room and walked over to the entrance of the island. I poured myself a glass of bourbon as I made my way through the bar towards Joe.

Damn. There was nothing like bourbon to take the edge off.

    My uncle Joe had noticed my arrival, smiling and giving a sigh of relief as he walked over to me and grabbed a hold of my shoulder.

"Thank you for getting here, Ad. You have no idea how much I appreciate it."

    I popped a couple pretzels in my mouth from a serving dish on the bar. "No es un problema." My uncle rolled his eyes out of habit pretending he was annoyed. But I could tell there was a small speck of a smile there.

    "So where is she?" I asked as I finished my drink and placed it into the sink at the bar.

He nodded his head over to his left, toward the curved booth in the corner.

Jesus. This wasn't going to be easy.

    "Be warned, she's thrown up three times." I threw my head back in disgust.

Fuck. This girl was already annoying the hell out of me and the only thing I could see about her was her black converse shoes.

    One thing that I couldn't stand? Someone taking advantage of my uncle Joe's kindness. Joe was a bit naive; always choosing to see the better side of things and people. He was always so optimistic, despite the loss we both had suffered, and he was kind to everyone, *always*. But, those traits will die with him, and sure as hell weren't passed down to me.

    I was always more of the rough type; I'd sneak out of mom and dads house when I was just ten years old. I liked adventure, I liked feeling the thrill of life. Nothing could or would ever stop me. Until something did.

When my mom passed my entire earth shattered, and what little hope of humanity I had perished along with her. After she was gone, I didn't see a sense of saving myself anymore, and let life choose my path. A path which led me here; twenty six years old, single, and a washed up drug dealer who still lives with his uncle. And not to mention, now had to take care of this dumb little shit of a human who thought they could come drink underage in my tío's bar.

Not that I'm against underage drinking.. fuck, I was ten when I had my first drink. But to blatantly walk into a bar, knowing you're risking yourself and the whole staff at said bar? Well, that was damn stupid.

I turned to uncle Joe, who was on the other side of the bar now with his eyebrows raised and arms crossed tight to his chest.

"Well Tío.." I cleared my throat, "Thanks for the wild night out.. being someone's taxi? Real nice…" I joked, but we both knew I had been serious. I could've been doing literally anything else, but here I was cleaning up messes. Messes that weren't fucking mine.

"Well Joe, I better get her home. Do you know where she lives?"

My uncle, the man of many words, simply nodded and pulled a piece of paper out of his pocket. "I found it on her real license." I read the small, white piece of paper.

1824 Scottsdale Way Covington, GA. How white of a neighborhood was this? It had to have been up in the suburbs; A place I wasn't familiar with considering I've lived in the apartment inside this very bar for fifteen years.

I figured this girl must have been far out of her territory, considering that her purse was a Prada and her converse had absolutely no wear and tear on them… not even a fucking scuff. It wasn't hard to figure out that this girl was the definition of entitled.

"Here are her keys. Take her car and park it at her house." He said, hesitating to hand me her car keys at first, but finally giving in: "And don't wreck it. It's an Audi."

Alright, this girl was way out of her element.

It made me wonder why she came here in the first place and the sudden thought piqued my interest, but I decided long ago to not question things I was asked to do. I was taught to just do the job: don't ask questions, don't get involved anymore than you already are… Just get done and move on. And that's how I planned to deal with this entitled pain in the ass.

I moved the silver round table enough so that I could reach for her and pick her up easily. Getting her home safe and sound was all my Uncle had asked of me, and I knew I couldn't let him down. That's when my eyes noticed the beautiful fucking mess of a girl sprawled out on the booth, snoring peacefully. Instead of paying attention to my immediate attraction to her, I simply decided to do the opposite.. I decided to hate her. I was disgusted by the way her cheeks tinted the softest shade of pink, I hated the damn Prada bag that probably cost more than what I will ever make in my lifetime, and I fucking couldn't stand the way my breath caught as her jet black hair fell perfectly along her neck, tracing her silhouette so perfectly, ending softly along the top of her breasts. I ignored my immediate attraction to her and cleared my throat.

I had decided that I was disgusted with everything about her, and I knew that the only way I could continue to do so was to pretend that whatever feeling that was making my heart race had nothing to do with her.

The thing was, though, that deep down I knew I couldn't hate her. And that's what made me despise her even more. I knew I couldn't hate her because of the innocent, peaceful look she had on her face as she slept so gracefully. Something about it made my stomach leap, and my stomach hadn't known of that feeling for a very long time.

I felt her warm, soft skin wrap around me perfectly as I smoothly picked her up in my arms. As I carried her, I began to notice her features a little more closely: the pearl complexion of her face, the freckles hiding along her cheeks, and the way her eyelashes fluttered while she slept. The curves of her face were only something you'd see out of a painting— chiseled around her cheeks but puffy and rounded around her chin, proving that she still had some growing in her facial features left to do.

She had beautiful plump pink lips that begged to be kissed, full and resting in a soft smile while she slept angelically in my arms.

The truth was, I knew I wasn't a fucking idiot. I knew she took my breath away in an instant. I felt my breath hitch deep in my throat as I forcefully reminded myself to breathe. She was beautiful, breathtaking, *angelic*. And I didn't think I had ever seen someone as beautiful as her— And that pissed me off, to no fucking end.

Fuck.

I brushed a single strand of hair from her eye as I enjoyed looking at the soft pink color on her cheeks. She seemed so peacefully asleep that I didn't want to even think about waking her.

Just as I walked to the front door, I heard my uncle clear his throat. As I turned back around, the mystery girl made herself comfortable and nuzzled her body closer to my chest. She tucked her head into the side of my neck, which just about ruined me.

What the fuck was happening?

"Make sure you get her home safe, Adam, I mean it. No side-hustle stuff on the way to her house, either. Here's some money. Call yourself an Uber once you drop her off."

My uncle Joe was always so protective of me and his close friends. But I wasn't sure why he was protecting some young girl who came here to drink illegally at his bar.

The thought of how contradicting he was made me laugh. He hated what I did, and I didn't even tell him what I did, he just kind of figured it out. He would always give me lectures about how illegal activities would "*get you nowhere in life except for prison*", and now he was helping a girl who did a lesser version of the same thing. And only then did I realize that I didn't care about how beautiful she was.. because the whole situation was entirely fucked up.

I decided to not bring that up to my uncle, so I thought it best to just reassure him in the best way I knew how. "Está bein, tio." I said that with a wide smile on my face, knowing just how much that got on his nerves. The thought of him rolling his eyes at me made me laugh.

I didn't want him to worry though, I always come through on my jobs, and I considered this one to be one of them. "I'll get her there in one piece, uncle."

I smiled at him once again and turned back towards the front door. I walked out the main entrance and felt the cool air hit my face, it wasn't normally this breezy here in Georgia. The sky was full of dark clouds, and the low distant rumble of thunder filled the sky. I knew a storm was coming, even if I wasn't prepared for it. I quickened my pace, knowing that I didn't want to get caught up in a storm driving someone else's car and going to a place I've never gone. I needed to get her home before the storm came. I needed to get her there before I started to panic at the familiar sounds of the thunder and the rain. I typed her address in my gps on my phone and waited for the route to load.

46 minutes to get to 1824 Scottsdale Way...

Where the hell did she live? Kentucky?

There was no way I was driving 46 minutes without the storm hitting; it already looked close enough. I knew I was completely and utterly screwed at this moment, but nothing was going to change the fact that I'd be driving a twenty year old girl in her car in a storm. Fear crept in as I placed her in the passenger seat of her car and buckled her in. The constant repetition of my mother's screams from fifteen years ago rang in my ears with every sound of thunder.

I may have lived through that crash, but all I knew was that fear took over my life, storms became my enemy, and without fully acknowledging it.. somehow I was still alive. But what I did know was that an eleven year old boy had died in that car with his mother That night and all that remained to this day was an empty carcass of a kid living without his heart; without his mother.

*

I hated that I agreed to even take this damn girl home. It's not like I felt entirely confident to be driving a stranger's expensive ass car through a thunderstorm. And not to mention that this damn girl was sound asleep in the passenger seat...*snoring.*

It wasn't like I was pissed at her for being oblivious to the loud sounds of lightning and thunder, but the damn girl could wake up and distract me from this fucking anxiety I felt.

I never enjoyed driving during a thunderstorm- in fact, I hardly ever did it. That meant I had to really love my uncle to be doing this shit right now.   Instead of allowing myself to feel the full sense of panic rising in my chest, I gripped my hands on the wheel and started thinking of the fond memories I had of my parents. Ones that would distract me from the thought that both of them were gone, and that I was a twenty six year old man whose life never would be what they had hoped for me. Despite being a disappointment to them, I knew my parents loved me, and I knew my parents loved each other... and that was one of the greatest things that I've been able to hold onto.

But I also had to hold onto the painful memory of them dying. And despite having my dad for nearly a decade longer than I had my mom, the pain of losing them both never went away, and I knew that it never would.

That's why I hated storms.

That's why I was such a little bitch and couldn't man up right now.

That's why I didn't want to be alone right now. The 11 year old in me was screaming and having a panic attack and the 19 year old in me just felt numb.

Sure, I could meet clients who carried rifles and I had regularly run from the police, but I couldn't fucking handle a thunderstorm.

Fuck, am I a little bitch?

Yes.

You are.

I let my hands gripped the wheel so hard that I felt my hands start to burn.

No way was I going to let anything happen to us tonight, and no way was I about to let anything happen to this car. As I turned onto the highway, I switched the knob for the wipers to increase their speed. The rain had picked up, and there were several lightning strikes. This girl must have been really drunk if loud lightning strikes didn't wake her up.

All I wanted to do was drop her off and go home, and truthfully I was fucking exhausted. I looked at the clock on the dashboard that read 1:34am. I was used to being out around this time of night— I was always going somewhere with Ricky, or I was on a supply run. But never in a million years would I think I'd be put this late because of a girl. A dumb girl, actually.

A fucking girl who couldn't control her liquor.

It felt too quiet here. I could hear myself breathe.

Worse, I could hear myself think.

I turned up the volume on the radio, which automatically connected to the girl's music from her phone. I was expecting some fruity girly-girl pop music like Justin Bieber or the Jonas Brothers, but it wasn't. It was the music I liked. A familiar track played on the radio from the Black Keys. I was genuinely surprised by her taste in music. It was something that I didn't expect from her girly pop exterior.

As surprising as her music genre was, I felt myself starting to wonder what other artists she liked. Maybe she liked Red Hot Chili Peppers, too.

What was her favorite song?

I wanted to know what was inside of her head, and it really fucking irritated me. I couldn't figure out why I cared so damn much based on one song on some random girls playlist.

Maybe it's because she seemed like she had more depth to her than she actually showed. Maybe because she was someone who looked like she wasn't just another spoiled brat. She looked like she had a story, and I was surprised when I realized that I had wanted to hear every single word of it.

I took the exit off of the highway and continued to follow the gps onto a back subdivision road. I had hoped I was going the right way. I couldn't believe that I still had 25 minutes left to drive. This was bullshit.

Just as I was about to turn onto a backroad, a strike of lightning shot down right in front of the car which scared the absolute shit out of me. I cut the wheel and swerved off of the road into a small patch of dirt that headed towards the woods.

This was God's way of fucking me over.

This was the way I was gonna die.

I sat on the side of the road for a minute listening to the beat of the wiper blades shifting back and forth on the rainy windshield, and I tried to catch my breath and calm down from this almost fucking nightmare. Not to mention that it felt like my heart had just dropped out of my ass. This whole thing was insane, and I was seriously regretting my involvement in this. But then I heard her voice.

"What happened?"

She rubbed her eyes with her knuckles and stretched her arms and torso out in an attempt to fully wake herself up.

I didn't know what to say.

We were safe, and no damage was done, but I sure as hell saw my life flash before my eyes. I didn't know how to explain any of it to her without sounding like a complete and total dumbass.

"Uh, everything is okay. There was a lightning strike in front of us, so I pulled off of the road for a minute."

She softly nodded her head and gave me a kind smile.

That fucking smile.

    What it did to my insides was fucking insane. My pulse quickened and adrenaline rushed through my veins.

    "Oh, no worries. I drank a little bit too much at the bar. I'm glad I'm feeling a bit better now." Her focus shifted to me, as her eyes took me in. Her eyes skimmed up my torso, to my tattooed arms, and eventually met my eyes. Her eyes pierced into mine with such intensity that my skin began to feel as if it were on fire. The way her eyes looked into my soul felt thrilling, and yet, fucking terrifying.

    I didn't know what the hell she was doing, but she needed to quit. I didn't have the time to feel like this. I didn't *want* to feel like this, and whatever the fuck I had been feeling since the moment I saw her needed to stop.

    The only thing was, I didn't fucking want it to.

    She suddenly snapped her eyes away and pulled her phone out of her pocket frantically. She let out a large huff and covered her face with her hands.

    "Oh my god. I didn't know I was out this late! My dad called me like six times! He got called out to the hospital a little bit ago— He's probably freaking out right now.. Shit. Shit. Shit."

    She bent over in her seat and wrapped her arms around her legs for a moment as her pony tail flopped over in front of her face. It gave me a chance to notice the small semicolon tattoo on the back of her neck; small enough to miss if you weren't looking for it, but something I could definitely notice.

    Her olive skin was perfectly accented by the moonlight, making her look as if her entire body was gleaming. There was no doubt that she was breathtaking.

What the fuck was wrong with me?

She continued hugging herself for a moment, as I admired her arm and back muscles, noticing how strong they appeared— like she used them constantly. Her hair was like a dark brown which almost resembled black, which went perfectly with her fair skin. But as beautiful as she was, none of that really compared to the way she looked into your soul.

It was a look that could kill if it wanted to. Her ice blue eyes could ruin me at any second and I would be fine with it.

"Don't worry, I'm taking you home. Call your dad and let him know you're safe."

She popped her head up then, and met my gaze once again. Her stare lingered this time, like she wasn't sure whether to believe me or not.

"Um, this is a little bit of a late question to ask, but who are you?" She continued to stare for a few more seconds, her eyebrows furrowed together in confusion before she bursted out into laughter, then slapped her hand over her mouth to stifle it.

It was the fucking cutest thing I've ever seen.

I felt myself holding in a laugh of my own, but she made me want to let it out. Every part of my body relaxed when I heard that laugh of hers. Her angelic laugh made my lips form into a small smile as my heart took somersaults in my stomach.

"I'm Adam. You went to the Skull tavern, the bar my uncle Joe owns. You had too much to drink, so my uncle called me to drive you home."

She had ceased all laughing by that moment, and her face went serious. I had clearly gained her attention. Her expression had gone from serious, to worried, to calm in a matter of seconds. All I wanted to know was what was going on inside that beautiful head of hers.

"So you're not gonna like... drive me deep into the woods and hack me to pieces, right?"

She said as her ice blue eyes skimmed from my eyes, and slowly burned down my body once more. Her eyes had stopped on my hands, as she admired the skull tattoo on my right hand. She slowly reached for my hand, and studied the tattoo with her fingers, gently tracing it with her own as if she was in a trance. Her fingers skimming along the ink on my skin caused my skin to shiver, and goosebumps formed on my arms. She seemed to notice my reaction to her, as her breath hitched, knocking her out of her trance, and she snatched her hand away from mine then closed her eyes for a short moment. Her cheeks reddened and she took a deep breath, then opened her eyes to meet mine.

"And it was only you who was there at the bar right? Like no cops or anything?"

I tried to stop myself from smiling. I knew exactly why she was asking.

She was afraid she had been caught drinking underage. It would have been really cute had she not almost risked my uncles livelihood just for some alcohol.

"No, no cops. Joe figured out you were underage though. That's why he called me. Didn't want a bad rep for him, or for you. He's a caring guy like that… but *me*?— Not so much." It took her a moment to fully process what I had said, but her eyebrows furrowed and she nodded her head a few times in understanding. "Oh...okay then."

She nodded again and pressed play on her phone connected to the radio.The Black Keys softly lingered in the background as we both focused our eyes back on the road. There was so much silence, but it felt like there was so much to be said.

I waited a moment before speaking my opinion, and knew that no matter how beautiful she had been, she still did something irresponsible that would have affected my uncle's livelihood. Joe was all I had left, and I wasn't going to let anyone, not even the prettiest woman I had ever met, hurt him. She needed to be aware of that. "So—Uh I just wanted to say that if my Uncle Joe hadn't been so understanding tonight, you'd probably be in jail. Just to throw it out there... That bar is all he has, and you seriously could've fucked his life up back there if you had been caught."

She looked up at me with sorrowful eyes before speaking. "I didn't know— I really like Joe, I didn't mean—" Her words cut off as if she was thinking. There was a moment of silence as I continued to keep my eyes on the road ahead of us. After a moment, she sighed softly and then continued. "You know what? Hold on a minute..." Her voice grew stronger, filling with annoyance. "... One, you're driving my car, and you choose *now* to bring up the fact that I could've risked your Uncle's business? *And* I don't even know you!" She spat.

"How dare you say that to me when you have *no clue* about what's going on in my life. So what if I needed a drink to take the edge off? So what if I used a fake ID? You know how many other underage people do that? Millions!" She was talking so loudly that I couldn't hear the music anymore, but I knew she wasn't even close to being done with her rant. "Look *buddy*, I didn't know that I was putting your Uncle's bar at risk when I went in there. I talked to Joe, and I really like him. Had I known that beforehand, I wouldn't have drank there. Okay?" She turned her whole body to face me now, waiting for my response.

I couldn't explain why, but seeing her so riled up about my comment grew some sort of satisfaction in me. I liked her mad side, it was ridiculously sexy.

A small smile played on my lips again, but I didn't let it linger. Instead, I decided to play into her little fit of anger.

"Okay, I understand. I just think you should think a little more before you go out and do that. Drinking and driving isn't worth the risk. You shouldn't be so irresponsible…" My voice wandered off as I looked over to her, her eyes full with rage.

"And you shouldn't be such a dick…" She fired. "… why do you care, anyway? You don't know me."

I hated to reveal my truth, but I knew she wouldn't understand, even if I tried to explain it. But I knew it was worth a shot to try. She needed to see that she would have affected everyone's livelihood. She could've killed herself if she drove, and my uncle would've been in trouble for serving her. That much was clear.

"Listen…" I raised my voice as I gripped the steering wheel, in hopes for her to take a moment to listen. "… Do you know what it's like to be an orphan? Probably not, considering the car you drive. You probably don't even know what struggle is."

She huffed and crossed her arms and tears began to well in her eyes as she turned to look out the window. "You don't know me, so don't claim to think you have it all figured out."

She sat there in silence, continuing to look out the window as I drove.

"Listen…" I said softly, "I know I don't know you. I know I might come across as a total asshole. And fucking I get it. But unless you watch someone you love die because of drunk driving, you'll never get it."

Her gaze shot to me then as a small tear rolled down her cheek. She quickly wiped it away as I continued.

"I am very overprotective of my Uncle Joe. He is all I have…" I glanced over at her, her ice blue eyes deepening to a darker blue. "… When I was eleven I went out to dinner with my mom after a soccer game. She had a few drinks with dinner, which usually wasn't a problem, she did that a lot. The thing that made it different was that she had just started new depression medication that week, and we were driving and got caught in a bad storm. She couldn't see very well, and we hydroplaned. Ended up hitting into the guardrail and spun around into a tree..." My breath felt heavy and my heart ached as I told Tara my story, but I continued on, "... My mom died instantly. I was pretty banged up, but I was in the backseat... Another car had swerved into the guardrail and into a ditch to try to miss our car. That young couple died, too and the family ended up suing the restaurant that served my mom the alcohol. That's why I am saying this. No amount of drinking is going to cure whatever the hell you've got going on in your life, and driving only puts you and everyone else on that road with you at risk." I gripped the steering wheel as I finished my story, but Tara remained silent. The only thing I heard was the small sniffles coming from beside me as she continued to look back out the passenger side window.

After a few minutes, the GPS route told us we were almost to our destination, and she finally broke the silence. "Oh, the GPS will take you the wrong way from here. Turn left up here instead."

I followed her directions enough to know that she could hold her own if she needed to. Other than her giving me directions to her house, the only thing I heard was the purr of the car engine and the faint music on the radio.

I decided to turn off my gps on my phone, since Tara was giving me directions anyways. My phone suddenly vibrated, alerting me that I had a notification.

It was from one of my buyers, Diego.

As I read the text, my mind was being a little bitch again and told me not to text and drive, but this text was important.

Diego: Hey man, so I need the usual hook ups for tonight. I need some moons if you can deliver, oh and bring Bernice too dude.

I rolled my eyes in disgust.

I never did any of this shit myself, but I made pretty good bank on selling it to other people. Sometimes it got too fucking overwhelming, though. Like people wanted too fucking much and expected too fucking much. I wasn't a damn drug lord, I couldn't just magically get Molly to pop up out of nowhere. That would require some real intel business. That would mean I'd have to call up Jerome and his crew again in Atlanta before I could even give Diego the hookup.

It was already 2 am, and I couldn't stand this shit. I knew I wasn't going to get to bed anytime soon, I had to hit up Jerome after dropping the excruciatingly beautiful princess off at her castle. I let out a huge huff of air that I had been holding in for the past few minutes, and slouched back in the drivers side seat, trying to get as comfortable as I could and enjoy the last few minutes of driving with a beautiful girl in a sick fucking car.

It still didn't change the fact that this was about to be one of the longest nights of my fucking life.

Chapter Five: Tara

I had been asleep for a long time, I guess.

I wasn't really too aware of what was happening, but I knew I was carried out of the bar and put into my Audi's passenger seat, and soon we were driving. I didn't really care about what was happening, until I felt the car jerk and my tires squeal. It was a nightmare to wake up to, and it made me scared for my life. I remember waking up, and felt more consciously aware of my surroundings.

Maybe throwing up all those times was actually a good thing.

I looked at the person sitting next to me, a stranger and yet my savior all in one, wanting to know what he looked like; eager to look into his eyes. It took me a moment to fully understand his presence.

His skin had a natural tan tint, and his hair was a chestnut brown that had been cut short, but the top of his hair was long enough to form curls at the ends. It was almost too much to handle at how instantly attracted I was to him.

What threw me for a loop, though, was how chiseled his features were. His jaw could break a saw blade if it wanted to. His long, muscular arms had tattoos cascading down them, the black ink weaving around his forearm like a vine.

We had been driving in silence for awhile, ever since he told me about his mom dying. I couldn't form any words to explain how much my heart broke for him, and how right he was about the whole thing, so I stayed quiet.

I thought about the fact that my dad would freak out when I got home, but instead it was not talking to a stranger that I didn't know. The stranger introduced himself as Adam, which was a great name to me.

Adam.

It sounded like the most perfect thing in the world. And I was also glad that he wasn't planning on hacking me to pieces in the woods…which made me relax a little bit. I noticed myself glaring over in his direction several times on our drive back to my house, knowing that I couldn't help myself, it was like my body had an automatic instinct to pull towards him. He felt like a magnet to me, pulling me in with his soft brown eyes and strong, intimidating presence. I tried my best to tell myself to not be this type of girl; to be smitten over some guy she literally met like 30 seconds ago.. but there was something about him that was different than any other person I had met.

It felt like I was supposed to know him somehow. I could feel it in my gut, but I didn't know how to feel about it. Something was telling me that this had to have been fate; that the universe was finally starting to work in my favor. But I had been let down frequently before, and I didn't want to be let down ever again.

We were about ten minutes away from my house when I noticed he grabbed his phone off of the dash and was reading something. It worried me because I didn't know this guy, he was driving my car, it was thunder storming, and yet he was texting and driving. No way was I going to let him wreck this car.

No, I don't think so.

"Hey, um, maybe you shouldn't be texting while there's a storm." I said it quietly, but got my point across. I wasn't going to end up in a car wreck because he was too careless.

He looked up at me from his phone then, meeting my gaze, and I felt my breath catch.

His dark brown eyes felt like they were melting my own. I felt like I was lost in a dark, wanting place that filled every single one of my senses. It was amazing and terrifying all at once.

"Lo siento, chica." I knew what he said to me, I had been taking Spanish in high school for three years now.

It's not like it was hard to figure out what he was saying anyways.

He had a small sly smile on his lips, like he was testing me. Like he was using his second language to fool me; like I was completely oblivious to what he was saying.

With every fiber of my being, I wanted to prove him wrong.

I knew I wanted to start a conversation with him anyway, but this was the perfect moment to do it.

"no hay problema, dijiste Joe es tu tio?"

That caught his attention. My Spanish was a little sloppy, but I thought I had gotten my point across.

"No problem, you said Joe is your uncle?"

He looked directly at me, his eyes burning into mine like a soft ember.

I knew he was surprised. I'm sure he was wondering how a girl like me knew how to carry on a conversation with him in another language. The side of his mouth turned upward, into a crooked smile then, but he took his eyes off of me and placed them back on the road. "Okay then...." He said as he rubbed his tattooed skull hand on his slightly grown out beard. There was a long pause, which seemed to have gone on forever.

"And yes, Joe is my uncle." I smiled, but kept my eyes on the road, knowing that if I'd look at him again, I might not be able to control myself.

"Well that's great. He's really a nice guy."

He didn't say anything for a moment, and just kept his hands on the wheel and face towards the road. A few seconds later, a small "mhmm.." escaped his throat.

We drove the rest of the way in silence, but I kept my smile on my lips, secretly celebrating my small victory.

Once we reached the suburbs, I told him to turn into the entrance of my subdivision. "It's there on the left." He did as he was told, and pulled up to the entrance gate.

"I'll be right back." I said as I opened the passenger side door, got out, and ran over to the entrance keypad.

As much as I appreciated this guy driving me, I didn't want him to know how to get into the gate. You can't trust everybody. I learned that during my early years in the system with my old foster mom. She would always scam people and would ask the neighbor girl down the hallway in our apartment to watch me, then would never pay her. I mentally shook my thoughts out of my head; I didn't want to have to remember that right now.

I finished entering my code, and lightly jogged back to the passenger side of my car. "Sorry, I just needed to put that in, and I don't really know you that well."

I said as I swung my feet in the car and closed the passenger side door.

I looked over at him to catch his reaction,

But all that he did was simply nod his head and give me a half smile. "No, I understand." We pulled through the gate and down the road to the first stop sign.

He listened to direction very well, turning everywhere I told him to, and didn't mess up once. My subdivision could be a little bit tricky at times. There's a lot of stop signs and subdivisions to the subdivision, and there are little side roads that go off to a path up to a few houses.

Once we arrived at my house, I told him to pull my car in the driveway and to cut the engine. "Well...This is me." I hated how awkward I sounded. It wasn't like I was out on a date with him or something. He whistled in reply as he leaned forward in his seat, gazing out the windshield, taking in the sight of my home. He looked completely amazed. Honestly, I was, too. I would never get used to this large 3 story home I lived in that had 8 guest bedrooms and 6 bathrooms.

"This is crazy." He said as he admired the outside of my house from the driver's side window. My dad must've known I was going to be late, he left the front door light on to make sure I could find my way inside.

I loved him so much.

I opened the door, and the mystery guy followed my actions, opening the drivers side door as well, then following me up the stairway to my front door. As I reached the door entrance, I turned back to look at him standing just a few steps down with his hands in its pockets. "Um, so thank you for driving me home." I said softly.

He smiled and nodded before answering: "Yeah, no problem. Have a good night." I gave him a small smile in return and reached in my purse for my front door keys. I panicked for a quick moment, trying to find where they were, before realizing that they're on a keychain with my car keys. I turned back around to face the stranger, and walked down a few steps to meet him.

"I, uh— kinda need my keys." I laughed lightly and rubbed my forehead.

Why am I so awkward?

He laughed in response and pulled my keys from his pocket. "Yeah I guess you do." He reached out his skull hand towards me with my keys in hand, and I met him halfway with mine. As I grabbed my keys out of his grip, our fingers slightly touched, sending a spark through my fingertips. It was like static electricity as it traveled throughout my entire body. It was exhilarating to me and I had a feeling that he felt it, too because after a moment, he jerked his hand back and slid it into his pocket.

I wanted so badly to be able to touch him again.

Even one more time.

"Yeah, so thank you... um—"I held my other hand out, gesturing to him that I wanted to shake hands to thank him. My face filled with embarrassment that I couldn't remember his name, but I was still drunk, and I had a rough night. His soft chuckle made my spine tingle. I felt a sense of warmth come over me like I was stepping out into the sunlight. "Adam, Adam Rodriguez." He replied, and his eyes burned fiercely into mine. I couldn't help but blush and smile. The corners of his mouth formed dimples into his tanned skin, and it made my heart flutter.

"Nice to meet you, Adam. I'm Tara Evans."

We stood there for a moment, our eyes locked into one another's gaze, and our hands still held into a handshake. I felt like all time had stopped and slowed down, and we were just there. Being us. I had a strange urge to get to know him, I wanted to know everything about him. I also knew that I was being completely ridiculous, and that I had just met this guy, but he made me feel like I was on an adrenaline kick, and I wanted more. So much more. "Do you have a way to get back home?" I asked, how fully remembering that he was stuck here. He pulled his hand away from mine, and time seemed to resume, making our moment quickly pass. "Yeah, I'm gonna call an Uber."

His hands went back into his pockets, which seemed like a nervous habit or something. I didn't fully know why I was allowing myself to think this way, but before I knew it, I said the words that I immediately second guessed. "No, don't." I said, biting my lip. "You can stay, if you want." Those were the words I wish I could take back, or at least could have changed. I sounded like a desperate whore who wanted him to come in with me. I hated the way I sounded. I was so embarrassed. I could tell he was confused, too.. his thick eyebrows were arched upwards and his lips were slightly parted, like he was in shock.

I needed to fix what I said, and I needed to do it as quickly as possible. "I didn't mean it in that... I meant you can come in and sleep with me— shit, not *with* me, but like in the house.. if you want, not that I'm telling you that you should... or that you have to... we have eight guest rooms.... but like I said you don't have to... I just thought you could stay.. but totally not in a sexual way, I'm just trying to be nice."

What. The. Hell.

I was a complete and total disaster.

He took his skull hand and rubbed the back of his neck as he bit his lip, trying to fight a smile. "I appreciate the offer...." he said, still rubbing the back of his neck.

I knew what he was going to say, I had been rejected plenty of times from guys to know when they didn't want anything to do with me.

I stopped him in his tracks before he could say anymore. "No, no, nope. Don't worry about it. I just was offering you a place to stay if you needed it, to thank you for bringing me home. But don't worry about it, no big deal." This was the most awkward moment I've ever experienced in my life. I didn't even know this guy and I was offering him a place to stay? I don't know what was going on in my head.

I waved goodbye to him, as he still rubbed the back of his neck, and turned to face my front door. I rolled my eyes at myself, I really wish I could have saved myself from that shit show. I unlocked my front door with my key and pushed it open, then turned the inside lights on in the entryway. I kept the door open as I attempted to take off my converse and put them in the correct cubby. I suddenly felt my body begin to feel the gravity testing me, pulling me towards the ground. I stumbled, and caught myself, holding onto the door for dear life. I must have still been drunk if I couldn't even take my shoes off. "On second thought..." I heard a deep, sultry voice behind me, and I quickly associated it with Adam. "How about I come in for a little bit while I wait for the Uber? I can help you get to bed and make sure you don't fall or hit your head off of something."

I heard his voice come closer and closer as he reached the front door, and soon he was directly behind me. I turned around to meet him, but I hadn't known just how close we were because I hit the side of my head off of his mouth while turning to face him.

"Ow, fuck."

He lifted his hand and placed his fingers on his mouth looking for any blood.

"Oh my god! I'm so sorry." I reached out to him to make sure he was okay.
My hands landed on his chest, on his dark gray v-neck t-shirt, and I could feel the hardness of his pecks beneath it. "I'm really sorry... I'm a klutz, I do stuff like this all the time, believe me." I reached my one hand to his face to remove his so I could check the damage on his mouth for myself. I hadn't noticed that he was still standing in the doorway, looking directly down at me. He reached his skull hand up to meet my hand that was placed on his chest, and he just kept it there. The tension I felt could cut a knife. I felt like every part of me was on fire.

 I met his gaze then, and felt a major sense of heat from his eyes. I knew what he wanted, and he was trying his best to hold himself back. What he didn't know was that I was trying too. I didn't know why this stranger named Adam had an immediate, yet strong hold on me, I couldn't quite figure it out. Guys like him weren't usually my type. I was usually seen around jocks, not dark, brooding guys who had tattooed sleeves and rock hard muscles.

 He must have read my mind though, he must of known what I was thinking: What I wanted to do to him..What I wanted him to do to me. He lightly licked his slightly blushed lips, and gripped my hand a little tighter.I was ready for whatever happened next, with the not so stranger, with Adam. And I was perfectly okay with it. He reached his skull hand up to my face, grabbed a piece of a loose strand of hair, and tucked it behind my ear. That gesture alone set my skin on fire. He closed his eyes for a brief moment, shook his head, and then stepped back.
"I think you should get some sleep."

 He scratched the side of his head and turned around. He walked down my front steps and onto the main street, as I stood there in complete shock. And there I was, standing in my entryway, annoyed, turned on, and feeling completely and utterly alone.

Chapter Six: Adam

What the fuck?

I had to get out of there quickly. It was like my body was acting and my dumbass head was nonexistent.

I continued walking down the street at a high speed. I wanted to make sure that my dumbass mind still worked and hoped that my body wouldn't tell me to turn back around right now, knock on her door, and kiss the shit out of her soft, plump looking lips.

There was no explaining what the hell was happening to me. I was used to meeting girls in bars or on a supply run, hanging out with them for a while, get a little drunk, or in their case, high, and hook up...but this was different. The attraction was immediate; I noticed it as soon as I picked her up out of that bar. To be honest, I didn't like that feeling, it made my stomach turn. I hadn't had this feeling in a long time, not really ever.

Not since Vanessa.

Dammit.

It took everything in me to continue to walk down the road, but I did it anyway. I texted the Uber driver and told him to meet me at the entrance gate. No way was I walking back to the house and waiting for the Uber there. I couldn't risk seeing her again. I walked out of the exit gate and stood there in the dark. I needed to get home as quickly as possible. I needed to drive to Atlanta to meet Jerome for the moons, and bernice, so that I could make the supply run to Diego. To fucking hell if I wasn't going to do the supply run to Diego. What he was asking for was selling for good ass money... Money that I needed to pay my bills. Money that I needed to help keep Joe's bar standing.

The Uber came and dropped me off at the skull about an hour later. The time was now 3 am, and I knew my ass would be getting an upcharge on the pills for this guy to be driving this late. I pulled the cash that tío Joe gave me out of my left side pocket and handed it to the driver. "Keep it." I shut the passenger side door, and walked to the back entrance of the bar. I walked to Joe's back office to retrieve my car keys and my gym bag, but I was stopped by Joe sitting in his office chair with his arms crossed and my bag, along with my supply sitting all over his desk.

Oh Fuck.

"Are you going to tell me what the hell all of this stuff is, or am I going to have to take a wild guess?" He was pissed. *Really* fucking pissed. There was no denying it. I knew I shouldn't have left my fucking gym bag in his back office, but of course I did. I was always fucking up somehow with him. "It's just some stuff I got from Ricky." I didn't want to explain exactly what it all was, so I just blamed the shit on Ricky. It's not like Joe liked him anyways. Couldn't hate him anymore than he already does.

He let out a large huff, and shook his head.

"I never knew exactly what you were doing. I figured at most it was weed. But this, Adam.. this is serious. You could go to jail for a long time for this. How careless are you?"

The thing was, Uncle Joe didn't know anything about my life, or what I chose to do with my time. He was a nice Man, he put a roof over my head and helped me since mom and dad died. I owed him a lot. But I didn't owe him an explanation. If I did, I knew it would destroy him.

The bar hadn't been making any money; Obviously he could see that. The bills from years ago still haven't been paid, and I have been catching them up.

If I hadn't, I wouldn't have anywhere to live, and Joe would lose his business.

I couldn't let that fucking happen.

The truth was that I had been in this business since I was in high school. I was a rebellious teen in my *I-have-a-dead-mom* phase, and got caught up with the high school druggies. That's where I met Ricky. Ricky's brother was the one who introduced me to the business of dealing when I was 19, just after my dad died. This had been my income for 7 years, and luckily I hadn't been caught yet. It started out with simple things, weed, pills like addies, but that was about it. I was able to handle those things so well at such a young age, that I kept getting involved with different dealers in my early twenties.

As I got older, I climbed up the chain of command, making the ability for me to change the path I was on impossible. Once I had been at the top of the line, I knew I was going to be in this for life. I was in too deep.

Now I'm one of the biggest dealers in the Covington area, and I'm dealing with just about any drug that they'd let me get my hands on. The problem was, I couldn't decipher what we would get for our supply, because my upline worked directly with the King.. and the King wasn't to be fucked with. My upline was Jerome, my boss so to speak. He would meet with the King, who most of us never met, and decide what shipments were coming in, and where to distribute them for the best profit.

Dealing drugs may have been illegal, but it was a business.. just like anything else. We'd buy the supply for a base rate and distribute it to our customers for double the price. That's just the way it worked. And I was in charge of that now.. making sure everything go distributed correctly, and our money wasn't fucked up. But that was because when I had gotten into business with Jerome, I learned pretty quickly that he was no dude to fuck with. He taught me how to get the best deal out of the buyers, make them feel like they were cutting a deal with us, when in reality we were benefiting. He also taught me to never fuck up the money, and to always have it even out. If your money didn't even out at the end of the night? You'd be as good as dead.

I remember it had happened when I first entered into the business with Jerome.. one his buddies, Jinx, came up short after a supply run. He was out over five hundred dollars, which wasn't surprising giving his fucking name. He was always playing games with his buyers, but I never knew he'd have the balls to do it to Jerome. I remember it like it was yesterday, there I was, standing in a room with all these guys, watching Jerome beat the shit out of Jinx:

"You're gonna tell me why you fucking shorted me you little bitch."

"Jerome, I swear, I counted it three times. I wouldn't fuck you over like that. We were selling for $60 a pop. How could I fuck it up?"

"That's where you fucked up. I raised it to $90"

"I-I didn't know that, J. I swear I didn't. No one told me before I left. I'll never do it again. I swear to you I won't, I swear!"

"That's right, Jinx. You're never gonna fucking do it again."

*

I can still hear the gunshot ringing in my ears. It had been years since that night happened, but I never forgot about it. What I learned from that moment on was that you didn't fuck around with Jerome.

Joe had known since I was in my early twenties that I was doing something suspicious with Ricky. He could call that shit from miles away. But I don't think he knew just how big this was. He'd never understand why I started this in the first place, and he sure as hell didn't understand that I was too far in it now to get out. It didn't help that Joe's attitude and constant questioning made me incredibly annoyed, either. I had somewhere to be. I wasn't going to get on Jerome's bad side and be a no show just to try to get my uncle to be less pissed off than he already was. No fucking way.

"Tío.... Tío..."

All I heard was Uncle Joe's constant lecture. I couldn't get a word in edgewise. This was insane. Joe had no fucking right to ridicule me like I was a child, much less go through my things. This was going to stop, now. "Tío, Deténgase, Por favor." *"Uncle, stop, please."* Joe still wouldn't stop. His reddened face and constant yelling had filled the entire room and I had enough. "has terminado de quejarte?" *"Have you finished complaining?"*

Uncle stood up then, packed all of my supply back into the bag and threw it at my face. "You better get the hell out of here right now, son. I don't want to see your face right now." The way he called me son made my blood boil. He was the farthest thing from my father. He was my fathers brother, but he couldn't talk to me like I was his kid. I wasn't his son. He would never even come close to comparing to my dad. And the fact that he treated me like a child when I was well into my fucking twenties? Fuck no. Fuck him. "Don't call me son." He walked around his desk toward me at full speed. I thought he was going to hit me, but he didn't. He just stood a few inches from me, looking at me with eyes filled with rage."Get the fuck out of here now, Adam. And don't come back until all of this is gone. For good! And I swear to God if you bring this shit back onto my property, so help me God I will call the cops on your ass. Do you understand?!"

I stood there, frozen; angry that he screamed at me like he was my father, annoyed that he treated me like a damn child, and utterly fucking embarrassed that I got caught.

He slammed his office door shut, and left me by myself in the hallway.

This night just keeps getting better.

Chapter Seven: Tara

The night that he left me standing in the doorway kept circling in my mind like a damn merry-go-round. I don't know why I couldn't get him out of my mind, it was like he was branded into my brain. I thought about him as I got into bed in a sports bra and my undies, I thought about him while I fulfilled my own desires and needs with my fingers. I thought about him the next morning, the second I woke up. I kept telling myself I needed to think rationally, to push the thought of him out of my mind.

I tried my best, but I couldn't help but think about his body, his dark curly hair, and that smile of his. That smile was a killer.

*

Speaking of killers, it was hard to go through a fucking Monday morning with a hangover from hell. I was up at 4:10, like I always was. I packed a bag of my school uniform, soap and shampoo, and other items to get ready for school after swimming practice. I re-pulled my now messy pony up into a high bun, put on my one piece, and placed a swimming t-shirt and sweats over my swimsuit. I hadn't felt this shitty in a long time. I don't think I had ever drank that much, either. I grabbed my bag and ran down the steps to my dad talking on the phone in the kitchen. "Yeah, okay. Well hang a new bag of Cipro, and I need a new round of labs; I'm ordering him a chest XRay as well, let's see if that pneumonia is clearing up...yep.... Yeah, Kristin, thank you.... yeah just make sure to get radiology up there for the X-ray... okay, bye."

I tried to steal a bottle of orange juice out of the fridge and an apple, and then sneak out of the house, but G caught me. "Uh, where do you think you're going, young lady?" I squeezed my eyes shut and threw my head back in disgust. I knew I was about to get a lecture. I turned around to face my dad, who was still wearing his lab coat and stethoscope. He must have just got back from the hospital. His eyes bulged and a worried expression appeared on his face. "Honey... you look awful." I rolled my eyes at him. He was just being dramatic. "Wow, thanks dad. The three words every girl wants to hear." I took a quick drink of my orange juice and sat it on the kitchen counter.

Dad walked over to me from the sink and pulled me into a comforting hug. "What time did you get home last night? You look exhausted."

I rolled my eyes again, trying to brush off my dad's concern. "I got home a little after midnight, why?" My dad pulled away from me, and placed his hands on my shoulders, still wearing his concerning look. "You knew you had practice this morning, kiddo. Why'd you stay out so late? Does this have to do with your mom leaving?...Do I need to worry about you rebelling?"

The thought of him freaking out made me laugh.

He was sort of panicking, but it was cute of my dad to worry so much about me.

"Dad...stop, I'm fine. I wasn't keeping track of time, and Rylie kept us there late talking about the competition. By the time I got home, I didn't even realize what time I had to get up." He stood there just staring at me, now with his hands on his hips.

He fixed his square modern glasses on his face, and placed his hands back onto his hips. "Okay, just don't do that again on a school night, kiddo. You get it?"

Me and dad always used our saying whenever we could, and I would always be so grateful that we could share it together. He'd always talk to me and at the end say, *you get it?* And I would always reply with *"I won't forget it."*

I smiled at him, walked up closer to him and kissed him on the cheek before I left for practice. "I won't forget it, dad. Thanks for caring, love you." I kissed his cheek, grabbed an apple out of the bowl on the island, and ran out the door.

By the time I got to the gym, it was 4:45, which was perfect because I had to do my stretches and some practice warm up laps before we started. I opened my locker in the locker room, put my duffle bag in there, and closed it behind me. I made sure my bun was secure before putting on my swimming cap and walked out towards the pool. As I approached the other swimmers, I saw one of my good friends, Haley. "Good morning Tara!" She said waving at me with a huge smile pressed across her face. The way she said it was super nice, but super loud. I felt a huge pang against my head…This hangover was going to be the death of me.

Obviously Haley knew something was wrong, because she jogged over quickly and rubbed my shoulders. "Are you okay? You look like fucking shit." She whispered softly towards my ear. She knew better than to cuss around Coach Eric, he would kick her out of tomorrow's meet if he heard us even say "hell." I simply nodded, and rubbed my temples with my index fingers. "Just a rough night, had a little bit too much to drink."

I opened my eyes then to see her reaction, and she was laughing while covering her mouth. "Well that explains it. How are you enjoying that hangover?" She said before continuing, "Practice is going to beat your ass, I promise you." She tapped my shoulder lightly, then walked away to her post. We were about to begin warm ups, when I saw a familiar face across the hall and through the window at the basketball court.

Adam.

No. No no no. This can't be happening.

I ducked my head, in hopes he wouldn't notice that I was in here. I hoped that he didn't remember what I looked like. What confused me the most was why he was coming to the gym to play basketball at five o clock in the morning... like who would *willingly* do that?

I knew I needed to avoid making any contact with him whatsoever, so I would try my best to keep away from that side of the complex. Haley and the rest of my first team teammates got on their starting blocks, and then the second team stood behind them, waiting for their turn. I walked over to my starting block, took off my shirt and pants, and made sure my swimming cap was on securely. I stepped up on the block, moved my arms back and forth, stretching my arms out, and cracked my neck. I was ready for this warm up. I was ready to have a great practice, despite my hangover. I knew that I was going to kick ass at the meet tomorrow, too.

I got into my starting position, ready to do a 100 meter freestyle for my warm up. My team member behind me, Blake, was someone I could always count on to give me feedback. Even though I was on the first team and he was on second, he always was honest about my form, and honesty was what mattered to me most.

Coach Eric stood at the end of the line, waiting for all of us to finish getting into our starting positions. "Morning everyone. Let's get to it. 100 meter freestyle to warm up, then we will do relays, then individual races. You know the drill. We got to be on our game for our meet tomorrow against Harrison College. Let's do this." Coach Eric blew his whistle once, signaling for us to extend our knees into a good push off position, then blew it again for us to dive in.

The second my body hit the water, it was like all of my worries went away. It was like I had no care in the world. Cheering drove me nuts, but swimming calmed me down. It was my own version of therapy. I felt the burn of my lungs begin as I picked up my speed towards the other end of the pool. Once I was close enough, I flipped, and kicked off into the other direction. I didn't really even know where I was in this warm up race, but I considered every event in the pool a race. And I needed to win. I pushed myself harder, moving my arms faster, picking up the speed of my breaths above water to compensate for my burning lungs.

 I reached the starting block where the rest of my teammates were, flipped over and pushed off the wall, back towards the opposite direction. I focused in on my goggles, looking to see if anyone was close to me.

There was no one in sight.

 By the time I ended back to the starting block, I knew this was the moment to really push my momentum. I knew I needed to get to the end. My body began to feel tired and weak because of the night before. And I knew it was going to hit me hard through the rest of practice. I touched the wall and popped up out of the water, to the side of the pool.

Coach Eric blew his whistle, to signify that everyone had finished.

"Great job first team. Go take a water break. Second team, you're up."

 Blake and the other second team members got up on the starting blocks, and waited for Coach Eric's signal. I ripped off my swimming cap, knowing that I needed to get the excess water out. It felt like a pocket of water was stuck and was sloshing around by my ear. I shook my swim cap out to dry, and then grabbed my water bottle and towel from the bench. "Good warm up, Evans." Corey Henderson walked over towards me, and slapped my shoulder blade. Corey was the typical swim jock type of guy. Him and I even went out for a couple of months my freshman year.

It was totally a nightmare.

I broke it off after 2 months; I was a virgin at the time, and he continuously tried to make me have sex with him. Even though he had a really nice six pack and beautiful sandy blonde hair, he was a major…douchebag. Even to this day he was a jackass, but he also hasn't given up on having sex with me. He makes sure to remind me of that every time he sees me at practice. "Hi, Corey." I said in a monotone voice, trying to show my disappointment. I took a drink from my water bottle, finishing the last drop of water before even acknowledging his presence near me."You're looking hot today, as always." I rolled my eyes at his comment. He always tried way too hard.

That was another annoying thing about him: he walked around like everyone wanted him and drooled over him, but he seemed to be the one doing the begging more than anyone. "Thanks...." I say looking towards the window at the basketball court. I suddenly remembered that Adam was over there playing basketball with two other guys. That made me curious. "Listen, Corey. I'm gonna go take a walk until my individual race, so I'll see you later." He smiled his million dollar, trying-to-hard smile, and patted my shoulder. "You got it, babe." As he walked away, I couldn't help but roll my eyes and feel a large wash of embarrassment flow over me for even talking to him in the first place.

*

I *wasn't* being a stalker. I had promised myself that over and over as I made my way down the hallway to look for *him*.

Was he still here? I really wanted to know.

Usually during practice I just sit on the bench when it isn't my race event, or I go for a short little jog around the track to finish warming my body up. But today was different. Today I walked along the hallways of the gym, looking slyly into each indoor basketball court, hoping to see him again, but also hoping he wouldn't see me.

So I kind of *was* stalking him.

What is wrong with you? Get your shit together Tara Elizabeth Evans.

I passed a water filtered fountain in the hallway as I passed the one court. I knew it was probably smart just to fill my bottle up now, instead of later. I filled my bottle up with the cold water, as my mouth began to salivate for more. The alcohol from last night must have made me more thirsty today for some reason, I don't know. I put the large cap back on my bottle and placed the water bottle to my lips. I turned and started walking back towards the swimming pools when suddenly my shoulder hit against someone.

I've done it again.

There were hardly any moments where I didn't feel like I was a constant bull in a china shop. "Oh, sorry m'lady, I didn't see you there." I look up from my bottle and meet his gaze. I didn't recognize this face. His skin was dark, as was his hair, which had a buzz cut. He was much taller than I, possibly around 6'4, and his cut off t-shirt showed off his biceps. "Yeah, no problem." I say, smiling at him kindly, then starting to walk away.

"Hey Platz, we told you to go get us Gatorade, not hit on the high school girls." Another male voice came from behind me, and continued with a loud laughter. I heard another laugh chime in, and that one seemed a lot more familiar to me. *Platz.* No fucking way.. I stopped in my tracks, feeling like I couldn't move.

I still had to walk down the rest of the corridor to get back to the pool, and I knew coach Eric would wonder where the hell I was, but I physically couldn't move.

"Shut the fuck up, Ricky. You're a dick."

They're laughter was closer to me now, and I knew that at any moment, I would be faced with seeing him again. "Hey, you." A familiar voice said.

"We're sorry if our friend here bothered you, or hit on you. We know you're probably here with the college swim team, and we don't want any trouble. I know you could probably do it yourself if you needed to, but I'll happily beat his ass if you want." His words alone made my entire body feel encapsulated in warmth, causing my legs to shake in response. It was like I could feel myself burning at my core with every word he said.

I started walking slowly, forcing myself to move, and hoping that he wouldn't recognize me in any way, whatsoever. "Mhmm..." was all I got out confidently. I opened my water bottle again and took a large drink of water from it. I had hoped they would get the idea that I didn't really want to be bothered with, and that I could walk the rest of the way to the pool in peace. But of course it wasn't working out that way. "Hey, wait up..."

His voice said, close behind me. I felt my spine begin to shiver again. It was too much to handle. I probably looked like a hot mess from swimming, and from my terrible hangover, so I didn't want him to see me. That was the last thing I ever would have wanted.

He softly reached out and touched my arm to get my attention.

"I'm really sorry again."

It's like my mind told myself one thing, but my body did another. I turned around then and met his gaze. At first it was blank, like he didn't fully recognize who he was looking at, but after a few moments his face filled with shock, and he took a major step backwards. "Oh fuck..." he said breathlessly, like I knocked the wind out of him all at once. "It's *you*."

Chapter Eight: Adam

Imagine my fucking surprise when the underage *princess* from the night before was now standing in front of me, drenched from head to toe in a one piece swimsuit.

God was *really* fucking testing me.

I promised myself that I wasn't going to see her ever again, let alone in a one piece swimsuit.

Fuck.

She was standing in the hallway, eyes bloodshot and water dripping from her body, but she took my breath away even then. It was like my gut automatically knew how to react to seeing her. My heart felt like it jumped out of my chest.

But I quickly came back to reality.. I knew I had to. I had to think clearly about this girl just once.

The truth was that this girl had not only been drinking underage, but she was drinking while doing college sports. She could have easily gotten caught which meant she had a level of immaturity that I didn't want to deal with... But quite honestly, I couldn't expect anything less from the perfect, spoiled princess who lived in the suburbs. Of course she could afford to make mistakes; Her family would save her with all the money they had.

A part of me would really fucking hate her for being such a spoiled brat if it hadn't been for the way she made me feel. And to be honest, I kind of hated that, too. I felt myself thinking back to the moment I first met her; seeing her long, Auburn ponytail, flipped over her face in the car as I admired her sleeping so peacefully.

I remembered thinking that she could easily drop someone to the ground with how muscular she was. Now that I saw her again, I finally realized where she got her back and arm muscles from: She was a swimmer.

And even though I knew absolutely fucking nothing about the sport, I knew that she must of done it well. She looked perfect. My eyes couldn't help but skim down her swimsuit. I tried to tell myself to stop, but she looked too fucking beautiful and I couldn't help myself. She recognized what I was doing just after a few seconds because her face suddenly turned red and she shifted her gaze to the floor.

The last thing I wanted to do was to embarrass her, but I was still dumbfounded that the girl who stood in front of me, who made my heart fucking skip a beat, was the very same pain in the ass, beautiful mess that I had met last night. God was really doing a number on me.

This had to be my fucking life, right?

The second I start to feel shit like this, I get overwhelmed and I back off. That shit is easier to do than to get hurt again. I didn't want to let myself get hurt as much as I had with my previous relationship. What I learned over the years is that relationships aren't meant to heal you, they're meant to teach you. And in the business I'm in, I don't have time to be taught any extra lessons. I don't have the time.

The problem was, though, that I thought I had some control over myself. I thought I finally could hold my shit together, do my job, help Tío out at the bar, and maybe have some casual hookups whenever I needed them.

Until I met her.

Within a couple of hours, I felt old feelings rise again out of the darkness. It was almost unexplainable and I fucking hated the feeling. I hated feeling weak, like my emotions were going to take over my fucking mentality. Like it was going to take over everything I've worked so hard to control. But I also didn't want it to stop. Not with her. She was like a drug to me, constantly pulling me in any second she could. "What are you doing here?" I said, trying to pull myself away from my thoughts. As if her wearing a bathing suit wasn't apparent enough to give me the answer I was looking for, I went ahead and asked the most dumbfuck question.

She scratched her nose lightly, but continued to look at the ground. "Um, just practice for my meet tomorrow. What about you?" She looked up after she asked the question.

She looked right into my eyes and I instantly felt like I was done for. Like time could end and I would accept it. Like my world could come crashing down, and it would be fine as long as she was there.

This girl was making me feel things within a twenty four hour period that I hadn't felt in years. I couldn't let her get inside of my head. I needed to quit being such an emotional wreck and man up. I wouldn't let someone hurt me again, or let someone even get close to me again. No fucking way.

"Just shooting hoops with the guys. You look nice, *princess*." Her eyebrows furrowed in confusion, and I felt myself clearing my throat from her reaction.

"So uh, I know you probably have to get back..." I started to say to her. She quickly nodded her head and said "Oh yeah, right. I better get going. It was nice to see you again, take care Adam." The way she said my name made the heat inside me shoot up like a cannon. I wanted to hear her say it again and again. I wondered what it would be like to hear her say it on my lips. The thought of that alone made me clear my throat and start coughing.

For fucks sake.

She started to walk back down the hall from me, but I knew I needed to talk to her more. I needed to find out more about her, and I needed to figure out why I was so interested. I wanted some answers. "Hey, wait. Um. What time do you get done with practice?" She turned her body back around to face me and a smile spread across her lips. "Well..." she said softly, "I'm here until 7, and then I get ready for classes at 8. I'm done by 4pm, and then cheer practice from 6 to 8."

Dammit.

This girl was fucking busier than the Pope. I still wanted to make time to talk to her. I didn't care what it took. "I'll meet you after your practice then. I'll pick you up at 8. I'm driving a corvette, you can't miss it." I smiled at her and winked, hoping she would be flattered by my initiative to take the leap of faith.

She stood there for a moment in silence, so I did too. I wasn't going to expect her to answer right away. Normally girls would immediately jump to the opportunity to talk to me, but I could tell Tara was different.

It was refreshing.

"Dude. C'mon..." Ricky moaned from behind me. I honestly forgot that those assholes were still behind me. "You can hold the fuck on." I looked in the guys direction, showing them that I was the one who called the shots and these motherfuckers weren't going to tell me to hurry up.

They knew I was serious by my facial expression, and immediately backed down.

This was one of the benefits of being Ricky's upline. I could tell him to do whatever I wanted, and he had to simply shut up and listen.

I didn't use my power much, but when I did.. it was fucking epic.

She continued to stand there, quiet as can be. She opened the cap to her water bottle and took a small drink, then rubbed her forehead. "It was really good to see you." She replied *nicely*. Almost too nice. The way she said that made my tongue hurt. It made me hate the way it was said. I hated that it sounded like she'd never fucking see me again.

Before I could process her rejection, she was walking away from me and into the enclosed pool area. I kept my eyes on her body as she walked closer to the pool. She put a hair cap on her head and sat her water bottle down, and I could only hear muffled voices, but I could make out one in particular: the coaches.

"Okay, 100 meter freestyle race, let's go. The top 3 will be competing freestyle tomorrow. Let's hustle today." I watched her as she stood up on the block, pulling her body down into a position. A whistle blew, and she rose her legs up into a starting position. A whistle blew again, and that's when I saw her dive into the water and take off. She was so flawless and beautifully perfect.

I was knocked out of my trance when my buddies came up behind me and smacked me in the back of my head. "Rodriguez, are you drooling?" Platz joked.

"Yeah, buddy I think your heart stopped beating there for a few minutes. Are you good? Do you need CPR? If so, I'm sure I can find a certain girl in a swimsuit who can do mouth to mouth." I elbowed Ricky in the side really hard then, showing him that no matter how funny he thought he was, that he'd better not fucking try talking about it now.

"Let's just go." I grabbed the basketball from Platz's hands, and walked back toward the basketball court.

Today had already been entirely weird, and it hadn't even begun.

Chapter Nine: Tara

    I jumped into the water for my individual race. This wasn't just any race though, it was the semi-final meet for districts. Yesterday had been one of the most difficult days for me; both physically and mentally. I tried to put all of my focus into swimming at practice yesterday, but all I could think about was Adam's facial expression when I disregarded his question to meet up after cheering. It hurt me to even think about it now.

Luckily, I won my practice freestyle race yesterday, so I was one of the three who got to compete today. I had one of the best time averages among the other six swimmers, so I had hoped that would give me an advantage for the race today.

    I felt the cold water hit every fiber of my skin as I flew through the water for my freestyle. The normal feeling of burning, tight lungs came back, telling me to regulate my breathing better for the race. I stroked my arms at a steady pace, trying to stay ahead without pushing myself too hard. I needed to wait until the final lap to push myself. When you're in the water competing, there is so much high intensity. You want to win.But there's a difference to swimming than any other sport: It's also completely and amazingly peaceful. I can sort out my thoughts while I swim, I can make decisions, and I can push worries and anxieties out of my mind. In that moment, even though people were watching me and expecting the most out of me, it was really the only moment I got to myself.

This was really the only moment that I felt both intensity and peace.

    The race was finished, and I tried my best. It still wasn't good enough. I was in second place by one-fourth of a second. It was stuff like that that drove me crazy. It wasn't always about winning, but it was about giving my best, and apparently I didn't.

I tried not to get too inside my head, but I knew that I couldn't fully stop myself. Everyone else was hard on me, so I was extra hard on myself.

    I walked over to the bench to grab my towel and took off my swimming cap. "Hey good job today, Evans. I know you did your best. You still made it to districts, so don't beat yourself up about it, okay? We'll keep practicing to beat your times." Coach Eric was strict, but I knew he fully supported us and he was always sure to keep our heads on straight. "Thanks, Coach." He simply nodded, patted my back, and walked towards the locker room.

"Honey!" A familiar female voice called out behind me. As I slung my towel over my shoulder and turned I saw my mom briskly walking towards me.

Great.

    I was mentally prepared to expect her listing my flaws of today's race, even though she knew nothing about swimming herself. I rolled my eyes at the thought as I turned my back, pretending not to hear her. "Tara!" She continued to yell.

    I grabbed my water bottle and slipped on my flip flops before turning back around to meet her gaze. Once I did, a large smile spread across her face. "Honey! You did such a great job!" Her arms flew around me now, gripping onto me for dear life in one of those overbearing mom hugs. As she pulled away, I felt the tenseness in my shoulders begin to relax.

She *always* made me tense.

    "Apparently not great enough, J." I dried my hair a little bit off of my towel, then looked at her, waiting for a reply. "Well honey..." she began, "no it wasn't the best but you should still be proud you made it to districts! We'll just have to keep practicing your form during extra sessions in the next couple of weeks."

We'll.

Like she knew what it took. Like she knew the amount of shit I had to do on a daily basis. Like she knew that my schedule was already busy as hell, and I couldn't fit more swim practice times in because of the cheering conference this weekend. All of this could've slipped her mind, I mean it's not like she was living at home anymore.

"Mom, why did you even come?"

I felt a new sense of power within me that I never knew existed. Maybe it was because I was finally done with her bullshit. The look of shock that she had on her face not only solidified my smartass remark, but also made me feel extremely guilty for even saying it. "Tara, that's an odd question to ask. I'm here to support you." I tried my best not to roll my eyes, but they always did out of habit every time she talked to me in her second language: bullshit.

The truth was, I thought I could deal with my mom and dad being separated. After the Sunday night fiasco at the bar, I thought I had my emotions in control. I thought I could get used to just me and my dad in the house. I knew I could be okay with my mom not constantly drowning me with her expectations every 30 seconds. But seeing her now, her long, curly blonde hair, her dark green eyes, the tall, thin figure dressed in designer clothes, and the Gucci bag on her arm that my dad bought her for her birthday two months ago, I couldn't help but feel my blood start to boil.

Seeing her again after the separation made me realize just how peaceful things could be without her there. I know deep down that even having those thoughts sounded wrong, but it was true,

I loved my mom, and I loved the life that G and her had given me, but I hated her constant expectations and the digs she made about me to her friends. I hated the way she acted like she knew what I had been through, and what it was like to struggle. She didn't even know the meaning of the word struggle.

She had grown up in the suburbs her whole life, had happily married parents, a trust fund, and then married a doctor. She had everything.

I started out with nothing. She would never know what it was like to have absolutely nothing. I held myself back from saying any of that, though. I was still a good and respectful daughter, even if I didn't think that way all the time.

I took a deep breath and rubbed my forehead. "Yeah, mom I know. It's just weird seeing you here without dad is all."

Her face turned a blood red, as if she was embarrassed and hurt by my comment. Her lips formed into a small pout, as if she was holding herself back from crying.

But it wasn't like I was the one who caused their separation. She did that all by herself.

"I know..." she let out a large huff of breath, "Listen, I know it's hard, honey. It's hard for me to think that I'm not going to see you every day for awhile. But this between your dad and I is needed. I made a mistake and I know you may never forgive me for it, but all I ask is that you still let me be your mom and support and love you. Because I love you, so so much, Tara." She wrapped her arms around me again, but this time with a tight grip, as if she needed me for support. I continued to stand there without a word.

It was the first time my mom had shown me any real affection. It was the first time I had ever seen real emotion from her. And as odd and unsettling it was to see it, it was kind of refreshing. I just let her hold onto me for a while as people passed by and the swimming arena emptied. I just let her hold onto me for however long she needed.

And to be honest, this time.. I held on, too.

*

It was finally Friday, and I couldn't have been more excited. The past few days I had been going from swimming, straight to class, and then to cheering practices afterwards. By the time I got home, I would have to do my homework for my lectures and study for any upcoming exams. It was like I never could catch my breath. Today, I didn't have cheering practice at the practice field. Instead, we got to drive up to the fairgrounds for practice and to stay in cabins for the weekend with the squad. We all had our own rooms and shared a cabin with four other girls. Luckily for me, I always got stuck with Riley as one of them.

Great.

As dreadful as staying in a cabin for a weekend with Riley sounded, I was excited to finally get a little break from things. I had no swimming on the weekends, and after our cheering competition on Saturday, I wouldn't have to worry about cheering anymore because it would officially be the end of our season. And that was something I was looking forward to the most; not having to cheer for six months.

As the day came to an end, I couldn't help but anticipate what would happen this weekend with our competition. It made me nervous, and even though I hated cheering, I knew that a lot of the girls were really excited and we had worked so hard for this moment that I wanted to do well for them.

I drove home in complete silence, I knew that I needed to get there quickly so I could pack a bag and get ready to head out to the cabins. I opened the driver's side car door, and grabbed my book bag out of the backseat as I noticed my dad's car was parked in the driveway, which made me very happy that he was home and not on rounds at the hospital like usual. I would get to tell him goodbye before I was off to the fairgrounds for the weekend. I opened the front door and slid off my dress shoes, then placed them in the correct shelf of the shoe cubby and ran upstairs to shower. After setting out the stuff I needed for my shower now, I packed the rest for the weekend. I knew I needed to pack one more outfit and a dress for our formal team dinner. We always would go to an Italian restaurant up there called Le Vite on that Saturday evening. We decided to make it a mandatory formal dress attire. I never understood it, probably because I always ended up with spaghetti sauce down my dress, but I still did it anyways. I grabbed my stuff for a shower, and walked down the hallway and turned the corner towards my bathroom.

 As I walked past my parents old room I couldn't help but hear a muffled noise from the other side of the door. My dad *never* cried. Sure, he expressed his emotions moreso than my mom, and I felt like I could open up more to my dad because he wasn't as cold hearted as Jen, but I didn't think I had ever actually seen him cry.

 And that's what's so scary; that your whole life you view your parents as some kind of superheroes, but as you get older you realize they're just human, experiencing life just like you. It really puts everything into perspective. And that perspective made my heart hurt so much for my dad, because if he was crying, he didn't want me to know it. And he deserved to know that I'd love him no matter what state he's in… he's my dad.

I opened up the door to check on my dad. Maybe he was really upset about everything with Jen and was crying. I wasn't entirely sure why, but the noise from the bathroom sounded muffled, so I decided to fully enter his room and knock on the bathroom door to check on him. I passed the bed and the dresser with all of my moms and dads belonging placed on it, frozen in time. I knocked on the master bathroom door and softly whispered, approaching the situation calmly in case he did do something to hurt himself. "Dad? Are you there?"
No answer.

The muffled noise continued on the other side of the bathroom door, as I now recognized the familiar noise of the water running in the shower. "Dad? Are you okay?" I walked into the bathroom, in fear of my dad hurting himself or passing out. And despite the thought of seeing my dad indecent made my skin crawl, all I could think about was my dad hurting himself. My anxiety would get so bad that I snap my wrists with rubber bands, but my *dad*? He has cut since he was thirteen years old, and even though he hadn't done it in so long, major life changes have a habit of bringing forth unhealed traumas. I thought that maybe he was having a really rough time with the separation from my mom. With my mom having an affair, I knew it couldn't have been easy for my dad to hear about that, let alone having to try to move on from it. But what I expected was nothing compared to what I saw when I opened the bathroom door. There was my dad submerged in the water of the bathtub, looking completely and utterly lifeless.

Chapter Ten: Tara

My brain was fried. It felt like my throat was closing up and my eyes began to water. But no matter how much I wanted to move, it was like I was frozen there, unable to. My brain couldn't fully process it, so I continued to stand there for a couple seconds in absolute shock.

I knew that I needed to act, I knew that I needed to move.. for my dads sake. I ran to the tub and pulled my dads head out from under the water, gripping onto him for dear life. "Dad!!" I screamed, tears now streaming down my face as I did my best to pull him out of the water. "Dad, dad!! Please, Dad!" I locked my arms under his and tugged his cold, wet body from the tub the best I could, until he was on the bathroom floor, lying deadweight, under my legs.

My body was now soaked from the tub water, as I tried pulling my legs out from under him. I continued to struggle with his body weight on top of me until I was able to wiggle my way out. I laid a towel under his head and dialed 911 on my phone. I listened for any sounds of him breathing, but I couldn't.

How could he do this to me?

"Daddy please.." I cried out as I began pressing hard on his chest to get his blood flowing again. I continued to do compressions and breathing air into his lungs, all the while I felt as though I was no longer breathing myself.

"911 what's your emergency?"

"I need help!" I screamed as I continued to do compressions on my lifeless father. "I..I found my dad in the bathtub, he's not breathing!"

"Okay honey, help is on the way. First I need some answers from you.." the lady spoke calmly, *"What is your address?"*

I continued to cry out, feeling my heart ripping out of my chest at the sight of my dad's body laying on the floor.

"*1824 Scottsdale Way Covington*" I cried, "please!! Please hurry!"

"*I have a few first responders close by, they are on their way. Is your father breathing?*"

I could barely breathe between hyperventilating from seeing my dad this way, and doing multiple rounds of compressions on him. "No he wasn't when I found him… I'm doing CPR now."

As the lady continued to talk to me, all I could hear was a constant ringing in my ears that kept getting louder each second. "Dad.." I whispered, not wanting to give up on him. "Dad, please don't do this. Please Dad."

I blew a couple breaths into his airway, causing him to choke and spit out water. His eyes went wide as he continued to cough in a state of panic.

I turned him on his side to get the rest of the water out as I took the first real breath I had in a few minutes.

We didn't speak another word to each other, I just continued to watch him until the ambulance arrived.

Once the ambulance had taken him to the ER, I felt tears beginning to surface. The truth was that I knew I needed some answers from him, but I wasn't going to get them right now.

I just wanted out of here.

I couldn't handle this, not now. I couldn't even fathom what my dad had been trying to accomplish, but I wanted no part in it.

I grabbed two dresses out of my closet, packed them and a pair of heels in my duffle bag, and threw some toiletries in my bag. I rushed around frantically, trying to avoid the thoughts of my dad altogether, and to get out of the house as fast as I could. I grabbed my duffle bag and headed down the stairs and into the entryway. I slid on my converse shoes, grabbed my keys and my purse, and packed my cheering tennis shoes in the side zipper of my duffle bag. I wasn't sure how I managed to get all of that packed within a two minute window, and normally I would be proud of myself, but in the moment I was running off of adrenaline, trying to make my escape from the reality that just occurred.

As I opened the front door to head out, I almost ran into the last person I expected to see. My mom.

"Tara, wait..." She said with tears in her eyes. I didn't want to even look at her or be near her right now. I slid past her at the front door and walked towards my car in the driveway. All of the details my mom told me about her cheating ruined everything. It ruined our family; it ruined my dad.

Whether my mom did it because she wasn't happy in her marriage anymore, or simply because she was bored; none of it mattered in my eyes. She ruined everything that mattered to me, and she caused my dad to go over the edge. I knew that I would never forgive her for this.

By the time I made it out to the driveway, my mom had reached me and tapped my shoulder to get my attention. But I wouldn't turn to face her. I refused. "Tara, please talk to me." I told myself not to turn around. I told myself that I couldn't do it. I had now made it to my car, feeling her presence following me with every step I took. I unlocked my car, and opened the driver's side door. J attempted to reach out to me again, but shook her hand off of mine.

"I have absolutely nothing to say to you, Jenifer." And with that, I jumped in my car and drove away as quickly as I could.

I drove out to the end of the drive by the exit gate. I pulled over on the next street in front of a large white three story home, full of beautiful Victorian accents. It was one of my favorite homes since I had lived here, and I found myself parking in front of it any time I needed a moment to think. I usually would pull over to think about things like school, or past boyfriends.. not *this*. This was something that I couldn't wrap my brain around. I felt so overwhelmed and so confused, and I started to convince myself that maybe I was in a terrible nightmare and that if I woke up, all of this would go away.

The sad part about that though, was that reality was disappointing, but it wouldn't change the fact that it happened.

I felt the innate habit of needing a release, needing the pain from the band to kill away the anxiety. It had rolled up my arm when I rolled up my sleeves and I felt myself urgently pulling on it to get it to my wrist. As I pulled and tugged it down my arm, the band made a familiar snap sound, but this time it wasn't from me attempting to push away my anxiety and fear.. no, this time it happened because the band had broken.

I let the broken band fall to the floor as I desperately tried to find a replacement. I looked in my dashboard, in the center console, but nothing was there.

This can't be happening.

How stupid are you?!

I began to panic, not knowing what to do next. I had never forgotten an extra band before, and the fact that I had only made my anxiety that much worse.

The only other thing I could think of was to call *her*. The only one who was able to talk me down from a panic attack, even though half the time she was the one that caused them.

As the phone rang, I felt my pulse speed up. I didn't know what I was going to say to her. I didn't even know if she would answer. "Hello?" I felt my breath hitch at her voice, suddenly a loss for words. I didn't really think this through. "Tara? Are you there?" I cleared my throat and suddenly my mouth felt as dry as sandpaper. "Riley?" I choked out, trying to hold in my tears.

The weird part about Riley? She could always tell when something was wrong, and I knew the second I called that she could. She could tell by my voice alone when something happened. Despite her being overly annoying nowadays, it was hard to forget that there was a time where she knew me better than anyone.

She used to be my best friend.

"Tara, are you alright? What's going on?"

A sudden burst of tears escaped my eyes and I felt my vision starting to blur.

"Tara. Calm down, it's okay.."

I felt pain in my chest because I felt betrayed by both of my parents in different ways.

"No Riley, it's not okay...." I started speaking while tears streamed down my face and a rosy pink hue highlighted my cheeks. "I got home from school and went to pack for the cabin and I heard my dad in his room, I heard weird noises.. he..he....was.."

I couldn't get it out. Every fiber of my being wanted to get the last few words out. But I couldn't.

"Jesus…Tara what's going on? What did he do? Is he okay?" A soft whimper came from the depths of my throat and more tears streamed down my face. I could hear her breathing from over the phone, like she thought something dangerous happened. I mustered up all the courage that my body would allow before I spoke:

"My dad, he..." I felt my voice begin to wiggle nervously "... I think he tried drowning himself."

There was a moment of silence, but it felt like a stabbing pain occurring over and over again. The silence was too much for me to handle, but after a few moments, I had heard what sounded like sniffling on the other end of the phone.

"Riley?"

No answer.

"Are you okay?"

I heard Riley clear her throat, and she sniffled a few more times before she spoke. "Yeah, I'm fine. It's just I'm not sure what to say other than, is he okay? Are you?" There was a long pause before I spoke; I was trying to hold back tears. "Yes he's gonna be fine, I'm pretty sure. And I'll be fine."

A long silent pause filled the spaces, and I was left there sitting in my car unsure of what was going to happen next. After a few moments, she finally spoke again: "Well, I mean, do you want me to call my dad? Do you want a ride to the hospital?.." I felt speechless. I knew that deep down Riley was a good person; I had known her most all of my life. Her parents and my parents were good friends, and at one point she had been my best friend… up until middle school when she decided to become friends with the popular girls, and I became closer with the girls on the swim team. She used to bully me incessantly for being a swimmer, even though she knew I was good at it. That was when we stopped being friends, and she started to be a pain in my ass.

But at this moment? She was the Riley I remembered. Kind, thoughtful, and a great listener.

"No, I can't ask you to do that." Was all that I could get out of my voice at the moment.

"Well, is there anything I can do? I know we're not close but your family is like my family ."

While I struggled with understanding why Riley was being so nice to me at this moment, I couldn't help but feel guilty. I thought of her to be the bad guy, but there she was, offering to help me. I wasn't sure of what to say, or if it would even fix any of the animosity we had between us, but I knew that I needed to speak from the heart. I knew that I needed to tell Riley that I truly appreciated her.

"Riley, I'm so sorry.." I started, not sure what to say, "I shouldn't have bothered you, but I didn't know who else to call. It seems like you know me and my family more than anyone else does." I put my head down now, feeling remorse for losing our friendship, and despite wanting to talk about it, I couldn't. I never had been able to, and that was the biggest embarrassment of all.

"Tara, it's okay. You're not bothering me. After everything you've been through in your life, it's hard not to want to reach out to someone. Trust me I get it. There's been a lot of times where I've felt myself wanting to call you.."

She let out a large sigh as if she was trying to hold in tears of her own. "But I have to remember that we're in different places in our lives now. We're never going to be how we were, and it's just easier to accept that.." she continued, "But if you need anything, please feel free to call."

There I was, still sitting in my car with the engine running. Though, I didn't care; The air conditioning was helping to dry my tears. I didn't care how late I got to the cabins. I didn't care that I never got a shower and I was still in my school uniform. What I did care about, though, was how I was meant to go on like nothing had happened.

A couple of moments passed as I collected my thoughts. The hardest thing for me lately was figuring out how to keep my composure. "And Tara, as much as I want you to go up to the cabins and have fun tonight, the squad will understand. Go be with your dad."

Surprisingly, I had a deep feeling of anxiety thinking about seeing my dad in that state again. A part of me felt guilty for not wanting to go see him, but another part of me wanted to avoid it all together. And it wouldn't be like he was alone… J would have gone to the hospital out of guilt. Still, he was my dad.. so I knew I should at least go see him.

"I'm going to the hospital to be with him now, Riley. But I'll be there later. I think I need to get my mind off of things, and we have our competition this weekend. I've got way too many people counting on me."

Riley sighed and took in an audible large breath before answering.

"Do whatever you feel is right; If you need to be with him, then go be with him. If you feel like you need a distraction, we'll be at the cabins. Either way, you need to make sure to take care of yourself. If you're feeling that anxious about your dad, I don't want you to start hurting yourself— and before you deny it, I know you're still using the bands, Tara."

I let a few moments of silence linger before she spoke again. "You've done it since we were kids… Did you think I was going to believe you when you said you didn't do that anymore?"

I felt tears beginning to well into my eyes again, feeling utterly defeated that somehow, Riley Turner still knew me, and she knew me too well.

"Riley, I…" She cut me off before I could say anything else. "Listen, Tara. I don't need an explanation. It's none of my business. I just want you to know that I see it, and that I know it's not good for you. But you know that, and you still do it… and that's something you need to get help for from someone else, because you never listened to me back then and you won't listen now..." she continued, "but like I said.. it's not my business. I'm gonna go, but if you need me feel free to text me, okay?"

And with that, the phone call ended and I was left to sit with my darkened scars and the bands around my wrist, suddenly feeling sickened by the sight of them and utterly disgusted with myself.

Chapter Eleven: Adam

I felt like a little bitch.

Actually, I *was* a little bitch.

I saw Tara for the second time this week on Monday morning during her swimming practice. I was happy to see her again, but something inside of me told me to keep my distance. Was it because I'm too fucked up in the head to get involved with a girl who has a busier schedule than me? Or was it because she just had gotten out of her teenage years and hadn't even been old enough to drink yet? Maybe it was because I knew that the second I saw her, I couldn't fucking explain how she had such a hold on me, and that familiar feeling scared the fuck out of me.

Being attracted to Tara was easy, though. Her eyes made you gravitate towards her. Her smile was so bright it radiated warmth throughout my body. Her kindness and selflessness showed instantly; She wore her heart on her sleeve, just like I once did.

But unlike Tara, I was no longer naive. I hadn't felt that way in years. I kept my guard up, I kept my distance, and I did my damn job. I owed that cold shoulder and new way of life to my ex, Vanessa.

Vanessa was a few years older than me, and we met when I began in the business. She was a family friend of Ricky's, and she had been in the business awhile. She taught me the ropes, as well as Ricky's brother, and they both were quite surprised when I started making more money on sales than Ricky. Vanessa became my first girlfriend, showing me what it was like to be in a real relationship at such a young age. She pulled me in, made me her little bitch, and really made me believe that she loved me. Until she disappeared one night with Ricky's brother, and neither Ricky or I had ever seen either of them again.

I couldn't help but think that Tara was completely different than Vanessa, though. I couldn't even put into words the difference of energy between Tara and Vanessa. Vanessa always had a motive, and you could tell that the instant you met her. But Tara? She didn't have a bad bone in her body.

She was somehow all that had been in my mind the past few days. Even if I didn't want to think about her, I thought about her, and it was starting to get exhausting.

It was taking a lot out of me and fucking up my mind. It fucked up my mind so much that I found myself repeatedly calling Natasha to hook up so I could get my mind off of it and to stop comparing and contrasting her to my past relationships. But calling Natasha for a quick fix didn't work, either.

It seemed as though Natasha meant what she said on Sunday. She was done with me. It was now Friday, which was enough time to get my head on straight.

At least normal fucking people would think so. But I couldn't, no matter how hard I wanted to. Her ice blue eyes were branded into my mind. I saw them on every supply run I went on, almost like a signal telling me to stop. But I ignored it. I knew I was going crazy over a girl who probably forgot I even existed…I believed that much to be true. And what a fucking shit show I was for not being able to get her out of my mind.

Ever since that Wednesday night when I took her home, she had been on my mind constantly. She was even on my mind when later that night Ricky and I went out on a supply run in Atlanta for Jerome. He wanted us to go to the North Side supermarket and deliver 200 pounds of dissolving roofie powder. It was pretty fucking disgusting to know that Jerome was supplying the supermarket manager with dissolving drugs to put into the slushie machines. In my head I was wondering what the fuck the purpose was, but I didn't ask questions.

I just did my job and kept my fucking mouth shut.

    Once we got the money for Jerome, I had Ricky count it three times, and then I counted it three times. I needed to make sure that the manager didn't rip us off, or both his and my ass would be dead.

Literally.

    There was no way I was gonna fuck this up. No way was I going to end up like Jinx. I knew I was the best supplier, and Jerome needed me to succeed. He reminded me of that on Wednesday after I had left Tara at her doorstep, wondering if I had made the biggest mistake in my life by walking away. Jerome had a way to brand into my memory that there was no room for a fuck up because of how big of a job it was. I knew that if I messed one thing up, not only me but also my downline would be fucking screwed.

    I would never forget that night, the one that made me realize that if I fucked up, I'd be killed the same way Jinx had been:

    I got out of the car and pulled the bag of cash out of the trunk as Jerome walked up beside me and looked at me with a serious expression.

"So what, brother. Did you get the supply there for me?"

I simply nodded and handed him the bag of cash. "You know it. The cash is there. Full." *He nodded in reply as he passed the bag off to one of his guys to count the cash. Jerome let out a sly laugh and hit me in the shoulder with his fist as he passed me.* "Rodriguez, you've been looking a little fucked up this week. You good?"

Jerome didn't ask me because he was worried about me; He wasn't sincere like that. He wanted to know if I was capable of keeping my deliveries up to his disgusting ass standards. Before I was able to say anything, Ricky came up and wrapped his arm around my neck, putting me into a headlock.

"No, Jerome, Adam here is not okay. He's a little bit of a mess. The dude is now whipped by a chick he doesn't even know." His laugh rang in my ears, and he tightened his grip around my neck as one of Jerome's guys whistled to him and called him over.

He whispered something to Jerome, and he simply nodded in reply. I noticed as he adjusted his gun in the back of his pants, and then fixed his gold chains that sat loosely on his plain black t-shirt. The moment that he walked back over to the Camry without a word and just stood there, I knew I would never forget it. That moment was one that would change my life.

That's when I realized something wasn't right. Something, or someone had fucked something up. Lord please tell me that I didn't fuck this up. Jerome pulled out his gun from the back of his pants, and his crew behind him followed. Ricky let go of his arm now, and stood next to me with a face full of fear. This had never happened to us before...everything always went smoothly, so this didn't make sense.

Ricky finally spoke up and broke the silence: "Is everything okay, J?" He nodded his head and formed his mouth into a small pout. His dark tanned complexion now turned blood red, signaling that he was pissed.

Fuck. "'No man, it's not okay.." he started to speak, as he checked to make sure his gun was loaded. I felt my blood begin to boil with anticipation.

"You see, Rodriguez and Sloane, I've relied on you two for years. So I know you wouldn't purposely fuck me over.." He approached us slowly, slithering closer like a snake to its prey. "You wouldn't fuck me over, right?"

He walked closer to me now, and my hands started to shake slightly. I don't know what the fuck I did, but I knew I was done for. Both Ricky and I shook our heads "no" signaling that we wouldn't fuck him over.

He laughed then, and looked down at the ground, then at his gun. He stepped closer to me so that he was right in front of my face. "Well you see, I don't think so. Maybe you two would fuck me over. Cause it looks like you just did..." He put his finger on the trigger, and pointed it to my forehead.

This was it.

"Did you dumbasses really think I wouldn't know this cash is counterfeit? How dumb do you think I am!?" One of Jerome's guys walked up with his gun in hand, now facing it towards Ricky's face.

Counterfeit? There was no way in hell. I was taught early on how to check for counterfeits, so I knew I didn't fuck up.

That cash looked legit.

I needed to save myself; I needed to at least give him another option instead of killing us. "J, wait. Wait. We counted and checked it six times between the two of us. That money didn't even check as a counterfeit. I used the polish test and everything before we left, man. I would've known if we were being fucked over. That dude back at the supermarket must have had a good system for that to look and run as real cash."

Jerome's anger was building with each second, but not enough to let him pull the trigger. Instead, he took the barrel of the gun and bashed it off of the side of my temple, causing blood to trickle down from my eyebrow to my cheek bone. As much pain as I was in, I didn't move. I couldn't. I stayed there with my eyes glued shut in pain. Jerome was screaming now, but it was hard to make out what was being said; my ears had been ringing following the swift blow to the head.

Once I opened my eyes, I saw Jerome pacing back and forth in front of Ricky and I. I wasn't sure what he was thinking, and that had to have been the scariest part of the entire thing. Jerome was so hard to read. Finally, he raised his gun to my head again, taking the pistol and pressing it into my forehead. "Be careful with your next words, Rodriguez…" he said with certainty, "…or you'll be seeing your parents again, real soon."

At that point, seeing my parents again hadn't seemed like a bad idea.. at least all of this bullshit would be over with and I could finally be at peace. Too bad Jerome thought he was scaring me with those words.. too bad he didn't understand just how much I needed my mom and dad. The only way I'd accept being killed is with the knowledge that I'd be seeing them again.

I grabbed onto the barrel of the gun now, wrapping my other hand around Jerome's hand that was placed on the trigger. I shoved the pistol further into my forehead, causing it to break the skin.

I looked Jerome in the eyes, not wavering from my fired gaze as I said the only words I knew to say in that moment. "Do it, Jerome.." I said, my eyes blazing with frustration and adrenaline. "…fucking do it, man, I dare you.." silence filled the room then, and I noticed Ricky's head slightly turned toward me in complete shock. But I didn't care. "…You'd be doing me a favor anyway."

My breath quickened, ready for it all to be over. But just then, Jerome's face went serious, as if he was thinking. His face formed into a sly smile, and then he slowly lowered his gun and placed it in his back pocket as a sinister laugh echoed through the warehouse. Once the gun was lowered, I finally felt myself start to breathe again. "Mhmm, okay..." He nodded as he stared at the floor. "…you almost had me there, Rodriguez.. I gotta give it to you." He said as he shook his head and a small smirk appeared on his face. "Here's what's gonna happen. Instead of me killing you, you're gonna do some extra jobs for me. One of them, you'll do for Tommy here." He said as he patted the man's chest standing next to him. "You're going to distribute some molly for me to a buddy of mine at the Newton county fair this weekend. While you're up there, you're gonna do some research for me…That supermarket manager also runs a shitty ass food truck. I need you to scope it out for me." I wasn't sure where he was going with this, but I continued to listen. I was glad I was given another opportunity to fix this instead of immediately getting killed.

"At the end of the night, make sure that bitch is alone, take all the cash you can find in that truck. Anything valuable, too…That's the first and last time He'll ever fuck with me." He let out a deep sarcastic laugh before continuing, "The last thing you're gonna do is bring him here. I want to know how he came up with this fake money. I don't care if we have to beat it the fuck out of him. Once we get the information, I'm done with him.
Then you can get rid of him." The last sentence he said stopped me in my tracks. Never in the seven years that I've been in this business had I killed someone. Ricky never had, either. I've busted some asses, sure, but I never killed anyone.

That moment was a big life changer for me. Everything was on the line, and no matter what, someone would be dead by the end of it.

*

Everything changed in that instant. I was now going to become a killer, and I couldn't get that shit out of my mind. It's not who I was, and to be honest, it fucking terrified me. I knew this business was risky, and I knew I couldn't get out of it, but I was proud of the fact that I never had to kill anyone. It was something I had been proud of– something that would never compare me to Jerome. But that was about to change.

It was now Friday, the first day of the weekend fair. Ricky and I were getting ready to go up tonight to deliver the molly to Jerome's friend and scope out the fair. We needed to know exactly where this guy's food truck was, and how we were going to approach robbing him and taking him without anyone else noticing. This was going to be one of the most difficult moments of my life. I looked in the full length mirror, looking at my v-neck maroon t-shirt, and my pair of jeans. I had hoped I looked normal enough to not be recognized. Hopefully I wouldn't be recognized and this weekend could go smoothly without a fuck up. If there was any, well I could just consider myself to be dead.

I was in my studio apartment above my Tío Joe's bar, finishing packing my bag, when I heard a knock on the door. A surge of fear ran through my veins. "Adam, it's me." On the other side of the door was my uncle Joe. I let out a huge sigh of relief. I really needed to get uncle Joe a gun to keep her now for his safety. No one and nothing was safe. "Yeah, c'mon in Tío." He walked in and looked around the apartment before meeting me at the seating area. The studio apartment was kinda small, but it didn't matter, it was home. "So I see you came back to the apartment, did you get rid of the stuff in the duffle bag?" I had to lie to Joe, I couldn't tell them that I stashed it in the ceiling tile at Ricky's apartment. I did get it out of *here* though.

"Sí, Tío."

    That was the first time he smiled at me speaking Spanish. But I doubt it was because of that... he was happy that I had gotten rid of it. "Good, I'm glad."He stood there staring at me, and I felt the awkward tension start to build. "So, Tío, did you need something? I'm about to head out for the weekend to the fairgrounds." Uncle Joe looked at me strangely then, raising his eyebrows and crossing his arms. "Why are you going out there? You always hated that place. Your mom used to have to drag you there with your cousins every summer." He was a great interrogator, I'm sure he could work for the FBI if he wanted to. I'm glad he didn't though, cause then my business would be totally fucked. "Yeah, I know Tío. I just was going to meet Ricky and Platz for the weekend. We were bored." My excuse wasn't good at all, but I hoped that it worked. I couldn't let him find out what was really going on. I wouldn't get him involved.

    His suspicious expression still carried, as if he didn't believe me. As a few minutes passed, he must have given up because he let out a large sigh and uncrossed his arms.

"Okay, Adam. I will try to believe you this time. You know how I don't like you with Ricky, but I obviously can't control you." This was true, I was glad he knew his limits. I would always have Ricky in my life, he did too much for me growing up, I couldn't just drop him. He was family…He was the only brother I had. "Yeah, Tío. Què necessita?" His common annoyed expression formed on his face again. I couldn't help myself, I always felt such satisfaction by using Spanish against him. He always was pissed off for it, too. "Don't start with me, Adam." He had his finger pointed at me now, but I could tell he was trying to fight a smile. I think he secretly enjoyed it. I couldn't help but laugh in reply. "I just asked what you needed, Uncle."

He shook his head and smiled, shaking off the annoyance he always felt when I did that to him. He pulled an envelope out of his jacket pocket, and walked over towards me. He patted me on the back, and handed me the envelope. "I love you, Adam..." he said, tightening his grip on the top of my shoulders now, "but you've got to stop lying to me." I looked down at the yellow envelope, wondering what on earth it could be. I had no clue.

Uncle Joe must have known I was confused, because he closed his eyes in frustration and rubbed his forehead. "A couple of men with guns came into the bar last night. They kicked out my customers and told me to give you this first thing this morning. One of the guys stayed here the entire night with it until this morning to make sure I didn't open it. They told me if I did, then they'd burn the bar down. .I don't trust these guys, Adam. I don't at all. So whatever shit they've got you into, you need to get out now, son." I felt a pang of guilt hit my chest and my heart began to feel heavy. He knew I was lying, and he knew I was in way deeper than I told him I was. "I'm scared for you.. I just want you to be safe." He patted my shoulder one last time, and then brought me in for a brief hug. As he broke away, he patted my cheek softly and turned to walk away. I needed to tell him something, before it became too late. "Tío, wait..." I walked closer towards the door and my uncle as he turned around to face me. "I just wanted to say thank you. For everything, really. You've done so much for me over the years… and I appreciate it..." I breathed in heavily before I finished. This shit was too emotional for me, but I knew how I felt. "..and I just wanted to tell you I love you too." I was glad I got that out without vomiting or bawling my eyes out. I never was one to let out my emotions, I liked to keep a cover and not reveal anything. But it was Tío, and this could be the last time I ever see him again if this weekend doesn't go as planned, so it was a lot different.

This meant a lot more.

Joe gave a simple smile, nodded his head, and then was out the door. As soon as he was gone, I grabbed the large yellow envelope in my hands and opened it.

I wasn't very surprised about what was in there, honestly. The familiar colored molly in a small baggie sat inside, assuming that it was for Jerome's friend that we were dealing it to. Sitting right next to the molly was an AR-15 Rifle. Jerome really thought of it all, I guess. He knew that this job could be taken to extremes, and knew that I needed to be prepared.

The thought of being prepared to possibly kill someone scared the hell out of me. I never wanted to even think about attempting it in my life. To me, there were other ways to get the point across instead of killing. But now? there's a possibility that Jerome will make me end this random man's life. I remained in my studio apartment now by myself, with my thoughts, a bag packed, and the thought that I may never be in my home again.

Chapter Twelve: Tara

    As I pulled up to the drive of our section of cabins, I couldn't help but feel a sense of peace. I had driven here right after seeing my dad at the hospital. The doctor said he was stable and everything looked good for him to be observed for a couple days before getting transferred to a Psych facility to get help. Once I was able to talk to him, despite him being very drowsy, it allowed me to breathe easier again for the first time all day.

    Now I had a little bit of time to myself. I was excited to get to spend some alone time here with my thoughts, and I knew it was going to be beneficial for me to think everything through with my parents, and about my future.

    I was also excited to go to the fairgrounds. Not because of the cheering competition, but because of the carnival that they have every year before officially opening the fair tomorrow morning to the public. The ceremonial carnival is sort of like the opening ceremony for the olympics; except way less important, and way more cheap. I was excited to have the entire fair grounds for just a select few of us; the cheerleaders, the other entertainment members for the weekend, the music artists, vendors, and the organizers of the fair. Even though there was always a good number of people, it still was less overwhelming compared to opening day at the fairgrounds.

    Seeing the fairgrounds wasn't the only exciting part of this weekend. In fact, most of this weekend could completely obliterate, and I would be okay with it. What I was looking forward to the most though, was going to my special place. I only visit my place once a year, twice if I was lucky. I found the small lake with an old wooden dock about a mile away from the fair grounds and ever since I declared it as my special place. I knew others probably had found it, there was a clear path to the lake from the wood trails back at the cabins. I was sure fishermen went out there constantly to go fishing in the mornings, but at night, every single time I went, there was no one in sight. Just me, the lake, and the lightning bugs that lit up the surrounding trees. That had been what I was most excited about and what I was looking forward to the most. I made a plan, after my time at the carnival with the team, I would quietly sneak off without a word and go to the lake. But for now, I needed to seem like I was focused on tomorrow's performance. I needed to impress Riley and make sure that I didn't get on her bad side. She turned into a cheer-zilla around competition time. It was like a menstrual period that never ended with her, well at least until cheering season was over. I never understood why she was so god damn tense all the time. I wondered, though, if she maybe just maybe felt like she needed to be perfect and had people expecting a lot out of her, too.

I pulled up to the cabin that read #4, knowing that according to Riley's cheering competition email, that it was my assigned cabin. I put the car in park, got out, and grabbed my duffle bag for the weekend. I made sure to grab my cheering uniform up on a hanger that was sitting in my back seat. I really wasn't sure when I found the time to do that between the constant anxiety I felt naturally, and the whole *'dad attempting to drown himself' thing.*

I felt a quick surge of anxiety as the thoughts of my father lying lifeless on the bathroom floor crossed my mind. I not only felt like I couldn't breathe, despite the branded memory in my mind, but I also felt a huge heaviness in my heart.

Things were not going to be easy for my family, and I knew that. But I needed to focus, even if my mind kept drifting off to other topics that shouldn't have held my concern. I needed to listen to Riley's advice for once and focus on me.

I walked up to the wrap around porch of the dark wooded cabin. I had noticed a welcome letter from the maintenance office hooked on the front door. Most of that letter was unimportant, usually just welcoming us as a team, what the expectations were as far as taking care of the cabin and cleaning up after ourselves, and wishing us the best of luck. But they did that for everyone, it wasn't like GSU got any special treatment from the maintenance team. I looked at the bottom of the letter, the most important part, for our roommate assignments for the weekend.

In the past few years, I got stuck being roommates with Riley. Luckily, though, there were enough rooms in each cabin for each one of the girls to have their own. As I read through the names of my roommates, I couldn't help but feel a little bit annoyed. It wasn't like they all were annoying, but I just had the weirdest luck ever.

My roommates for the weekend would be a sophomore, named Caroline Booth, who was one of the quietest girls I had ever met. She hardly spoke ten words in general during our practices in the past two years she's been a member of the squad. It's not like she needs to talk, though, she did what she needed to do to be a valuable part of our team, and she did it well. The next cabin mate had been a Junior who was one of my good friends on the squad. I was glad to have Danielle in the cabin with me, and I felt comfort in knowing that the whole weekend wouldn't be a complete disaster now that I knew she was in the same cabin as me. Danielle was such a kind person; she and I had been in cheerleading together ever since pee-wee's and we've always stayed pretty good friends throughout the years.

The last name that I read on the room assignments made my vision blur out of familiar annoyance, and yet also a new feeling: guilt. Although, I really wasn't surprised. Riley was the final roommate on the list, and there was no doubt that she would be complaining and trying to dictate everything about our stay the entire time we stayed here. She had done this every year, but as her power grew with each upgrade in cheer rank, so did her ability to treat us all like we were nothing.

But this time was different; Riley knew a secret no one else knew, and I had reached out to her because she had already known so much about me and my family, that it was an automatic reaction to want to tell her. But now the feeling of guilt from involving her came forth and I also felt guilt for all of the annoyance I had felt towards her in the past. But that wasn't something that could easily be fixed, and with everything else going on in my life, I told myself to take things day by day. I grabbed the key from the mailbox and opened the door with my duffle bag hung over my shoulder.

The cabins were always maintained so well. The kitchen was breathtaking with its rustic themed cabinets and stainless steel appliances. There were brand new leather sofas sitting in the living area, placed in front of a television and complemented with a dark brown wool rug in the center. I walked down the hallway and scoped out the bathroom. It was always so awkward sharing a bathroom with three other girls, but this bathroom seemed to have enough storage, so I wasn't too worried about keeping my things in there. I sat my duffle bag on the top of the sink and pulled out my toiletries, towels, and shampoo for the shower. I grabbed a change of clothes and underwear, too, knowing that I needed to get a shower quickly if I wanted to be done before the other girls got here.

I looked at the time on my cell phone, I still had a half an hour before the other girls would arrive, so I could settle in and be at peace for a moment. I walked to the bedroom next to the bathroom and sat my duffle bag on the dresser. I could finish placing my stuff where it needed to go after my shower. I was still in my clothes I had worn to lecture all this time. Even though the forty minute drive out to the fairgrounds, and the other ten minute drive through backroads to get to the campgrounds for the cabins. Wearing a dark blue jean skirt and white dress shirt wasn't the best idea for a county fair.

I walked into the bathroom then, locked the door behind me, and started the shower. The immediate warmth radiating from the steam made my skin form goosebumps. It was like an immediate reaction of comfort. I undressed out of my clothes, pulled my hair out of my messy bun, and stepped into the shower. This place was where I could finally be myself; with my thoughts, my fears, my insecurities…everything. I never got much time to myself in the past few years, but it seemed like the only time I did, it was when it involved water. I always felt a sense of comfort and relaxation while swimming, but I understood that feeling when I showered, too. This was the perfect time to collect my thoughts and mentally prepare myself for the weekend ahead.

*

"Tara *lets gooo*, we're gonna be late!"

It wasn't my fault that the other three girls in my cabin didn't like my outfit tonight for the carnival. I wore leggings and an old Covington High t-shirt from my high school days. I had my hair combed through, now resting against my shoulders. Riley was *of course* the first to disapprove. "You look like you're about to go rent a movie, binge-watch a shit ton of tv, and spill butter from a large bag of popcorn all over you." The other girls had unfortunately agreed, so I was now back in my room changing my clothes.

"I'll be out in a second, I'm almost done!" I pulled up my high waisted jeans a bit farther, making sure they were in the right place and that I felt comfortable enough to wear them for the rest of the night. I changed my completely worn Covington High School shirt for a Black Keys logo tee, and put on some charmed bengals on my wrists to dress up my outfit a little. I opened the door and walked out into the living room of the cabin. "How's this? Good enough?" Caroline and Danielle were smiling now, giving me their approval. It wasn't a drastic change, but it was an improvement. Riley though, was not amused. She was wearing a pretty white floral romper, her long blonde hair was flowing in curls, and she wore three inch block heels, like she was going out to a wedding. Of course she wouldn't approve of my outfit whenever she would wear outfits like that. "Well, it's not as terrible, but I'm not waiting anymore so it'll have to do." She slung her pink Gucci bag over her shoulder, and led us out of the cabin and to her mustang convertible.

*

I was now waiting in line to get my entrance ticket and had felt awfully odd walking around with my four cabin mates, feeling like the carnival was the last place I wanted to be. I waited in line like any self-respected person would for my free ceremonial carnival ticket. The organizers offered us free passes for the entire weekend to the fair and for all the carnival rides.

I was the last of our group of four to get my ticket pass, so the other three girls walked ahead of me and greeted some other girls on our squad. I continued to walk alone, slowly catching up to the other girls who were waiting in line for the circling cyclone. Even just looking at it made me want to hurl. I never did well with rides that would spin you around constantly in a circle. And as much as I hated them, I didn't want to seem like a wimp…so the sooner I could get it over with, the better.

There was a long line by the time I got to the cyclone, but I remained right behind Danielle and the other girls. I just kept quiet as I waited, I had no interest in pretending to be someone that I wasn't. I noticed right next to the line was a funnel cake vendor. My parents, or should I say my mom, never let me have many sweets growing up. I never knew what an m&m tasted like until two years ago. I partly felt deprived of a childhood and all of the sugar crashes that everyone else experienced, but I also felt lucky because I never had that craving as bad as other people. Every memory I had made at the fair always consisted of me and my dad riding carnival rides together, visiting the goats at the petting zoo, and sharing a funnel cake to end the night. My heart began to feel like it was made of glass, and it was beginning to shatter with the painful reminder from earlier today. It was hard to think about my parents at the moment. I knew it was always going to be hard from here on out, everything was changing. I couldn't stop it though, everything in life changes at one point or another.

    I decided to distract myself, and walked over to the food truck to stand in line for a funnel cake. I was excited to buy myself something I thought was well deserved, but also something that held such a close memory to my heart. Next to me, the cyclone ride stopped and the passengers that were on the ride began to exit the gate as the people in line began to climb on. *So much for wanting a funnel cake right now.*

    I would just have to get one after this nightmare of a ride was over.

    I walked away from the food truck and back towards the line of the cyclone, hoping I could get on at the same time as the other girls, but mostly, at least Danielle. She was the only one who accepted me and never judged me for my crazy and irrational fears.

I began to pick up my pace, slightly jogging to the line entrance to make it in enough time, but my field of vision was disrupted and I felt a strong force of energy rush through me as my body slammed up against someone. I kept my focus on the ride, still trying to make it in time, but also wanting to apologize for running into that innocent person. It wasn't their fault that I was in a rush to get on a stupid ass ride with a bunch of girls; The majority of them didn't like me. But the reasoning sounded so stupid once I thought about it.

I turned around to face the person, and noticed it was two tall men, one with dark— almost jet black hair that was short but curled at the ends by his ears, and another with sandy blonde short hair that spiked up in the back. I gently grabbed the back of the dark haired man's arm to apologize, but once he turned around and my memory began to recognize his features, my senses intensified and my heart began to flutter at an uncontrollable rate. "Adam.." I said, almost breathlessly. "Hi."

I couldn't believe it, it was almost like God was testing me. It was like God didn't want me to go another day without seeing him. The way his soft, pink lips formed into a wide smile made my heart skip a beat. His big, soft brown eyes were now burning into mine. "Cuidado chica.."

The way his perfectly articulate Spanish rolled off his tongue made my spine tingle, and my insides burned with desire. He placed his hand on top of mine, moving it to the side of his arm that I still was holding onto. "You better be more careful Tara, or you're gonna end up hurt."
Yeah, tell me about it.

My heart desired him, and it made my body want him so badly. I so badly wanted to rub the stubble on his chin and comb my fingers through his dark curly hair, I so badly wanted to study his sexy skull tattoo on the top of his right hand and I wanted to continue to discover more. I wanted to discover everything about him.

But my head knew better.

My head was more logical. My head believed what Adam had said, but instead of it just being about running into him, it became more real. It felt like a warning signal going off in my head.

"*You're gonna end up hurt..*" Those five words continued to ring in my ears as I still stood there, staring at him as my heart pounded out of my chest, and the sound of the cyclone ride began to spin along without me.

"So, what are you doing here?" He asked, projecting his voice now that the cyclone ride had started and the loud sound of the machine took over. "Uh, I'm here with my team. We're performing tomorrow for cheering." I didn't want to admit that I was a cheerleader to him. He seemed like he lived on the dangerous side of life, and yet here he was, talking to me, a college cheerleader whose only excitement each year was going to a hidden dock to be alone.

He simply nodded, and put his hands back into his pockets like they were a place of comfort from the awkward tension. "Ooh, a cheerleader, huh?" The sandy blonde guy stood next to us, smiling from ear to ear. "I'm Ricky...." He held his hand out to shake mine. I smiled and shook it, noticing how different it felt to shake someone's hand that wasn't Adam's. When I shook Adam's hand that night, it was like my entire body started to tingle with excitement. Shaking Ricky's hand now felt completely different.

"And I'm guessing your Tara." I nodded and didn't say anything else. I just kept my eyes on Adam, the familiar safe haven that I confided in. " 'Riguez, did you hear that? She's a cheerleader. I'm sure she dances and flips and everything.. Am I right?"

Ricky's eyes skimmed down my body and I felt a strong sense of nervousness as he did so. He made me feel uncomfortable, very different from what I felt when Adam was around. "Uh, yeah I guess so. It's kind of required..." my eyes locked with Adam's then, and I noticed he was trying to ignore the words escaping from his friends mouth.

"... Yeah, see Adam? I'm sure she's very flexible.." He winked in my direction and nudged Adam in the side with his elbow. I could see he was taunting Adam, but I didn't know why. I couldn't quite put my finger on it, but I knew Adam's face had suddenly filled with anger by how red it became.

He grabbed Ricky's arm and twisted it behind his back, sending Ricky into a deep searing pain. "Say shit like that again about her, Ricky. I swear I will break this lame excuse for an arm." Ricky laughed in response, just as Adam twisted again to prove his point, which sent Ricky into a world of pain yet again.

"Okay, okay! Adam let me go." Adam finally had let go of Ricky's arm, and I couldn't help but feel like he was my protector. He had made sure I was okay, and that no one would say anything like that to me. It made me feel safe, but it also made me feel special.

What I found amazing was how quickly men got over things so fast; it's like their problems don't even exist after five minutes. Adam took his hand and ruffled up Ricky's hair before pulling him into a light headlock. I smiled in response to their boyish actions, lightly pushing one another for torment. I could tell they were close just by those few minutes of seeing them. It made my heart feel full knowing that Ricky and Adam had been so close, that nothing would ever ruin their friendship.

I had forgotten what was going on, though, because before I knew it, Danielle, Riley, and Caroline were getting off of the ride and walking over towards me with confused expressions on their faces. Riley was the first to notice that I was standing with two good looking, older guys who had a crap ton of tattoos on their arms between the both of them. Her face formed into an sly grin, and she cocked her eyebrow. "Well, well, you know Tara, I was wondering where you were... but now I see why you didn't come on the ride. Looks like you have two of your own standing right here." She eyed Ricky and blushed as his eyes skimmed over her and stopped to stare at her long legs.

I rolled my eyes from her comment. It made me seem like I was some desperate whore and made me feel a type of anger that I had reserved deep inside me, only to come out for her.

Danielle must have noticed, because she quickly offered support by patting my back and glancing at me with a genuine smile. "You missed a good ride.." she said, almost in a whisper, "…but who are these guys?" Danielle was by far the most protective person I knew. She cared about everyone's safety, and was kind of like the mom of the group. Her fair skin with freckles and strawberry blonde hair made her look way older than us, like she was in her mid twenties. She never had an issue with getting alcohol, but she would always make sure we had a way home or had somewhere planned out to stay before she bought us anything. She was a really great person.

Adam broke the silence then, and smiled as his hand reached out to shake Danielle's. "Hey, I'm Adam. Nice to meet you.." he smirked and kept looking between me and Danielle, like he was trying to win her approval. She bit the side of her cheek and glanced between the both of us.

I could tell by her expression that she knew there was something between Adam and I. Hell, even I knew…But I couldn't quite figure out what.

"I'm Danielle, nice to meet you too, Adam." Danielle was studying him like a damn rubix cube. There was a moment of silence before she spoke. "…So how do you two know each other?"

I didn't really want to explain that I was wasted in a bar and we met because he was forced to drive me home. No way was I going to embarrass myself in front of Riley. I eyed Adam, trying to form a secret communication, trying to signal him to make up a lie.   Luckily, he was smart and read my face the exact way I wanted him to. He slightly nodded his head, enough for me to notice, but no one else. "We met at the gym, she was swimming and I was playing basketball. We kind of keep running into one another." I smiled in response as a nonverbal thank you, and he formed his lips into a small grin in reply. Danielle just nodded her head then, and focused back on Riley and Ricky, who both had found their way closer to each other, continuing to stare at one another and flirt.. It was pretty evident that they were into one another. "Oh shit." Adam said quietly, leaning down to whisper in my ear, "We're in trouble with these two, aren't we?" He said with a small laugh.

The way he whispered in my ear made my ear tickle and my skin suddenly goosebumps formed like a second skin. Just those few words did that to me and I couldn't help but wonder at that moment… What else could he do to my body if only a few words sent such a shot of adrenaline through me?

I nodded and bit my lip, trying to fight a smile.

Riley and Ricky were lost in their own little world, oblivious to what was going on around us. I had barely noticed, but Danielle had pulled Caroline away to one of the food vendors to wait in line. All that was left was me and Adam standing side by side as the carnival music and the voices of strangers conversing filled the background.

Adam looked around the fair as if he was looking for something. His eyes were scanning the crowd, the vendors, and even people on the carnival rides. It was very strange.

Was he looking for someone? He looks like he's searching for something.

I felt my eyebrows furrow to express my curiosity, but then I spoke too soon.

"Are you looking for someone?" I couldn't help but ask. It was like I didn't have a filter when I was around him… I couldn't hold in my thoughts when I was in his presence.

His attention snapped back to me, as if I had caught him doing something he shouldn't have been. "Oh no..no. I uh— I was just looking around, I thought I heard a familiar voice or something." He continued to be preoccupied, now gaining the attention of his friend Ricky, who started looking around too.

After a moment, they both looked at one another, and then looked over at a food truck serving curly fries. I was visibly confused, but I let it go. I knew Riley wasn't going to let his attention stray away from her that easily, though. "Umm.." she said, clearing her throat in a high pitched manner, trying to get Ricky's attention. "Ricky, do you want to walk over with me to the Ferris Wheel?" She smiled and walked towards him, then grabbed his hand. He was knocked out of his trance of staring at the fries from the food truck, and smiled back to her. "Sure thing, sweet cheeks. Let's go." He said, intertwining his fingers with Riley's. "'Riguez, I'm sure you can keep Tara here company, yeah?" Ricky winked in Adam's direction as Riley pulled him in the direction of the Ferris wheel.

A few moments of silence passed before anything was said. In fact, I really didn't know *what* to say. Now that all of my friends had left me, I didn't want to be here alone because I didn't know how to act in front of Adam. Every single time I ended up making a fool of myself.

I decided maybe it would just be good to get away from the noise of the carnival and the mixed scents of food and go for a peaceful walk. The truth was that I secretly had been hoping for a moment of peace since I got out here, and maybe, just maybe, my favorite place would make me feel less awkward.

"Do you want to go for a walk with me?" I wasn't sure how he would react. He seemed too lost in the food truck vendor that was selling fries. Even though it didn't make much sense to me, it was obvious he was behaving like a typical guy, ogling over food. But if he wanted fries, all he had to do was go up and order some…but he didn't.

I was also nervous about asking him because of the day I turned him down at the gym. I didn't want to, hell, I wanted to see him again and again but when he asked me to meet him after practice, I suddenly panicked and my heart felt like it was racing.. I had to say no because I felt myself start to clam up and felt the familiar feeling of anxiety creeping in. The normal intrusive thoughts then began to take over, and I was soon reminded that I wasn't good enough. That I wasn't worth enough. And I wasn't going to put myself through a position that allowed me to feel that vulnerable.

But things were different now; We were left alone and despite feeling anxious, I wasn't going to let this situation become awkward. It wasn't like I was asking him to marry me, I just wanted to go for a walk.

I walked closer to Adam, and put my hand on his wrist, the one that had the skull tattoo on it. The thought of the tattoo being right under my grasp made my adrenaline pump. Something about that tattoo in particular drew me in.

He noticed my presence and the placement of my hand on his wrist as he looked down at our hands. A small smile formed on his perfectly smooth lips, and then he lifted his head to meet my gaze. His smile could have allowed him to speak a million words if it wanted to, instead, he remained silent a moment, just letting his smile speak for himself.

"I'm so sorry, I got lost in thought.. What did you say you wanted to do?" He reached for my hand then, twisting his wrist enough to intertwine our fingers together. I felt my heart flutter with anticipation and my cheeks warmed.

Adam was holding *my* hand, and I was holding *his*. It felt like it belonged there... like his hand was meant to mold into mine.

I glanced down at our hands as his thumb danced around, caressing the top of my hand. I couldn't help but smile at the small act of intimacy between us. It was a moment that I would cherish forever. "I wanted to see if you wanted to go for a walk."
I squeezed his hand gently at first, and then he squeezed back in response.

His deep chestnut brown eyes didn't leave mine. Our eyes were magnets; pulling towards one another with an unspoken intensity. "*Por Supuesto*" He said fluently, and I knew it came out without any force. The thought of him speaking Spanish to me made me blush, and so I put my head down to cover the new redness of my cheeks. I didn't want him to know that I was a fool for his accent…even though I absolutely, *totally* was.

"*Vamonos*." He said quietly, the sound of his smooth husky voice was enough to cause my spine to shiver. I looked back up at him and smiled, feeling completely relaxed and energized all at once. Even though the rest of my life was a mess, it was good to feel like something was starting to finally fall into place.

"Okay let's go..." I said, pulling him slightly behind me as I walked towards the exit of the carnival and towards the familiar dirt pathway. I looked back at him as I wandered us out to the path, knowing where I was leading him, but wanting to let his mind wonder.

He simply smiled at me, but it was like it stung my heart. His bright smile reflected off of the moon's light and I felt my heart flutter almost instantly. "So, are you sure that you're not going to take me out to the middle of the woods and hack me to pieces?"

He was tormenting me now, using the same words I had used the night he drove me home from the Skull. The fact that he remembered that made every part of my body envelop into a comforting amount of warmth. I gave him an ornery smile and playfully stuck my tongue out at him, giving into his silly little torment game.

"No, I'm saving that for later..." I grinned in response, "I just want to show you something."

Chapter Thirteen: Tara

Once the familiar sight of the wooden dock had come into view and I was able to see the beautiful glimmering lake on the horizon, I smiled. This was where I wanted to bring him. This was my special place. The way his eyes glistened against the moonlight on the lake made my pulse quicken, causing me to feel nervous all over again. He was breathtaking, and he didn't even know it. "We're here." I said as I squeezed his hand, and motioned him to sit down on the edge of the dock with me.

I let go of his hand and sat down, making sure that my shoes didn't get wet by the water. Soon he followed suit and scooted closer to me so that our arms were touching as we stared out to the lake. "What is this place?" He began looking at his surroundings, causing him to smile at the sight of the lightning bugs making the trees glow. I let in a huge breath and held it as my body scooted closer to him. "This is my special place." I murmured softly, trying to hide the blush that was now tinting my cheeks.

"I love it here, it's so beautiful." His voice was deep and sultry, but had such a softness to it that you felt so comforted by the sound of him.

I followed his gaze up to where he was looking, and admired the familiar sight of the glowing trees with him.

This view had always amazed me, and it was one of a kind. I never got tired of it, even after all these years.

I was sure that many people had known of this place; it was never overgrown, and the dock was always well maintained, but still... I was happy to pretend it was mine.

A moment passed between us where there was silence. The only noise we heard was the soft chirping of crickets around us and the sounds of us breathing. I felt my eyes slowly moving towards him, wanting to see him, wanting to study his eyes and smile so I could keep it as a memory. This feeling was so strange and it wasn't one I had ever experienced before. I had noticed this feeling the first time we met, and no matter how scared I was of this unfamiliar feeling, I knew that I wasn't making it up; it was absolutely real.

There was no doubt that I was attracted to Adam, but the strong pull I felt towards him was something that was foreign to me. It was an uncharted territory in my emotions, but I didn't want it to stop. I continued to want more of him in any way I could get it, even if it meant that I had to sneak glances at him every second.

As my eyes traced up the bridge of his nose, I could tell that he was already staring at me. His eyes were focused on my lips, like he was holding himself back from crashing into me. That's all I wanted to do, too.

But I held myself together.

That was until his hand reached over to mine and gently pulled it over to his lap.
He intertwined his fingers with mine once again and the warm, familiar feeling of his hand made me smile. He leaned in closer to me, his lips slightly touching my ear, and he whispered as he spoke, making his voice vibrate through my entire body.

"God.." he said, his voice cracking like he was being tortured, "You are so beautiful."

I turned my head slightly, trying to make eye contact, but by the time I turned my head I could feel the heat of his breath on my lips. We were just a few inches away from one another, and I could feel that magnetic force drawing us in together. I wanted his lips to be on me more than anything.

For a moment we lingered there, our lips almost touching. The way my heart was jumping out of my chest made me want to run for the hills, but it also made me want to jump on top of him and kiss him until I couldn't breathe. There were a lot of things I wanted to do to him and I began to feel impatient. The sexual tension was building higher and higher between us as the moments passed. He licked his lips as both of our breath became synchronized, one waiting for the other to make a move.

He moved the slightest amount, placing his forehead on mine, knowing that we were there with each other, both wanting, both knowing how we felt without saying a single word. Without knowing hardly anything about Adam, it was amazing to see just how much of an impact he had on me already. I was overworking my heart too much with what this man was doing to me, and he hadn't even kissed me yet.

I lifted up my chin, signaling him, begging him to take his lips onto mine, but he didn't move. His breath became quicker and more shallow, but he didn't give into his need. I could tell just how nervous he felt by the way his fingers were shaking slightly while resting on top of mine, but I was sure that he was trying to brush it off. It was almost comforting to know that I wasn't the only one who was always in my head.

He lifted his hand and cupped my chin with it as he stared into my eyes, mesmerizing me with his deep chocolate brown eyes. We lingered there a moment, knowing that this moment was about to happen, and yet just as he went to lean in, his phone rang.

Shit.

He cleared his throat as the moment had passed and we both had missed out on it. At that moment, I decided that I didn't want to miss out on another chance. Not with him.

He was looking down at his phone as he texted intently. I knew that I needed to think of something else for us to do so that I didn't jump on top of him like I had wanted to ever since I saw him at the fair earlier. "Do you want to swim?" I stood up and took off my converse shoes.

He stopped texting at that moment and looked up at me as he continued to sit on the dock. I rolled my eyes and playfully nudged his shoulder with my hand. "Hello? Adam? Are you there?" I cupped my hands around my mouth as if I was calling out to him, but couldn't see him. The small chuckle that escaped his lips made my heart dance in the familiar rhythm whenever he was near. He stood up and walked closer towards me. He reached out for my hand, trying to seize the moment and take the reins. But I wasn't going to give up that easily. "Well if you aren't, then I am."

I pulled off my Black Keys t-shirt and jeans, leaving just a black pair of undies and a matching bra on, exposing the rest of my body to him. I looked over my shoulder at him and shrugged my shoulders before jumping in. I had a sudden feeling of embarrassment because the water was colder than I expected. The impact of the water was shocking. It was like a thousand needles were stabbing into my skin at first, but after a few seconds the intensity wore off.

The water was cold, but it was slowly becoming bearable. He had a wide smile now, and shook his head as if I was amusing him. "You're making things hard for me, woman." I could tell he let out a small groan as he said those words. "But you know that, don't you?" He chuckled in amusement. It made me happy to hear him say that, to have that kind of impact on him, so I decided to torment him.

"Well, you're just making things harder for yourself, since you won't come in and join me." I playfully splashed the water in his direction, and he backed away, trying not to get his maroon t-shirt wet from the impact. He was checking his jeans and shirt for any water, making sure that he was still dry. This was such a bad idea to spice things up, but I knew that it was too late now, I had gotten his attention.

Well. No time like the present.

I reached around to my back and unclasped my bra, then pulled off my undies and rolled both of them into a ball with one another. I felt a surge of power and confidence that I never had before. Butterflies swirled around in my stomach, making me feel the intensity and anticipation of the moment. "Are you coming in?" I asked, batting my eyes at him. His gaze directed back onto me now, following me around as I gently moved around the water. "*mujer de ninguna manera*" "No way woman". After a moment of silence, I decided on a new tactic. I started to pout, holding onto my bra and undies as a final pawn. The pout must not have been working, because a smooth vibrato laugh came from his throat. At least he was amused."No mama, I don't swim."

The way he called me mama made me want to moan out loud. The way he said it with a tiny little twinge of an accent may have been the sexiest thing I had ever heard. I didn't know what he was doing to me, but he could destroy me in every way and I would be fine with it. There was too much tension, and I couldn't take it anymore.

If he was playing hard to get, well so could I. I felt my lips curve into a smile and I cocked an eyebrow, trying to signal him that I had more tricks up my sleeve.

He was staring at me with his arms crossed, like he was unbreakable.

I grabbed my bra and underwear from under the water and turned around, ringing it out so that I could throw it farther. I turned back to face him and tossed my bra and underwear at him, which landed onto the dock.

He looked down at what was left of my clothing, fully realizing what I had just done. He cleared his throat and began taking off his Adidas tennis shoes. I knew I had won our little challenge, and what a wonderful feeling it was to win. I began to dissolve into a fit of laughter as he struggled to quickly take his clothes off. Once he jumped in and his head was above water we continued to wade around in the lake, gazing at one another without saying a word.

He decided to break the silence then, and started to speak: "So, can I ask you a question?"

I felt puzzled, but intrigued by the question he was preparing to ask. "Yeah, absolutely." He moved his arms in a slow motion back and forth at his sides, creating movement without actually going anywhere. "What made you go to the Skull that night? Why were you there?" The question had been a little personal, but I soon realized that I was swimming around naked in the water with him, so anything goes at this point.

"Um.." I started, trying to find the right words. "I kind of needed a break. I'm always so busy with swimming, cheering, and school that I don't have much time for myself. So it was that, and also I had gone home from practice that day and found out my mom had an affair." I gazed down at the water now, focusing on the moonlight's reflection off of it. I didn't know how he would react to what I had told him, but I had felt so much better just talking about it to someone, anyone. "Hmmm." He hummed softly, probably not sure what to say to that, but I didn't blame him. "Makes sense I guess. Are you okay with your mom?" My heart felt like it was twisting inside. *Was he asking questions because he cared?* It was super sweet and I had never had someone who paid so much attention to what I had to say. "Funny story about that.." I try not to laugh, but I couldn't help it. My life is just too much of a shit show now not to laugh. "My mom cheated, and my dad has suffered with depression most of his life, so it was a little too much for him. He ended up trying to drown himself in the tub.." I let the silence between us linger for a moment, letting a chuckle out to cover up the pain. "That wasn't even the plot twist, Adam. Are you ready for this one?" He simply nodded his head, studying me and my reactions. "Turns out my mom found out, and attempted to come to the house to *help*, but never came to the hospital. Not once."

It was kind of funny now that I said it out loud. But, It wasn't funny at all. It was like I was in denial, but I knew I'd be affected by this for a while. "Oh shit." His eyes went wide in shock, unsure of what to say. "I'm sorry that all happened at once." His eyes showed so much empathy that It was like I was seeing him clearly for the first time. "That's gotta be tough on you.." his voice trailed off, like he wasn't sure what to say next.

How did such an amazing guy like him come into my life?

"It's okay, things will work out.." I said softly as I moved my eyes back to the moon's reflection on the water. "What about you? Any crazy parents who randomly have an affair or try to self harm and make you be the one who witnesses it?" I attempted to laugh away the hurt, but it was still there. All I knew was there was no way his parents could be worse than mine. I could already tell how great of a person he was within these few encounters, and the great person he is comes from how he was raised.

His parents must be so proud of him.

The empty silence made me realize that I may have said something I shouldn't have, because his expression went dark and his eyes clouded over.

His expression changed, no, his entire being changed the second I asked that question. Embarrassment washed over me and I knew that it wasn't my place to even ask. Something about his parents must have caused him so much pain for him to react the way he did. "Adam?" I tried my best to get his full attention, but he wouldn't budge. It was like he was in a fog, and he wouldn't break out.

I swam over to him until my face was right in front of his. He looked off into space like he was anywhere but here.

I did this to him.

I will never forgive myself.

You are an awful person.

The familiar thoughts came creeping into my mind, right on time. I never went longer than a day without hearing my inner thoughts emotionally knock me out.

Despite those thoughts resurfacing, all I could do was focus on the empty shell of a man that was wading around in the water. And knowing that I triggered this reaction scared the shit out of me. "I'm so sorry, I don't know what's going on…but whatever it is, I'm sorry I asked. It's none of my business." I said as I placed my hands on his shoulders, gently beginning to squeeze them. "I'm sorry Adam.."

He wouldn't look at me and I could tell that the amount of pain in his eyes had lingered there for a long time. It broke my heart to see him this way, and to have turned this way so quickly. I cupped his jaw with my hands, hoping me touching him would knock him out of the dissociative fog he was in. "Adam..." I said, my voice becoming a little more worried. "Adam, please." I pleaded. "Look at me." I lifted his chin up for his eyes to meet mine. His eyes gazed into mine and it was like he told me everything without saying absolutely anything. I didn't need to know, and I understood. I accepted it.

"I'm here.." I said softly, as I combed my hands through his dark, curly hair. "I'm here Adam." He reached under the water and grabbed my legs to hoist me around his lower waist. I continued to comb through his hair as he placed his forehead on mine, taking a moment to just hear us breathe together. He looked up at me and gave me a small, sad smile. He tucked a wet strand of hair behind my ear with his skull hand and held his hand on the side of my cheek, trailing my skin with his cold, wet fingers.

"Thank you for being so patient…" He said, stroking my cheek with his thumb. "It's hard for me to talk about, so sometimes I go to this place that is hard to get out of. But since we're being transparent here, I'll tell you.." He continued, "Is it okay if for now it's the short version?" I nodded, feeling all kinds of emotions rolling out of me at once. "My parents died.." He sucked in a large breath of air, closed his eyes for a moment, and then let it out slowly. "It's really hard. Tío Joe has been taking care of me ever since my mom died when I was 11. Dad was diagnosed with cancer two years later…" He continued, "He ended up passing away when I was nineteen. My Uncle Joe took me in and has been with me every step of the way."

A single tear fell down my cheek, but there were no words that I could say that would take away the pain that was so clear in his deep brown eyes. I wanted him to understand just how sorry I was for him.. just how much my heart broke. All I wanted to do was to cure his heartache.

To be the one who gave him the happiness he deserved. And It shocked me because I didn't even really know him. But I wanted to.

I appreciated him being so open with me. I couldn't imagine the grief he must've gone through every day. Even though my parents had a lot of issues, I couldn't imagine my life without them. That was what made hearing this so hard; Adam didn't deserve that,

He deserved to be happy.

His life has been centered around his parents death, and it was completely consuming him. I could see it in his eyes. My heart mourned for him, wanting to carry some of that weight for him.

A slow flow of tears escaped my eyes, and a small sob escaped my throat. I didn't know what to do, I felt like I couldn't help him. "I'm sorry, I didn't mean to make you upset..." a quiet moment passed as we both looked into one another's eyes, knowing that whatever this feeling was, it was more than just physical attraction.

There was a small twinge of hope there, like we both could see something more than anything we could have ever imagined. "Thank you for telling me, Adam." I took my hand and traced his lips with my thumb, wanting to memorize every part of him, forever.

His warm caramel eyes gazed into mine, which made my heart race like I was a teenager again. The corner of his lips lifted into a small smile, as he mimicked what I did with my thumbs over his lips. He traced mine with his thumb, and then placed a kiss on my forehead.

"Where have you been my entire life?" He gazed back into my eyes as he placed his forehead on mine, now cupping my cheeks with his large, slightly rough hands. We had never been as close as we were right now. He lifted my chin up with his skull hand's index finger and he let a moment linger between us before he leaned slowly, studying how I would react to him making his move, before he crashed his lips into mine.

I was in shock at first; I wasn't sure what was happening to be honest. Before I knew it, he was walking me out of the lake, both of us entirely naked, as he placed soft kisses along my collarbone, my neck, and my cheeks. I let my body take control and soft moans escaped my lips from the pleasure those small kisses of his gave me.

He walked up to the small shore and gave me a quick peck on my lips before parting. He grabbed his maroon t-shirt and placed it over my head before grabbing the rest of our clothes. He slid on his tennis shoes quickly and I couldn't help but giggle.

He was trying his best to hurry, all the while lifting me up to hold me around his waist. He showered me with kisses with every word he spoke:

"Where." *Kiss*. "Do." *Kiss*. "I." *Kiss*. "Go." *Kiss*.

My lips felt swollen and my skin felt hot, even though we were dripping cold water from the lake. "There's a path over there.." I pointed. "Back to the Sherwood cabins." I stared at his beautiful brown eyes, not wanting to give up this moment we were in. It felt like my entire body was on fire.

I loved it.

A playful grin tugged at the corners of his lips then, which made me smile. "How'd you know the name of the cabin I was staying in?"

I shook my head in dismissal and kissed him softly on the cheek. "No, I don't.. That's where I'm staying, I'm in cabin #4." My legs and arms were still fully wrapped around him as water was dripping down both of our bodies.

All he was wearing was his boxers and a pair of shoes. He was clinging onto the rest of our clothes as he held me up over his hips. I suddenly realized that I didn't even have underwear on, just his t-shirt. I felt his entire body right up against mine.

I could tell that he wanted me just as much as I wanted him. I could feel him through his boxers, practically pulsating. "Great." *Kiss*. "I'm in #16." *Kiss*.
He broke away for a moment, staring intently into my eyes. It was like he immediately thought of something.

"Tara..." He said, lingering on the question.

I just wanted him to hurry the hell up and take me to his cabin. "What?" I snapped, starting to get sexually aggravated.

"Are you sure we're not.." his voice trailed off, but I knew what he was about to say.

I kissed him softly, trying to allow me entrance into his mouth, as I slid my tongue in to meet his and they began to dance with one another. I parted my lips from his for just a moment, to study him through my ice blue eyes. "No, we're not rushing it. I want to. Do you?" The lake water had been cold and there was a breeze in the wind. Any other time I would have been freezing, but right now at this moment, I was burning up entirely. The frustration alone was enough to make me roll my eyes and throw my head back in agony.

"I do want to, God, I fucking want to." He said, as his eyes darkened and his dark brown eyes scanned from my eyes to my lips— studying them, taking them in, and his gaze became drunk; mesmerized by the sight of my lips. He kissed his lips softly and began to nibble at the nape of his neck. I moved my hips into him, showing him just how bad I wanted him.

No, just how bad I *needed* him.

Our breathing became synchronized, our chests rising and falling at a fastened pace together. "Good.." I said to him, as I placed soft kisses on his cheek, and ran my hands along his perfectly formed and tattooed chest. "I want this, Adam." I looked into his eyes once more and nodded, giving him permission to continue this beautiful moment. "Let's go." He kissed me softly, and then deepened the kiss as he started walking again.

*

We laughed with one another on the way to the cabins as we continued to stop to kiss; we both knew that we couldn't stop the hunger we had for one another.

We both knew there was no point in multitasking; walking and kissing at the same time wasn't the best thing to do in the dark, as the moonlight had been the only source of light we had to direct our path. He stopped a few times on the way, pulling me closer to him and tugging on my lips with his teeth. Every single time he did I felt a spark of desire shoot through me, causing me to move against his hips. It was like my body had a mind of its own. We needed every bit of time that we had together. We didn't want to waste a single moment.

Just as we approached his cabin, he stopped for a moment and looked at me, now stroking my hair with his hands. "You carried me this entire way." I stifled through the laughter and kissed his collarbone that connected to his neck. "You're like my own personal tattooed Clark Kent." I smirked as I pressed my lips to his and bit his lower lip to gently tug with my teeth.

It was like that one small thing had sent him into orbit… he let out a moan so loud that it had echoed through the woods.

I couldn't help but burst out into laughter.

There were cabins all around us; we could've easily gotten caught. "I think the whole fair could hear that.." I said as I wiped my laughter filled tears from my eyes. "Want me to make you do that again?" I said, wiggling my eyebrows in a moment of torment.

His expression grew dark again, signaling to me that he was ready for me, just as I was for him. "Shh…" He said as his lips trailed down my neck. "..Stop. Talking." And with that, he hoisted me up higher on his hips and walked me onto the cabin porch to the side door, and into his bedroom.

Explicit content

You have the option to skip past this Chapter and resume on Chapter 15.

No important plot details are in this scene

Chapter Fourteen: Adam

As if I couldn't think she could be any more sexier, I watched as she fell into a deep sleep and snuggled herself under the thick covers. Her perfect curves were highlighted by the moonlight beaming through the window and I couldn't help but feel a rush of adrenaline. The way her delicate and yet confident presence could intimidate just about anyone scared the hell out of me. The only other person who made me feel this way had been Vanessa, and it had been years since her.

The thought of twenty year old me being so in love with Vanessa made me draw in a breath, fearful of the past and fearful of letting that in again in the future. I had guarded myself for six years; to the point where I thought I didn't care at all. I was quick to learn to not care much about anything when being a drug dealer, and especially after Vanessa. We had been together for three years, almost until my twenty-second birthday.

I had thought she was it for me, and I was more than happy to spend the rest of my life with her. Little did I know that she was cheating on me with one of my best buddies from high school. And what was hilarious about the whole thing was that I introduced them.

I still felt so frustrated whenever those memories resurfaced; She caused my life to fall apart, and I fully planned on never letting a woman let me be as weak as I had been.

That's why I was so damn conflicted now.

Already having feelings for Tara seemed like a damn reach. I could never give her what she deserved, and it was better for my heart to not get so damn invested. I had seen that happen with a lot of guys I had worked with over the years; They'd fall for a girl & finally think they could change their outcome.. but they never could get out of this business; no matter how hard they tried, they were stuck. This business would ruin you or kill you before you even thought about leaving.

I knew I could never leave, either. As much as I wanted to get out of this situation and get a real job, or maybe start a family.. I knew it wasn't in the cards for me. And even if I desired the woman laying in my bed, I didn't want to be the cause of her suffering.

I glanced out the large window pane that displayed views of the woods from my bedroom. Thoughts seemed to find their way in my head, spinning around like that damn cyclone ride over at the fair. Thoughts came in about all kinds of things…but mostly my thoughts resolved around the beautiful woman who was sleeping soundly in my bed with a small smile pressed on her lips.

I felt my heart tighten at that exact moment.

God, she is breathtaking.

I wasn't sure what this twenty year old girl was doing to me, but I knew the moment I put her in the passenger side of her car to drive her home that I was utterly *fucked*.

She had changed my life in a matter of days; just her presence alone set my world on fire. It was torture to think of what life was before her, and it was torture to think about how there would never be anything outside of this. This moment, this *thing* was all we had, and all we could have. So for now, I was going to bask in the idea of pretending.

I'd pretend that we could have something more than just *this*. I'd pretend that she could change my entire life just with her company and I wouldn't have to worry about dealing drugs ever again.

But there were real things, too. She was *real*. And she was *here*.

Now.

It was like she had known all of my strengths and weaknesses without telling her them. It was like she knew me, without really knowing me at all.

I began to think about the moment she stripped in front of me to jump into the lake, the way her fair skinned body reflected off of the moon made her look fucking angelic. And I wasn't proud of it, but it made my stomach flutter like I was a goddamn teenager.

I couldn't control myself. She drew me in so quickly, so easily, that I struggled so much to hold my shit together. She had no idea how much I wanted her at that moment. I wanted so badly to see her fully naked body, to know what she tasted like, to know how it felt to be inside of her.

She teased me at that lake and I let her, which had brought us back here; to my cabin. I thought about the moment I brought her into my room; She was so energized and ready for me. I could tell by the positioning of her body on my hips; I could tell by the way she kissed me. She was eager for me to fuck her. And I was eager, too.

Fuck, I was so eager.

The thought of me pushing her up against the wall as I kissed her burned into my mind. The way her soft moans made me want her more as she tugged on my bottom lip with her teeth. The way she laid in my bed, gazing up at me with such wonder in her eyes knowing that she trusted me to make her feel a way she never had before.

She was different from the other women I had been with in my past, and the bliss I had felt with her was like a drug, and I wanted all of it.

The truth was, that every single time I wasn't near her, all I did was think about her. And every time I was with her, she made my pulse quicken and filled me with desire. She was also absolutely breathtaking.

Her striking eyes were like two blue pools, pulling you in and taking you under. Her dark hair laid so perfectly along her soft pink cheeks, and drifted down to her collarbones. And her smile, *damn*....That smile was enough to stop a man from breathing. Every damn moment where she had been put in my life, randomly by the universe, God, whomever... well it took my breath away.

I continued to look out to the blackened night sky, thinking about a few hours before when we both had been on my bed kissing one another, filling each other's every desire. The sound of her loud but smooth moans against my ear, and the way she said my name was enough to end me.

My favorite moment was when she looked right into my eyes during that special moment for us. As soon as I was inside her, thrusting through the tightness, I locked my eyes on her. Her eyes started rolling back and closed tightly as she arched her back on the silk sheets in pleasure:

"*Holy shit..*" *she said, breathlessly, "Adam, please."*

She was begging for me, wanting me to fasten my pace... to send her into a flood of ecstasy. She had looked so sexy in just my t-shirt that it made me feel heated, unable to tame the fire that I needed from her. I suddenly found myself needing to see her beautiful blue eyes.

"Tara.." *I said, trying to speak clearly, but unable to form too much of a sentence. Her eyes shut tighter as her hands were grasping and pulling on my bed sheets. She was enjoying this too much. I needed her bright blue eyes on mine, I needed to know we both were feeling the same way at that moment.*

"Look at me." *I ordered.*

I continued moving deeper into her, showering her in pleasure, knowing that I was close to finishing. She opened her eyes then, and her blue eyes burned into mine. Her breath synchronized with mine, causing my chest to rise and fall at the same time as hers. It was something completely different than I had ever experienced before. I wanted to see her in all of her beauty as I was inside of her. I didn't know why, but this moment with Tara hadn't been just another fuck. It had been confounding. It had changed everything.

Somewhere deep inside of me, I hoped she thought that, too.

"Adam, oh god." She yelled, starting to moan louder, letting me know she was close, too. "Shhh, baby." I covered her mouth with my hand, hoping that Ricky wasn't here, hearing her calling out my name in the middle of the night. If he heard us fucking, he would have never let it go. We continued like this for a few more minutes, her wrapping her legs around my waist. I couldn't take it anymore, I couldn't hold it. She felt too good, too ready for me. I was going to explode. I needed to pull out, now. "Fuck, Tara." I rasped, loving how good it felt to be inside of her. To see her beautiful blue eyes gazing into mine. She set my soul on fire. Soon, a familiar shock overtook my body and I quickly pulled out of her, attempting to hold my body from its release.

I knew she had been close, but I couldn't risk coming inside of her. I wouldn't do that to her.

I slid two fingers inside of her, moving them in a steady rhythm, one that she copied by moving her hips. "Adam, I can't take anymore!" I grazed my thumb over her sensitive skin. "Finish for me, baby" I growled, I was getting harder just by her rocking against my fingers and hearing my name on her lips.

As she sighed out my name, I felt her grab onto me, stroking me from the tip all the way down in such a swift, yet incredibly sexy way. I felt my release coming as she continued to stroke me and I fastened my pace for her. She let out a long sigh and released around my fingers; her body *trembled around me as she finished stroking me while riding my fingers, sending us both into an aftershock.*

I couldn't help but smile down at her. She was so beautiful. I leaned down and kissed her lips softly, then kissed her forehead "That's my girl" I hummed into her ear. She let out a small laugh and cutely pushed my face away with her hands, making me laugh with her.

*

I remember us laying there afterwards, her head laying on my chest as her small fingers traced my skull tattoo on my hand, then another tattoo for my parents of two doves that was inked on my chest. She let out a small sigh, which made my stomach flip again. She seemed to be doing that quite a lot. I found myself actually caring for this girl, and yet I didn't know why. I kissed the top of her head softly and smiled at the sight of her. Even with her damp, wavy hair from the lake, she was the most beautiful woman I had ever seen. Her eyelids had become heavy not long afterwards— letting herself fall into a quick, somber sleep.

Thinking back to that moment earlier, I had felt like the luckiest guy in the world. I knew that maybe I was getting in way over my head, and maybe I was fucking pathetic to be looking at her and thinking about her the way I was, but I allowed myself. I didn't get many moments to truly enjoy myself anymore, so I let myself have it.

I heard a faint strum of a guitar next to the window, out on the back patio. I moved the curtain to look out of the window, noticing Ricky sitting there, playing his guitar and sitting in front of a bonfire. Ricky had been like a brother to me,, and I knew that this weekend wasn't going to be easy for either of us, but I worried about him. I wanted to make sure he was okay, even if that meant taking the blame if something went wrong and getting killed by Jerome. had hoped nothing this weekend would get in the way of our plan; we had a job that we needed to do, and it was time to get serious.

I decided maybe it was a good time to go talk to Ricky, to map out our plan a bit more for tomorrow night. The last thing I needed was something to fuck it up.

I opened the side door to my room out to the patio, when I heard a small, yet high pitched sigh from behind me.

Tara.

I looked back over at her on the bed; she was rubbing her eyes with her fingers.
She stopped and looked over at me, her lips forming a wide smile. I felt my lips pull up into a smile too. I felt like I was beaming, like the sorry son of a bitch that I was.

"Hey, beautiful.." I said, my voice raspy and dry. "... you go back to sleep okay? I'm going out here to talk to Ricky."

She nodded her head, still with a smile pressed on her lips. She hopped off of my bed, my shirt hanging slightly over her knees, which made it look like a dress on her. She did a small, but cute skip over to me and wrapped her arms around my neck.
It was the cutest fucking thing I had ever witnessed.

She kissed me quickly once, and then kissed me again, this time deepening the kiss and flicking her tongue against mine. I felt a groan escape my throat.

What the fuck was she doing to me?

I broke away from her before my body reacted and I threw her back on the bed to fuck the shit out of her.

"As much as I don't want to, we have to hold that thought.." I groaned in agony as I spoke. "Go ahead to bed and I'll be there in a minute, mama." She blushed then, and nodded as she bit her lip. She kissed me once more, and walked back over to my bed, climbing in on the left side where I sleep, and covering herself up with the comforter.

I smiled at her once more and winked at her as she closed her eyes, and then finally made my way out to the patio to talk to Ricky. I needed to make sure he was protected, and that we were on the same page about how this transaction was going to go down.

There was a lot that we needed to discuss.

Chapter Fifteen: Adam

I open the side door of my bedroom and walk out to the back patio. Ricky was still in the same place I saw him last, humming along as he strummed his guitar.

Ricky was always the creative one of the two of us; He could have made it as a musician. He was a part of a band a few years back, but he quit to work full time for Jerome. It was a shame though, a few months later the band Ricky was with got a record deal and moved to Nashville.

I can still see in his eyes how much he regrets not sticking with it, but it really wasn't like he had much of a choice. He couldn't leave, not when Jerome had him wrapped around his finger. He still fucking does to this day, that's how I know we'll never get out.

But the truth was, neither one of us would ever get out. Not unless we were lucky enough to get shot. I rather that be my way out then to be stuck in this shit for the rest of my life.

Did I want to die? In retrospect, fuck no. I wish I could live a full life; One where I could have a wonderful wife to come home to, and maybe some hellions. Maybe even a dog; a Golden Retriever and name him some kind of generic name like Buddy or Cooper. But that was all just a dream; In reality, the closest I would get to a family was Ricky.

Ricky noticed me walking out on the patio, slightly nodding my head when I caught sight of him. He nods in reply and his face fills with a cocky smirk. "Hey, dude." I sighed heavily as he reached his hand out to do our handshake. "What's up brother?"

I sat down next to him, my eyes getting lost staring at the bonfire in front of us. "Nothing much, couldn't really sleep." Before I could realize what I had said, Ricky started coughing and laughing loudly.

Adam, you fucking idiot. You walked right into that one.

"Yeah I bet you didn't get much sleep." He mimicked loud moans and humped the air. "Shh! Shut the fuck up, Rick." I said as I hit him in the chest and looked back to the room to signal that she was still there. I couldn't help but laugh along with him, though. If I was going to get tormented about this, I might as well enjoy it.

"Were we really that fucking loud, Rick?" I rest my head on the back of the chair, becoming more relaxed in the warm Autumn air.

"Dude I was across the cabin in my room and I heard you. I swear people in Atlanta could hear Tara. Not to say that it didn't sound hot, but fuck it was loud. That's why I came out here, but it didn't help much." He reached over and playfully punched my bicep.

I wasn't embarrassed, Ricky had heard more than enough of the hookups that I've had in the past years, especially Natasha. I did, however, feel embarrassed for Tara. I don't know if she wanted anyone else knowing, and it worried me that he invaded her privacy in a way.

Or… Maybe I was just whipped already.

I shook the thought out of my head and focused back on Ricky. "So, how did the rest of your night go?"

I eyed him and wiggled my eyebrows, wondering if he was interested in that girl he left earlier with. He smirked and shook his head at my question.

"Well let me tell you, that Riley girl that Tara is friends with is batshit crazy." He made a full smile then, and then looked back at his guitar as he played a few chords.

"But I like crazy, so I like her. She gave me her number at the end of the night and ran off with her friends. I didn't even get to kiss her. I think she's playing hard to get..But it's cool, cause trust me I *will get*."

I smiled at his comment, but what he said didn't need a reply. Ricky was always confident in whatever he did, especially when it came to women.

A moment of silence passed, I personally was enjoying the quietness of sitting next to my brother, knowing that this could be my last night to enjoy his company. I knew I needed to talk to him, I needed to get everything out on the table now, before it was too late.

"So, tomorrow." Is all I said, knowing he'd catch on quickly. "Tomorrow is gonna be a tough one, brother." His voice sounded nervous, but he just looked down at his guitar and continued strumming.

I nodded my head, knowing he wasn't looking at me, but I knew I agreed completely. "I was thinking we should deliver the molly to his friend tomorrow night, then wait until close, after most of the vendors shut down for the night. I'll park the Camry close so that no one sees us. Then we'll get the guy when they're closing, put him in the trunk, then drive straight to the warehouse. Deal?"

Ricky stopped playing his guitar, and looked like he was dazed. He continued to stare at the trees in the distance for a few minutes.

"Rick?"

He snapped out of his daze, and turned to look at me. He cleared his throat, as if he was trying to hold himself together.

"Uh, yeah sounds good. Except we'll deliver the molly to his friend during the day. There's that cheering competition tomorrow, so most everyone will be there. That'll give us a chance to do the exchange somewhere private where we won't get caught."

I shook my head, that wasn't going to work, it was too obvious. "I like the idea of doing it during the day, but if we go somewhere private, there's an easier chance that someone will notice…" I thought more in depth about this. *How would it be easy to hide it during the daylight?* There weren't many options. A few moments of silence lingered before I was able to think of an idea. "…No, we aren't doing that. Text J's guy and tell him we're meeting him at the cheering competition. We'll stand by the bleachers and do it discreetly there. No one will be watching us, all of their eyes will be on the cheerleaders."

Ricky simply nodded and got his phone out, quickly texted a message to Jerome's friend, and then sat his phone back down on the arm of his lawn chair.

He looked over at me again, and met my gaze. He gave me a small smirk before speaking: "I don't want to sound like a pussy, but incase tomorrow doesn't work out—" He paused, not wanting to finish the sentence.

But I knew exactly what he was trying to say. I knew what he wasn't saying, because I thought the exact same thing.

There was a fear that both of us hadn't experienced. The fear of getting caught, like usual, but also the fear of the plan not working out well, the plan of not delivering the man to Jerome properly, the fear of possibly having to kill this man, and the normal daily fear of getting killed.

There was a lot riding on us this weekend, and I'd be lying if I said that it didn't scare the fuck out of me.

I didn't want to die, that much was true. But I didn't want Ricky to die, either. And if I had to choose between the both of us, I would never, in a million years, let my brother die. It would be me.

That's why after Jerome told us our mission for this weekend and Ricky got in the car that night, I pulled J to the side and spoke to him quietly. We made a deal: I pull all the cash from the vendor's register to help make up for the counterfeits, and I deliver the man and money properly. If all goes well, then we don't have to kill the man, and we're able to walk out alive.

But if somehow we fuck this up, I'm the one who gets punished and Ricky walks off and gets out of this business for good.

Jerome was hesitant of my request of letting Ricky get out, but he said he was "all about fairness" and "keeping his word", so he agreed to my terms.

Knowing that Jerome didn't back out on his word gave me at least a little bit of comfort, knowing that Rick would be okay, no matter what happens tomorrow.

That, at least, gave me some peace.

Even if it meant that I had to die, I would know that my brother was safe, and that was all that mattered. I cleared my throat and focused back on Ricky.

"You don't have to say anymore, Rick...." I say, barely audible enough to sound like I wasn't getting emotional, ".....Lo se hermano." *".....I know brother."*

The both of us sit there for a moment, both with a simple, understanding smile, knowing how much we've appreciated each other all of these years. Understanding that we were, in fact, brothers. Regardless of fucking genes, or blood, or whatever other dumbass references people use. He was my brother for life, and he always will be.

We both nodded at one another before facing our direction to the new sound behind us; the side door to my room opening and closing.

Tara.

She walked out of my room and onto the patio, still wearing my maroon t-shirt, but now with a pair of my gray Nike sweatpants on, too. Those had been my favorite sweatpants, but *damn*, my clothes looked so much better on her so I didn't give two shits. Her dark hair was laying against her shoulders in waves, now completely dry from the lake.

The second she saw the both of us, she blushed and a small smile appeared on her face before she walked closer to the bonfire. "Hey, Ricky." She says softly, as she waves at him in the cutest way possible.

"Hey, Tara. How are you? Tired?" Ricky smirks, and winks at her, causing me to automatically hit him hard in the chest so he could learn to shut the fuck up. Her eyes go wide and shoot over to me, the pink on her cheeks forming into a bright red.

"You told him?" She snapped, as if I should've known not to say anything.

Before I could reply, Ricky saved my ass.

"No…You have it all wrong, Tara. He didn't need to tell me, not when I heard *everything* to prove it." She covers her face with her hands, showing that Ricky embarrassed the fuck out of her. Ricky was a great guy, but he was a cocky smart ass and constantly tormented people.

I learned to enjoy this side of him, but a lot of people who didn't know him felt uncomfortable by his blunt and cocky personality. "Rick, knock it off.." I order, immediately shutting him up. "...Tara, come sit over here with me."

She uncovered her face, her color returning back to normal, and walked over towards me as I reached out for her. She reached my chair and grabbed my hand, as I guided her to sit on my lap.

She gave me a small smile, then snuggled herself up onto my lap and wrapped her arms around my neck, gently combing through my hair with her fingers.

"So what were you two talking about out here anyways?" She was curious, I could tell by her face. Her eyebrows were furrowed and she was looking between the both of us. Ricky sat there, frozen, as if he had no idea what to say.

I pulled her face towards mine with my hand and kissed her softly. A small smile appeared on her lips afterwards, which sent a jolt of electricity through my chest. I decided to speak up and answer her, since Ricky looked like a fucking deer running in front of a car

"We're talking about what we wanted to do tomorrow at the fair." I said simply, trying to cover up what we were actually talking about.

"Oh well, come to the competition tomorrow!" she says excitedly. "I'd love it if you guys came!" She smiled at both of us, hopeful, like a little kid on Christmas morning.

A moment passed before she spoke again, now her face full of confusion.

Fuck.

She knew something was off.

"Not to get into your business, but the reason I asked.." she said softly, "... is that the both of you were looking at each other when I came out here.. like you're in a bromance or something."

She giggled as she looked between us again, and Ricky's lips formed into a small smirk as she laughed. "Well, Tara..." Ricky spoke, "…We do, Adam and I are deeply in love with one another." His answer even made me laugh out loud. This dude was such a smart ass. Tara laughed too, though. It was obvious that she was starting to catch on to his humor. That made me happy.

"Sorry, Ricky..." She kissed me softly and then looked back at him as if she meant business, "But he's mine now." I couldn't help but stare at her while she said that.

Any time she spoke, I was captivated. But this time when she spoke, it was different. Not only did she have my undivided attention, but she made me *nervous*. Like my heart felt like it could jump out of my chest at any fucking moment.

She said I was *hers*.

Something about that sentence gave me a new sense of warmth, but a part of me felt fearful. It was easier to hook up with women than it was to have a connection with them. But Tara was different. I wanted to know everything about her. I felt drawn to her, like she had been a magnet that pulled me in constantly. I couldn't even get away if I wanted to, that much I knew.

The way her soft voice sounded when she would say my name, or maybe it was the way her eyes would light up whenever she looked at me— whatever it was, all I knew was that I was completely in it, and I never wanted to leave.

She looked down at me again, this time with a full faced smile, and kissed me gently. She had no idea what she was doing to me. No one had any clue about just how fucked I was.

Ricky smiled and looked at the both of us, before strumming his guitar again. Tara admired Ricky playing the guitar and started humming along with him to the familiar song, *Big Jet Plane* by one of Ricky's favorite artists, Angus and Julia Stone. The way that they quickly accepted one another made my heart full. As dumb as that sounded, I felt complete in that moment. I finally knew that things would fall into place the way that they should be.

*

The rest of the night we sat on the patio and talked about our lives, the nerves that Tara felt for the competition tomorrow, and the fact that Tara couldn't believe how much Ricky liked the girl, Riley.

We laughed and sat in front of the bonfire until it went out at about three in the morning. Once the fire went out, we said our goodnights to Ricky, and went back into my room.

We both were tired, but too interested in one another to sleep. We had sex again before Tara fell asleep as she cuddled in my arms for the rest of the night. I had never felt so close to someone as much as I had with Tara in one night. The feelings were fucking terrifying, and this whole thing was unexpected. I watched her as she slept peacefully in my arms and couldn't help but think about tomorrow. We had completely different levels of playing fields that we had to endure tomorrow.

She was worried about a cheering competition and I was worried about possibly being killed. But my worst fear was that if tomorrow didn't go smoothly, I would never see her again.

My thoughts overflowed my head for the rest of the night and I was unable to fall asleep. I would have been pacing had it not been for Tara's relaxing presence and her body wrapped around mine. I admired her soft, fair features as her leg wrapped around my torso.

Even though Tara's presence kept me relatively calm throughout the night, the thoughts I had in my head never went away. All I knew was that I needed to be in the moment with Tara, so I kissed her forehead and moved my body closer to hers, completely engulfing myself in her warmth.

Chapter Sixteen: Tara

As I opened my eyes, I noticed the bright sunlight shining through the curtains of the patio doors. I noticed that my eyelids felt incredibly heavy; I didn't get a lot of sleep like I had been hoping I would, but I also didn't care; I got to spend an amazing time with Adam.

I turned my head to look at Adam laying on his stomach, bare chested and only half of his body covered with the blankets. I took a moment to admire his features.

His skin was a beautiful tan, his hair started to become longer than I had remembered in such a short amount of time. There were more curls on the edges now.

His biceps were flexing as he held onto the pillow to support his head. He was truly the cutest thing ever when he was asleep.

I yawned and stretched out my body, trying to wake myself up. Today was competition day, and I knew that I needed to prepare for that the best that I could, even if I was exhausted.

I grabbed my phone off of the nightstand to check my notifications and the time. I pressed the button to turn my screen on, and read my notifications.

I had twelve missed calls from Riley, several texts from Danielle, and a few phone calls from other girls on my squad.

I checked the time to make sure I was still on time, but my heart began to race and a surge of fear shot through me as I noticed what time it was.

10:48?! No no no no this can't be happening.

I was supposed to be at our tent at the fair at 10:30 for hair and makeup. I was supposed to be in my uniform by now.

I jumped out of bed quickly and found my underwear thrown on the floor and put them on, then a pair of Adam's sweats. I began to run around his room tin an attempt to find my converse. I couldn't find them anywhere.

"Shit. Shit. Shit."

I knew I must've made a bunch of noise, because Adam's head popped up and he rubbed his eyes as he yawned. "What the hell are you doing, Tara?" I stopped for a moment and smiled at him. The second he spoke, I felt like I was lost in our own little bubble. I always got lost in his eyes, too.

I quickly snapped out of my daze and started to look around for my shoes again."¿Que esta mal?" *"What's wrong?"* I looked up at him again, noticing how wide his eyes were, as if he could tell I was panicking.

"I'm late.. I have to go get my uniform and get ready." I looked at the bottom of the bed and found one of my shoes.

Thank God.

I fastened my pace as I looked around the room, behind the dressers, under the bed, anywhere I could.I finally relaxed when I saw the tip of my shoe sticking out from behind the curtains of the French doors. I slid my other shoe on, walked over to Adam, and climbed on top of him; my legs straddling him down to the bed. He let out a deep sigh and those warm brown eyes of his met my gaze.

"Thank you for last night.." I smiled and kissed him softly. Once he broke from the kiss, he kept his burning eyes on mine as his hands gently ran up and down my back.

174

The way his fingers caressed softly against my skin gave me such a sense of familiarity now. His touch made me calm, and I felt in complete peace when I was around him. "Thank you too, beautiful." He replied, with a small smirk forming on his lips.

I kissed him once more, letting it consume me entirely. I felt my breath lighten, my lungs now burning for air, just like it did every time I was swimming. I felt myself begin to desire that feeling, like it was a part of me, like I needed that feeling more and more each time I felt it. I knew that I didn't want to leave him, that much was true.

It was agonizing to think that I had to crawl off of him and leave him behind as I walked back to my cabin. I kissed him quickly once more, then kissed his forehead. "I really have to go.." I said, now placing my hands on his bare chest and rubbing my hands on him gently. I climbed off of him and walked towards the side door. I looked behind me at him again and smiled at the perfection that was Adam.

"I'll see you later, then." I said softly, putting my hair behind my ear.

His lips pressed into a full teeth smile, and his deep brown eyes glared at me for a long moment. "See you then."

And with those final words of perfection, I walked out of his bedroom door of the cabin, and made my way down the path to mine to get my cheering uniform.

I had totally messed up by not waking up on time. I tried to pick up my pace to reach my cabin, passing each and looking at the numbers as I went. I finally reached cabin #4, and unlocked the front door with my key that was in my back pocket.

I ran in, brushed my teeth, grabbed my makeup bag, and put on my uniform in full. I made sure I remembered to wear my white ankle high socks and my cheering shoes. Our regulations for this competition seemed so strict and pointless, it was just a county fair. But I also knew that I needed to follow it strictly, Riley would have my ass if I didn't. I looked at myself in the mirror, still looking tired from the long night before. I grabbed my blue glitter scrunchie and put it around my wrist, knowing that I would soon have my hair pulled up so high that I wouldn't be able to move my eyebrows.

I was already about a half an hour late, and I felt the common feeling of anxiety come to the surface. as if I didn't already have enough as it is. Because of this, I knew everyone on the squad would probably panic that I wasn't there. It was sad that I knew what to expect: Riley was going to tear me apart for this, and I had to just accept it.

*

"It's about fucking time, Tara."

Riley's high pitched, nasal voice yelled over everyone talking as I ran over to the tent, which made me really uncomfortable and very annoyed. So much for me believing she was redeeming herself.

"Where have you been?" She asked, invading my personal space with that question. "What were you even doing?" It was like she thought she had the right to know.

Bitch.

She walked over to me as she skimmed down my body, looking at my uniform to assess it.

"Well, telling by your tangled hair and your pasty complexion, I guess I should ask you *who* you were doing?" She looked at me now with a cocky expression on her face and her hand was on her hip, as if she ruled the place. She let out a nasal laugh and did a slight snort at the end. It was the most annoying thing I had ever heard.

"Let me guess.." she said as she walked closer to me, "...it was that crummy looking hoodlum that you went off with last night."

I tried my best to compose myself. I did what I could to control myself at that moment. She was the epitome of what it meant to be a cold hearted bitch. When I thought she was becoming her old self again after our phone call, clearly I was wrong; there was no saving someone like that.

I was late and I was the last to get ready, so I knew she was pissed off. Yes it was my fault, but I still wasn't in the mood today for Riley's bitchiness, not to mention her uncalled for bullshit. She had taken it way too far. No one should ever say those hateful things, and I wasn't about to let this cold hearted dumbass make fun of Adam.

"You know what Riley?" I said with courage, finally standing up to this bitch after so long of keeping quiet.

"I didn't think you could go any lower than you already are, but here you are— always surprising me."

I smiled at her, showing her my full blown sarcasm before I spoke again. "It's people like you that cause our world to be so fucked up. And you know what? I feel sorry for you…truly. But don't fucking take it out on me just because everyone and their mother thinks you're a crazy psychopath."

I walked over to put my makeup bag down and noticed all of the other girls on the squad staring at me, whispering to one another in hushed tones.

Riley's cheeks blushed a bright pink, like I had embarrassed her; like she was hurt by my words but she was trying to hide it. "Whatever, Tara. You're a loser. A loser to this squad, a loser at the school— Hell, you're even a loser to your parents. You're probably the reason they broke up and you're probably the reason your dad tried to *off* himself. So it's no surprise to hear that the loser herself picked a loser to fuck, *and* you hurt yourself, too just like your crazy father."

She scoffed out a smartass laugh and turned towards the end of the tent, flipping her pony tail in my face. She thought she had won by bringing up my family's private situation, to which she only knew because her parents and mine were so close. She knew what she did, and she knew it would sting.. and yet she did it anyway.

In front of the whole squad.

Before she got too far, I tugged the back of her arm, and pulled with such force that she immediately spun back around to face me.

I inched closer towards her, to make sure she knew I was serious. I had waited years to finally get this moment; I wasn't going to let it pass me now…*not today*.

"Be thankful that this time I didn't pull your arm out of your socket…" I spat, a fire in my eyes, ready to cause an inferno at any moment. "…Oh, and Riley?" I said, pretending to be innocent at first, before I let the monster in me make her way out.

I let go of her arm, but sent it with a tight squeeze

"…I might have a lot of personal issues going on, but at least I'm not a cold hearted bitch that everyone hates. And before you get confused since your brain is the size of a pea, yes I'm talking about you."

And with that, I turned around, walked over to the table to get my hair curled and pulled up, and plastered a happy, and meaningful smile on my face while Riley stood there dumbfounded. I had *finally* won.

Chapter Seventeen: Tara

Today must not have been a good day for Riley.

We had arrived at our competition around noon, we were all getting ready to start our performance, when Riley had looked like a long lost puppy, staring at the audience.

She had looked for twenty minutes prior to us going on, while three other small colleges went ahead of us in the smoldering Georgia heat. I couldn't help but glance over to her as she skimmed the audience before our performance. She really wanted someone there, but they all seemed to be no shows.

I felt a little guilty; A lot of people were here to support their loved ones for the cheering competition. I even spotted my mom and grandma within three minutes of looking out into the crowd. The thought of seeing my mom and Grammy made me really happy despite my ongoing struggle with my mom.

The one person that I was yet to find, though, was Adam. He told me he would be here. It wasn't like we were together, but I knew there was something there.. something that couldn't quite be explained. I had felt suddenly disappointed, considering that I really believed him when he said he would come to my performance.

I found myself quickly relating to Riley's situation. Her parents were a no show, whereas the one person that I wanted to be here to see me, wasn't here either.

As depressing as it was that Riley's parents weren't there, it wasn't really surprising. Riley's dad was the COO of a corporate office for Scripp's Smartwatches in St. Louis. He would constantly fly out every week to meetings and business proposals, so he was never home. And

Riley's mom, well she had opened up a Pilates studio in both Atlanta and Savannah, so she was always traveling between the two cities.

Riley's parents weren't around that much for her and her younger brother, Julian. The sad part was that Julian went to a boarding school three hours north of Covington, so he was never home either. Thinking about Riley's home life… It was kind of heartbreaking.

Yeah, she had maids and private chefs that waited on her hand and foot. And yes, she got to drive any car she wanted and was able to manipulate her dad into buying her anything she wanted, but she didn't have something that she needed desperately: attention and love from her parents. Maybe that's why she was so cold all the time, and why she was constantly seeking attention.

I couldn't help but feel bad for the girl who I had just told off an hour before despite the things she repeated out in the open. Telling her off liberated me in a way, but that wasn't who I was deep down;That wasn't how I was raised to be. I could tell the way my comments rolled off of my tongue like they were nothing, I could tell the reaction I got from Riley had really hurt her. And the sick part about it was that I was proud of myself for it, and I enjoyed telling her off.

I had dazed out into a major thought of guilt for so long that I could barely hear our squad being announced to walk onto the mat. My nerves shot through me like a cannon and goosebumps raised on my skin. As annoying as Riley could be, I knew that she wanted to win. She wanted to feel proud and accomplished. And we all had worked so damn hard, we all deserved that feeling, too.

I searched the crowd again for Adam as we made our way onto the mat. He was still nowhere to be found. Before we got into our starting positions with our Pom-poms on our hips, I glanced off to my right and I noticed a man walking towards the bleachers toward the competition. It didn't take long for me to recognize that the one guy was Ricky.

I then saw a strange man that I hadn't seen before. He was tall and resembled the height of an NBA player. And to be honest, I had wondered who he was and why he was next to Ricky. I looked over to the left of Ricky as I noticed one more guy standing there, wearing dark black aviator sunglasses and his body facing towards me on the mat.

I knew immediately who it was just by his dark curly hair.

Adam.

The sight of him made me smile, and made my insides dance far more than any feelings of nervousness for this competition ever could.

I *loved* that feeling.

It was like he noticed how much he made me squirm when he looked at me, it was like he knew what kind of spell he had me under. He placed his hands into the pockets of his leather jacket and beamed a full smile in my direction.

He took his one hand out of his pocket then, and stuck his thumb up to wish me good luck.

I couldn't help but smile at that, either.

I heard Riley's throat clear, obviously signaling me to get into my starting position. With a roll of my eyes, and moving into my starting position, I focused in on the cheering of the crowd and the announcer's voice. I closed my eyes and tilted my head towards the ground. This was a moment I had to give myself a pep talk to focus. To recognize the strengths of this squad, and to know how hard we had worked to be here.

The fast pop music began to play and I felt my body begin to move to the beat out of memory, knowing each movement I needed in order to line up with the beat. I crossed over the mat, making a "Z" shape with my Pom-Pom and quickly got to the other side of the mat within a quick eight count. I stood in the corner of the mat as I watched the other girls do their part of the routine.

I sat my Pom Poms down and prepared myself for my tumbling. This was an important part that needed to be perfect, and I knew a big part of the score would come from our tumbling.

Caroline crossed over to the mat in the corner next to me, and started her roundoff back handspring, landing it perfectly in the opposite corner of the mat.

I got myself into position and made a running start to do two backflips and then used my feet for leverage for my next tumble; a double twist. This was the hardest flip that was in our competition, and I was the lucky one who got to do it.

I landed in the opposite corner of Caroline, making sure to land perfectly, and put an overexcited expression on my face. We all danced back into the center of the mat, then we all simultaneously did a triple toe touch stunt before dancing one final move and finishing with a timed back tuck, which ended with some of us girls on one of our knees, while the back row stood standing, holding our arms up into a high "V" position.

The crowd cheered loudly for us, louder than I had heard for most of the other squads. The adrenaline that shot through me after that performance was incredible. I felt like I was on cloud nine, and nothing could bring me down. The only other time that I had felt like that was when I was with Adam last night. Out of habit, I looked over in the same direction of where I last saw him. He wasn't there anymore, which made me incredibly sad. It made me think that maybe he was uninterested.

I skimmed the crowd and landed my eyes on my mom, who was jumping up and down in the stands as she clapped for me. I was glad she was happy; I did this for her, not me.

I noticed the familiar dark curly hair nearby and I immediately darted my eyes down to the side of the stands where not many other people had been. Ricky, Adam, and the strange man were there discussing something, and I noticed Adam was nodding his head in agreement with what the man had said. Adam patted the book bag that hung off the side of the rando's shoulder. Ricky leaned in and gave the man a bro hug and Adam quickly did the same, then gave him a handshake at the end. Except it wasn't just a normal bro handshake.

It wasn't like the ones where they close each other's fingers around the other hand to both form a fist before sliding their hands out.. No, this one was different because it was clearly hiding something. Apparently they weren't hiding it well, because I could see what happened.

I noticed as Ricky placed something into Adam's jacket pocket and the random guy pulled cash out of his pocket to hand to Adam. I couldn't tell just how much it was, but it must have been quite a lot for me to notice it had been a wad of cash.

Once Adam went in behind the man, who had the book bag now latched on his back, blocking Adam from anyone's view.. apart from mine. I noticed him put a small box into the open part of the book bag, then reached into his pocket and slid a small bag of something white into the book bag.

It wasn't hard to tell what they were doing, but I didn't want to believe it. I wanted to forget about ever seeing any of it, And I tried to convince myself that maybe I had gone crazy.

Yeah, that's it. I'm going crazy.

I turned my head away and walked off of the mat, to look for my mom.. I wanted to distract myself from the dark, irrational thoughts that were just put through my mind; The crazy thoughts that I, Tara Evans, might have just had the best moment of my life last night with Adam, who definitely just looked like he had been a drug dealer.

*

"Hey. Thanks for coming." I said as I kissed my mom's cheek and gave her a quick hug. I was still having a hard time accepting her, but I wasn't going to embarrass the both of us by not acknowledging her.

I turned towards my grandma and hugged her, too.

"Thanks for coming, Gram." They both seemed to be super enthusiastic after cheering me on.

They were so proud of me, and it made me happy to know that. My grandma handed me a bouquet of yellow roses, and I held them in my right arm as I admired the fresh scent coming from them.

We had waited for the results of the competition to see what place we got, but we were allowed to go say hello to our families before the judges made their final decisions.

I stood there for a moment, noticing all of the other girls excitedly waiting for the results. I was excited and nervous, too, but I didn't have any doubts; I knew we would win.

"Excuse me, if all the cheering participants would make their way to the mat with their teams, we will begin the awarding ceremony." One of the female judges spoke into the microphone very loudly, ensuring that all of us knew to go back to where we needed to be.

I hugged my mom and grandma once more, and kissed my grandma on the cheek. I was grateful for them both being here to support me despite everything going on.

I walked back down towards the cheering mat, as I attempted to find the identical uniforms that my other teammates had on.

I didn't even bother to look for Adam while I was out there. I had just felt so confused; I didn't even know what to think at the moment. I met up with Caroline and another girl on the squad, and walked over to the rest of the team who were sitting in a circle on the mat.

As I sat down next to Danielle, I couldn't help but notice Riley's disappointed expression. She had no one here for her.

Even though she was a total bitch, and I had told her off earlier, I knew that she didn't deserve this. No one did.

She deserved to be proud of herself.

"Hey, Riley.." I was reluctant at first, but I swallowed my pride and did what I needed to do. "...you did a really great job with the choreography."

I smiled in her direction sincerely, meaning every word that I had said. "Also…" I hesitated, "...I'm sorry for the way I was earlier. It wasn't right of me to say those things, and I know we all have been stressed."

Riley's eyes went wide, like she hadn't expected me to own up to being wrong. It was like she had never been apologized to. Her face quickly went back to the full, bitchy glare that she normally did, quickly trying to hide her surprise.

"Whatever, Tara." She rolled her eyes then, as if she could care less about what I had to say. But I noticed there for a small moment, her lips forming into a small smile as she gazed in my direction.

We weren't best of friends, in fact, we hardly got along nowadays. But it made me feel better to know that we finally had an understanding, even if Riley didn't want to verbally admit it.

We sat there in silence as we waited for the announcer to walk to the center of the mat. She held an envelope in her hand now, getting ready to announce the runner ups. She got to her spot on the mat, looked around at all of the cheering teams sitting down with a large smile on her face, then looked out to the crowd as she spoke into the microphone:

"Thank you everyone for coming out this afternoon to see these wonderful teams compete. We have so much talent here in our county, it's amazing!" After she said that, a loud roar of applause occurred from the audience.

"So let's get to it then, shall we?"

The noises of clapping and whistling came to a stop right at that very moment, making the entire place go silent, as everyone grew more eager for the results.

"In third place.." she said with anticipation in her voice, "... the Tigers at Morehouse College!!"

A flood of relief washed over me. I was happy to not end up in third place, Riley would have thrown a fit.

The Morehouse College cheerleaders ran up to the awards table and accepted their award before sitting back down in the circle, smiling at the fact that they even placed.

"In second place, and the 1st runner up, the Jaguars from Spelman College"

The crowd erupted into cheers for the Jaguars, knowing that they had been working so hard this year and finally made it to states for a cheering competition. Being a part of this state fair competition was something that was enjoyable for them… It was like an exciting start to the semester. They were definitely our biggest competitors when it came to competition cheering, so my confidence felt like it was bouncing off of the walls knowing that the only other team that could beat us was in second place.

That only meant one thing...

"And last but not least.." she said into the microphone, creating a high rate of tension throughout the audience and the team members.

"In first place, the champions of the Georgia State Fair, and the overall Grand Champs..." she lingered for a few minutes before she spoke again, "Congratulations to the GSU Panthers!"

I felt success and happiness fill every fiber of my being. It was like all at once every girl on our squad jumped up and began hugging one another like our lives depended on it. Moments like this made every single ounce of pain and hard work worth it, especially for the seniors graduating next semester; It was a bittersweet moment for them. The six seniors walked up to the table to receive our trophy for first place. The judges then handed them the trophy and a banner for overall grand champs.

I felt myself looking out to the audience to look at my mom, who was hugging my grandma with such a wide smile on her face. Through everything that had been happening recently, it was nice to know that she never gave up on me. I felt blessed to know that she was supporting me, despite the tough relationship we have.

I scanned the rest of the crowd, my eyes scanned the same spot where Adam and Ricky exchanged drugs for money with that Unknown man.

I looked straight ahead of me in between the bleachers and saw his bright white smile and his arms crossed over his chest, allowing just a small speck of his skull tattoo on his hand to peek out from under his other arm. His curly dark hair now created even more curls at the ends due to the Georgia heat. I could tell he was sweating through the black leather jacket he was wearing, but it still didn't stop him from looking so damn sexy.

A few moments passed where I got distracted and hugged by strangers telling us congratulations, and people I didn't even know were giving me high fives as I made my way off of the mat and into the deep sea of the crowd.

I kept my focus on Adam, knowing that he was my end goal. I would do anything to get to him, I needed to see him. It was like my entire body was shooting shocks of electricity through me and my entire body was urging me to get to him.

Just get to him.

That's all I kept telling myself. *Just get to him.*

The constant need that surged through me to be near Adam was motivation enough to keep my eyes locked on him. As I made my way through the crowd, I noticed a familiar blonde spiky hair cut and soft, dark brown hair with curls all over the ends of it. *Ricky and Adam.*

I no longer cared about the strange exchange that they had earlier with the unknown man, in fact I wanted to throw it out of my mind completely…it didn't matter in the scheme of things. Not to mention that it wasn't any of my business.

I caught up to them, now seeing Ricky's bright smile from a bit of a distance, as I still pushed through the large number of people that were filing out of the bleachers.

Once I reached the two of them, I felt my entire body spring towards Adam, an unconscious reaction to wanting to be close to him. He lifted me up as I tightened my arms around him and wrapped my legs around his waist. The position we were in reminded me too much of our perfect night last night.

I couldn't help but smile at the thought of it.

"Hi, beautiful." Adam whispered against my shoulder, still holding me close to him, rubbing his hands slowly up and down my back to provide comfort. "You did amazing out there."

He moved his head away from me for a moment to look at me as he smiled. He then leaned his head upwards to kiss me on my forehead, so I automatically lowered mine to meet his soft kiss, like it was a familiar habit that had been formed between us already. And I found myself longing to keep doing this habit as many times as we could.

I had only hoped I could continue to do so.

I jumped off of him then, now turning myself towards Ricky to give him a quick hug. "Thanks for coming, Ricky." I was happy he came along. He was a great friend to Adam, and I knew he valued Ricky being in his life as much as he valued his Uncle Joe.

"Girl you're crazy if you think I came here just for you.." He said in a smartass high pitched voice for emphasis, "I'm here for Riley, too. She basically told me she would ghost my ass unless I showed up today."

I felt myself laugh at the thought of Riley's bluntness. She sure as hell wasn't afraid to be herself.

I shook my head in disbelief, "Wait, you actually liked her?! I thought you said she was crazy!" I spoke loudly as the crowd continued to pass by us. Adam's lips turned into a slight smirk as he wrapped his arm around my waist and pulled me into him.

Ricky shook his head and laughed, "Hell yeah I think she's crazy!! But I like it, it makes things exciting…" He continued, "She texted me earlier to ask me, *"Do you think I'm a crazy psychopath?"* And I said *'Hell Yeah, but you're the only one who could get me on a Ferris Wheel and get me through my fear of heights, so I want to see you again.'* And now we're going out later tonight." He shoved his shoulder into Adam's as him and Adam quickly did a handshake they had both seemed to have memorized. "Although, Tara.." Ricky said, "…It's nice to finally know from that routine that you're a badass at doing backflips and shit. I don't want to mess with you, cause you'd probably be able to drop kick me so fast!" He let out a small laugh before he continued, "Damn, I'm scared of you… I can see who'll wear the pants in this situation." The wide smirk on his face as he pointed between Adam and I made me want to laugh again, but I held it together for Adam's sake. Adam's eyebrows were now slightly furrowed, like he had been annoyed with his best friend. It was obvious that a small part of him was trying to hide the fact that Ricky was simply being humorous.

Ricky started to laugh at his own joke, which made him look like a complete weirdo, but it was also understandable. He patted Adam's leather jacket on his chest, where the tattoo of two doves for his parents would have been if his chest was bare.

My stomach swirled around at the thought of him laying naked in bed next to me as I traced his tattoos with my fingers. Everything about him made me feel like I was on a high and I couldn't get enough of him.

I just couldn't believe that I had these feelings this soon. I had only known him for about a week, and yet, it was like I'd known him my whole life.

But sometimes things like this happen; life is one big crazy mess and you can either run away from it or embrace it. And with Adam, I wanted to embrace every single moment.

I noticed Adam quickly nodded his head at Ricky and gave him a small smile, before he bent down behind him right under the bleachers to pull something out from under them. As he reached for them, I was able to see the enormous bouquet of red roses with baby's breath intertwined in the bouquet. The beauty of these roses made me gasp, and as if Adam couldn't have been any greater— he went ahead and did this sweet gesture for me.

He handed me the roses, and I reminded myself to smell them before placing them in my arm. "Thank you." I said, trying to fight a smile. I felt myself bite the inside of my cheek, trying too hard not to show him that I was blushing. He came closer to me then, and pulled me in for another hug.

This time he held me so tightly, so securely that I never wanted to let go. I felt like he was claiming me as his, like he needed me close to him just as I needed him close to me.

"These are for you. As a congratulations for your competition.." he said in a low whisper, "...and also a thank you for the best night of my life last night."

I couldn't agree more that it was the best night of my life. I didn't get to have that many moments of intimacy; Only a few times with ridiculous guys who only cared about themselves.

Last night was completely different though, it was something I hadn't experienced in my entire sex life.

It was kind of magical, really.

It was one of those stop your heart, make your spine tingle, *feel-it-in-your-bones* kind of moments.

I wouldn't trade the memory of last night for anything.

And I knew that he wouldn't either.

He pulled away from me, then put his hands into his pockets, as if he was trying to find a comforting place other than my body to put his hands. "So, do you have anything to do tonight?" Adam was looking at me through his aviators, but I could feel the intensity even through his sunglasses. It made me blush, knowing how much we wanted to be with one another.

"Well I have to go back to my cabin to take a shower and get ready for my team's formal dinner. What about you guys?"

I looked between the two of them, and although I had tried to fight it, I couldn't help but think of earlier this afternoon when they were with that strange man.

Ricky and Adam looked at one another then, like they were trying to figure it out, too.

"I think we're gonna go shopping and just explore the fair for a little while. But we'll probably go back to the cabin for a little bit first to catch up on some sleep.." Ricky jumped in with an answer before Adam could even speak. "...Lord knows that I need my sleep, since I didn't get any last night thanks to you two."

I playfully smacked him then, knowing that he was joking and being his smartass self. I was catching onto his humor pretty quickly and it made me proud of myself.

"Well, maybe you guys would want to meet up for a little bit after my dinner?" I had hoped I could see Adam again tonight. That's all I wanted out of my last night in my little weekend getaway.

I just wanted to be near him.

"Yeah, maybe." Adam's response became serious and distant, this small little moment made the insides of my head go wild, it made me start to second guess myself entirely. Ricky must have known the awkward tension between us, because he began looking back and forth between the two of us.

"Hey Tara, What time is your dinner?" He gave me a questioning look as if he was trying to help me out.

I decided *what the hell*, I would play along with Ricky's weird game. "It's at seven, why?" I knew that it was just after three right now, which meant I had time to go back to the cabin and take a short nap, then get my shower and get ready for our formal dinner.

Ricky smiled at me then, and raised his eyebrows, as if I was supposed to automatically know what was going on in his weird brain.

"Tara, I'm sure you can have guests, right?" He placed his hand on my shoulder, knowing that we were both absorbed into a strange conversation run entirely by Ricky, while Adam just stared at the two of us in confusion.

I had finally realized what Ricky wanted me to do. To be honest, I wasn't sure why I didn't think about it sooner. We were always allowed to bring a plus one, the school had automatically paid for it. Except for the fact that on this year's RSVP, I put that my dad was going to be my plus one. I didn't even think about having to go there alone now that my dad was recovering in the hospital.

"Adam..." I said shyly, almost afraid of the answer. "Do you want to be my plus one for dinner tonight? I mean you don't *have* to.. just if you *want* to.. like not as a date.. unless you want it to be, but it doesn't have to.. totally not a date.. just wondering if you were bored and wanted to go.. unless you're busy... "

Why was I always a rambling, pathetic asshole when it came to asking Adam something important?

The memory of the night we met and the similar and embarrassing situation of asking him to stay came to mind. *Jeez, I was such an embarrassment.*

His skin turned a light pink color and he shook his head slightly, revealing a small smile on his lips. "You drive me crazy with all of your nervous talking, woman..." He walked closer to me, and grabbed my hand as he intertwined his fingers with mine. "…But if you want me to go with you tonight, then I'll be there."

The feeling of satisfaction his answer has brought me couldn't be summed into any words. Truthfully, it was like a pinch me moment. I couldn't think of what to do next or what to even say. All I knew was that I was a little shocked but even more excited for the night ahead.

After a moment, I composed myself and attempted to calm down my heart rate by slowing my breathing.

I looked up to meet his gaze, as he was smiling his beautiful smile.

"Okay, I'll be at your cabin at 6:30. It's a formal dinner. Did you bring anything like that to wear?" I didn't want to sound rude, but I knew that his sweatpants and jeans that he brought to the cabin weren't going to cut it.

He needed a good pair of pants and a blazer for this.

"Don't worry about it, I'll call Tío Joe and go pick something up from him. We're gonna get going so I can drive back to Covington." He quickly kissed the side of my head, and smiled at me once more.

"I can't wait to see you later."

He must have enjoyed whispering into my ear, or maybe he knew just how much that turned me on, I don't know, but either way it worked, oh *damn* did it work.

I hugged Ricky once again, and then he patted me lightly on the head. "Good job today, T. I'm gonna go find Riley before we head back to Covington. See ya later maybe." And with that, they both walked out of the small little arena and towards the parking lot back to their cars.

Seeing Adam here today really showed me just how amazing he truly was. I knew that I could now rely on him to be there for me, and to find that out so quickly was something that you don't find often.

I felt like I had truly lucked out meeting him. Even if it happened because of a stupid drunk night at a bar.

I smelled the red roses Adam had for me, really taking in the scent this time. Admiring the thought of him going into the store to pick these out especially for me. The thought warmed my heart entirely.

I turned around to go back to our tent to get my tote bag and makeup, but I hadn't noticed just how long I had been talking to the guys.

The bleachers were almost completely empty now, and the gravel road was full of walking feet towards the rest of the fairgrounds. I walked a few feet past the bleachers as I let this afternoon sink in until the moment that I was stopped by the familiar color of tan heeled boots standing right in front of me.

Mom.

I forgot that she was still here.

   I looked up towards her and my grandma and noticed both standing there with concerned looks on their faces.

I had never felt more intimidated in my entire life.

   "What?" The confusion on my face and the furrow of my eyebrows made my face hurt, but I wanted to know why they both looked so concerned.

   What I didn't know was that I would soon realize why they were so upset, and what was worse was that I couldn't give them a good explanation:

   "Tara, who was that young man you were talking to?" Gram looked at me with her hands placed on her hips, as if she expected an instant answer. "Do you want to explain to me why that guy was kissing your head and hugging you, or do you want me to take a wild guess?"

   And it was at that moment, I realized that I was about to get yelled at.

Chapter Eighteen: Tara

My alarm went off on my phone for what could have been the twentieth time. I just continued to hit snooze; I had been enjoying my nap too much.

This time though, I didn't get much past hitting the snooze button, because just as the room went silent again, Danielle and Caroline barged into my room banging pots and pans from the kitchen to wake me up.

"Get your ass up girl, *let's goooo*." Danielle screamed through a funnel like it was a megaphone.

"We're grand champs, Tara. C'mon, we gotta celebrate!" Caroline chimed in with excitement. This had to have been one of the first times I've seen Caroline out of her comfort zone and being friendly.. This was completely different from the timid and shy girl I had known.

"Okay, okay I'm up. I'm up." I put my hands up in surrender and pulled myself out of bed. Getting out from under the soft blankets was torture. Today was such a crazy hectic day, not to mention the night that I had beforehand which left me physically drained. I felt like I couldn't even blink without feeling sore.

I walked over to the dresser and pulled out a pair of shorts and a cheering t-shirt for my shower. Just as soon as I had gotten up from the bed, Caroline and Danielle disappeared and started banging the pans in another room, which I assumed to be Riley's by the high pitched scream going on. "*Get the fuck out you lunatics!*" She hadn't sounded too happy about that, but the thought of her resting bitch face made me laugh a little.

I grabbed my other items and a bath towel before walking down the hallway and into the bathroom. I let the hot water run for a few minutes before completely undressing from my sports bra and gym shorts.

As I stepped in, it was like my entire body began to relax and my sore muscles became less stiff. I let out a soft sigh in relief from all of the tenseness I had felt in my entire body.

After I finished my shower, I grabbed my towel and wrapped it around me as I stepped out. My dark hair was hanging down my shoulders, dripping droplets of water down my shoulders and as I looked into the mirror, I noticed deeper dark circles and bags under my eyes.

I truly must have been exhausted, my face looked so drained. I began moisturizing my skin while looking in the mirror, dried off my body, and then quickly got dressed. I walked out into the living room of the cabin and sat down on the couch as I waited for the steam to evaporate through the vents of the bathroom. There was nothing worse than trying to dry your hair or apply your makeup in a hot, sticky bathroom.

Gross.

I fiddled on my phone for a couple of minutes, until I heard what sounded like a herd of wild animals pounding down the stairs of the loft. "Beware, Cheerzilla is *pissedddd*." Danielle laughed through her words. I shook my head in a playful response, trying to fight a smile, but one creeping up anyway. "You guys are terrible. You know she can dish it out but can't take it."

All three of us, Danielle, Caroline, and I bursted into laughter, which made all of our eyes water and hold onto our stomachs from the laughter. I, for one, hadn't noticed Riley walking down the loft steps as we continued to laugh.

"What are you losers laughing at now?" She said as she brushed through her long blonde hair with a brush. Our funny moment had quickly subsided since she walked down the stairs. Caroline's face went serious, and she walked over to the kitchen counter and sat the pans down before sitting on a stool.

Danielle looked over towards me and widened her eyes, then stuck her tongue out, making a funny face.

"Well, since you three are down here.." the familiar nasally voice of Riley began, "It's 5:10, So we all should be getting ready now to go to dinner. I can drive us to the restaurant if you want. *La Vite* is about a half hour drive from here but they were the only ones who would accept reservations of more than twelve."

Rylee had her kind moments. Not often, but small moments like these were ones that shouldn't be forgotten. I almost accepted her invitation to drive, until I remembered a certain someone that automatically made me burn with desire and my stomach swirl with butterflies

"You girls go ahead, I'm meeting up with someone. But thank you."

I couldn't help it, I felt a warm sensation fill my cheeks.

I was *blushing*.

"Well... do we know this certain someone?" Danielle smirked at me and wiggled her eyebrows. "Yeah, a dark haired cutie perhaps?" Caroline added excitedly. I softly nodded in reply, not giving more details than I wanted to share to the group, especially Riley who usually hates anyone else being the center of attention.

I really wasn't in the mood to take that away from her, but she made sure of that when she spoke: "Of course! you just have to bring the Mexican loser.."

The way she so haphazardly talked about other people in a rude context without having any sympathy for others' feelings was astounding. The way she said that with such ease made me want to throw up. In fact, I did a little bit in my mouth.

"Yeah, says the one whose mother came from Venezuela."

Wait... what?

    I had met Riley and her parents when I was only six, and I remembered her parents vividly; her dad was white as snow and her mom was a bit on the tanner side, but Riley never brought up anything to do with her family heritage, and at this moment she seemed embarrassed by it. I didn't really understand why, but I kept my mouth shut.

"Shut up Danielle." Danielle had shut Riley right up, making it hard for her to come up with an insult. "My stomach hurts, I'm going upstairs." Riley marched herself back up to her loft bedroom and into the private bathroom and slammed the door,

    "Danielle, I always wondered, but she never says anything about it." I hated to admit how embarrassed I was, but it was the truth.

    Danielle nodded her head at me simply, while putting the pots back into the cabinets. Caroline must've thought that it was her cue to leave, because she smiled softly and walked back down the hallway and into her room. "Yeah, her mom is Venezuelan. She used to have her whole family come visit them here, but as Riley's family got more wealthy they stopped seeing her family anymore. Her dad is from Ireland, but that's all I know. She doesn't tell people that much… I only know because her mom told me one time after Riley had us over to swim." I rolled my eyes at the irony. She had been harshly making fun of Adam's family history in Mexico, but she was similar to him in more ways than she realized. And at least they knew their family history, I was left with not knowing any parts of my ancestry, but knowing plenty about my drug addict birth mom.

    I sat there for a few more moments trying to figure out just how I never knew her story. I was at peace, sitting with my curiosity until fingers snapped me out of my daze."Let's go, Tara. You need to get dressed. You have a big night tonight with your dark and sexy mystery man." Danielle pulled me up off of the couch, not too easily might I add, and dragged me into the bathroom.

We both were facing the mirror now, me waiting for her instructions and help with styling my hair and applying my makeup. "Okay, first things first..." Danielle said as she brushed through my damp hair. "We need to fix whatever is going on with your hair. It's seriously a mess." I didn't bother to stop Danielle, it was too late now.

She loved doing all of these different things with style and makeup, but here I was, standing in front of the bathroom mirror feeling like a basket case. I sucked at being able to figure out how to fix my hair properly.

"Okay, Danielle. Just don't put any tight braids in my hair like you did last time.. I could feel my head pulsating for a week afterwards." A sinister smile placed on her lips as she continued to brush through my hair, combing out each knot repeatedly. "How long have you known me, Tara..." she said in a serious, and yet extremely happy voice. She smiled at me then, making sure to grab my attention with her pearly white teeth reflecting in the mirror. "...No promises."

Chapter Nineteen: Adam

It was 6:15 the last time I had looked at the clock on my phone. The anticipation was killing me, and yet I didn't really know why. This girl had changed me from a cold hearted dick to someone who actually gave a fuck In just a matter of days.

All I do know now is that my heart catches fire at the thought of her. Her beautiful long dark hair, her bright ice blue eyes when they look at me like I'm the only person in the entire universe almost had me completely undone. And those lips— the lips that send me to heaven every time I touch them, all parts of her sends my heart into an all consuming ecstasy.

As I tie my sky blue patterned tie around my neck, I couldn't help but double check my appearance in the mirror. I wasn't used to looking like this kind of guy;

The guy who wore a white button up shirt with a navy blue stupid suit jacket. The only semi-normal thing about me was my choice of shoes. No way in hell was I giving up wearing my all white Nike's that I had gotten for Christmas from Tío. These were my favorite shoes, and I only wore them during special occasions.

I looked down at my khakis, trying to smooth out the wrinkles when I heard a knock on the door.

"Excuse me, Princess Adam?"

Ricky was such an asshole. I loved him and his humor though. "Go to hell, Ricky."

As he opened my door and let out a small throaty laugh, I couldn't help but shake my head at his joke.

He really was a fucking moron, but he already knew that.. I had told him that before. That was our friendship, we just jokingly made fun of one another all the time. We had to keep things as light as we could considering how dark our lives are, and how difficult our jobs were.

"Dude, you're taking longer than a girl to get ready." With a swift eye roll, I double checked myself in my mirror. "Rick, I usually don't do this shit, I'm just trying to make sure I look okay. So respectfully..fuck off, brother."

He came behind me as I looked at him through the mirror, and he patted his hand on my shoulder; he knew I needed a bit of comfort. "Adam..." He said as he glanced into the mirror behind me, "...You really like this girl, don't you?"

I didn't want to admit it, or seem like I was already whipped by some girl I just met, but yeah. I really did.

I couldn't wrap my head around it, and I knew it made no sense…but from the moment I saw her face in the bar, well I was irrevocably and undeniably hers.

I simply nodded my head and gave him a small smile. The only one who truly knew me was Ricky. He had known me for too long not to… so lying to him or pretending wasn't on my list of priorities. And it's not like I'd get away with it if I did lie anyway, the man could weed me out within a one hundred mile radius.

"Well, then.." He said as he backed away towards the bedroom door, "Let's hope tonight goes smoothly so you can continue to see her, man."

I turned back around to look at him, fully realizing that tonight was the night that could change everything. It was like I was in a daze and let my emotions for Tara gloss over the fact that I could die if this job doesn't go smoothly.

Ricky must have known my sudden fear, because he gave me a look with a deep sense of sympathy in his eyes. "Don't worry *hermano*, everything will be fine."

I didn't know whether to believe Ricky or not; Anything could happen tonight and no one but God was in control. I just had hoped that Ricky was right: That everything was going to be fine, because it had to be. I wasn't going to accept anything less.

*

I felt my entire body fill with nerves as I looked at the clock. It was six thirty. Tara should've been here by now.

I started to pace around the small, dark living room of the cabin, letting my dumbass thoughts get the best of me. It started to get so bad I considered taking one of Ricky's Xanax. I tried to slow my breathing and to calm down the best that I could, but that was fucking useless. I found myself walking to the fridge and grabbing a beer.

I started chugging it down as I heard a knock on the door.

Shit.

That was her.

I walked over to the door and opened it, expecting to see the beautiful girl I had the pleasure of knowing standing there waiting for me.

But no, it wasn't her.

"Ricky, you fucking asshole..." He started laughing hysterically, apparently thinking his joke was funny. "You should have seen your face, you're so fucking nervous."

I had known that Ricky had gone back to his room to get some sleep. We both knew that we weren't going to get any for awhile with the high intensity bullshit Jerome was making us do. I didn't know that he was playing such a nice trick on me, though. It was a good one, though... I had to admit it.

"Get the fuck in here, man. Go get some sleep." With one last laugh, Ricky shook his head and walked past me through the front door. I followed him in the house, with my beer still in my hand. I drank a bit more and started to close the front door when I heard the sound of a car pulling up on the gravel road. It was really her, now.

I watched her from the front door as she pulled up in her black Audi. I thought back to my first impression of her; how I thought she was some stuck up princess because of the things she had. I couldn't have been more wrong.

She quickly stepped out of the car and came rushing towards me at full speed. "I'm so sorry I'm late, Danielle was helping me get ready and she braided my hair but I hated it so she had to do it all over again, and it was a disaster..."

She had looked exasperated as she continued mumbling her reasons for being late. "... Then I couldn't get these damn wrinkles out of the dress so I had to iron it out. And guess what?! don't know how to use a damn stupid iron that well and I burned—"

I couldn't stop staring at her. It was like I was frozen in the position that I was in. Like I couldn't move, I couldn't breathe, I couldn't even fucking think. I stood there without saying a word, admiring her familiar dark hair, now curled loosely, laying perfectly against her shoulders. My eyes gazed down to her neck, where she wore a silver necklace with the letter "T" on it for her name. My eyes skimmed down her chest, trying to compose myself at the thought of her naked. Knowing how beautiful she looked with no clothes, but knowing how breathtaking she was regardless.

I felt my body heat up and my insides begin to swirl as my eyes followed the curves of her body, her soft pink dress laying tightly on her hips, showing off her beautiful curves. I felt a groan escape my throat before I tried to control it.

This woman was making me weaker by the second. I was complete puddy in her hands; willing to do anything, be anything for her. Whatever she wanted, I would do it without hesitation.

I admired her soft, long legs as I felt her eyes burning into mine, knowing that she could tell how taken aback I was by her.

God, she made it hard to breathe.

She slowly walked closer to me, her hand reaching out for my beer bottle, and as she wrapped her fingers around the base of the bottle, she swiftly lifted it to her lips and took a large swig of my beer. She had it finished within a couple of seconds and then laid it gently on the ground.

Fuck.

Who was this girl, and what the hell was she doing to me?

There was no doubt that she was sexy, I already was very appreciative of that, and all I wanted to do was kneel before her and worship her like she deserved. But the way she just chugged down a whole bottle of beer effortlessly? Well it was safe to say, that had been the sexiest thing I had ever seen… and I hardened at the thought of just how breathtakingly sexy the woman in front of me truly was.

She placed her arms around my neck, and I found my hands reaching out to grab ahold of her hips. The way my hands sparked as they touched her body sent me over the edge. I tried to control my breathing, knowing that this wasn't the time to give into what my dick was telling me... no matter how much I wanted to. "Whatcha thinking about?" She asked in her soft, beautiful voice of hers. I cleared my throat, trying to keep my composure.

"Just thinking about how beautiful you are." And it was true, she really was. Regardless of if she wore sweatpants or a killer dress like this, she really did take my breath away.

She kissed me softly with a smile pressed on her rosy pink lips. "Well I think that you look very handsome." She gazed down at my body, admiring my outfit for the night. The way her eyes burned down each part of my body made me react to her every glance. Each part of my body now had tensed up, and my mind began wondering what she could do to the parts she was looking at.

Holy shit.

I knew I couldn't take it anymore, I had to give in.

I scooped her up, pulling her legs around my waist for old times sake, and crashed my lips onto hers. I was giving into everything I wanted at that moment; I wanted her, completely and entirely. I wanted every inch of her.

I deepened the kiss, sending soft flicks of my tongue into her mouth, tasting the sweet, familiar taste of honey from her mouth. She danced her tongue with mine, sending shocks down my body and into my groin.

I let out a deep growl, wondering what in the fuck was happening to me, and how I became so fucking weak when I was with Tara. She let out a small laugh in response before she broke away from my lips.

Her face was pink, blushing so much at the way we made one another feel. My hands ran up and down her back, allowing myself to get comfortable with the idea that this was something I could get used to. She smiled at me with her beautiful white smile and cute side dimples on her cheeks. "As much as I'm enjoying this.." she said, beginning to pull away and trying to get down off of my hips, "… We have somewhere to be."

I took my hands that were on her waist and pulled them towards me in a jerk, making her gasp. "Adam.." she said, breathlessly. I started to slowly find my way to her back, beginning to unzip her dress as her legs hugged my hips. I could feel my groin throbbing for her.

I needed to be inside of her right now.

"You know what.." she said as she kissed me softly, her hips now moving in rhythm against mine, "…*fuck dinner."*

Warning: Explicit Content

You now have the option to skip to Chapter 20.

No significant plot details are mentioned.

I walked backwards into the cabin, trying not to trip as I made my way through the hallway, and into my room. Once we were there, I slammed the door so we could have some privacy. "As beautiful as you look right now in this dress.." I was so turned on by everything about her. She really had no fucking idea how bad she made me want her. "... I want to get you out of it." I said as her lips brushed against mine. I felt her hips shift into me, making both of us moan in pure lust. "Adam.." she said breathlessly as I laid her on my bed and she shimmied her way out of her tight dress.

I could see the darkness in her eyes, the ones full of lust and hungry for more. I knew what she wanted, but I wanted her to tell me herself. "What do you want, Tara?"

She bit her lip and her eyes sparked as she heard me say her name. Without warning, she pulled me down on top of her, and switched positions so that she was straddling my lap. She laid me down on the bed and started to unbutton my shirt as her hands glided down my torso.

"I want you.." she began to say softly, as if she was afraid to admit what she really wanted. She looked down now, unsure of how to say it. I took my hand and reached for her chin, lifting it up with my fingers so she could meet my gaze. "Tell me what you want, baby."

She bent down to kiss me, deepening the kiss on my lips, then tugging on my bottom lip with her teeth.

I took control now, turning her over onto her back as she let out a small laugh. I unbuckled my pants and threw them across the room, hitting the side door window out to the patio. She couldn't help but laugh as her bright pink cheeks turned into more of a red color.

I held myself up over her to look into her beautiful eyes. My fingers fell to her face, touching her lips softly as she closed her eyes. Her hips were moving forward, calling for me, *needing* me. My hands started traveling down her body, touching her breasts and letting my fingers slide over the curves of her body. I loved the way her body reacted to mine. With every touch, every breath, her body reacted to mine like a mirror.

She was breathing so heavily as my fingers skimmed down her navel, making her squirm. She couldn't take it.

"*Please*." She whimpered, her lips were brushing against mine as she said it. I deepened the kiss as I allowed my fingers to move down farther, to the top of her panties. I pulled them down, exposing her fully, allowing me to take in her beauty. Everything we both needed would be coming soon. My fingers traveled down farther, dancing to find an entrance into her. I began teasing her with my fingers, feeling her fully wet and ready for me as her hips moved in rhythm with my fingers. "Oh my god.." She said with a loud moan. "Please, Adam, please." She begged. The thought of her begging brought a smile onto my lips. I liked making her feel this much pleasure.

It made me want to show her more. "Tell me what you want, Tara." I breathed, her hot breath panting on my lips as her eyes rolled back in her head.

She let out another soft moan, enjoying my dancing fingers inside of her. I pulled my fingers out of her, her face now growing aggravated. She opened her eyes and stared at me, obviously confused at why I stopped.

"I'm not going to continue until you tell me what you want." She let out a large huff of air as her ice blue eyes burned into mine, like the hottest part of a flame in a fire. She was meeting me with the same desire that I had for her, there was no doubt in my mind.

"I want you inside of me, Adam.." she began to speak, but she trailed off, like she wasn't done. "… I *need* you inside of me."

And with that, a small smile crept up onto her lips, showing that she was finally happy to admit what she wanted. I smiled and kissed her, filling my senses with the sweet taste on her tongue as she opened her legs for my entrance. I positioned myself over her and entered inside of her, sending us both into a world of complete bliss.

Nothing was more important than this moment with her; To spend this time with her was better than anything I could've imagined.

Tara was completely right.

Fuck dinner.

Chapter Twenty: Tara

Adam and I walked into *Le Vite* about an hour late from everyone else. I knew they would still be there, considering that most of the parents didn't care if their daughters drank, and a few of the other girls like me, had a fake ID. The squad had a plan to go eat, and then walk down the street and go to the club. So that meant that most of the girls were wearing short dresses and high heels, making it easy to see almost *everything*.

We entered the restaurant, both now freshly cleaned up, and attempting to seem like we hadn't done the nasty just an hour ago.

"Where the hell have you been?" Danielle ran over to us with a glass of what I'm assuming was moscato in her hand. That girl had a serious problem with wine.

I couldn't help but blush and glance at Adam, who had a small smile on his lips. "Sorry, Danielle. I wasn't ready on time, and we got kind of lost with the directions."
I was so thankful for Adam coming up with an excuse, because honestly, I had nothing.

Danielle looked at the both of us with a small smile forming on her lips "Mhmm...I bet you did.." she laughed as she took a sip of her wine.

She seemed to let go of her questioning and grabbed my hand, pulling me along to wherever she wanted to go. "Come on, I saved you guys a seat over here by me." I glanced back at Adam who was chuckling behind me at Danielle's assertiveness.

We sat down at the round table and the server came by with small garden salads and glasses of water. Adam looked up at the waiter and was quick to order our drinks. "Hi, can I get a Whiskey on the rocks, Blanton's if you have it. And a glass of the 1998 Constantia Moscato." The server hesitated before speaking, "Uh, sir… We only sell Constantia by the bottle." He said sheepishly, scanning over Adam's tattoos and dark stare like his life was flashing before his eyes.

Adam met the young waiter's gaze and nodded "Bottle, then." Adam closed his menu and handed it to the server before he stalked away to get our drinks.

I was surprised that the waiter didn't even think to card me, but I was way more intrigued with how facile Adam was with ordering our drinks.

I was even more surprised with how easily Adam didn't seem to care about the price of the bottle of wine. That was something that I couldn't accept. "Adam.." I leaned over to whisper to him, keeping my voice hushed. "Thank you for being here and being so romantic, but I can't let you buy that bottle of wine.." I said, hoping he'd meet my gaze. Instead, he reached for my hand and squeezed it lightly before intertwining our fingers together on his lap. He gave me a small smile before looking me in the eyes; his milk chocolate eyes melted so intensely into mine that I began to forget anyone else was in the restaurant with us.

He leaned in and kissed my temple and whispered with his lips still close to my skin. "The wine is a gift…" He continued, "...And I think we both know that if I could buy you the world, I would." He lingered; his warm breath against my skin sent shivers down my spine. I held my breath at his comment; The intensity of just being in his presence was enough to send me over the edge. It was thrilling, yet terrifying.

"So..." Danielle knocked me out of my trance as she sat down next to me, holding onto her wine glass for dear life. "Tara you've been gone this weekend.. *Ahem*.. Thanks Adam" she coughed and then gave Adam a playful evil stare before turning back to me, "Anyway, you haven't stayed at the cabin so you didn't get a chance to meet him. This is my boyfriend, Aiden."

I smiled as I looked at the young man sitting next to Danielle, stuffing a dinner roll in his mouth.

Danielle realized he wasn't paying attention to our conversation, so she nudged him with her arm and cleared her throat. Aiden quickly looked in my direction and smiled.

"Hi, I'm Aiden. You must be Tara."

He reached in front of Danielle to shake my hand as I met him halfway. He looked next to me and simply waved in Adam's direction.

"Hi, I'm Aiden." He said, clearly talking to Adam.

The waiter had brought our drinks back, but I hadn't noticed until I saw Adam take a drink of his beer.

He put his glass down and nodded, giving Aiden a friendly smile. "Adam. Nice to meet you."

I could tell that Danielle didn't enjoy how Adam and Aiden hadn't become best friends in five seconds, so she brought up a topic she *never* would talk about any other time to engage them in conversation.

"Hey, Adam. Aiden here plays basketball… I remember you telling me you played it at the gym when you ran into Tara there that one time..." she drifted off, hoping Adam would catch on. She made wide eyes at us both, using her nonverbal to make a point.

Adam cleared his throat and nodded, trying to fight off the small chuckle he let escape his throat.

But only I heard it.

"Uh, yeah. Aiden, what position do you play?" Danielle smiled and nodded at me, then looked over towards the women's bathroom. "Come with me." She whispered quietly.

I stood up from my chair and rubbed Adam's shoulder, upset that I was leaving him alone with Danielle's quiet boyfriend. I heard Aiden's response in the background, answering Adam as Danielle and I walked towards the bathroom.

"Yeah, man I do. I play forward. Did you play in high school?"

Danielle and I walked into the bathroom, both of us holding our glasses of wine in our hands. She quickly checked the three stalls in the bathroom before turning back to face me.

"I need your help." She said, almost in a whisper. A cloud of fear took over her eyes, and a soft tear rolled down her cheek. Whatever it was, it was tearing her apart.

"Yeah, Of course.. What is it?"

She swallowed hard and then took a large gulp of wine before she spoke.

"Tara...", barely saying my name loud enough for me to hear, she said, "I think Aiden was going to propose this weekend" Shock hit me like a tidal wave and my heart warmed with excitement for her.

No fucking way.

I snatched her wine glass from her hand and sat it on the counter as I reached for her to hug her.

"Danielle, Oh my God!! I'm so happy for you" I screamed with excitement, only to be *shhh'd* by Danielle. She shrugged and rolled her eyes at me, before turning to face the mirror above the sink.

"Tara..I don't know if I'm ready to get engaged, let alone married.." Her voice trailed off, overcome with nerves. "...I'm scared out of my fucking mind, okay?! That's why I needed you here. I don't know what to say if he asks." Her whole body began to shake now, worry filling every fiber of her being. I pulled her into a comforting hug, trying to console her all the while trying to calm down myself, too.

"It's okay, Danielle. We'll figure this out." She simply nodded her head and wiped a tear that was rolling down her cheek. "I know— trust me, I know how bad this sounds. I love Aiden, but I don't think I want to get engaged to him, or anyone *ever*. It was never something I thought about." She took a big deep breath in and wiped a tear that was coming to the surface. "What should I do?"

She walked into one of the stalls to get some paper to blow her nose and I heard a soft sob escape her lips as I waited. "It's okay, Danielle. I'm here." A couple of minutes passed and she walked out of the stall. "I think…" I waited, attempting to collect my thoughts. "I think you should just tell him the truth. If you love him like you say you do, and he loves you, then he should understand. But if he wants to get married one day and you don't, that's going to be a really hard conversation to have, and it might mean that you two don't continue your relationship.. Do you think you can try to have a conversation with him tonight?"

I was super proud of the way she was trying to keep it together. I wouldn't have been able to if I was in her situation.

I'm sure people saw us walking to the bathroom together and wondered why the hell we were in here so long, but I also didn't really give a shit either. "I think you're right, Tara, but I just don't think I'm ready to lose him." I let out a large sigh and grabbed my purse off of the floor. "I just think you should have the conversation now instead of later; It would save a lot of hurt for the both of you if you talked to him now." She smiled at me softly and nodded her head.

I hadn't noticed that someone had walked in during our conversation, but I was surprised when I saw her long blonde hair swaying as she ran into the stall.

I felt my breath hitch at the sight of Riley, running into the stall with blood dripping down her legs which had stained her dress. Danielle released me and turned to see what all the commotion was, noticing the red spots forming on the bathroom floor from Riley running.

"Oh fuck."

*

The night had gone by relatively fast. I didn't want to go to the club with the rest of the squad as the dinner had been abruptly canceled due to Riley's emergency. I was tired and I had almost had a heart attack because of how terrified I was for Riley.

It had been a heartbreaking moment to witness; seeing Riley experience a miscarriage right before my eyes. She hadn't even known she was pregnant, and I couldn't imagine the horror she felt when she noticed the blood.

After we helped to calm her down and got her cleaned up as best as we could, Danielle called 911 to take Riley to the hospital. It was clear she had already lost too much blood, and it didn't seem to be slowing down any.

As the paramedics got her into the ambulance, I heard Riley's soft voice call out to me. "Tara, please don't tell anyone what actually happened. And don't tell Ricky, please.." She begged as her cheeks dampened with tears. "...He just thought it was my period when I first noticed.. Please don't tell him." All I could do was simply nod to her as she shut the ambulance doors, and all I was left to see was the flashing ambulance lights fading off into the distance.

Those words echoed in my mind on the way back to the cabins. *Please don't tell him.* I was sitting in the passenger seat of my Audi, letting Adam drive the car back to the cabin. Normally, if I would have known a guy for a week I would have still had the thoughts of the guy driving me off into a forest to kill me, but the amount of trust I felt when I was with him was amazing.

I had grown to trust him so quickly, and while people could think it was crazy, in my head I knew it was crazy, too. That's the funny thing about it; I knew it sounded insane, but in my heart I didn't care. Things happened so quickly, and yet, it had been like we had known one another our entire lives. It's funny how one day someone could be a stranger passing you by on the street, and the next moment, they could be the most important person in your life.

Once we reached his cabin, I grabbed my bag and my jacket and walked into the side door that led to his room. The beautiful moments from today circled in my mind, and I was beyond grateful to have had such a wonderful time with Adam. I couldn't have been happier, apart from the heartbreaking situation for Riley, and the one small moment from today that kept replaying in my head.

The moment of him and Ricky looking as if they were a part of some kind of drug deal. And although I tried to shake the thought out of my head, I was too curious, I needed to find out what had gone on during that moment.

"Hey, I've been meaning to ask you.." I said, a little hesitant at first. His beautiful brown eyes shifted from the door as he locked it behind him, and landed on mine. A small smile played on his lips as his gaze pierced mine. "Go ahead, mama."

I cleared my throat and thought about ending the conversation all together, but as a woman who had goals and ambitions, I needed to truly know who Adam was and what I was getting myself into.

The feelings I had for him had burned into an inferno now, ready to burn into a wildfire. Whenever I was with him everything about my life was different. He awakened my soul in a way no one else ever had; he made me feel passion and peace all at the same time and I knew that no matter what, he would always be etched in my mind.

But the rational side of me took over, which caused me to question his motives entirely. And I couldn't see myself continuing forward with him, despite my feelings, if I didn't know the truth. "So, at my cheering competition this afternoon, I saw you and Ricky with some guy. I was wondering who he was?"

His hand gripped the back of his arm and squeezed it, but the rest of his body didn't move a muscle. "Oh yeah, that's a friend of ours…" he lingered, still massaging his tricep. "…Well I should say that he's more of a friend of a friend. His name is Dustin. We ran into him in the parking lot and he just stuck with us.."

We lingered in silence for a moment before he spoke again: "Why did you want to know?"

The strong sense of annoyance and sadness took over my mind. I felt like I had been lied to. I knew that couldn't be all of the story; I had clearly seen them pass something to one another.

Adam made his way to the bathroom and began to undress himself, leaving just his boxers on. He wasn't paying much attention to me at the moment, so I sat there on the edge of the bed as I decided what to do.

Instead of questioning him further, I decided to come up with an easier solution: I was going to prove that Adam Rodriguez was most likely a compulsive drug dealing liar. I wasn't sure how, but I knew I could eventually get enough information to call him out on it.

"Oh, it's nothing…" I spoke loud enough for him to hear from the bathroom as I fiddled with my bracelets on my wrists. "…I just thought he looked familiar."

I turned my body towards the French doors out to the patio and watched the starry night sky as the minutes went by, surrounded by complete and utter silence.

A few moments later, Adam returned on just his boxers, and lightly kissed the top of my shoulder.

"What are you thinking about?" He asked, his voice softened just enough for me to barely hear.

I stood up from the bed and walked over to the nearby chair to grab my purse. "I'm actually going to head back to my cabin; Riley wanted to have a girls night now that they are back from the club." I tried to play it off as though the reason I was leaving was no big deal; but little did he know that catching him in a lie this quickly really shifted things, and now it was hard to gain my trust.

I walked out of the bedroom door and walked to the gravel driveway next to the cabin. I could feel him walking behind me, following my steps as I moved. He called out my name a couple times, but all I could hear was the muffled sounds and the feeling of tears coming to the surface. I stepped forward to get into my car, but Adam grabbed onto my waist and turned me around to face him.

"Wait wait wait.." His voice rushed, "…Somethings wrong. What's wrong?" His hands still gripped on my hips, causing butterflies to dance through my stomach. I smiled softly, but didn't look at him. I knew if I had, all my defenses would crumble into oblivion, and I needed to remain strong.

I was clearly bothered by his lie, and I felt it in my bones. I knew something more was going on, and yet, he stood there and lied to my face. I wasn't sure how to feel at that moment, and I wasn't sure what to do. It was going to take some time for me to think it all through.

His voice knocked me out of my trance as his fingers found their way to my cheek, softly caressing it with his fingers before resting on my chin, lifting it up to meet his gaze.

His smile radiated from under the moonlight's beaming light, almost making him blinding to look at, but at the same time entirely captivating.

I smiled shyly, not fully used to all of his compliments, but now not entirely believing them all, either. He pulled me in for a long, warm hug before parting and trying to meet his lips with mine.

The truth was, no matter how much I wanted to; I couldn't do it. I couldn't think about kissing him knowing that he was lying to me. I felt the lie burn into my bones, and I knew that I needed to stand my ground, no matter how captivatingly sexy he was.

I quickly maneuvered my head, so that I could kiss him on his cheek before pulling away. "I'm tired, I'm gonna go to bed. I'll see you."

I got into my car before he decided to pull me into him again, and before I decided that I wanted him to.

I drove down the road and towards my cabin, ready to get into bed. I had a stressful and eventful weekend and I deserved a good night's sleep without constant stress about cheering, my parents, or Adam.

My plan to go to bed was suddenly ruined by Danielle's text message:

Danielle: heloooo Tara, I'm not felling well. I came with some girls to ghe club. Aiden and I got into a fight and he left me all alome. :(. The other grls got a ride and now I'm all by myself (Cue that one Celine Dion song lolll) I can't drive my car, I'm too drunk from the glub.. fuck, I mean club. Come me pick up? I want s corn dog.

Tara: Stay where you are, I'm on my way.

I picked up my speed as I headed towards the fairgrounds to pick up Danielle. Through all of the shit we've been through today, I was surprised I was still awake to do this. But I also knew that I couldn't leave Danielle alone, drunk and stranded. She had been my friend, and I wasn't going to let anything bad happen to her. She needed someone to be there for her right now, and I was glad she reached out.

*

I got to the entrance of the fairgrounds about ten minutes later, feeling a sense of relief that the cabins weren't too far away from here.

I pulled out my phone from the center console to text her that I was out in the parking grounds, but I didn't hear my phone alert to go off because she had texted me about five minutes ago.

Danielle: nvermind, Caroline had her and her dad come pick me up. Were going to the cabinet now, see u there.

I continued sitting outside the entrance of the fairgrounds and let my car run. I had no reason to be here anymore and yet, here I was. Part of me grew annoyed, but another part of me was just glad that Danielle got back safely. I pulled my car into one of the open spaces by the front of the entrance. No one was here this late; The only ones here were some of the workers cleaning up for the night.

    I thought maybe, just maybe, I could make it to the funnel cake stand in enough time. I never had one this entire weekend, and I had to keep the tradition alive for my dad even though the thought of my dad also brought my heart pain. I reminded myself to go check on him once I got back into town. I had texted him every day, but I didn't expect him to answer; he had just gone through hell and was recovering.

    I shut the car off and grabbed my wallet before getting out of the car. As I walked towards the entrance, I noticed a single car parked a few yards away, completely alone in the parking lot. From a few yards away I could tell that it seemed to be an old beat up Toyota.

    I was sure it belonged to one of the vendors, so I shrugged it off and walked towards the funnel cake vendor. As I passed the cyclone, I couldn't help but feel uncomfortable at how deserted and creepy the fair was without anyone here and anything running.

    The carnival rides looked abandoned; it looked like most everyone just up and disappeared, leaving everything the exact same way as the day before.

I looked for the funnel cake truck, feeling utterly disappointed that I had missed it yet again.

    I walked around for a few minutes until I ultimately decided to make my way back to my car. I slowly walked back towards my car from the back path, which was full of grass and a lot easier to get around in with block heels instead of gravel.

    As I turned the corner, I noticed the tail end of my car, feeling a sense of relief when I saw it. I looked down the lot as I noticed the Toyota from earlier with its lights on, sitting a few hundred yards away toward the other entrance for the petting zoo.

I decided to ignore it, but continued to increase my speed to my car. The innate feeling I had of being a woman late at night alone with a strange car running nearby wasn't something I took lightly; I could sense the energy, and I didn't like it. I grabbed my key fob and held onto my pepper spray, *just incase*, and continued to walk to my car without a second thought. That was until I noticed two men with the familiar dark brown curly hair and spiked blonde hair emerge from the end gate, pulling someone through the gravel.

I focused my attention on them now, looking at the man they were dragging.

He was older, bald, and incredibly skinny. They had his hands tied behind his back, a white cloth tied around his mouth to keep him from screaming, and a bandana around his eyes.

Panic set in, and if I had been stronger, braver, and had more testosterone, I would have felt determined to help this person. But I couldn't move. I couldn't even think about moving. I stayed exactly where I was on the grass path, now hidden behind one of the entrance pillars, as I continued to watch Adam and Ricky kidnap the poor man.

They dragged him the rest of the way towards the Camry, and as soon as Ricky let go of him, the man attempted to run off and kicked Adam and Ricky repeatedly as they attempted to grab ahold of his arms.

I felt myself hold my breath. I was frightened by the entire situation, and in any instance, I would have been. But seeing Adam and Ricky doing *this?* Well, it was a whole new territory of betrayal.

Adam kicked the man's legs out from underneath him, and walked over the man as he laid on the gravel ground, scrunched up in a ball. Adam kicked him in the stomach once more, until the man stopped moving, and laid unconscious on the hard gravel. I noticed Adam looking around him now, as if he was checking to see if anyone had noticed what they were doing, and then called Ricky over.

Ricky opened the trunk and quickly looked around the premises himself to make sure they were being discreet.

No, no, no. Please do not tell me they are about to put this poor man in a trunk. I thought to myself. I couldn't help but think about the horror I was witnessing. How Ricky and Adam could abuse a man and stuff him in the trunk like it was nothing was something completely unfathomable.

I had let them into my life. I grew to like them and to trust them, and *all for what?* For *this?* To get wrapped up with some guy who dealt drugs and abused people?

What the fuck did I let myself get into?

Why the hell did I let myself get involved with him?

I focused my attention back on what they were doing, trying to make sense of it the best I could; but I couldn't. There was no explaining a situation like this.

Ricky picked up the man and tossed him into the trunk like he was a bag of trash.

The scariest part about it, though, wasn't anything else that I had seen. In fact, I felt kind of numb during the situation. It felt like I made this whole thing up in my head. There was no way it was actually real. That was until I saw Adam pull a gun from his back pocket. As Ricky walked over to pick him up, Adam held the gun to the man's forehead, and was screaming at him words that I couldn't make out.

Ricky shut the trunk and Adam got on the phone, seemingly having a serious conversation with someone and then abruptly ended the conversation and stuck his phone into his back pocket.

Things had never made any sense in my life, but this was on a whole other level of crazy. I noticed Ricky and Adam talking, looking more like they were arguing about something. I tried to sneak to my car and get away before anyone had noticed me, but plans never work out the way you want them to, *do they?*

*

Before I knew it, a strange, yet strong hand covered my mouth, preventing me from screaming. I kicked and screamed anyway, trying to wiggle my way out of the strong grip. I even tried to bite the person's hand, fully aware that I was being dragged away from my car and taken somewhere. Tears flowed like they had ripped open the sea, causing my vision to blur with the tears welling up in my eyes.

I didn't know what to expect, or who was doing this to me. All I knew was that I hated it, but I couldn't do anything to stop it. No matter how many times I tried to pull away, the strong hands became stronger, grabbing onto me and pulling me closer towards the running engine of a vehicle.

Someone opened a sliding door, as I tried to figure out my surroundings and took a moment to tell myself that I needed to remember everything that I had seen. As the strong man pulled me back into the van, he spit his tobacco chew on the ground and laughed in satisfaction.

The creepy man behind me sat me down in front of him in the strange bus, and moved closer to my ear. I flinched, trying to get away from him, but was stopped by him as he grabbed hold of my chin and tugged violently as my body followed suit, forcing me to sit closer to him, and forcing me to live out the darkest fear I had ever come to know.

"This is what you get for snooping on business that ain't yours, baby girl." Before I could even fathom to let out a normal breath, the man behind me cocked his gun and shoved it against my head as he laughed. "We're gonna take you somewhere special. Don't worry, you'll be dealt with there…" He lingered as his bandana covered his mouth and nose, leaving only his eyes to be seen. "…J probably won't let you go anywhere, though *Chica*. You are very beautiful."

    I closed my eyes, letting the tears continue to fall, as my mouth became overly dry from a rag being shoved into my mouth after being shoved in the van. This was the worst moment of my life. And having a gun to my head was one of my worst nightmares, but I had begun to think that being killed would be better than to be in whatever the hell this was.

All I wanted to do was go home, and go to bed.

I wanted to hangout with Danielle and Caroline.

I wanted to be able to watch reruns of friends in my living room at home.

I wanted my mom and dad.

I really just wanted to be an innocent twenty year old again, and yet here I was, coming to terms with the fact that I may never be able to do any of those things, or see any of those people again.

    My breath began to feel shallow as I felt my body shudder. My adrenaline was on overdrive, making my breath quicken to the point I felt lightheaded.

Whatever was happening, all I knew was that there was a possibility that I wasn't going to make it out of this alive.

    I swallowed what little saliva I had left in my throat.

I could die tonight.

Chapter Twenty One: Adam

I pulled the Camry up to the warehouse, feeling a huge amount of nerves for what we had just done. Ricky was breathing heavily, as if he was about to hyperventilate.

Fucking Jerome. That dude could honestly fuck off.

He enjoyed making his little servants squirm, and he controlled them well. I guess that made me and Ricky servants to him, too considering he made us do his dirty work for him. I got out of the car and typed into the garage keypad as I waited for the door to open. Once it did, I pulled into the familiar warehouse, then killed the Camry's engine.

I knew that Jerome would be finding a new place to set up his business, especially if the cops were onto him. We wouldn't be in this place for very much longer. I got out of the car as I noticed a few of Jerome's men had surrounded the car, all staring either at the Camry, or Ricky and me.

Rick and I made our way to the back of the car to get ready to open the trunk for Jerome. I had noticed Jerome and his two main guys as they walked through the small crowd towards us with a wicked smirk on his face.

"So, how did it go, amigos?"

Jerome smoothly rubbed his hands together, looking down at the ground with a smirk still on his face.

I cleared my throat as I walked closer towards Jerome and his guys, and gave the cash I had taken from the cash register to one of them.

"It went fine, J. We got everything done." Ricky said with his hands behind his back as his eyes remained on the trunk. Jerome nodded his head in agreement, then looked back to one of his guys who counted the cash we brought him.

The guy nodded to Jerome, and then he looked at me.

"Good job with the cash man, not a whole lot, but good enough. And looks to be no counterfeits either.. But we'll test it out to make sure– you know that." He nodded his head, as if he was pleased with how I followed through.

Ricky nodded towards Jerome's men, and they walked over to the trunk. Jerome and I walked back to meet Ricky, as we all stood there waiting for Jerome to give the go ahead to let the man out.

Jerome waited a moment, causing the silence in the air to be deafening, and then nodded. Ricky popped open the trunk, all of us noticing the man inside was still out cold. I was glad that the kick in the stomach I gave him had knocked him out for that long, not to mention the sleeping pills Ricky shoved down his throat as we dragged him to the car.

The guys pulled the store manager out of the car, still perfectly tied so he couldn't run away or scream. They dragged him by his tied hands and sat him down in a chair as they tied his hands to it.

"Good job boys… you followed through." Jerome patted me on the shoulder, before telling his guy to "*do it*".

I wasn't sure what those words entailed, but I knew they weren't going to be pleasant, and I didn't really want to watch. Not after what I witnessed with Jinx. The guy grabbed a bucket of water and tossed it towards the guy, waking him up and sending him into a state of shock. Jerome's sinister laugh made my stomach turn as I suddenly felt the urge to throw up. He didn't care how he had to do it, or who he had to kill in the process, when he wanted something done, you had to follow through.

The store manager's eyes went wide in realization of where he was, and who he was talking to. One of Jerome's guys pulled the cloth out of his mouth for him to speak.

"J, man, what am I doing here?"

Jerome rubbed his hands together again, before reaching in his waistband for his gun. I could tell by the expression on his face that he was beyond pissed; He was seeking vengeance.

He made sure his gun was loaded and cocked it, as he walked over to him and put his gun against the man's head. "You really think you can out play me you little bitch?" He said as she shoved the gun further into the man's head, leaving indents on his skin. "Who the fuck do you think you're messing with?"

The man's eyes went wide as he realized that Jerome figured it out about his counterfeits. Ricky and I just stood there at the Camry, not willing to speak, move, or even breathe. "J, I can explain—" Just as the words left his mouth, one of Jerome's guys pulled his head back and reclined the chair, making him face the ceiling, and grabbed a large bucket of water as they began waterboarding him.

Witnessing this was fucking hard. There was no way around it, either. It was painful to watch. I felt my throat close up, feeling as if I could feel the pain the man felt; feeling like I was drowning.

As much as I felt bad for this man, he deserved it. He fucked with Jerome, and he messed things up for me. I wouldn't have been in this situation if it wasn't for him. I wouldn't have had to have panic attacks about getting killed if it wasn't for him.

The man spit water out and sucked in a large breath, trying to get oxygen in his lungs. Jerome's guy lifted him up into a sitting position, allowing Jerome's gun to be placed on his forehead where he had it previously.

"Since you messed with me, Vince, you're gonna do me a favor. You're gonna tell me how you get those counterfeit to check right in the system, and then we'll be good. You'll be free to leave. If not, well, then I might have to give a call to Elena and little Chris.." as he said this, Vince's bloodshot eyes filled with tears.

"...I have a man at your house as we speak, *amigo*. One phone call and they're dead. You either tell me, or I call my buddy. Choice is yours."

Vince didn't speak a word, he just sat there with tears in his eyes as Jerome gave him an ultimatum. After a moment of silence, Vince let out a sigh and met Jerome's gaze, tears streaming down his face.

"J, I swear to you, I didn't give those guys counterfeits. All the cash evened out when I gave it to them, they probably switched it, man I don't-" Like a strike of lightning, Jerome's fist slammed into Vince's face, making him spit blood out onto the floor.

"Lie to me again, Vince, and the next thing you'll be getting is a bullet in that hollow ass thing you call a head."

I wasn't surprised when Vince immediately shut up after Jerome had said that. You don't fuck with him. Simple as that.

"I've known these two guys longer than I have known you. They have *never* fucked up. Not until I send them to meet with you. I've had my issues with you before, so you goin' and blaming my boys when I know they don't fuck up… well I don't even do that, my man…" His voice echoed through the warehouse, sounding like a siren. "...So that tells me that you're the problem. And you know how I am, Vince. I'm a tit for tat kind of man… and you've gotta pay your dues."

Jerome nodded to his boys again, now tipping Vince back and waterboarding him for a second time.

This could take all night if he wanted it to.

Once Vince sat back up, he gurgled up water and spit it out of his mouth, mixed with his blood. "Fine!! Fine-" Vince begged, his voice barely sounding audible, "Javier Cortez." The name rang in the warehouse like a gunshot. All of us feeling poisoned by the name.

Javier used to work for Jerome. In fact, we all were good friends at one point, and Jerome and Javier became romantically involved. A few years back, Javier started ripping Jerome off— taking his supplies, taking money. Javier thought he was sly though; He thought he was a real boss for doing those stupid ass things. It wasn't a surprise, though, when Jerome found out that it was Javier who was stealing from him. That was about the only time I ever saw Jerome show any emotion. But he shut that down real quick. And it was at that moment I learned that you can't show any emotion in this business, because if you do, you don't run the business— the business will run you.

Hearing Javier's name, Jerome's face turned a dark red color as his body filled up with anger. He still hadn't gotten over it. I guess I wouldn't have gotten over it either if someone you loved stole two hundred thousand from you.

Soon after Javier left, we had heard talk about a new gang in Atlanta. We didn't know who was running it, or what their strict business was, but we knew we had some competition. This new gang was taking some of our most important clients.

But as soon as Vince coughed up Javier's name? We knew who was doing it now, almost as clear as day. It all made sense.

Jerome cleared his throat, and his face went back to normal after a few minutes.
"And what about him, Vince?" Vince shut his eyes for a moment, knowing he had lost in this scenario.

"Javier has been working for the King, Jerome. He's been working for him personally. It was Javier's idea to get some of the guys in Atlanta together. He started creating counterfeits that could run through the system like it was real cash. I don't know who makes it or how it gets distributed. I honestly don't know. But most people don't think anything of it, because most people don't check it. That way we get the supplies we need, give them fake cash and keep the real. Then we use the supplies we get and sell them for real money. I didn't know how the process had worked until recently. Javier and his guys came in and told me they had a proposition. They said the King would get me out of this business and would pay me what I was owed. He said I could move and start a new life. I just want Elena and my son to be safe. That's all I want." His voice drifted off and there was a moment of silence as Jerome was thinking about something.

"And what proposition did Javier and the King give you?"

"They wanted me to give you the counters, and to continue to do so. I was supposed to eventually get on the inside and find your clients. The plan was that every time you guys distributed, you'd be getting fake cash because we'd get to them first. The king and Javier were trying to flush you out. They're trying to get rid of you."

Jerome began to laugh then, like he had been watching a comedy show. His laugh echoed for a few minutes as the rest of us remained quiet.

"They're trying to get rid of me? *Of me?*! Nah, man. It doesn't work like that…" He spat at Vince's feet before shoving the gun a little further into his forehead, breaking the skin and causing a trickle of blood to run down his forehead. "... Remember this Vince," he continued, "A King with no kingdom is no King at all. So I don't work for the King, and I sure as hell don't follow him. And the King without a kingdom is as good as dead. So— I'm gonna take out his kingdom. Starting with you..." His voice was steady now, knowing that every word he had said was true. He let out a light laugh before speaking again, his gun still pointed at Vince's head:

"Oh, and don't underestimate me, Vince. Fuck your *King*."

And just as fast as Vince opened his mouth to speak, Jerome pulled the trigger and the gun fired, making my ears ring. It was over. And Vince was dead.

Jerome nodded to his boys to get rid of the body, turning around to us with some blood splattered on his t-shirt. He nodded at Ricky and I once and then walked past us, back into the back room.

I knew that I was never going to be able to get that moment out of my head. Seeing Vince's brain being blown out with a bullet really did me in. And I thought seeing Jinx getting killed all those years ago was bad.

It didn't even compare to this.

I walked back to the driver's side of the Camry as Ricky walked over to the passenger side, following my lead. As far as I knew everything was good with Jerome and us, so we were free to leave. As nerve wracking as tonight was, and the entire weekend of anticipating it, we had done our part, and we came through.

I got into the car and was about to start the engine when Jerome came back out of the back room.

This time, he was with two guys that I didn't know the names of, but who had looked familiar, and another guy, who was Dustin. Dustin was the guy who we had given Molly and Coke to at the cheering competition. Everything was good between us, so I was confused as to why he was here. I knew we didn't fuck up.

"Hey Dustin." I said, nodding my head in his direction. He nodded his, then went back into one of the back rooms.

Jerome had his arms crossed over his chest, looking at me intensely. "Rodriguez, you did good tonight. You too, Ricky." I gave a friendly smile, and nodded, then attempted to get back into the car.

I was stopped when one of Jerome's guys pulled me back out, making me stand next to the car. Someone on the passenger side of the car did the same to Ricky, and walked him over to stand next to me.

"I've got a question though, boys."

Jerome scratched his cheek with his fingers, but continued to make eye contact with me. "You said everything went smoothly for you out there. No one saw you, did they?"

Ricky and I both shook our heads, knowing that we had waited until after the fair closed to get Vince. "No, J. No one saw us. We made sure of it. Everyone was gone by then."

Ricky's voice was shaking now, knowing that something was wrong if Jerome wasn't allowing us to leave.

Jerome clicked his teeth together, and his lips formed into a familiarly vile smirk. "Ahhh, no boys. I don't think so. I don't think you were safe enough..." He trailed off, nodding at the guy who was guarding the door that Dustin went into.

"...Someone saw you. Which means you did, *in fact,* mess up. Now, I'm a forgiving person. I *promise*. But you're gonna need to get rid of the problem, because I can't have any snitches. Even though this young, sexy looking bitch is something I'd like to get my hands on, I can't have her as a snitch. I took care of Vince for you two, so now you're going to take care of this."

Dustin walked out, holding onto someone, the supposed girl who had seen us at the fairgrounds.

As he got closer my breath caught in my chest.

"Now Dustin tells me you know this fine little mama, Rodriguez. Do you?"

I felt my vision become blurry, all of my senses highjacking themselves. It made me feel like I was hallucinating. But I wasn't.

The dark black hair of hers swayed side to side as she was pulled by her arms towards the center of the circle of people. She still had her light pink dress on, now covered in dirt and spots of blood.

Her makeup was running down her face, as were tears. There was blood trickling down from her eyebrow, a bruise forming on her face from being punched, and a small cut on her left arm and her chin.

I felt my body tense, and I clenched my fists. My anger had formed into a rage.

Jerome was going to fucking pay.

Just as I started to move, Ricky pulled me back toward him. Ricky wasn't going to let me move and put all of our lives at jeopardy. Jerome let out a dark, soulless laugh as his eyes darkened. He made his way over to where Dustin was holding Tara, as her arms pulled behind her in Dustin's grip. "Ahh, so I'm guessing this is the girl who has you whipped then, 'Riguez. Good to know."

Dustin brought her closer to Jerome as her ice blue eyes met mine for a brief moment. The panic in her eyes made me want to rip Jerome's head off.

I'd fucking rip him to pieces and kill every son of a bitch in here if I had to– I'd do that for her.

Her life was all I cared about, and nothing and no one was going to stop me from protecting the only thing left that I cared about: Her.

He placed her right next to Jerome as he turned to her and placed a stray hair behind her ear. I pushed forward, attempting to break away from Ricky this time, and ready to kill the bitch for touching her. He was already dead in my mind, I just needed to carry it out.

Ricky held me back as I fidgeted out of his grasp, my blood boiling with fury, causing me to turn around and drove my hands into his chest, pushing him away from me. I loved Ricky, but that was the last time he was going to hold me back. I looked at him, a fire burning in my eyes full of rage. Our noses were almost touching as I was ready to fight anyone who stood in my way. My adrenaline was pumping through my veins and all I could see was red.

"Stop.." Ricky urged "..you'll make it worse."

Ricky's wide eyes glared into mine, as if to warn me. Although I was ready to give up anything and everything to save Tara, I knew that acting on my anger alone wasn't going to fix this problem. And that's why Ricky was my best friend, because he knew how to handle situations a lot better than I did. I hesitated before obeying Ricky's request. I stood there, feeling utterly helpless as Jerome looked at her like she was a piece of meat, and was enjoying torturing me by hurting her. He made his way over to her and reached for his knife in his back pocket, as he began to run the blade lightly along her skin. He started at her forehead, leaving a small cut right on her temple. She winced away from him as bright red blood began to trickle down her temple. He made his way with his knife to her ear, nicking the tip of it with the blade, causing her to scream out in pain. I tried to control the tears that I felt rising to the surface the best that I could– but I realized that anything involving Tara made my rational judgment fly out the window. The only thing I cared about, the only thing I breathed for now, was her. And I couldn't help her.
My baby.

I kept my eyes on her as her eyes gleamed into mine, begging for help. I felt a lump in my throat as I swallowed. My throat felt dry, and I felt dizzy as Jerome combed his fingers through her hair as she tried to pull away from him again. He grabbed her by the throat, causing her eyes to water, and whispered something into her ear as his hand made his way down her body, running the knife lightly down her skin once again, and then slicing the top of her thigh. Tara screamed out in agony as she beveled over in pain, only for Dustin to pull her back up to him with a forceful grasp.

I couldn't bare to watch Jerome hurt her; I would rather him torture me for weeks rather than him even look at her. Every fiber of my being wanted to go over and help her, to make this stop, but I knew Ricky had been right– If I went after any one of Jerome's guys or him, he'd kill her instantly. And I couldn't let it happen; I wouldn't let that happen. I had to think of something else, but my mind was drawing blanks, so I did the only thing I could do as I stood there, forced to watch them torture her. I mouthed a few words to her, knowing that I couldn't do much else. "Baby, I'm so sorry."

Chapter Twenty Two: Adam

As we stood there in the warehouse Ricky continued to have his hand on my shoulder to hold me back from slaughtering Jerome into fucking pieces. And I would do it with a smile on my face. Dustin took the rag out of her mouth, and she began involuntarily licking her lips; they had looked dry and cracked. She coughed out a dry, hacking cough, and her beautiful blue eyes watered.

"Now, now.. don't cry beautiful." Jerome said in a hiss, just like the snake he was. She clinched away from him as his hand stroked her cheek. "Get away from me!" She yelled, fighting back with her words now.

This made Jerome laugh. She didn't know who she was dealing with.

I couldn't take my eyes off of her, though. I knew that she was here because of me. I knew that this was all my fault. "Jerome, I had no idea she was there. Please, we did what you asked— just let her go…" I begged, and I didn't care how desperate I sounded. I just wanted her to be okay. "... If you want someone to punish, then punish me. Just let her go." I pleaded, knowing that this was a long shot, but I was desperate. I needed to protect her.

Jerome shook his head and gave a coy smile. He was playing with me like a little puppet. And he knew it. "Nah, man. I ain't gonna do that. By punishing her, I'm punishing you, get it?" He walked closer towards me until he was directly in front of me, and our faces were close enough to the other to feel one another's breath. He was trying to intimidate me. "I've relied on you, amigo. Usually you don't go making mistakes like this. Now… you should have made sure there was no one around— No way to get caught. You messed up. So you take care of it. Once you do, we're good.."He put out his hand, giving me a gun.

I refused to take it.

I wouldn't do this.

   He forcefully grabbed my hand now, and put the gun in my hand. He walked back over to Tara, standing dangerously close to her, as she continued to cry in fear. "You either shoot the gun, or I'll take her back into the back room and I'll do some things to her that you wouldn't be too happy about…" He hissed, "…You know how I like mixing torture with pleasure." As he said that, he grabbed Tara by her cheeks as she struggled to turn away from him, but he was too strong, and she was forced to turn her face towards him.

   He kissed the side of her cheek, and then placed his lips on hers. He started demanding her as he pulled her away from Dustin and toward him. Tara continued to try to break away from him all the while tears fell from her face.

The vile pit in my stomach got rid of any care I had about what Ricky wanted me to do. I didn't fucking care what he wanted me to do or not do. That was *my* girl, *my* Tara. And I wasn't going to stand by while someone violated her and hurt her like this. *Over my dead fucking body.*

   I cocked the gun and put my finger on the trigger.

I wonder how he would feel if I shot him. I wonder how he'd feel if I lit all of his limbs on fire.

   I aimed the gun towards Jerome's head, ready to kill the motherfucker. He broke away from Tara, noticing the gun pointed onto him. He began laughing so hard that he bent over in hysterics.

This guy was certifiably insane.

   "You're going to shoot me? *ME?* After everything I have given you? No, man, that's not how it goes—". I was no longer able to think clearly. I was in the fight or flight mode of adrenaline. I wanted to fight. In fact, I wanted to *kill*. I would have done anything for her, I would burn this entire warehouse down to the ground with all of these useless motherfuckers inside. *Anything to save her.*

"Yeah man, that's how it fucking goes!" I spat with the gun pointed in front of my face directly at him, "I have listened to your ass for *years*. I've done everything you've asked me to, no question. I've proved my loyalty to you. One minor fuck up doesn't take away what I've done for you— What Ricky has done for you! You said earlier that a King isn't a King if he doesn't have a kingdom…" I paused as I felt my heart beating out of my chest and sweat began dripping from my forehead. "… If you didn't have us, half the shit you've made us do wouldn't have been done! I've earned my fucking keep, so don't fucking start with me!" I yelled, causing Ricky and Tara to both flinch. I didn't care how much of a joke Jerome thought this was, if he wanted to hurt what mattered to me, I'd hurt what mattered to him.

"Now you're going to let her go, and you're going to let us leave or I'll blow your fucking head off, I swear to God, J." I was completely honest in that moment, and by the look in Jerome's eyes, he knew I meant every word.

I knew what I needed to do, and I only had so much time to act before this became ugly. I shot the gun, hitting the bullet right into Jerome's thigh. He hurled over in pain and screamed out. "Fuck you, Riguez!" All of Jerome's men pulled their guns on me, ready to kill me easily. I had five guys on me with guns, so I knew that I didn't stand a chance. I looked over to Ricky, who had pulled out two rifles from his back pocket the second I pulled the trigger. It was now two against five.

We all held the guns towards one another. Standing there, waiting to shoot.

Jerome took a second to get used to the pain as he limped over to me again, this time dragging Tara along with him.

"I know who you're loyal to now. I just never thought it would be to some *slut*. But I have faith in you, Riguez. At least I know you show loyalty. Take your little bitch, or should I say both of your little bitches and get out of here before I have my men get rid of all three of you."

He threw Tara at me as I caught her in my arms and dropped the gun. I pulled her over into the car and placed her in the backseat.

Ricky ran over to the closest door he could get into. I got into my car and backed up out of the garage, now spinning it around.

"Let's make this interesting!"

Jerome yelled as I pushed my car to a halt. He walked up closer to the driver side window with his men behind him, including Dustin.

"You go.." He said nonchalantly, "..You try to take her somewhere.. but I'll find her." He laughed maniacally, then continued, "I've always liked the thrill of the chase— It's all about the chase for me, baby. If you hide her, then good for you. But I always find people, and I always get what I want." He leaned in closer, this time close enough for his spit to hit my face as he spoke. "You think I'm letting you go? *Just like that*? There's not a nice part about me, Riguez…" He paused and moved away from the driver's side window to look around to his men as he spoke, then directed his attention towards me.

"I'm making this a game now. I'll fucking come after *you* and *her*. And I will make you watch as I kill her— slowly. I will do everything in my power to make you suffer now that you broke my trust. Consider yourselves dead." He stepped away to walk back into the warehouse and slammed the garage door. I drove away quickly, as the wheels caused a hazy smoke to surround us from spinning.

I glanced back into the back seat, as Ricky untied Tara's hands and took his shirt off to wipe her face. "I'm *so* sorry." Ricky murmured to her.

She looked at him and a soft sob escaped her throat. She leaned into him and let herself cry, hard. She let herself wail out as she cried on his shoulder.

What have I done to her?

I continued to drive, heading back to the cabins to get her stuff and mine. We weren't safe here, and we needed somewhere to hide. "We need to go somewhere. We need to leave. Guys when we get back to the cabin, hurry up and pack your stuff immediately. I will switch cars to my Camero. They don't know I have that car.." I glanced back in the rearview mirror as Ricky looked up and met my gaze. Tara still cried on his shoulder, not moving an inch. "We'll need to leave as soon as possible. I have some money, so we don't need to worry about that. But we need to go tonight. If not he'll find us…" I couldn't bear to think of the next words I spoke, hoping that these words wouldn't manifest into the truth, "... He'll find *you*."

My eyes glanced back into the backseat, looking at Tara resting her head on Ricky's shoulder.

She had composed herself enough to meet my gaze, but it took her a moment to process my words. Once she did, her head immediately shot up from Ricky's shoulder and she began to protest. "*What?!* What the *hell* are you talking about? I'm not leaving."

She was brave, and that was one of the things I loved about her, but it wasn't safe here for her. Jerome made it clear that he was coming after her, which meant that his entire crew was, too. It was too much of a risk.

"Tara, I'm so sorry for involving you in all of this—"

She cut me off, anger now forming on her face as she looked at me: "What the *hell* was that? *What the fuck* Adam?!..." She continued ranting in a straight path of fury, directly aimed towards me. "...You know what? I thought you doing a drug deal with that guy at my cheering competition was bad, but this?-- This is just fucking *crazy!*"

Fuck.

She knew what I was doing at the cheering competition. She even questioned me about it tonight after dinner, and I blatantly lied to her, which meant that she knew I lied, too.

It all began to make sense, how she turned cold after our conversation, how she was so eager to leave. I could tell by the way she was looking at me in the mirror of the car now, too, and I hated the way she looked at me then.

She looked at me like she didn't give a shit about me. Like I disappointed her.

It made my stomach drop, and the nausea had suddenly creeped in. I never wanted to make her feel like that *ever* again.

"I am sorry, Tara. I never wanted this for you. I *never* want anything to happen to you…" I felt my voice trail off, unable to find the words that she needed to hear. "...I need to get you out of here. I know a place we can go." She scoffed then, pushing her body up through the center console to sit in the passenger seat.

"You're fucking crazy if you think for a second that I would go with you anywhere! Look what you caused! I was kidnapped by your little drug deal friend and punched and thrown around like a fucking ragdoll! You kidnapped an innocent man and I watched it as you threw him into the trunk— Adam, you held a gun to his head!..." Her anger took over, and if it weren't so serious of a topic, I maybe would have smiled. That's how cute she looks when she's angry. "...Is he still in your trunk?!... You know what— Don't tell me because either way I absolutely do not trust you. I want to go home now." I huffed out a large breath.

I completely understood that she felt overwhelmed and terrified. She wasn't even at the legal drinking age yet, and she was focused on sports and academics. The shit I was involved with didn't even come close to comparing to it.

We drove the rest of the way in silence, and once we got to her cabin, I put the car into park. She slammed the car door on the way inside to get her bag, her car nowhere in sight.

I couldn't just leave her alone without explaining to her that it wasn't safe for her to be here. I needed to tell her how much she meant to me, and that I would protect her with my life. I'd kill anyone who dared to come near her, and I wanted her to know that.

I ran after her, hoping she'd hear me out. "Tara... please" I said as I reached for her hand. She yanked her hand from mine and looked into my eyes. Her bright blue eyes were cold now, giving a deadly glare. "Let go of me! I want nothing to do with you, *leave*."

She ran into the cabin, as I stood there stunned, confused, and unsure for the first time in my life.

Ricky walked up behind me and patted me on the back. "I'm gonna go back to the cabin to pack our things. Just give her a few minutes, she'll come around."He started to walk down the path towards the other cabins, and then stopped and turned to face me.

"I know you need to protect her from Jerome. I know how much you care for her, but she was just introduced to our entire fucking world in *one* day. I've been a part of it for ten years and I'm not even sure I still know what the fucks going on. Be patient with her."

He left me there, baffled at how right he was. When Ricky wanted, he could really give good advice.

He was my best friend— My brother, and if he was telling me to give her some time, then I needed to listen. He was the only one who could give me advice that I'd willingly accept.

I had felt terrible for bringing him into this situation, too. But if I tried to apologize, he wouldn't accept it. He would deny that I did anything wrong. He was always so much wiser about the business than I was, so I shoved my feeling of guilt down deep.

I walked into the cabin, following her into the house. I walked to the nearest room I could find. The cabin she was staying in was similar to mine, so I picked the luck of the draw and found myself walking into the back room of the hallway, hoping she'd be there.

I walked into the room, and immediately felt my heart shatter. She was laying on her bed, bawling her eyes out. Her short breaths in between her sobs caused her whole body to shake. At that moment, there wasn't much to say. She noticed me in the doorway, and instantly cried harder. I walked over to the other side of the bed and climbed in. I pulled her closer to me as she continued to cry, and I continued to hold her tight, letting there be a moment where we didn't feel the need to say anything. I rubbed her back to soothe her, finally coming to terms with how traumatic this must have been for her to witness all in one day. *No wonder she hates me right now.*

"I don't know what to say.." I whispered, laying my chin on the top of her head, "I'm so sorry for the pain I've caused you, baby."

She lifted her head to look me in the eyes. The soft blue eyes that I remembered were looking into mine— all traces of the cold, dull look she gave me before had melted away.

I placed my lips on her forehead, leaving them there for a lingering moment. She let out a soft sigh and then nuzzled her head into my chest. The way she scooted closer towards me reminded me of the night I met her in the bar. She did the same thing in my arms then, and it warmed my heart to know that she did it again. "I'm sorry.." she whispered quietly.

I looked down at her now, confused as to why the *hell* she would apologize to me. "Why would you say sorry? You have nothing to be sorry for."

She made a sniffing noise, like it was stuffy, trying to compose herself.

"I'm sorry I got so mad at you. I don't even know anything about you and why you're in this and I judged. But I trust you.." She reached for my hand now, intertwining her fingers with mine. "It's okay, I understand that all of this is overwhelming and fucking terrifying.. Trust me, I get it." I said, feeling her soft whimpers on my chest.

"I know this is hard. And I will explain everything to you. All you need to know right now is that I got in when I was a teenager. My mom had died in a car accident when I was a kid, and then my dad died from cancer a few years later. I ended up hanging out with the wrong crowd, and one thing led to another…" I trailed off, unsure if telling her the truth was going to save whatever this was with her. I hoped it would. "...I've worked under Jerome for years, but he's gotten worse over the years. Power has a funny way of changing who you are, and Jerome has changed a lot. And the Jerome he is now— He wasn't lying when he said that, Tara. He *will* come after us.."

I let a few minutes of silence sit between us so she could process it and understand it a little bit better. "..I just want to protect you."

She lifted her head up and kissed me softly, gazing into my eyes once again, but this time I could tell that she trusted me and that she understood that all I wanted to do was to keep her safe.

"Okay." She simply said, trying to form her words together. "Okay. We can leave and go somewhere. But I need to come up with some lie to tell my parents. I can't just disappear…my mom saw you at the fair. She would guess that you took me or something. I need to act like I'm leaving on purpose.." She was thinking now with a face full of concentration, all the while shaking with anxiety. "But you won't leave me, right? I want you with me." I nodded to answer her question and kissed her head again. "No, I won't leave you."

I got off of the bed, and grabbed her duffle bag. I packed all of her things for her, and gave her the sweatpants of mine that she had worn and a t-shirt to change into. As she reached to grab the sweatpants, I noticed a darkened scar on her wrist, which scared the hell out of me. Jerome did all of this to her, and I was going to make his life a fucking living hell; I'd shoot him right between the eyes if I had to. I reached for her hand so I could get a closer look, but she quickly tugged her hand away. "Did he hurt you there, too?" I said, looking down at her wrist. She softly shook her head no and began twisting her wrist in her other hand nervously. "No, It's nothing." She seemed distracted in thought, looking for other things she needed to pack, but all I could think about was those marks on her wrist. I walked toward her, but she moved away as she continued to search for something.

"Are you sure?" I couldn't help but feel as if she had been hiding something; Like there was a large part of her that I had yet to come into contact with. And while part of it was intriguing, part of me didn't like the feeling that I was being lied to.

Tara looked in my direction and gave me a soft smile, but it didn't reach her eyes. "Yes, Adam. I'm fine, I promise. We have other things we need to worry about right now, like getting the hell out of here." She grabbed her clothes and walked toward the bathroom, as if she was in a rush.

"I guess I'll finish packing your stuff up while you shower, then." I hesitated, still wondering why she had quickly changed the subject off of her markings on her wrist. I began folding her clothes and placing them into her duffle bag, attempting to take my mind off of it. "And I'll think of something you can say to your parents. But we need to get some supplies to last us and get you extra clothes, then we need to hit the road." She nodded her head in agreement and got off of the bed. She grabbed her shampoo and soap, a towel and the clothes I put on her bed and walked to the bathroom to shower.

As I heard the water starting, I felt overwhelmed by the panic that had set in. I didn't know where to go, I didn't know how to keep her safe from Jerome.

I wasn't cut out for this— to put my all into protecting someone else. My entire life I had protected myself, even when I dated Vanessa. I always shielded myself and I kept my distance from any girl who tried to wiggle their way in. But with Tara– everything was different. I had never met anyone like her; She gave me a new sense of peace– One that I haven't had in forever. She gave me the freedom to feel for the first time in a long time. She's changed *everything*.

I didn't know what to do, but I needed to do something discreet, something that no one, not even

Jerome would expect. I found myself dialing a familiar number, knowing that she probably didn't want to hear my voice, but I still tried.

She picked up and her coarse, high pitched voice answered the phone. "*Adam*? Why are you calling me?" I didn't know what she could do for us, but she was the only person I could go to who I trusted. "I'm not calling for what you think. I've met someone…Somehow Jerome found her and is coming after us."

I closed my eyes and hoped that she would understand. There was a long moment of silence, I thought that maybe she had hung up on me– not that I would blame her.

It took a lot out of me to even call. But I knew that no matter how much I didn't want to involve her, the only person who wouldn't make anything *obvious* was her. "Natasha.. Please. We really need your help."

Chapter Twenty Three: Tara

Adam told me where we were going for a while: to Savannah, GA. He told me that he called up one of his friends he had met during a drug deal, and her name was Natasha. He said we could trust her, and that her and her fiancé Harry lived in a safe environment for us. He also told me that they were more than welcoming us to stay there.

I couldn't help but hear the anticipation in his voice, like he didn't know what to expect from going to Natasha's house. It wasn't hard to put two and two together; I had quickly figured out that at one point, the two of them must have been involved in some way or another, but it wasn't important to ask about the details now. What was important was packing up some of my things back at home, and leaving my parents and the town of Covington, for now.

I hadn't known what to do about my parents. I knew that being rude to them and leaving would break their heart. I knew that I couldn't be too drastic with my story; I was Twenty, going to be Twenty One soon, and although I legally am an adult, I still live under their roof.

I had wanted to tell Adam of my complications, but I felt like there was too much going on to bring up my *very detailed* home life, and how I was adopted at age five. So I made up a plan myself, and even woke up Danielle at the cabin so she could back me up with it, too. I had simply told her that I was going on a romantic getaway with Adam, to which she suggested that her and Aiden should come along, too. I ignored it though; I was trying to focus back on my plan.

Before we left, I gave her my car keys that I had in my bag with me when I had gotten kidnapped. I don't know how I kept my clutch on me that whole time, but I managed to do so. I asked her if she and Caroline could pick my car up and drive it to her house for the time being when they leave tomorrow. Danielle questioned it and complained, but she eventually agreed.

Once we were packed and met back out front of the cabin, I couldn't help but feel like this had been a bittersweet moment. As I walked to the car, I noticed a beautiful, yet wilted red rose laying on the ground near the driveway. I knew the girls had gotten flowers for the competition, but seeing flowers die had always made me sad. It proved that time for everything is fleeting. I picked the rose off of the ground and smelled it, inhaling the wonderful scent, then placed the wilted rose on top of an old flower pot outside of the cabin.

As I got into the car, I knew that this was something I had to do. It didn't mean it wasn't difficult, though. I had to remain safe from Jerome, and I knew that Adam and Ricky were hell bent on keeping me safe. And I knew that regardless of what was going on with my parents, that I would miss them. Another thought that went through my mind was the fact that I would miss the first few weeks of classes, which scared the living hell out of me. I would actually miss going to physics class every day to annoy Mr. Cain. I would miss a lot— I knew that.

But I needed to do what was best in order to survive, and this was it.

*

We had dropped the Camry off at Ricky's apartment, and picked up Adam's Camero from Ricky's garage. Adam said he felt upset that we couldn't take his Corvette that he loved so much, but he knew that Jerome had seen him in it before, and we needed a car that no one would recognize.

On the way to my house, Adam called his uncle Joe and told him he would be out of town for a few weeks tops. He said he had to take care of something, but never specified. I was almost certain that his uncle Joe knew what he was talking about, though.

I was sitting in the passenger seat during that call, so I could hear Joe's voice clearly on the phone. He was beyond worried for his nephew:

"*Please tell me where you're going, Adam.*" Adam continued to ignore his questions.

"*Adam Richard Rodriguez, you answer me right now!*"

"*Lo Siento, tío. I won't be too far away, I'll come back as soon as I can.*"

"*Adam, son....*"

"*I know Uncle, I'll be safe. I'll call you when I get there.*"

The sorrow in his eyes of talking to his uncle broke my heart. He didn't want to leave him, and yet he was, because of me. Guilt built up in my chest, causing an unfamiliar tightness.

"*I love you, Adam.*"

"*Te amo, tío.*"

I looked back to Ricky in the backseat, already looking in my direction. He glanced at me with sympathy in his eyes. He knew what was going on in my mind, almost instantly. He placed his arm on my shoulder and rubbed it gently, and gave me a small, reassuring smile. With only knowing Ricky for a short amount of time, it was hard to think of Adam and I going on without him. I never fully realized how close you could get to people in such a short amount of time—It was truly surprising.

Adam hung up the phone, and looked back at me. He gave me a soft smile, and then reached for my thigh. "We're almost to your house. Do you want to stop by the hospital and see your dad?"

His words were steady and strong. Like he would support me through whatever decision I made. "Sure, I want to see him before I go. I won't be too long, though. I promise. I'm going to pack my bags, tell him I'm going to stay with Danielle for a while or something, and then I'll call my mom as we drive out and tell her the same thing."

"That's a good plan, Tara." Ricky said from the back seat, giving a reassuring smile.

We stopped by my house so I could quickly grab a few more items before heading to see my dad. Once we arrived at the hospital, I began to feel as if my nerves had gotten the best of me— just like they always do. I unbuckled my seatbelt and let in a large breath of air. Adam smiled and squeezed my hand with his. "You've got this mama. We'll be out here, come when you're ready." I glanced back at Ricky, who was smiling just like always.

I got out of the car and walked to the entrance of the hospital, and found myself walking towards the familiar elevators. The ride up to my dad's floor was agonizing, mostly because I hadn't seen him since his accident, and I wasn't sure if I was strong enough to say goodbye to him right now.

I hesitated to open his room door, feeling a new sense of being in a foreign territory. I had planned on talking with him more about what happened once I got back from the cabins, but now that I was leaving— I wouldn't have as much time. I didn't want to focus on all of the negatives, I just wanted to say goodbye.

I opened the door, and my hand began to shake as I grabbed the door handle. The door made a familiar squeaking sound, bringing me back to reality and out of my thoughts. "Kiddo?" I heard my dad's faint voice coming from behind me, just as he turned the corner, walking with hospital staff. He looked so much better since the last time I saw him: His skin color was back to normal, he didn't look as tired or worn down, and he was conscious. So I considered that a win.

I stood in the doorway of his room and smiled in his direction. "Hey, dad." He walked over towards me and pulled me into a hug, squeezing me hard enough that the sore parts of my body sent shots of pain through me. But I tried my best to hide my pain. "I've missed you, little T-bird." My dad hadn't called me that nickname since I was in middle school and obsessed with Grease. I smiled at the memory of us watching Grease over and over until I passed out on the couch, covered in popcorn. "I've missed you, too."

I moved away from him, now looking around the hospital hallway awkwardly. Things had changed since the last time I was here, and I was so happy to see him improving. It was hard to think of how to start a conversation with him, with his attempt hanging over our heads. "...Dad" I started, knowing that I needed to quickly get to the point, because I was leaving, and I had to leave soon. But in order for me to feel safe in knowing my dad would be okay, I needed some answers. "I don't want to overwhelm you.. You seem in a good place, but would you mind telling me what I saw on Friday?" He scratched the back of his neck, showing that he felt just as awkward as I did. "We really have to talk about this, huh kiddo?" I nodded my head in response. I think the both of us deserved some answers.

"Well then..." He said, gesturing for me to sit down in the recliner chair in his hospital room. He walked a few feet away and sat on the edge of his bed as he looked out the window for a few moments– collecting his thoughts. "About a year ago, your mom and I were in a pretty bad place. We had considered getting a divorce…" His voice was barely above a whisper, as if it was hard for him to admit. "We pretended to do okay for the sake of not wanting to hurt you. We both know how much you have been through— We didn't want to do that to you. Although we didn't get along about anything anymore, the one thing we did get along about was you."

He coughed, and I heard a large gulp after he finished.

"So around that time a year ago, I was out with my buddies at a falcons game. We were drinking beers and having a fun time. I had to go to the bathroom, and I went by myself. That's when I ran into Donny Miller. I knew that he was the guy that everyone on the block thought was trying too hard to keep up appearances of having money, when in reality he was dirt poor most of his life, but I didn't want to treat him differently for it— There was no reason to. We started out our conversation about how his kids go to the same school as you, Paige and Will. We went to one of those restaurants inside of the arena to get a beer and were chatting about our lives, like how he had gotten really lucky to land such an amazing government job in Atlanta due to his military training. I really enjoyed his company, and he seemed to be a good guy. But things changed once we had a few beers, and I should've known then." He took a large breath in and held it for a moment, before continuing to breathe normally. "…After that, he told me his wife had left him a few years ago and he had always lived near us and thought your mom and I were a great couple, but that we didn't *make sense*." He continued, "He said he never really knew how to express feelings, but ever since his divorce to his wife, he had been talking to your mom more at PTO meetings, and started having feelings for her but that he's never *acted on it* for the sake of our marriage."

I couldn't believe what I was hearing. I wasn't sure how my dad listened to any of this without wanting to beat him up. But I didn't ask any questions, I just continued to listen.

"And believe me, I was ready to kick his ass. But I had too much to drink, and decided to leave right then, without saying anything.." He sighed once more, and then looked at me. "So I went home that night, and called your mom. I called her out on it and wanted her to explain what was going on, and if she ever *acted* on it. That's when I found out they had an affair for four months prior to that conversation I had with Donny that night. That next morning was the day you walked in on us fighting and your mom left." "I knew that one day, you would find out the truth anyways and regardless of how upset you would be with it all, I knew you would always come around.." Tears streamed down his face, but he was quick to blotch them with the box of tissues on his bedside table.

"Friday night was a new low for me, Tara. I had done so well for so long with my mental health problems. I stopped self harming, I wasn't having any suicidal thoughts anymore– I didn't have them for a long time. My medication was working really well for me. But Friday I went out for some drinks with my buddies after rounds at the hospital, and guess who we ran into." He broke his gaze and looked down at his hands as he fiddled with them nervously.

"Your mom and him were all over each other– I couldn't take it. I apparently was about to cause a scene— I must've had too many beers. But my friends got me out of there, and got me home safely. It wasn't until I turned on the TV and your mom's favorite movie came on... fucking *Weekend at Bernie's*..." He sighed and rolled his eyes before continuing, "That's when I spiraled. I don't really know what happened after that. I drank some more beers, took my night time meds, and went to get a bath. I don't remember what happened after that. I must've blacked out." We sat in silence for a few minutes as I tried to process my dad's story. It sounded as if his attempt was actually an accident, and that he didn't really attempt to end his life at all.

"Well.. has mom visited you since you've been here?" My dad scoffed and shook his head, telling me everything I needed to know. Just like a forest fire burning in California, my anger built up and spread over my entire body. "No sweetpea, she did call though and made sure to tell me she was engaged." He shook his head again and let out a disbelieving laugh. *Engaged? Engaged?* It took everything in me not to scream.

It didn't have anything to do with the fact that they were planning no divorcing– I could understand and sympathize with that... but for Jennifer to not only cheat while my parents *still* were married, she went ahead and got *engaged*? That was next level bitchery.

I stood up from the recliner, not sure if I could hear anymore. I couldn't let the tears fall from my eyes, I was stronger than that. I had been through more than that. I grabbed my purse and headed towards the door, until my dad's voice stopped me. "Tara, where are you going?" I shook my head, unable to process everything he told me in just a few seconds.

"I can't stay here, it's too much to process.." I continued, "I'm going to stay at Danielle's for a while. I can't be in that house, Dad."

He stood up from his bed and opened the door, and kissed the top of my head.

"If you want to talk about it more later, we can Tare Bear." He smiled softly as I walked towards the hallway. "You better come see me in a few days— Do you get it?" I turned back around to face him, tears now falling down my face like a heavy rain.
Even though I could tell he felt a little relieved by finally telling me the truth about my mom's affair, my heart shattered with sadness for all of it; For the information, for the betrayal, and for leaving him. This was the hardest thing I had to do.

I nodded my head in reply, I wanted to give him just a little bit of happiness and a little bit of hope, too. I wiped a tear from my cheek, and turned back to face him before I walked away: "Yeah, dad..." I said softly, the words coming out in a whisper ".... I won't forget it."

Chapter Twenty Four: Adam

We arrived in Savannah during the early morning, just before sunrise.

I, personally, was fucking exhausted, so I knew that Ricky and Tara must of been, too.

Ricky stayed up with me the entire time through the drive, but Tara nodded off here and there, only soft whimpers from dreams waking her.

We parked my Camero in the back driveway of Natasha's new home. This was not what I was expecting her life to become at all. The house was similar to Tara's in a sense; It was a three story old Victorian home with a large backyard and a swimming pool with a slide connected to it. It was far from the old beat up trailer we met in.

I killed the engine and got out of the car, both Ricky and Tara following me to the back door with our luggage. Natasha opened the door, a wide smile on her face as she waited to greet us.

"Hey, strangers." She said, reaching out for Ricky and pulling him into a tight hug before coming over to me to do the same.

It was weird now— being friendly with her without being anything else. But it wasn't anything I thought about now; Natasha had become a friend I could count on, but that was all. I had come a long way in just a few short weeks.

"Hey, Tasha, Thank you for helping us out." She smiled and patted my shoulder, before her eyes focused onto the beautiful, dark haired girl who was behind Ricky and I.

"...And who is this?" She said happily, walking towards Tara with her arms reaching out for her.

"Tasha, this is Tara." Tara smiled shyly, and let Natasha hug her before pulling away and glancing at me. "You must be Natasha." Tara said quietly, looking between the both of us.

Natasha clapped her hands in excitement and jumped up and down before speaking.

"Okay, I know you guys are in a pickle, but you're more than welcome to use anything in the house. Except, just don't drink my wine— that's to *you*, Ricky." Ricky laughed then, and shook his head in amusement.

"You bet your sweet ass I'll drink it." He winked at Natasha and then gave her a sly smile, which was typical of Ricky.

"So..." Natasha said, looking at all of us now, "We have a lot of rooms, but I thought you two could use some privacy. So Tara and Adam, you can have the guest house right over there. It has a kitchen and everything! That way you can wine and dine in peace. Ricky, you can stay in the basement. It has a kitchen too, so don't feel left out. You'll have privacy– *mostly*. We have been having a little bit of a mouse problem, so fair warning."

Tara's eyes went wide at Tasha's comment, clearly shocked that she'd put Rick down in the basement with mice. But Tara didn't catch onto Natasha's humor just yet. I was confident that Tara and Natasha would be great friends once they got used to one another.

Natasha noticed Tara's concerned look and burst into a fit of laughter. "Oh, honey I'm kidding!" She said, gently reaching to squeeze Tara's arm. "We just like to mess with Ricky here as much as we can, ain't that right, Adam?" I nodded my head in agreement, and looked over to Ricky who had already started helping himself to Natasha's food on the counter. Tara lingered, clearly she was uncomfortable around Natasha, but she remained in the same spot, not even trying to move before she spoke. "Natasha, if you rather the boys stay in the guest house, I'd be happy to use the basement instead. That way I could study a bit for my online class?" Tara seemed anxious waiting for Tasha's reply, but what I didn't understand was why she didn't want to sleep with me; She knew she could still study in the guest house, so something wasn't adding up. I felt my mind wander to the moment where she had pulled her wrist away from me. Maybe she wanted to keep her distance; Maybe she was hiding something.

Natasha waved her hand to dismiss her comment, and then walked over to the counter and slapped a muffin out of Ricky's hand. "Oh nonsense Tara, you'll stay with Adam. You are more than welcome to study anywhere you want, but there is an office in the guest house, which I'm sure you'll like using. But if not, I totally understand. Adam tends to snore like a train, believe me." Ricky couldn't help but choke on the bite of muffin he had in his mouth as Tara's face instantly paled, and I was left there feeling the most awkward I had ever been in my life.

This was the worst shit ever.

Natasha finally realized what she had said; Her face turned beat red and she quickly walked to the refrigerator as if she were looking for something. I cleared my throat and grabbed Tara's hand, intertwining my fingers with hers. She grasped onto my hand tightly, and walked closer to me, as if she was claiming herself as mine.

It made my heart race. "Well, Thanks Natasha for allowing us to stay here. We're tired, So we're gonna head in for the rest of the night." I said as Tasha nodded and smiled kindly in our direction before turning her attention to Rick. "C'mon Ricky, I'll walk you down to the basement." She grabbed his duffle bag for him and walked with him to the basement.

I grabbed Tara's suitcase for her and walked towards the guest house. I felt her ice blue eyes lingering on me, and I knew what that meant: she had questions. I grabbed her hand for comfort, and squeezed it gently, as I guided her into the guest house. "We can talk about whatever you're thinking of, if you want." I said softly as I sat our luggage down in the bedroom, and watched her as she climbed into the bed.

She truly was exhausted.

I took my shirt off and sweatpants, getting into the bed next to her in my boxers.

It felt natural now to be around her— To be in bed next to her.

I made myself comfortable and laid down as she brought herself closer towards me, cuddling her body against mine. "Do you want to talk about it?" I asked as I rested my chin on her head. I felt the soft rise and fall of her chest as her breath synced with my own, and I began to feel myself relax a little bit more. "Nuh-uh." She mumbled. "Talk later."

I kissed her head and listened to her breathe as she started to fall asleep. I was finally able to take a moment to think about everything that had happened in the past twenty four hours. I wasn't sure what I was going to do, but I had decided to consult with Ricky and Tasha in the morning about it. I wouldn't leave them out of my plans; They were the only ones who knew the ins and outs of the business so I needed as much help as I could get.

I was snapped out of my thoughts when I heard a faint hum from next to me. Tara was tracing her fingers again on my chest, then sliding her fingers up and down my tattooed arm. I felt my hair rise up on my arms, feeling the electrical current surge through me from her touch.

I turned my head and pressed my lips onto her forehead, kissing her softly. "I thought you were sleeping." I whispered as I brushed her hair with my hand. "Adam?" She said quietly, as if she was whispering so no one else could hear us. "Yeah?"

She wiped a single tear that had fallen down her cheek, then met her eyes with mine. The familiar color of ice blue filled my entire visual field. It made my heart beat faster, but I couldn't quite explain why my body reacted the way it did just by the way she looked at me. It was magnetic, and the pull I felt towards her was something I had never felt before. I had always been able to keep control over myself in the past, but I had absolutely no clue what she was doing to me.

"Do you think that Jerome will find me?" I kissed the top of her head as I brushed my fingers through her hair. There was no way in hell that I would let him get close to her. That was a fact. I couldn't even fathom the thought of it.

I had decided when I saw her struggling from Jerome's grip in the warehouse, that I was going to kill that motherfucker one way or another.

I shook my head to answer her, and then spoke the only words I could tell her at that moment. I decided to be completely and utterly honest with her. I knew what I was thinking was a strong promise to give, but I had meant it.

I didn't care what plan I had to come up with, or how I had to get into contact with, if that meant keeping her safe. She didn't deserve any of this, the least I could do is protect her. I cleared my throat and gazed at her bright blue eyes, feeling the heating desire that I had learned to crave more than anything else.

"I will protect you from it all— without question, without hesitation, without a doubt in my mind." I continued, "I don't think you know the hold you have on me." My heart began to race as I felt as if I had been washed away in her bright blue eyes, completely taken aback by her. I cleared my throat; feeling a new sense of urgency for her. "I'd move the earth for you if I could."

She beamed back at me then, feeling reassured with my answer. Only thing she didn't know, though, was that my plan to protect her hadn't gone past the idea of bringing her here and my tired, overwhelmed brain felt completely fucking useless.

Chapter Twenty Five: Tara

I woke up to the annoying sound of a tractor mower outside of the window.

What the hell?

I got up from the bed and noticed that Adam was no longer in the bed next to me.

I had walked through the guest house, getting a little more acquainted with my surroundings, all the while still trying to look for Adam.

The simple, white interior of the guest house made the natural light shine in, lighting the house up without worrying about turning a light on. Most of the furniture was modern; A light blue couch with decorative pillows sat in the middle of the living room, facing towards the mounted flatscreen tv above the fireplace. The walls had simple frames of artwork, allowing for people who stay here to feel comfortable without making it look cluttered, and the kitchen had all stainless steel appliances to go with the white marble countertops and matching white cabinets.

This house had so much open space, and I really enjoyed looking around at the beautiful interior. So much, in fact, that I had forgotten why I had been walking around in the first place.

That was, until I noticed a figure running outside in the yard towards the main house.

I walked over towards the patio door to get a better look, now recognizing the gorgeous tanned body, the perfectly sculpted muscles, and the familiar dark, curly hair bouncing as he ran.

Adam.

I felt my breath become shallow, almost as if seeing him without a shirt on and sweat beating down his perfectly chiseled abs sent me into orbit. It was still the morning, so I had to keep telling myself to hold it together and not let my overwhelmingly hot and all consuming feelings for Adam take over. I rubbed my forehead and took a few deep breaths before walking over towards the main house.

"Hey Tara! Come on in, I have breakfast made here for you guys."

Natasha was yelling for me from the back porch of the main house with a wide smile on her face, waiting for me to go inside. I liked Natasha so far, even though I knew nothing about her or even about her history with Adam. She seemed like a really nice girl, and I wanted to form my own opinion of her before blocking it by my feelings for Adam.

As I got to the back door, she smiled and threw her arm around my shoulder, leading me into the main house. The main house was very similar to the inside of the guest house, except for it being *three times bigger*. The kitchen was so huge, it could have probably fit forty people in it easily.

"TARAAAAAAA, Hey girl, hey girl I know it must be you, when I see you comin' in the house with those eyes so blue. C'mon, get some eggs, cause you know what I'm about to say is true, I might not know you well but there's no one quite like you." Natasha, Adam and I couldn't help but bust out at Ricky's ridiculous attempt to rap. Ricky always knew how to make people smile. He was crazy, that's for sure, but he had quickly become a great friend to me. Ricky had become a breath of fresh air for me, and I was so glad that our paths had crossed— even if it happened to be in these circumstances. He got up from his seat at the kitchen table and walked over towards me with his wide smile on his face.

He grabbed me and hugged me tightly, basically squeezing the air out of me. "Good morning to you, too Rick." I choked. Natasha was still standing next to me, waiting for Ricky to quit hugging me.

"Alright, alright, man. Let my girl get something to eat." Ricky broke away from me now, holding his hands up in surrender. I looked over to the familiar voice I heard, and noticed Adam, who was standing at the island and eating an apple. All he was wearing was sneakers and a pair of gym shorts. His body was glistening still from the sweat of his run.

Looking at him made my face feel hot and I instantly knew that I was blushing. Not only did the way he looked make me blush, but the fact that he also called me *his girl*. I walked towards him now, probably looking like a blushing hobo wearing his sweatpants and a t-shirt, and wrapped my arms around his waist.

He pulled me in closer, wrapping his arm around my shoulder. "Good morning." I said with a bright smile on my face. If we hadn't been in the situation we were in, I would love to get used to this; a life with Adam. Seeing him every morning, looking as incredible as he does…Being able to wake up next to him every morning and see his beautiful smile… *yeah I could get used to this.*

A playful grin spread on his lips as he looked down at me, admiring me with his soft, brown eyes. "Good morning, Mama." He kissed the top of my head quickly, before grabbing me a plate from the center of the island and handing it to me. "You look beautiful." He leaned in as I lifted myself on my tippy toes to meet him, as he placed a soft kiss on my lips.

Just in the way he kissed me made my heart skip a beat and sent butterflies dancing in my stomach. I rolled my eyes, trying to fight a smile at the fact that he called me beautiful, even though I was about eighty seven percent sure that my hair was so messy that I looked like I got caught in a tornado. "*Ewwwww* guys get a fucking room." Ricky mocked, as he rolled his eyes in amusement and stuffed a whole pancake in his mouth.

I grabbed some sausage links from the pan, a spoonful of scrambled eggs, and two pieces of toast. I grabbed the glass that was sitting on the placemat for me and filled it with orange juice. I sat down next to Ricky at the table as Adam and Natasha both walked over to meet us there.

"So..." Natasha spoke, her question already lingering with anticipation, "How did you two meet?"
She looked between Adam and I now, sitting at the head of the table, opposite of Ricky. Adam and I sat on either side of the table, facing one another, and glanced at one another before looking at Natasha. "Well, I uh- I went to a bar one night for a drink and I drank a little too much, so Adam's uncle called him to come pick me up and take me home. Then we just kept kind of running into one another at the gym and at the fairgrounds.. And, yeah. We just kept finding one another." I glanced back at Adam whose eyes were on me the entire time I spoke. I could feel the intense heat from his gaze burning into my skin.

"Yeah, we ran into one another again during her practice for the swim team." Adam chimed in, not bothering to focus on anyone else but me. "Oh, that's so nice you guys. Tara I can't believe you swim competitively, I've always wished that I could've done that. Do you swim for Georgia State?"

I felt my face flush, realizing that Natasha knew nothing about me. It also occurred to me that I didn't know much about Ricky or Adam, either. I knew his parents died when he was young, but other than that, I didn't know much. "Yep! And I cheer, too. " I smiled, hoping we could learn more about each other.

"So how old are you, then?" She asked, inquisitively.

"Twenty."

"And how long have you and Adam been together?" She quizzed.

I noticed Adam and Ricky looking at one another in complete confusion, but I wasn't confused at all; She was testing me. "A few weeks" I shot back. Natasha's eyes went wide and her mouth formed into a large "O". I could easily tell just how shocked she was to find out that Adam and I barely knew one another, and yet he was risking everything to help me. "Oh.." her voice carried off and I knew she didn't know what to say. There was silence for a moment, so I did what I could to fill the silence and drink my orange juice. I couldn't even attempt to eat right now, my stomach was in knots.

Natasha finally cleared her throat, looking between Adam and I now, with her hands folded together and her elbows sitting on the table. "Well, Adam didn't tell me many details, so I'm sorry if my reaction was a bit rude. It just seems like this thing between you two is… a bit rushed."

Before I could reply to Natasha, she cut me off, obviously holding some pent up frustration.

"Adam, I don't understand. Why would you tell me you met a girl and you needed somewhere safe to go, but fail to mention that you've known her all of *what*? Two, Three weeks?! *And* you introduced her to the business?!... What are you, insane?!" Natasha's face heated now, clearly frustrated with the whole situation. "I really don't know what messed up shit you've gotten me involved in here, but you better start explaining. I don't care what fucked up bullshit J is trying to get you into this time, but I'm not falling for it. Bringing a girl into this life after a mere *couple of weeks*? It makes no sense, and frankly, it's really pissing me off. So explain now, or you'll need to leave."

Adam rolled his eyes, obviously annoyed with Natasha's sudden outburst. Adam reached out for my hand and grabbed it, and squeezed it reassuringly. "Tasha, calm down." He said slowly in a stern voice. "We met the way we said we did. It all happened fast– and if I remember correctly, that's the same thing that happened with you and your fiance. Sometimes things don't take a long time to figure out, sometimes you just know." He glanced back over at me, still rubbing my knuckles with his fingers. The small little act of affection relaxed me a little bit. I was truly grateful for his touch.

Natasha looked down at both of our hands, and crossed her arms. I could tell she wasn't completely sold on the story. "Well, let's say that this did happen the way you said, how did a twenty year old college girl somehow get involved with J?"

Ricky huffed, and got up from his seat, taking his plate to the sink and washing it before coming back to the table with a beer. "It's too early for this shit, I need a drink." He mumbled as he cracked open the beer. "Listen, Tash. I didn't want to believe it either, but I think it's legit. They really like one another. She got involved with J by mistake. It was our fault, but we didn't know she was there." Ricky stepped up and helped us, knowing that Natasha was having a hard time wrapping her mind around the thought of Adam and me.

"But I don't get how she got thrown into this shitty mess." I nodded in agreement. In my head, Natasha was right. I wasn't sure how I got involved in it either, really, but I wanted to be honest with her.

She was offering us a safe haven—– the least we could do was give her the truth.

"Natasha..." I said, softly, but still gaining her attention. "We ran into one another at the fair this past weekend. I was there for a cheering competition, and I'm guessing Adam and Ricky were there for whatever the hell they did with that man. They can explain that, I don't really know. Anyways, I was going to pick up my friend who was drunk after our team dinner and went to the fair. She ended up getting a ride back to the cabins, but I had already gotten there. I was walking around and noticed Adam and Ricky dragging a guy to a car, Adam kicking him, and holding a gun in front of him. They put the guy in the car and then before I knew it, a hand was around my mouth and I was being dragged into a van." I felt my entire body shake as I recalled the past few hours of my life. This had been the worst thing to ever happen to me, and I wasn't sure if I would ever get over it.

Adam tightened his grip around my hand, signaling that I didn't need to finish the story anymore. I knew he would deal with the rest of it, I found myself being able to depend on him.

"So, Ricky and I had *a lot* of fun last week. We delivered powder to the market downtown, and gave the supply to the store manager, his name was Vince. That night, we went back to give J the money, and it turned out it was counterfeit. But it wasn't regular counterfeit, the money he gave us checked out, passed the scans and everything. Whoever is making this cash is smart as hell. So J told Rick and I we had to go to the fair and deliver some supply to his friend Dustin. Then we were to pull the manager Vince from his food service late at night and bring him to the warehouse so J could get answers from him. He did get answers. He found out it involved Javier."

I wasn't sure when Ricky put his beer down, but he was now nodding along to every word that Adam spoke to Natasha, who now was listening intently. "*Javier Cortez*? Jerome's ex *Javier*? The one who stole all the money? *That* Javier?" She was taken aback by the name. I couldn't really figure out why, though. I wasn't sure who this person was. "Say Javier one more time, Tash, and I'm gonna bang my head through a wall." Ricky whined, and then took a sip of his beer. Adam reached for his glass of water and took a drink.

"Yeah, Tasha. Vince told J that Javier has been working for the King, he runs a new crew in Atlanta and makes the counterfeits. Vince was supposed to find out about our clients and convince them to give us counterfeits on runs for supplies, and then they were going to sell the supplies to get actual cash…They're trying to get rid of Jerome."

Ricky chugged another sip of his beer before speaking again. "J is fucking crazy if you ask me, he went all psycho on Vince and killed him, then dragged Tara out of the back room after he found out that someone saw us. He wasn't too happy about any of that, so he threatened to come after her. That's why we're here. We want to keep her protected."

When Ricky really wanted to show it, he was such a caring and loyal friend. He wanted to protect me just as much as Adam did, and my heart felt so full because of it. Because Adam was his family, which meant he was treating me like family, too. Natasha closed her eyes for a moment and rubbed her forehead. "So, basically Tara saw something she wasn't supposed to see, she got punished for it, and then somehow J just let you go?" I nodded my head, realizing now his crazy the entire night had been.

"Not to mention that Adam got so pissed about everything, he shot J in the leg." Ricky's hand slapped Adam's shoulder and shook it, smiling at Adam with a smile full of pride.

"Hold on, you did *what*?!"

Chapter Twenty Six: Adam

It took Tasha a good twenty minutes before she finally stopped yelling at me. She thought it was completely stupid that I shot Jerome in the leg, but I honestly thought it took some serious *gonadas* to do what I did. She didn't seem to care though, her face was still as furious now as it was twenty minutes ago.

"We know it's a lot to take in, Tasha.." Ricky said as he walked over towards her at the kitchen island, cleaning up her breakfast mess. She pulled away from Ricky once he was close enough to touch her. She wasn't in the mood, *clearly*.

"Oh, you *think*?" Natasha threw the empty carton of eggs in the trash and slammed the utensils down into the sink.

"I just have one thing to say to you two dumbasses..." she said, stopping what she was doing to look at Ricky and I.

"What the hell are you going to do now? No wonder he threatened to come after you guys, Adam *very very* stupidly shot him in the leg! What a great way to give him a motive. He will look into this… He will know you're here. You need a plan, and a good one." Tara and I still sat at the kitchen table, she was gulping down a glass of orange juice like her life depended on it. Had we not been in a life or death situation, I would've taken a moment to admire her; The way she downed the orange juice was fucking adorable.

I gave Tara a comforting smile and stood up from the table to wash my plate at the sink. "Don't worry, Tasha. Ricky and I came up with a plan earlier this morning." I gave her a proud smile as she rolled her eyes in annoyance.

"Okay, wiseass. Tell me this foolproof plan of yours."

I placed my plate and the dirty utensils that Tasha had thrown in the sink into the dishwasher, then turned around to face her, pressing my back up against the counter top. "So, Tara and Ricky are going to stay here for a few weeks, and I'm actually going to drive back to Covington tomorrow morning. I've got some things to clear up with Tío, then I'm driving to Atlanta."

Tasha snorted at my plan and almost threw the pitcher of orange juice out of her hand she began laughing so hard. "*This?* This is your plan? You're basically *begging* to be killed, Adam. C'mon, I know you're smarter than that.." She trailed off and let out a large huff before putting the pitcher in the fridge. "I wasn't done, Tasha..." I used a more serious tone now, knowing that all I wanted was to get to the important part, but she had to ruin it. "....I'm driving to Atlanta to meet up with Javier."

"*OH HELL NO, ARE YOU INSANE*? Adam what in the world are you th—" I cut off her yelling, holding my hand in the air to signal her to stop. "Tasha, enough."

She finally stopped her endless ranting and listened to me.
Thank God.

"I discussed this with Ricky, and it's final. I contacted him as soon as Ricky and I decided…" I breathed in deeply as I crossed my arms over my chest, then continued.   "…Javier said that it was all a big misunderstanding, and he has nothing against Ricky or me. His problem is *strictly* with Jerome. He said he'd have to explain more in person, but that he was sure that the King and his crew could offer us protection from Jerome, and eventually keep Tara safe enough to go home, too."

Tara stood up immediately then, obviously this had been the first time hearing about our idea, too. "Adam..." she said softly, jogging up to me and crashing herself against me. I wrapped my arms around her waist and kissed the top of her head, focusing on the sweet smell of her mango scented hair.

"Do you really think this is a good idea?" She questioned. Her sad eyes looked up at me then, her eyebrows furrowing in uncertainty.

"This is the best idea we could come up with, Mama. I will be gone for a few days– Maybe a week, but I'll be back before you know it. Ricky and I will be switching on and off for some jobs for Javier until I know it's safe enough for you to go home. That was one of the deals we made in exchange for discussing our situation and receiving protection. We now work for Javier."

I felt Tara hold her breath while resting against my chest as Natasha gasped at the information I had shared. I knew that this information was making them both a nervous wreck right now.

Tasha always knew what this business was like, but it didn't mean she liked the schemes and the dues that this business brought along with it. Once Tasha had gasped, Tara's body tensed against mine— Freezing us in time as she continued to hold on to me with everything she had.

"Whoever this Javier guy is, I'm not sure I trust him…" Tara sighed heavily, and took a moment to find her words. "I don't even know what's going on, really, but don't you find it odd that he's already having you do jobs for him?" As she questioned me, I could see Tasha nodding her head in agreement. "And what if it's a setup? How can you be sure that he'll protect us from Jerome?"

The questions Tara had were legit, in fact they made a lot of sense. I didn't know what getting involved with Javier would bring, but the possibility of getting protection from him *and* the King was far better than the alternative; Jerome finding us and killing us.

I wouldn't let it happen, I wouldn't let Tara get hurt again. I wouldn't let him come near her again. And if that meant that I had to make a deal with the devil, then so be it. For her, I would do anything.

"Mama, don't worry..." I pulled one of her arms that were wrapped around to my back, and brought her hand up close to mine, kissing it softly. ".... We've got a lot to discuss, you and I. But what I will tell both you and Tasha is to not worry. Ricky and I have it figured out and this is the best way to go in order to protect us." I looked towards the opposite end of the kitchen to Tasha, who was dialing a number on her phone. As if she could tell I was looking at her, she looked up and met my gaze. "Well if you're doing this, the least I can do is rent you a car so that you're Camero won't be identified by Jerome.."
She paused for a moment as she waited on the line for someone to pick up.

After a few minutes of what I assumed to be torture, she hung up and slammed the phone down on the counter. "I'll call back later..." she closed her eyes for a moment, and clenched her fists, slowly breathing in and out to control her anger. "....And about the Javier thing— I agree with Tara. I don't trust him, and I don't think you guys should be doing this." I shrugged, brushing off Tasha's opinions and worry.

She didn't have a right to tell me what to do anymore.

I turned toward Tara, only concerned about what her thoughts were on this whole situation. "Well... What do you think, mama?" I looked down into her sparkling blue eyes, becoming aware of how my body ignited every time I looked into them. It was like I was forming a habit, becoming completely captivated by her and everything that she is.

Her lips formed in a small smile at me calling her Mama, something that I've become to quickly enjoy. "I'm sticking with what I said, I don't know if I'd trust this guy, Adam..." Her face grew serious, almost scared for a split second, but then her face relaxed and that small little smile reappeared instantly. "...But I trust you and Ricky. So whatever you guys decide, I support it and I trust you… Just don't leave me for too long."

She smiled and blushed, obviously finding the humor in my facial expression. I could only imagine the look on my face right now, but I was shocked to say the least. I've never had many people in my life who had trusted my decisions, or fully supported me to follow through with them. This was something I've never experienced or expected.

This was something entirely new.

Forgetting about where we were, I dipped my head down as she lifted herself on her tippy-toes to meet me halfway. My lips crashed with hers, feeling the now familiar taste of her on my lips. Her lips were warm and soft, and had the sweetest taste of mango on them; They were enough to pull you in and drive you fucking mad.

I suddenly felt my phone buzzing in my back pocket, which ruined my moment with Tara. *Talk about bad timing.* I didn't even bother to look at the caller ID, I groaned as I broke away from Tara in agony as I reached into my back pocket for my phone. I wrapped my arm around her waist as I answered the call. "Hello?"

"Is this Adam?" A disguised voice came from the other end of the phone. There was no way in hell that I was going to admit who I was. It could have been one of Jerome's guys for all I fucking knew. "No, uh sorry, I think you have the wrong number."

The person on the other end of the phone ignored my answer though, because before I hung up, they replied again, with force this time. "Javier Cortez has sent a request requiring protection services for you and two others. We were given your contact information, and you are needed tomorrow night to discuss the logistics of your request, as well as your connection to Jerome Santiago."

None of this shit made sense. *Who the hell was calling me? What did they want? And how did they know I was in connection with Javier?*

I needed some answers. "And who *exactly* needs to meet with me?"

The person on the other end of the line lingered with an answer, but soon spoke confidently. "The enemy of an enemy is a friend, Mr. Rodriguez." The disguised voice echoed hauntingly before continuing, "You are officially summoned."

I knew what was happening now, like my life was flashing before my eyes. Javier really *did* get in contact with him.

This was his call to meet with me.

This was going to change everything.

"1397 Parkway East, it is an abandoned building. Get dropped off there, then walk under the bridge. When you see the wolf's mark, stay in position. Your discussion will happen once you are there." I felt like I couldn't breathe. In my entire seven years of being in his business, I had never met him. In fact, I always thought it was some washed up story the guys used to tell to intimidate us.

I thought it wasn't real.

But *it is*.

"Oh, and Adam..." The strange, deep voice came from the other end of the phone again, ".... Do not be late. He expects you at midnight." And after the last word left the disguised person's mouth, the other line hung up and I felt my entire body freeze.

No way did this just happen.

"Yo, buddy. Why does it look like you've seen a ghost? You turned whiter than Tara." He joked. Ricky walked to me now, clapping my shoulder with his arm, and Tara scooting her body closer to mine to provide comfort.

"*Adam?* What just happened?" Tasha's voice sounded wobbly and uncontrolled. She was nervous. She had no idea just how nervous I was. I was so nervous that my entire body felt completely frozen up. I closed my eyes for a second, put my phone back into my pocket, and rubbed my forehead with my hand.

"I've been summoned." Ricky and Tasha gasped so loud it was like those three words took all of the oxygen out of the room.

"Adam? You've been summoned? What does that mean?"
Tara was tugging on my shirt now, curious and asking for clarity. "Tare..." Ricky said, saving me from having to explain. "I don't think you understand how serious this shit is."

I was glad Rick stepped up; I was still in shock and could barely breathe, so I couldn't explain it to her right at this moment. "Understand? Understand what?" She said, her voice now sounding just as unsteady as Tasha's did.

"The King, Tara...." Tasha said, her expression dark and serious now, "....He's been summoned by the King."

Chapter Twenty Seven: Tara

I had never felt so overwhelmed and uninformed in my entire life. This was one of the few moments that I've ever felt both of those at the same time.

It didn't happen often.

I was just introduced to Adam's world, and to be honest, I was just trying to wrap my mind around what happened with Jerome, so adding all of the other stuff made my mind want to explode. I couldn't take much of what happened during breakfast yesterday morning with Ricky, Natasha and Adam. It was too much information to try to wrap around my head, and too much that I didn't quite understand yet.

All I could do was trust Ricky and Adam and hope that they knew what they were doing. I had to believe in that.

*

I stood there in Natasha's driveway, holding onto Adam as he did the same to me. It was time for him to go back to Covington while I stayed here with Ricky and Natasha.

It was hard not to be with him, even if it had only been a few days. I couldn't imagine not being here without him— it felt so awkward already. The rental car was right next to us as he stood there, leaning up against it. "I will be back as soon as I can, Tara. I promise."

This was one of the few times he's called me my name, so I knew how serious he was about it. I trusted that he meant what he said. "Okay..." I said quietly, as I tried to stop myself from crying and I pushed myself closer to him to feel the comfort of him.

I had known Adam for a few weeks and yet, it was like I had known him my entire life. And the truth was that I didn't want him to go, and I was afraid of what would happen if he did.

As I rested my head against his warm chest, the familiar aroma of him flooded my senses. The sweet scent of pine and mahogany caused a familiar chill to race down my spine. He made me feel safe, he made me feel cared for, and even—*loved*.

"I know this kinda sounds weird, but bare with me for a second..." I said softly to him, allowing the heat of the sun to warm my back and I continued to cuddle into Adam's arms. I felt his chest vibrate as he let out a hearty laugh. "Go ahead, mama."

I took a deep breath, and then pulled away from him so that I could look him in the eyes.

"Is it weird that I've known you for a few weeks and yet saying goodbye to you is the hardest thing I've had to do?" Maybe I was pushing it a little bit, but I couldn't help but be honest. It was true— I was going to miss him.

"No, that's not weird at all..." He said as his lips parted, as though he didn't know what to say. "... but can I tell *you* something that might seem weird?" He gave me a small smile before he spoke again. "I think... you might be the only person who would have this much understanding about what I do for a living.." He hesitated, "... and I want to thank you for that— for staying and trusting in me." He kissed my forehead softly and let his lips linger there for a moment. I felt the soft vibration of his voice as he spoke his next words against my forehead, "You're my girl... I'd fucking do anything for you."

I felt my heart soar at his words. That was all that I needed to know to reassure me that we both were on the same page. He had felt the weird, exciting, and exhilarating feelings that I did, and it made me feel less crazy. "I know I won't see you for a few days, but I will call you." He kissed the top of my head, and then pulled me in for a hug. He then grabbed my hand and walked us towards the car. "And don't let Ricky annoy you too much." He smirked, trying to fight laughter.

He opened the driver's side door of the car and stood there, looking as handsome as ever.

My mind flashed back to the night we met, remembering his strong muscular arms carrying me from the bar. It made me think of how our attraction felt immediate— a flame that blazed into a scorching inferno.

I walked closer towards him and kissed him softly, tugging at his hair in the process. He let out a small moan as he bit my bottom lip with such tenderness. I slid my tongue to meet him, and I was soon pulled into him with a force of passion, as if he needed to be as close as he could to me. Our tension had me overcome. His presence was all enthralling, all consuming, and I felt drunk on him.

He suddenly pulled away from me and stared at me with a dark, burning desire in his eyes; The same one that I had seen several times before.

"*Don't*." He demanded. His expression grew dark as he gazed at me with his dark, auburn eyes. "Or you'll make me stay." His lips formed into a small smile, but his eyes looked like he had been tortured by the thought of leaving.

"I wish you could stay."

I lifted my head as he leaned his forehead on mine and our breath moved in time together.

"I know, Mama." He whispered softly and hovered his lips over mine. It drove me insane at how much I wanted his lips on mine, and how easily I would give all of myself to him.

As if he read my mind, he kissed me slowly and deepened the kiss at his own pace. Our kiss was long, and full of everything that we wanted to say to one another without using words. Time seemed to stop around us, allowing us to be fully encapsulated by one another and proving that nothing else in the world could take us away from the connection that had been there since the day we had met.

It was infinite, and so were we.

Once he parted from me, he leaned down and placed his forehead on mine. We stood there a moment, as he shut his eyes tightly, like he was in physical pain. "I will do anything to protect you." He pulled his forehead off of mine, kissed me on the cheek, and got into the rental car. Then he was gone.

Two weeks later

"So Tare Bear, what do you want to do tonight?"
Ricky was sitting in the living room of the guest house— a normal occurrence that had been happening for the last couple of weeks— as he clicked through Netflix on the flatscreen.

The truth was that no one called me Tare Bear except for my dad. But Ricky very quickly became like family to me, and so him calling me my childhood nickname didn't seem like such a bad thing.

I plopped down on the couch next to him with a bowl of popcorn and grabbed a blanket near me. "Can we just watch *friends* or something? I need something that'll make me laugh. Adam and I haven't talked in like almost a week." He grabbed the popcorn bowl and put a few pieces in his hands. He chucked the popcorn at my face, for what— I don't know. Ricky was just being Ricky.

"What the *hell* was that for?" I said, my mouth hanging open as I tried to stop myself from laughing.

"Well I'm offended that you think the tv show *Friends* could make you laugh more than me." He mimicked being stabbed in the heart, and then laid there limp for a minute, being *dramatic*.

I laughed at his crazy, yet funny humor. He had always done whatever he could to make his friends laugh. He was such a source of light for all of us through the difficult times we were experiencing.

"Okay *drama queen*, you're the funniest person ever. Are we good?" I grabbed his arm and patted it, going along with the silliness that is Ricky.

"Fine, you win. We'll watch *Friends*. But I pick the episodes." He handed me back the popcorn and grabbed the remote, trying to find the show on Netflix.

*

We were now in the middle of our fourth episode, as we both started to recognize that we were becoming binge watchers.

It was the episode where Phoebe tries to seduce Chandler into proving that he was dating Monica. This episode was one of my favorites, but it wasn't surprising, every episode was.

"So..." I started off, trying to get some answers that I had been wondering about since I was brought into this entire drug dealing world pretty quickly. I was hoping that Ricky could answer some of the questions I had been having because I knew he would tell me honestly, no matter what I asked of him.

"I was wondering…" I asked curiously, "How did you and Adam get into the business anyway?" Ricky rolled his eyes jokingly, probably realizing that this was just the beginning of my interrogation.

"Welp, I should've guessed that you were going to ask questions sooner or later." He cleared his throat and repositioned himself on the couch to face me.

"So where do I start?" He looked puzzled, as if he wasn't sure where to begin, but any information I could get would help me understand the whole business better.

He coughed before continuing, "I've, um— I've always been kind of an unlucky guy. My birth mom was a single mother, and put me into the system when I was a baby. I bounced around from foster home to foster home for a while until I ended up in a permanent home when I was fourteen. The family wasn't bad…They were really nice."

"I got fed, I had clothes on my back and everything, but the family just didn't have a lot of money. One of the sons was a year older, so we always walked to school together. We became really close, so I started to call Matt my brother. I started to hang out with him because at the time I had been new to the school and didn't really know anyone."

He took a drink of his beer and gulped it down quickly. "And I became close with his group of friends, which were a bunch of stoners, but then my brother graduated and I was alone my senior year. I started dealing some light stuff with some guys, and then got majorly pulled in. It was funny in a way, though. Once I was really in the business, I got to meet the crew that we've been with up until now. Jerome was my age at the time, he was just a little shy bitch that hid behind his older cousin. It's funny how he is the way he is nowadays... He wasn't always on his high horse."

I sat there in awe, I was amazed to know that Ricky, like I was, had been in foster care. Not many people knew what that was like.

"I didn't know you were in foster care." I said, in shock. "I was too, until my parents adopted me when I was five."

I didn't make it a habit of telling people that... I wasn't sure if Adam even had known about that. But I had begun to feel so comfortable around Ricky, that I knew he wouldn't judge me.

"You hardly seem like a girl who was in foster care. You have a really lucky life."

I shook my head in argument. My life wasn't *always lucky*. It was far from it for the first five years of my life.

"It wasn't always easy, I still have crappy memories from my birth mother and the day I got taken away. I was really young and that stuff sticks with you."

He simply nodded his head in agreement, but didnt say anything else. We both fully understood one another, and knew that no matter how much time we spent in the system, we still both shared that similarity, and that was something that connected us in a way that I hadn't had with anyone before.

"Thanks for telling me about that. It feels kind of refreshing to know that someone gets it…" My voice trailed off towards the end of that sentence, still in disbelief that I had found a friend who had understood what I went through.

Ricky took a drink of his beer before speaking again, this time, looking like he was stressed.

"No, It's okay, I completely agree with you. It feels weird to be 100% candid with someone about your past… It feels weird to not have to hide it…" Ricky hesitated, but I found him staring at me, almost as if he had been in a daydream. I coughed slightly to get his attention, and he quickly got knocked out of his trance.

"Anyway, I had been in the business for around three years and I had met Adam in school. We became pretty close, but he was a part of the football team and the basketball team, and I was kind of a loner. To be honest, I didn't think I deserved to be his friend." He looked down at the floor for a moment, as if he was remembering himself and Adam during that time.

"He stuck with me…" He smiled softly at the thought. "He even convinced me to join the basketball team my Senior year when he was a Junior. We stayed good friends through the years, and he's like a true brother to me… I'd be lost without him." I smiled at Ricky's heartfelt words, knowing that Adam's and Ricky's friendship would last forever.

"When I was twenty, I was pouring in some serious cash from the new stuff I was selling. I got into selling coke and Molly. Adam knew something was going on, though. He worked at his uncle's bar almost every night and barely made half of what I did. So I introduced him to the business... very lightly at first. We started with weed, addies, sometimes we'd supply Xanny's too. I never felt completely comfortable introducing him into it, but he always insisted on it. He kept telling me that he needed to make sure his uncle Joe could keep the bar and his house. That's how I knew how awesome of a guy he was." Listening to how selfless Adam had been during that time, in order to save his family was both heartwarming— but also heartbreaking.

"Of course, Joe never knew what he was doing...He just lied and said he got a job with the city cutting grass."

"We kind of became a dynamic duo after that. We always went on runs together, and then eventually Adam caught up with me, and was bringing in the same amount of money as I was. Jerome ended up taking over the crew once his cousin died, and it's never been the same since. It's like everything shifted. Adam has always thought of the day when he would get out of this and be able to go to college and get a real job..." Ricky sighed; I could see the disappointment he had for his best friend. Adam was never able to get out of the business, even though it seemed as though in his heart he never wanted it in the first place. Ricky looked at me with sadness in his eyes, before he continued. "Adam..." he lingered, "He wants the wife and the kids to come home to... But this business... it takes everything out of you. It takes over a huge portion of your life and It's hard to get out once you're in it."

We remained in silence for a few minutes as we continued to watch the episode of friends and I munched on popcorn. I continued to stay in my thoughts about the whole situation. It was so heartbreaking to hear how Adam and Ricky were so young and made a decision without realizing that it would affect the rest of their lives.

All of this information had made a lot of my thoughts clearer, and I felt like I was starting to understand Adam and this business a little bit more. "But who is this Javier guy? And the King?"

Ricky grabbed his beer and finished it, then walked over to the small kitchen to throw away the bottle. He grabbed another out of the fridge before returning to the couch. "Javier is a guy that Jerome used to date. They got into the business around the same time as me, so I was around for all of it. Javier and Jerome we're constantly with one another. They were stuck up each other's asses— *quite literally...*" He smirked at his joke, and took another swig of his beer. "So a couple of years go by and our profits start decreasing. Jerome got really mad and thought that someone was ripping him off, so he went through each one of our deals to see which one it is that's ripping him off. It ended up being one of his good friends, Jinx. He died because Javier misinformed him about the price of the drug he was distributing… Javier set him up and got him killed." Ricky shook his head, clearly disgusted by the information he had just shared. I couldn't help it, but my stomach started hurting, too.

"That's when Adam and I realized how serious this was, and how we never could fuck anything up, or that could be us someday. And a couple of months later, Jerome found out that Javier was taking the money from him. Javier took off and Jerome tried to track him down, but by the time he got close, the King stepped in and it was like Javier fell off the face of the earth. Until now."

"We just found out that he's in charge of a new crew in Atlanta who buys supplies with counterfeits, then resells them to get the real money. It's pretty smart, actually. So the King and Javier are connected, and they're trying to wash out Jerome's business. They're trying to get rid of his crew, too. If Jerome's crew is out, then the King has control over basically the entire city of Atlanta and some of the other Burroughs in Georgia. That's what the King wants. He wants to be in control."

He glanced at his phone quickly before returning to the conversation, looking up to meet my gaze. "Are you overwhelmed *yet*? I don't want to keep talking about this all damn night." He smirked as he drank his beer, as he looked at me from the corner of his eye.

I stuck my tongue out at him, and shook my head. I still wanted more information. This was a great education lesson for me, and I was using it to my advantage. "Who's the King then?"

Ricky almost choked on his beer, trying to control the laugh he let out in that instant. "There's no stopping you, *is there*?" He said as he shook his head and was still coughing through his words, "But— I wish I knew. We've never met him. We've heard things about him. Jerome's cousin is the only one I knew of in our crew who met him. When you think of a King, you think of royalty, right?"

I nodded in response, attempting to follow along with Ricky's explanation.

"Well think of it this way: You can't request a meeting with the King unless you're high up on the social chain. If you're a nobody, chances are that he doesn't even know you exist. As long as you're pulling the money in and doing your job, that's all that matters. If he finds out about you and wants to talk to you, or you're invited somewhere, it's considered like an honor."

This was starting to make so much sense. I couldn't believe that I didn't catch on earlier. This business kind of seemed a little too easy.

"So when that person called Adam, and he said he was being summoned, that meant that the King wanted to meet with him, which was a good thing?"

Ricky nodded his head and smiled, then lightly tapped my leg.

"You're catching on quick, Tare Bear. I'm proud of you…" He paused, "Wait... are you sure *you're* not the King?"

We both laughed at that and I couldn't help but shake my head. He was a great person for filling me in on the things that I didn't know, but still making me laugh while doing it.

"No, Ricky, I'm not the King. I've asked too many questions about what you guys do to be the king. But it's easy to figure out, it's all quite midevil if you ask me." I shrugged my shoulders and grabbed a handful of popcorn and tossed it at his face, just like he did to me earlier.

"Alright, that's it. *It's on.*"

He grabbed my legs that were curled up on the couch and pulled them straight, and pulled me all the way down on the couch as I screamed and laughed in response.

He started tickling my sides as I tried to fight him off, as I continued to laugh hysterically, having fun for the first time in a while.

"Ricky... Stop it!!" I said through laughter. I tried to kick my knees up, but he had me pinned down like a wrestler on a mat. *Friends* was still playing in the background and the smell of popcorn drifted through the air. "Stop it. Stop it." I was trying to control my breath, but was overcome by a fit of laughter.

"Alright, I'm done. I'm done. As long as you say you surrender and I win." I opened my eyes then, as I realized that he was laying directly on top of me, and his dirty blonde hair caved into gravity as it flopped on his forehead.

His green eyes were gazing right into mine, but I wasn't sure what was happening at the moment. His lips formed into a small smile— one that was so genuine and *real*. I remembered that I only really got to know him well in these past two weeks without Adam here; He was someone entirely different with him gone.

The truth was, with Adam gone all I had was Ricky. He made me laugh, and when we talked he was truly present. He listened to what I had to say without question, and I really enjoyed his company. He seemed so grounded and at ease that no matter who was around him, he was a calming presence to be close to. I had begun to feel a comfort in that; having someone that I could enjoy the quiet with, someone who understood where I came from, and the experiences who had made me into the person I am. I had grown such a genuine love for Ricky over the past few weeks, and he had become such a great friend to me. The love I had for him wasn't romantic, but it was the type of love that felt genuine and real, and pure. He very quickly became one of my favorite people, and I was grateful for his friendship.

Ricky had looked lost in my eyes, like he was admiring them, and I could tell *whatever* he was feeling was more than what I expected. He leaned down, inching closer to me, as his lips started to move closer to mine. I panicked and tried to push him away from me, but then we heard someone clear their throat, startling us by the sound.

"Well…doesn't this look *cozy*." I looked to the doorway to see Natasha standing there with a tub of ice cream, bowls and a convenient store bag.

Ricky and I shuffled to both ends of the couch now, attempting to not make it obvious that we both were about to cross the line. "Oh, don't stop on my account." Tasha said as she walked to the kitchen to set up her little ice cream sundae bar for us.

"Sorry, Tash." Ricky grabbed his beer and swigged it down, now walking over to her in the kitchen. "Tash, it wasn't what it looked like—" I attempted to say, but she cut me off before I could explain.

"Well don't apologize to me, I'm not the one who is in Atlanta right now trying to find a way to protect your asses." She grabbed a scooper from the drawer and began scooping ice cream out of the carton and into the bowls. I continued to stare at Tasha as she stood there with a coy smirk on her lips, and Ricky looked like his life had flashed before his eyes.

"C'mon Tara, here's some ice cream. I'm sure that'll help to cool you down from that red blush you've got plastered on your face." It took everything in me to bite my tongue. I was a guest here, and I knew that if I said one wrong thing, Natasha could easily kick me out. I needed to learn to just keep my mouth shut. I felt my anxiety beginning to seep in through the cracks, pushing its way through, causing an infestation.

Out of habit, I frantically reached for the band on my wrist. I needed release, I needed to stop these feelings; the feeling of embarrassment, of shame, of fear. I needed to stop it all. But I realized that I couldn't do that here; I couldn't expose this part of myself to people who wouldn't understand why I did it in the first place.

Breathe.

In an attempt to distract myself, I walked over towards the kitchen to get my bowl of ice cream. As I walked closer to the kitchen table, my phone began to ring. I pulled my phone out to see Adam's name on the caller ID. I quickly answered it— excited to finally get to talk to him.

"*Hey, you.*" He said from the other line.

"*Hey.*"

"*I'm sorry I haven't called..*" He said with a deep, sultry voice.

I looked up from the floor to see Ricky and Tasha staring at me.

"*No, it's okay. I was worried about you.*"

I noticed Tasha snort as she focused back on scooping out the ice cream. "*Clearly.*" She said sarcastically. All I could do was roll my eyes at her comment; She didn't know anything.

"*So what are you guys doing right now?*" He asked, keeping the conversation flowing.

"*We're just watching TV in the guest house. What about you?*"

And before I could answer, the guest house door swung open and Adam walked in through the doorway with a bouquet of roses in his hand and a bright smile on his face. He held the phone back up to his ear, and motioned for me to do the same.

"You asked me what I was doing... Well, I happen to be looking at the most beautiful and amazing woman I have ever seen."

I felt tears spring in my eyes as I ran to the front door to see him.
God, I missed him.
I missed his beautiful brown eyes, and his curly dark brown hair. I missed his beautiful smile. I missed his voice.

"Well, *that* was a close one." Tasha said, clearly referring to the moment that she witnessed Ricky on top of me. Apparently she thought she was funny. "What was a close one Tash?" Adam's hands wrapped around my waist as he held on to me tightly, and then looked in her direction. "Oh— Uh, Nothing..." She said with a small squeak in her voice, "...Just almost dropped ice cream on my shirt.

Chapter Twenty Eight: Adam

The trip back to Atlanta was definitely interesting.

To be honest, I didn't expect to be gone as long as I was. I figured I would be gone a few days max.

Not two weeks.

Throughout the two weeks all I kept thinking about was the next time that I would get to see Tara. No matter what crazy shit I ended up in, I focused on Tara.

Ricky kept me updated every few days on what was going on in Savannah at Tasha's place, but all that I had been worried about was Tara; If she was handling things well, if she was eating, and if Tasha had finally backed the fuck off of her a little bit. Not being able to see or talk to Tara put into perspective just how much I fucking needed her. I craved her. Everything she did amazed me, every part of her made me breathless. I couldn't fucking understand it, and yet, I didn't really care to. All I knew was that, without her, my life had been a damn nightmare— she had been the one that turned it into a life that was actually worth living.

All of this bullshit had been for her; Every move I made from now on affected her, every little mistake I made meant harm would come to her. I couldn't allow it, I couldn't even fathom it. All of the trials I had been given by Javier so that I could prove my loyalty and worthiness to him had been worth it. I had to do whatever I could to prove to Javier and the King that I was on their side, and I would do whatever it took. I would do it a thousand times over if I had to.

Even though I had been summoned by the King, it didn't mean that I would *actually* meet him.

I had to prove my worth before the summoning could be validated. If I passed whatever tests Javier had for me, then it meant I would be *considered* to meet the King. Javier had a way to remind me that just because I had been summoned, it didn't mean that I would get the privilege of actually meeting *Him*. And while Javier took over an hour explaining all of the legalities, I was beginning to feel my brain twist into a motherfucking knot.

What Javier clearly didn't understand was that I was a simple guy— I always had been. I don't cause any problems, unless there's a problem to cause.

Luckily, the past two weeks had gone so smoothly that I didn't have to worry about repercussions or what information Javier had been giving to the King. I knew I was doing my part, and I was doing it well.

*

My arm was now wrapped around Tara's waist, her familiar smell of honey had been radiating from her, creating an intimate space between us. "I'm so glad you came back. I've missed you." Tara's angelic voice vibrated her whole body, allowing me to feel her sweet voice speak against my chest.

"I've missed you too, Mama."

Ricky stood in the kitchen by Tasha who was scooping out ice cream. I was sure that Tasha and Tara had time to get acquainted, and I found myself hopeful that Tasha's attitude toward Tara had finally stopped. Ricky looked over to me, nodded his head to greet me, and grabbed a bowl of ice cream off the counter.

"Hey man, how was it down in Atlanta? Everything good?" He took a huge spoonful of ice cream and shoved it into his mouth as he plopped down on the couch while Tara and I walked over toward the kitchen island to get ice cream. "Everything is fine. I'm gonna need to go down there by Friday. Javier's got a lot of supply runs this weekend and he needs you to catch them up. That's why I've been gone so long, I got the little bitch work of picking up everyone else's slack."

I grabbed a bowl of ice cream from Tasha, who looked up at me with bright eyes and smiled widely at me. "We've missed you, Adam." She leaned in and gave me a quick hug before handing Tara a bowl of her own.

"Well man, that sucks. I'm gonna hate to have to leave, I was just getting used to it here. But as long as we keep Tara safe and get her the protection she needs to go back home, then I'm all for it."

I'd be lying if I said that I didn't notice the awkward tension the second I walked in the door, or the way Ricky's eyes kept flashing towards Tara. I'd be fucking stupid if I didn't notice her cheeks to turn a light pink color, either.

I brushed it off, though, chalking it up to just being paranoid, and it was because I had missed so much that I was noticing tiny details and twisting them into what they weren't.

But a small part of me knew there was something I wasn't seeing. "So, Adam.." Tara began to speak, patting the couch cushion next to her, "what did you do these past couple weeks?" I noticed her scoot closer to me on the couch, needing to feel a part of me for comfort, just as I needed it from her.

I put my arm around her, completely ignoring my bowl of ice cream for the moment. "Well if I told you, you might not look at me the same way. This is a new world for you, I don't want to freak you out more than you already are." And that was true. Within the past three weeks, we had gone from meeting one another in a bar to running from a drug gang. This wasn't exactly something to be talking about freely.

Not that I didn't think she could take it, I knew she was strong, that much was fucking evident. I just didn't want to overburden her.

As much as I didn't want to admit it, I grew to care for her in a short amount of time, and I didn't want to say or do anything that would jeopardize that anymore than it already was. She proved me right, though— with the thought of how strong she was. She shook her head, not accepting my refusal.

"No, I can take it. Just tell us, we need to know." I let out a large huff, and softly rubbed her shoulder before speaking:

"Okay…" I hesitated before continuing, "So the day I left, I went down to the Skull and visited Uncle Joe for a day. I stuck around and helped him out with the bar, and he was short a bartender so I figured it'd be a good way to make extra money. That night was busier than usual, so I ended up making like two hundred in tips. I packed some extra clothes of mine, too. I didn't meet with Javier until the next night. We met in Atlanta in the abandoned movie theater building. The cops don't drive past there anymore, so they have meetings there I guess. By the way Rick, when you drive there, park in the back gate so that if someone were to pass, they wouldn't see you."

Tasha finally joined the group and sat down on the bench opposite of the couch. She was eating her ice cream but kept her attention on every word I was saying.

I guess it was important to tell them.

They had the right to know about my two weeks there.

"So, I met up with Javier and his crew at the movie theater. Let me tell you, it's so much more than we thought it was. They have an entire system for these counterfeits. There has to be around five million in counterfeits just sitting in stacks in one of the theaters. I thought that I shouldn't have been seeing that. I thought it was a little weird that they were introducing me to that right away, but they were testing me. They wanted to see if I'd repeat it back to Jerome. Javier was a little bit skeptical at first. He didn't know why I was there, but I told him about the need for protection and that J had gotten out of control, and he offered help. He said he would always come through as long as we did.

He completely acted like Jerome didn't exist though, so I didn't even bring anything up regarding him. I knew that they thought of J's crew as the enemy, but god, they *really* do. Javier set me through a series of trials. The first was that I needed to go on three supply runs an hour away, and make it through each of them and make it back within an hour and a half. I physically didn't think it was possible, but I did what I had to do. I wasn't going to ruin this for us. The second was tougher, I had to learn how to make the counterfeits and process over $50,000 by the next day without help. I was glad I learned how to make them properly enough to check through the system, because if they weren't, Javier said I would have been done, and we would have been screwed.

And the last trial— um, I don't know if I should repeat this."

The three of them were completely silent now, afraid of the words that I didn't say. "Adam, man, just tell us. We know how much you have to test your limits for the king. It's okay.." I nodded my head, and glanced down at my now melted bowl of ice cream. What I hadn't noticed though, was that no one was eating theirs any longer, either.

I felt Tara's arm wrap around me and her head rested on my shoulder. I was glad to be back here with her, and everything I had to do these past two weeks was for her. I want her to feel protected. I want her to feel safe enough to be able to go back home.

"Uh, well the third trial took the longest to prepare for.. that's why I was gone so long. We had to set up a plan and a roadmap so we wouldn't get caught. It took us about a week to fully construct a plan, and to feel confident in it. I didn't necessarily want to do it, but I've been summoned, so I need to meet the King. The other night, we had one of Javier's guys drive a service truck with $150,000 in counterfeits in the back.
Javier and two other guys met me, and—-"

"Dude..." Ricky's eyes went wide, clearly knowing what happened, despite me not wanting to admit what I did.

"I know, shut up I'm getting there. We— we robbed Huntington Financial and replaced the counterfeits in the safe for the real cash. It checks out in the U.S. registry. People will not know the difference about their money, unless they try to deposit money into their account through an

ATM. That's the only place it doesn't check out." I felt the air in the room get thinner, knowing what I did was a new level of crime for me- and I wasn't proud of it at all, I was disappointed in myself for doing it, but I knew that if I was successful, then everything would work out. "I didn't know Javier's plan included us holding hostages at gunpoint—" I cut off, unable to finish the sentence.

"So that was *you?!* Dude, they have a search warrant out for you guys. It was all over the news.." Ricky was breathing heavily, trying not to give away any idea of how nervous he was about going in next. "… There were casualties. Adam, did you—"

I stayed there silent, unable to answer the question. Ricky had already known that I wasn't proud of the things I had done these past few weeks, especially the past few days. I didn't need to say anything. He just knew. So did Tash. But Tara? I couldn't bear to see the look on her face when she realized that the old Adam had been quickly changed; he had now turned into a killer.

Tara pulled herself away from me, but I didn't blame her. I just hated the way it felt to have her pull away from me like that. I never wanted that to happen again.
I didn't want to disappoint her like that, ever. Her eyes went wide, but were glossed over with tears.

"Well, I'm not surprised." Natasha said from the kitchen, washing all of the ice cream bowls out and drying them.

"What do you mean you're not surprised?" Tara's voice got a little sharper, like she was on edge. Natasha shot daggers towards Tara before continuing.

"It's Javier Cortez. He stole money from someone he used to consider "the love of his life", what makes any of you think that he would view anything else differently? In my book, he's worse to deal with than Jerome. The amount of people he's killed just for the fun of it? I mean the man's a raging psycho. The only advantage you guys have in this case is getting close to the king. If it weren't for that, I would've told you to get out and your asses would be halfway to Denmark by now."

Although Natasha and I were no longer together, I was glad to have her rational thinking. She thought of things no one else would think of, and really made you get a new perspective on a situation. She had always done that since I've known her. That was one of the things I continued to admire her for.

Ricky must have thought Tasha was funny with her whole Denmark idea, because he was sinking onto the couch as he was laughing.
I was so glad he found some kind of light in this situation.

Tara got up from the couch, and walked over to the kitchen. She pulled a glass out of the cupboard and filled it up with water and took a sip of it before focusing back on my eyes gazing at her. "Ricky, I don't really think it's that funny."
She slammed the glass on the counter and walked over to us sitting on the couch.
"How dare you laugh at something this serious, Ricky. I thought that you actually grew up there

for a second. It's nice to know that the little immature asshole is still there." It was safe to say that Tara wasn't taking this whole situation well.

Just as I had suspected.

I couldn't blame her for being angry about it, she was used to her spoiled lifestyle with her perfect car and perfect school and her perfect suburb where nothing could ever go wrong.

I couldn't blame her because of her lifestyle. She wasn't used to this fucking shit that I was involved in. "Tara, listen—" I tried, but she cut me off. It wasn't good to mess with her now, that much I knew.

"No! No, don't even tell me to calm down! I have *every* right to be upset right now. I knew you broke the law by distributing illegal drugs, and I *still* allowed you to bring me up here to protect me. I have trusted you through this process to make me safe. I have done nothing but supported your decisions about this. But hurting innocent people for someone's acceptance? That is where I draw the line." Apparently she didn't care that there were two other people in the apartment, she was ready to fight. And the truth was that I knew just how bad it was. That I contributed to something that made three innocent people die. So I couldn't blame her. In a matter of weeks I had turned from someone who wouldn't think of killing anyone, to a murderer.

So I let her get her feelings off of her chest for a moment.

"Tara, listen, I am so so sorry. I would do anything to protect you, you know that. I had to listen to what Javier ordered. I had no choice."

I couldn't admit that I was in a nervous wreck when the whole thing went down. Hell, I was basically shitting my pants a week prior. But she truly didn't understand the gravity of the situation we were in. It's like she thought Jerome would come after her and that would be the end. It wasn't going to be. He would make her suffer to hurt me— He'd do whatever he could to make a show out of it and then he would kill her, and I could never let that happen.

Her ice blue eyes drew thinner, her hands began to shake slightly, and her face turned blood red.

"You had no choice!? You know what would happen if you get caught? Life in a state prison, or worse! I would *never* see you again, and not to mention, I wouldn't get the protection from the crew, so Jerome would come after me pretty easily. Did you think that through before you went to rob a bank and became a killer for Javier?!"

I stood up, ready to defend myself. I was ready to tell her that I had done *everything* for her; That I would end anyone's life for her, if that meant she was safe. I had risked my judgment, my conscience, my morals for *her*. Javier was a sketchy dude, sure. But the King was someone we could trust. The king was unbiased despite me previously being in Jerome's crew. I was sure that He was willing to accept me after leaving, and as much as I didn't trust Javier, I trusted the king with every fucking fiber of my being.

I walked over towards her, trying to reach out, but she just continued to push me away. "No, Adam. I don't want to talk right now. I can't even begin to understand why you thought you needed to put yourself in that situation. I just— I just need some time to think about this."

I grabbed her hand and pulled her back around to face me. I couldn't let this entire ridiculous process ruin what we had. "I'm so sorr— I'm so so sorry" I held her face in my hands as I wiped a tear falling down her cheek. I rested my forehead on hers as I plead for her to give me a chance. "Baby. Please listen to me, please. I love you, I promise I will do whatever I can to fix this, okay?" I tried to hold back the tears, to hold back the urgency in my voice. But I did *need* her. And I did *love* her. I felt my voice crack as I spoke: "Please, can we talk about this?" I had hoped she heard the seriousness in my voice. I had hoped she'd reconsider and finally give me a chance to fix this.

She reached up to my hands that had been holding her and slowly pried my hands off of her. She slowly backed away from me as tears began to stream down her cheeks. .

"You know— my birthday started out great, and my greatest gift has been you. But then you do something like that, and it makes me wonder if I ever really knew you at all." She sniffled as she spoke, but her voice remained strong. "I can't even look at you right now. Happy Birthday to me, right?" Before my brain would click with what she had just said, she ran into the master bedroom and slammed the door.

Due to my obsession with Javier's crew and trying to keep us protected, I had completely forgotten about something just as, if not, more important.

It was Tara's 21st birthday, today.
And I didn't think I could have ruined it anymore than I just had.

Chapter Twenty Nine: Tara

I needed to get out of here. I couldn't take it anymore. The thought of being so wrapped up in this crazy world drove me insane. It was something that I wasn't prepared for. It was something that I no longer wanted— even if it meant not being around Adam or Ricky. Although they had quickly become an important part of my life, I had to choose: either stay in this position and watch the man I love become someone I don't recognize, or get out of this situation all together and go home.

Going home sounded like the best option to me at the moment.

I picked my phone up off of the bed, needing someone to confide in, needing to hear that everything was going to be okay. I dialed my mom's number, but it went straight to voicemail. I dialed her another three times, and it did just the same. She had a habit of not answering me in the evenings, it was like she was always too busy to talk to me when I needed her the most.

I grabbed my bags from the corner of the bedroom and threw them on the bed. I would just have to call an Uber or something to pick me up. I could feel my anxiety rising with each passing second, becoming like an infection, taking over my body. It was like the walls were closing in, and I felt myself begin to panic.

I heard a light knock on the door, and saw Natasha's small figure squeeze through the doorway. "Hey, can we talk for a second?" Her eyes were full of sympathy, and her voice was soft and calm. I couldn't express what I wanted to say, so I just nodded my head.

I pulled my bags off of my bed and threw them back in the corner so we could sit on the bed. Although Natasha had me at my limit of annoyance today, I wanted to give her a chance to talk to me. I still didn't really know her, and I thought she deserved that much. She walked over to the bed and plopped herself down, now turning on her stomach and looking at me on the opposite side of the bed. "Adam was planning on running in after you but I stopped him." She glanced down at her nails now, checking to see if any of them looked cracked. "I figured we needed to have a girl chat." I smiled simply at her, not knowing exactly what to say.

"So all jokes aside, I don't really know what's going on between you and Ricky, I'm going to result that to being caught up in the moment. It's not my place to tell Adam, or to scold you guys about it. I've been there before, and I'm the last person who can judge." I felt my breath become heavy. If I was being honest, I don't know what really happened between Ricky and I either, but I knew I didn't have romantic feelings for him. I had realized, though, that Ricky and Adam were two completely different men, but at the same time, they both made me feel special in their own way.

With Adam, it was like I was the center of his world, like he was only focused on me and while I loved that commitment, it scared me because of how quick our relationship played out. And I felt as if I truly didn't know who he was becoming. Was this something that could last long term despite what he's done? I didn't know. All I knew was that I felt like a part of me was missing whenever he wasn't around.

Weirdly enough, the first impression I had of Ricky was that he was a pig, and then it grew into a great friendship. He was someone that I felt like I could be completely open and honest with, and I knew I wouldn't be judged for it. My mind was spinning in circles. I didn't know how to feel, I didn't know what I wanted. I knew that I loved Adam, and yet, he now terrified me. It scared me to think that he would literally *kill* for me—kill innocent people.

It was like Natasha read my mind; she knew that my head was spinning all over the place in confusion. "I just wanted you to know that regardless of the jokes I made earlier, I think you're a really nice girl. I think you have a good head on your shoulders, you're beautiful, and you're smart... I think you're good for him." She bit the inside of her cheek and looked up to the ceiling, avoiding all eye contact.

I tried to figure out who she was talking about though: *"you're good for him"*

Did she mean Adam or Ricky? I wasn't too sure.

I needed to know why Tasha was here, and I needed to stop thinking about the damn love triangle Tasha created in her mind.

"Thank you.." I felt myself hesitate, unsure what to say. "Did you need to talk about something else?" She nodded her head softly and then sat up to face me on the bed.

"Yeah, I had a feeling that you were a little upset with what Adam told us in there." I wanted to be the smartass that I usually am and say *you think*? But I didn't have the energy in me right now. I was too overwhelmed to make a sarcastic comment.

"Yeah I was." I left it short and simple. There didn't need to be a longer explanation about it; I was overwhelmed, anxious, terrified, and pissed off all rolled into one. All of these emotions were going to consume me and ruin me, and I couldn't think of a single thing that could stop it.

"Well. It's a hard business to be in. And I know that these past few weeks have been anything but normal for you. The stuff that you've been introduced to so suddenly unfortunately happens every day. I was lucky to not be as involved in it as everyone else. You think that it's just the dealers and the King that are the main focus of the whole operation; but there would be nothing if there weren't the people who buy the drugs." She paused for a moment to collect her thoughts.

"Did you know that before I got involved in that lifestyle, I graduated high school at the top of my class and was accepted into Stanford?" She shook her head as my eyes widened in surprise.

"Yeah it's pretty weird to think about that now. I ended up not going because of my dad getting sick, but that's not the point. The point is, I was kind of like you once— The girl who had everything: the supportive parents, the good high school education, the intelligent best friends, the weekend parties. Everything.

Things change when my best friends start buying ecstasy.." Natasha let out a big sigh, then continued. "…The most I've ever done is smoke weed. But when you're young and all of your

314

friends start using new shit and doing drugs, it's hard to watch, you know? I met Ricky about five years ago, he was the drug dealer to my friends. I hated him for it, too. I absolutely hated him and I thought that he was ruining their lives just to make money. But as the years passed and I got more involved into this world, I realized that it really had nothing to do with him. He was the distributor, sure. But he was a part of a much bigger game. He didn't control my friends, he didn't make them use the drugs: that was their decision. The fault was solely put on the drugs itself for making them addicted, and my friends for giving in to it. I was always so afraid to leave my friends, though. No matter what they did, I was right there with them. I did anything I could to make sure that they were as safe as they could be, but just like Ricky didn't control them, well, neither did I."

"Things didn't start to change until I met Adam. I'm not sure if he told you about us, but yeah, we were involved. I met him at a college party one night that all of my friends went to in Atlanta. He comes walking in with Ricky and I remember my eyes immediately darted onto him. I remember thinking *why is this guy here?* He was too cute and too healthy to be there. From the second I saw him, I knew he was a good one. We became really close friends as the time passed. We were there to keep one another company, and to give our honest opinions to one another. It was refreshing because we knew everything that was going on around us and within the business now. We knew about Jerome and the whole mess with Javier. We became so invested into this crew that it was like it ran in our blood. It wasn't until Jerome started going crazy after Javier left him that I knew that I wasn't safe. I wanted Adam to get out with me. I wanted us to leave and to not come back. By that time, I wanted Ricky to leave, too. But things like that never really work out. I had it all planned out to leave, but Jerome found out pretty quickly about the plan. He threatened to hurt my family if I left with Adam and Ricky. He said I was nothing but a spoiled little slut who thinks that I can always get my way. I remember that moment like it was yesterday. It terrified me to even be in the same room as Jerome after that. So one weekend I drove to Savannah to stay with my step mom and I went out for a few drinks with her. That's where I met Harry. We had been dating for two months, and I suddenly became so invested in him that I really wasn't around this life much anymore. It was like I was starting to disappear to Jerome. I can't even tell you how happy that made me— to think that I was not a person to watch out for. It made me want to disappear completely so that he would never hurt me or my family. I was so happy when Harry proposed. I love him so much and I know he's the one for me. But I had a huge moment of clarity once he proposed— the second he got down on his knee and I said yes, I was more excited that I was getting away from Jerome than I was about actually being in love. That moment of clarity changed everything. I realized that even if I don't do drugs, I was still involved in the business. Jerome was controlling everything, he was controlling my life. Hell, he even controlled what was supposed to be the happiest moment of my life."

"Out of fear and a lot of guilt, I told Harry everything about the crew. I didn't even hold back. I didn't want to be a part of this world anymore if that meant living in constant fear. So here I am now. Living in this beautiful house in Savannah, with the best fiancé ever. I thought I would never have to worry about anything ever again, and then God damn Adam calls me and tells me it's an emergency and he needs help. I immediately ask if he's okay, and you know what he said? He said *I'm not worried about me, I've met someone— Tara. He's after Tara and I'm scared.* The second those words left his mouth, I knew that I had to help my friends one last time. I knew I had to help him, because of you."

I didn't breathe the entire time she spoke. My entire body felt tense as she told me her story. It was unbelievable to think that she had a similar lifestyle to mine, and it all got ruined the second she got pulled into this world. I couldn't help but notice a deeper meaning— was she telling me this story to help me or was she trying to tell me that I needed to get out of Adam's life?

Either way, it didn't make me feel any better.

"Tasha.." I started to say, without really knowing where it was going to go. "I appreciate you telling me that, I do. I just don't know what you're trying to tell me from that." She huffed and got up off of the bed now, leaving me to sit on it by myself.

"I wouldn't have helped you guys if it weren't for Adam sounding so scared for you. I've never seen him care so much about a person as much as he cares about you. I've never seen him care this much so fast, either. He's so invested in protecting you and keeping you safe. Sometimes, I wonder if he's so blinded by liking you and protecting you, that he's willing to do *anything*. Just like what he did that night at the bank. I've never seen him go that far, ever. I just wonder that maybe by worrying about you so much, that he's not thinking of how much he needs to protect himself."

She had a good point, but It made me question everything. Every moment we shared. Every single thing we did together. The extremes that he's gone to already to protect me. I was extremely grateful for him, but what I failed to realize was that I was ruining him, and he could potentially be killed, all because of me. She seemed to have noticed the worry that caught my face. I could feel my face heat up, and was breaking out into a cold sweat.

"I didn't mean to freak you out, Tara. But it's my job as a friend to be honest…" She glanced over to my bags that had been thrown on the floor, and then met my gaze. "…I noticed you had your bags on the bed when I came in. If you're planning on leaving, I won't tell them. I just hope you get somewhere safe and you protect yourself…" She gently tapped my hand with hers, and got up from the bed. "…I just want my guys to be protected, too." She gave me a sympathetic smile, and then she was out the door.

She was right…she was right about everything.

I needed to protect Adam now, and I needed to let him go. It seemed that he had been taking things too far in order to protect me, and I couldn't let him ruin his life for the sake of protecting me. and the only way I knew how to fix this was by leaving.

I had made up my mind, I would go back home tomorrow and have an Uber take me to Atlanta. That seemed the easiest way to go. I would have to explain it to Adam, of course, but I just wanted one last normal night with him before I never see him again. I finished packing my stuff in the master bedroom of the guest house when my phone rang.

It was my mom finally calling me back. I mean, it was the least she could do, after all it was my birthday. I answered the phone, finally happy to hear a familiar voice. "Hey mom, thanks for calling me back." I knew something was wrong the second I heard a high muffled noise from the other end of the phone. It sounded like a muffled scream from far away. I knew that something was happening once I heard a deep, familiar voice speak to me.

"Oh for you honey, anything."

I felt goosebumps rise on my skin as I heard the evil from his voice. This was what I had feared all along. This was what I didn't want to happen. "You didn't think I'd find you, did ya?" He followed up with a sinister and throaty laugh. It took everything in me not to cry. I wanted to know what happened to my mom.

"Where is she?" I tried to remain quiet and calm so that Adam wouldn't hear me in the other room. I also told myself to not panic. He wouldn't hurt her; there was something he needed from me. "Now sweetheart, giving you that answer would be way too easy. You know that…" His raspy voice rattled through the speaker, causing it to ring in my ears.

"I thought you and your boys were smart. But apparently, not enough. It was pretty easy to find where you are. All I needed was for you to have your cell phone location on, and the rest was a piece of cake. I love technology nowadays. So easy to get in touch with the ones you love, and to find people…such as Jennifer here."

He started laughing again, knowing just what he was doing to get me to do what he wanted. "I swear to God if you hurt—"

His voice became more serious now, and he started yelling through the phone "Or what?! What are you gonna do to me?! *Nothing*. Now shut your fucking mouth. If you want her to remain safe, Imma need you to get down here to Atlanta, tonight. 815 Broadway Avenue. I sent Dustin to come get you, he's picking you up at 2 am... you remember him, don't you?" I heard him speak away from the phone, as if he was discussing something with one of his men.

"Oh, and one more thing, You better not speak a word of this to your boys. If you do, say goodbye to your mom." The phone line went dead, and all I could do was close my eyes. My tears weren't going to stop any time soon. All I could think about was my poor mother, fighting for her life because of me. For the stupid things I have done.

Natasha was right; my life was ruined because of this drug business, and Jerome has just made me more invested into it than I ever thought I would be.

But I promised myself something. I promised myself to be strong. I told myself to stay as calm as I could. I promised myself to put on an act in front of Adam and Ricky.

And I knew that no matter what happened, that I wouldn't give up without a fight.

Chapter Thirty: Adam

I woke up the next morning with the sun shining directly in my face. Apparently we must have forgotten to close them last night. I already knew by the way the sunlight was shining in my face that I was up earlier than normal.

I stretched my body out like I normally do every morning, before turning around to face Tara. Ever since I had been with her, I was always encapsulated by how beautiful she was when she woke up in the mornings. The way she laid there next to me in bed, so peaceful and beautiful, made my heart race.

I had thought from the beginning that she was driving me crazy, and she had… I had become completely fucking mad for her. It was like we had reached a point where everything was finally starting to make sense with us, and I couldn't have been happier or felt any luckier to have her.

I had the most beautiful girl to wake up to every morning, and while our situation was dangerous, I knew that I needed to be lucky for the good things that I did have in my life, and start to learn to cherish those things, and those people. I needed a day to be thankful for the things that I had instead of being so fucking miserable all the time about the mistakes I made.

I turned around to see her beautiful face, but I felt my stomach drop as I noticed that she wasn't there. Her side of the bed was a mess with the sheets, so I knew that I wasn't imagining it. She was here with me at some point last night.

Where did she go?

I began to panic when I noticed that the suitcase and bag were gone out of the room. She either left in the middle of the night, or was taken. Without even thinking, I raced over to the main house to see if she had gone there, maybe she needed to wash clothes. Maybe she went out for a run.

Maybe.

That's what I kept telling myself.

I opened the patio doors into the kitchen and paced around the house, looking for her anywhere I could, anxious and needing some kind of relief to this aggravating pain I began to feel in my chest. I had barely noticed Ricky sitting at the dining room table eating a bowl of cereal until I heard the familiar crack of a beer top and the sound of gulping in the same direction.

Normally I would take the time out of my day to remind him how fucking disgusting he was to mix beer with cereal, but I didn't have the time. I needed to know where she went. Ricky was my best friend, he had to have known something about where she had gone to.

"Rick.." I said in a panic, still pacing around the house and pulling my phone out to text her and call her as many times as I could until she would pick up. I called her cellphone five times straight, but it had gone straight to voicemail. The pressure in my chest started to build up higher and higher, making me feel like my air supply was going to cut off at any fucking moment.

Where was she?

I walked over to the kitchen, now thinking that it was my phone that was messing up. I wandered around the island a couple of times, searching for the best service spot in the house. The second Ricky turned around, he noticed the expression of panic that I had on my face, and the progressive shaking in my hands. He rushed over towards me, standing at the kitchen counter, and placed both of his hands on my shoulders.

"Adam? Adam?"

I felt my breath quicken, like I couldn't control my breath, like I couldn't control anything around me. It was like my entire sense of being just went completely numb, and other than the feeling of suffocating, I couldn't feel anything.

I couldn't feel my hands, it was like they weren't even there. I couldn't fully see Ricky in front of me as everything had begun to form into a large blur. "Adam, I need you to breathe, bud. You're having a panic attack. Take slow breaths, c'mon man you've got this. Let's go, ready? ...breathe in.."

I had my fair share of panic attacks when I was younger after my mom died, and I was never fully able to stop them until Ricky came around. He was the only one who knew how to calm me down and relax me enough to get back to normal. With his help and his guidance, I managed to stop taking my anxiety medications, and I hadn't had a panic attack in years.

This was the first time I had one in three years.

Once I began to regain my vision and felt the deep rush of oxygen hit my lungs, I grabbed a bottle of water out of the fridge and sat down at the dining room table. "Riguez, what's going on?" I was still trying to catch my breath, knowing that if I spoke too quickly or got too worked up that I would end up having a panic attack for a second fucking time in three years.

My words were breathless, barely able to make out, but I knew that Ricky would get the point. "...Tara....is gone...I.. can't..." I closed my eyes and breathed in and out slowly to compose myself as much as I could. The truth is, I couldn't even get the sentence out without feeling like I was being sent over the edge.I knew that Ricky understood exactly why I was having so many panic attacks, because before I knew it, he was sticking his tennis shoes on and grabbing his keys.

"Where the hell did she go?"

The desperation in his voice to figure out what happened to her sounded like it came from more than just friendly concern. It was like he was driving himself insane just as much as I was.

"I don't know-- she could have left, I don't know."

Ricky held up his index finger, signaling me to shut up and then gestured for me to follow him. He walked us both back to the guest house, his pace was fast with urgency. "Maybe she left something here to let you know where she went, start looking.."

I simply nodded and followed Ricky's orders, trying not to focus too much on the strange amount of concern he had expressed for her. At the moment, that wasn't important. The important thing was that we found something to let us know she was okay, and to maybe, just maybe give me a small amount of hope that I could get her back. So that we could go back to where we were before the crazy mess I brought her into. So that we could continue to get to know one another in a normal way, like fucking human beings.

If you had asked me a few weeks ago if I would be thinking like a romantic, I would have told you that you were completely fucking insane. To be honest, I never really understood why guys let themselves be wholly captivated by a woman. I used to think that the sex must of been pretty fucking great in order for a guy to stay with a woman that long.

I wasn't a total dick my entire life, though. I didn't originally think that way. I think I was more sensitive back then, when I was with Vanessa. My sensitive side and lack of confidence made me useless to her in the relationship, enough for her to go batshit crazy and hit me, cheat on me, and leave me like I was nothing to her. I always felt embarrassed in myself to have been so in love that I was blind to the way I was being treated, but I constantly reminded myself that I would never lay a hand on a woman, no matter how much she did it to me. That was the only way I could stomach the situation. It took for her to walk out of my life for me to realize that abuse in a relationship can go both ways; it's not always the male who abuses the woman. It also taught me that I needed to take care of myself, and solely focus on me. That's when I grew the new attitude of not giving a fuck about any one or anything besides my job and my family.

I grew to realize that people don't stick around; they use you until they get what they want and they're gone. It was so much easier for me to just behave the way everyone else did than to put effort in. I had been that way for awhile, actually, until I met that stubborn woman that got caught for underage drinking at my uncle Joe's bar. I knew I was falling in love with this girl, and it scared the fuck out of me and the man that I had forced myself to become all those years ago.

No matter how hard I tried to resist it, I couldn't help myself; I already began to miss those captivating ice blue eyes of hers and the way she looked at me when I made some dumb ass joke. I longed for her to call out my name, and envisioned her walking out of the bathroom with a towel wrapped around her head and no makeup on, taking my breath away. I thought about the need to be near her while I searched for something, *anything* to let me know where my lady was. I had tried to keep my cool and to not let myself return to the anxious man I was just fifteen minutes ago. I couldn't let myself go there again, because if I did, I wasn't sure if I would stop.

I tore up anything I could find within the beautiful guest house, starting with looking on our bed, trying to find a small note that could have gotten lost in the sheets. I looked on the floor under the bed frame, and in each nightstand. I told myself to check the closet, thinking that maybe I had gone crazy. Maybe she didn't even leave and she had put everything into the closet before going on a run. I pulled open the closet door, noticing the twinge of optimism fill my body, hoping that what I thought had been true.

Sadly, I wasn't right.

The closet was completely empty and bare, as if no one was ever here. I continued to check the other rooms with Ricky, going so far as to move the furniture in case I were to find anything. I knew that Tara wouldn't just leave without an explanation. No matter how upset she was about my job with Javier, I knew the kind of woman she was, and she wouldn't have left for something like that. There had to be a good reason.

"Hey Ad, I think I found something!" I heard Ricky shout from the kitchen as I searched the bathroom for anything I could find. I jogged out to the kitchen, knowing that there wasn't any time to waste, I needed answers. I noticed the refrigerator pulled out from the wall and all of the cabinet doors swung open. Ricky had really broken this kitchen apart. He must have been as desperate as I was.

"I found it sticking out under the fridge, it must have fallen or something. It's addressed to you." He handed me a paper towel with dark writing on it before he turned around and moved the fridge back to its proper place.

I walked away from the kitchen and made my way into the seating area, sitting down on the couch so I could properly read her goodbye letter to me. I knew that if she wrote me something, it had to be true-- she really did leave. I took in a large breath of air before reading her note, not sure what to expect but knowing that whatever it was, I wasn't ready for it:

Dear Adam,

I don't think I can do this anymore. I can't make you guys risk your lives for me, it's not fair to all of you. I arranged for a car to pick me up and drive me to the airport-- I'm going to be staying with my grandma for a while in Las Vegas. I will text you to let you know that I am safely there. It's not what I want, I want to be with you more than anything. It's just something I need to do. You probably won't see me again, so I want to thank you for everything you've done for me. I will never meet anyone quite as special as you, Adam Rodriguez. Thank you for showing me what true loyalty and love is. Please don't check up on me. I'm sorry. --T

P.s. tell Tasha and Harry I said Thank you, and please let Ricky know that I will truly miss him making me laugh all the time.

    I couldn't fully comprehend what that letter was supposed to tell me. She told me she went to live with her grandma in Vegas, but I wasn't completely sure that I bought it. There was no way this was real, that after everything we had gone through, she just up and left me. I felt a familiar sharp pain in my chest and the shallow inhales of breath hit my lungs. I knew exactly what that feeling was, I just never thought I would have it again. I thought I could protect myself against it.

I thought I could trust her enough that I wouldn't have to feel this fucking bullshit ever again.

"Esta bein hermano?"
"Are you good brother?"

    I heard Ricky's deep, familiar voice amplify as he walked closer towards the living room. He was the only one who truly stuck with me through everything, and he had been with me through most of the heartbreaks I had felt in the past. The amount of pain I felt in my chest made my nerves fill with anger, making me question why I let another woman betray me and use me like she did.

Fed up with it all, I ripped up the paper towel and threw the remains on the coffee table in front of me. "Si, estaré bein" *"Yes, I'm good."*

I couldn't tell him what the letter said, mostly because I couldn't bring myself to say it out loud. I knew the second that I did, my sadness and anger would grow, and I didn't know if I could control myself.

I couldn't tell my best friend, my brother, that the girl that I was in love with was no better than Vanessa.

I couldn't tell him that, yet again, my heart felt fucking shattered.

I couldn't tell him that, never again would I let a woman get away with doing this to me. Tara wouldn't get away with it, and I'd fucking find her… If it was the last thing I ever do.

To Be Continued…

Trouble Series: Book Two

In Too Deep

Coming soon

Trouble: Three Book Series

Trouble Series: Book One

Trouble

Trouble Series: Book Two

In Too Deep

Trouble Series: Book Three

Guilty As Sin

For other works, updates on book releases, and book signings please visit:

Mariadunbooks.com

Instagram: @authormariadun

332

Made in the USA
Middletown, DE
11 November 2024

64117950R00198